HARRY

Straight Eight

8

Fifth Detective Harry Taylor Thriller

Laurie Dicker

Dicker Books
PO Box 1304, Buderim, Qld, Australia, 4556
www.dicker-books.com
First published by Dicker Books, 2025
Copyright © Laurie Dicker 2025

ISBN: 978-0-6484128-7-8

Prepublication Data Service
National Library of Australia
Dicker, Laurie
Harry: Straight Eight
Cover: Marni Hinton
Crime mystery fiction—Australia

A catalogue record for this book is available from the National Library of Australia

Dedicated to Marjie and Rohan

my very special team

Chapter 1
Tuesday

Detective Senior Sergeant Harry Taylor had been called this morning to the zoology department of the University of New England at Armidale in northern New South Wales. On this 18th of April, 1950, the cool, dry autumn air was brisk and invigorating.

Harry walked tall; shoulders back; his head and brown felt hat tilted slightly to the left; his big shiny boots strode confidently towards the shed. As Harry opened the door to the old weatherboard building he stopped and took a deep breath as a strong musty smell punched his nostrils. A man's body was lying on the concrete floor in the middle of the room, face up, stripped to the waist and his trouser legs pulled up to the knees. The man's body lay parallel to the back wall, with his head to the left and his feet to the right. Some pieces of straw mixed with specks of animal droppings were scattered around the body. Two large cooked sausages were stuffed into the mouth of the grossly overweight man.

The man's white belly was so large it appeared ready to burst. The top of his trousers was hidden under the large flap of his overhanging gut. His biceps were flabby blobs of flesh. His oversized breasts resembled those of a fat elderly woman. His double chin hid his Adam's apple. His trousers were skin-tight around his thick thighs. A coat, two socks, a pair of boots and a crumpled shirt were on the floor near the body.

Standing behind Harry, Detective Constable Joe Simms pointed to the body. "Bloody hell, Harry, that bloke would have to pay a kid a penny to tell him if his trouser fly was undone—because he couldn't see it for himself over that fat gut."

"Hold your smart-arse comments, Joe," replied Harry.

Joe Simms was recently appointed to Armidale from Parramatta as Harry's offsider. He was young, raw and inexperienced. Harry couldn't help but compare him with Detective Constable Neil McNulty, his very capable former partner at Wagga Wagga. While Joe was street smart in the rough inner suburbs of Sydney, he had never lived or worked in the country and was very naïve about life here in Armidale.

Joe was five feet, eleven inches tall and very fit. In earlier years he had been a regular at the Police Citizens Boys Club in Redfern. He developed as a better-than-average middleweight boxer and, on most days, kept fit by weightlifting. In a tough suburb like Redfern he could hold his own against most of the bullies and knew the ways of city life but he was on a steep learning curve here in Armidale.

Harry blocked the doorway of the shed with his arm, preventing Joe and the laboratory assistant, Sue Ellis, from entering the room.

On the left-hand wall was a bench with a washbasin. A stained handtowel hung on a metal ring beside it. Next to the washbasin were two fold-up casual chairs and a small picnic table with two drinking glasses and an empty bottle of lemonade on top. There was a wooden stool just inside the door.

Banks of small wire cages on wooden shelves covered the back and right-side walls, floor to ceiling, with each measuring eighteen inches high by one foot wide and one foot deep. One or two large rats occupied each cage. Some were grey with black patches and others more brownish in colour. They were all highly agitated. They squealed as they walked over each other. Some stretched up the wire in an attempt to see what was going on in the room.

Joe turned to Sue. "What is this stinking place? Why the bloody hell would you be keeping giant mice here? We're in the middle of prime sheep-grazing and wheat-growing country. The New England region is one of the best farming areas in Australia. The last thing we want here is a bloody mouse plague."

Sue Ellis was of medium height and slim with her blond hair pulled back into a carefully formed single plait tied at the end with a blue ribbon. She was dressed in a starched white lab coat over a blue shirt and plain blue slacks. There were brown marks on the front of the coat. She wore sensible highly polished black wedge shoes. She fixed Joe with a piercing stare. Harry had already formed the view that Sue was a down-to-earth, no-nonsense woman who was not going to take a backward step after Joe's smart comment.

"The animals in those cages are not mice; they are Norwegian rats. This old weatherboard building is an ex-army hut that used to house soldiers during the war. It is now used as a storeroom for the university's Department of Zoology. This is where we breed the rats. The Norwegian varieties are excellent for use in scientific experiments and are used by the first-year zoology students."

"How do you kill them?" asked Joe.

"We euthanise them before pinning the bodies out on a hard wax base in a metal tray," replied Sue. "The students then proceed over the next few weeks to dissect out, identify and study the various systems such as the respiratory, digestive, circulatory and reproductive systems."

"Wouldn't they stink?" asked Joe as he turned his head and stepped back to distance himself from the smell.

"No. We preserve them in formalin at the end of each day."

Harry turned quickly as he laid a hand firmly on Joe's shoulder and snapped at him. "Enough of the small talk. Get your mind focused on the body over there."

He turned to Sue. "Before Joe and I go in, Sue, tell us what you found this morning when you opened this shed."

Sue drew herself up to her full five-foot-eight-inch height and pointed into the room. "On Tuesday and Friday mornings my first job is to clean out all the cages and put in fresh straw. When I arrived this morning I found the padlock to the hut was in the latch but unlocked. I locked the shed at five yesterday afternoon. I had definitely locked it last night. Someone either had a key or had picked the lock. As I entered, the rats were running everywhere and all the cages were open. The rats were running back and forth over the body and around the room. I quickly slammed the shed door to keep them in."

"Was anyone with you?" asked Harry.

"No. I was alone. When I saw the body of that poor man I could see he wasn't moving. So, I ran outside and rushed to the office in the Booloominbah building to call the police. On the way back I called Jimmy Sexton, the botany department's lab assistant, to help me get the rats back in the cages."

"How difficult was that?" asked Joe.

"Well, when Jimmy saw the body he fainted, so I had to do it by myself anyway. We have a net on a stick to assist us if any of the rats get out and run around. When I got them all back in I helped Jimmy and sent him to the sick bay. He was as white as his lab coat."

"Are you sure you got them all?" asked Harry. "Do you know how many there were?"

"Yes," replied Sue. "Every rat is numbered and photographed. None of them escaped."

"Bloody hell, Sue," said Joe. "How much do they pay you to look after these bloody rats?"

Harry spun around. He poked Joe firmly in the chest with all four fingers on his right hand. "Joe, keep your eyes and ears open and your mouth shut until I say otherwise. Keep your smart comments to yourself. Apologise to Sue—and we'll have no more swearing, thank you."

Joe stepped back, turned side-on, dropped his chin to his chest and raised his left hand as if he was about to lead with a punch, but thought better of it. He stared at Harry for a few seconds before turning to Sue.

"Sorry Sue. I meant no offence. It won't happen again."

"Thank you, Joe," replied Sue with a smile. "Not everyone can stomach working in this place. More importantly, I am a former nurse so I checked the man's body. There was no pulse and the body was cold. I could see that he was beyond resuscitation."

Harry tapped Joe on the shoulder. "I want your full attention here. Now let's get in here and see what's happened."

He invited Sue to stand just inside the door but to stay away from the body.

Joe pointed at the man's head. "Why has he got those sausages in his mouth?"

Harry stepped forward and gently removed one of the sausages. "This has not been eaten or chewed. It is whole."

Harry removed the second sausage. "This one also has not been chewed and it looks like it has some vomit on it."

The light from the oversized cream enamel shade shone brightly down onto the man's naked torso. The skin and dark hair of his exposed torso and lower legs glistened with an oily substance.

Harry pointed to the man's torso. "What do you two see on the man's skin?"

Joe spoke first. "He's all greasy. I know the sun's out but nobody would go out for a suntan in this freezing weather. And his skin is as white as talcum powder."

Sue stepped forward and pointed towards the floor on the other side of the body. "Over there is an aluminium bowl with the sieve lid next to it. It looks like one we used to have beside the stove at home to store the lard dripping after roasting a leg of lamb or beef. The sieve catches the hard bits and the fat seeps through and is kept for use later. On our farm we used the lard for butter during war rationing."

"Well spotted, Sue," said Harry. "We had one beside the fuel stove on our farm too."

"Why would he rub fat over his body?" asked Joe.

Harry pointed at the body. "We don't know if he did, Joe. It could have been put on by somebody else. Was he murdered or did he commit suicide? If he was murdered, the killer could have rubbed the dripping onto the man's body before letting out the rats to encourage them to eat the flesh."

Joe took a closer look. "But the skin doesn't look broken. There are no holes in the flesh and no open wounds. So Sue must have got here soon after the rats were let out of the cages and got them back in before they could eat him."

Sue took another step forward and pointed to the man's chest. "There appears to be a few minor lesions on the flesh. Despite what you might hear in legends or see in horror movies, rats rarely eat human flesh; and certainly not when they are well fed. They might bite in self-defence if threatened but their main diet consists of grains, fruit, vegetables and other plant material, not human flesh. If you study their teeth they are more suited to grinding and slicing through vegetation. And their bite is weak. The incisors are sharp and can cut through wood and wires but are not suited to tearing at meat."

Harry walked around to the left side of the body, leaned forward and placed his forefinger into the aluminium bowl. He lifted it to his mouth and touched the tip on his tongue. "That is definitely the drippings from roast lamb."

He waved his hand towards Joe. "Joe, go to the university main office and call Doctor Gregory Ebsworth, the government medical officer. We want him here as soon as possible. On the way back bring the fingerprint kit, evidence bags and the camera from the wagon."

Harry walked around the body again and spotted an object around the neck of the dead man. He moved in for a closer look and found a long leather bootlace. At first it was not easily seen as it was tucked under the fatty rolls of neck flesh. Harry used his pen to gently stretch it out. A piece of copper about two to three inches long by an inch and a half wide fell flat onto the floor. The top surface was marked with a number 1 in the centre, surrounded by bright enamelled colours.

"What could that be?" asked Sue.

"I don't know," said Harry. "It could be a piece of jewellery, but men in the country normally don't wear jewellery. This man, with his obvious obesity, would have been bullied out of town if he showed that fancy pendant hanging outside of his shirt in public. If this man was murdered I suspect the killer might have placed it there. He might be trying to tell us something."

"You said he, Harry. Could a woman be the killer?" asked Sue.

"It could have been, Sue, but we are looking at a victim who, at a guess, weighs well over twenty stone. For a woman to overpower a man of this size you'd expect to see a major wound to the body or head to knock him out, but I don't see any such wound. In fact, I can't see any wound or bleeding. When Doctor Ebsworth comes we will do a more thorough examination to assess the cause of death."

Harry walked back around to the left side of the body. He grabbed the man's trousers to turn him on his side. He saw the edge of a piece of white cardboard taped to the skin with grey masking tape.

"Sue, could you remove the piece of cardboard from his back? Try not to get grease on your hands."

Harry let the body roll back.

Written in large letters was the word:

Temperance

"What the hell does that mean?" gasped Sue.

"That's for us to find out," said Harry. "It might be some type of message."

"There is the Temperance Society in Armidale and it is a bunch of old wowsers who don't want anyone to have fun. They are a lot of old miserygutses and fuddy-duddies. They don't drink or go to dances or to the flicks. They need to be more tolerant of others. I'm not into heavy drinking, but people need to have a bit of fun."

"Do you recognise this bloke on the floor, Sue?" asked Harry.

"I've seen him around the university but I don't know who he is. He certainly was not studying zoology and I doubt he was in any science department; otherwise, I would have seen him in the laboratories. I know most of the science students by now. He's definitely not a staff member. He was probably a first-year student."

"It's a bit hard to tell the age of someone that fat," said Harry, "but I'd guess that he's about twenty."

Sue pointed to the small table and two chairs on the left. "Harry, those two glass tumblers on the table over there are not ours. The chairs and table don't belong here either. I don't know where they came from. I haven't touched any of those things this morning and I've never seen those glasses. We have our glasses in the staffroom; and I doubt other staff would have brought them here."

"Great. Thanks Sue. Here comes Joe. He can take the prints here now and then we'll get prints from all zoology staff for comparison. He'll send the glasses to the SIB—the Scientific Investigation Bureau— tonight."

As Joe walked towards the washbasin he noticed another piece of white cardboard lying on the floor. He picked it up. In clear black writing it read:

Their destiny is destruction.
Their God is their stomach.
Their glory is shame.

"I think they might be verses from the Bible," said Harry.

There was a knock at the door. Harry looked up to see a middle-aged man with carefully groomed brown-grey hair and wearing a tweed suit and highly polished tan brogue shoes.

"Hello Harry. What have you got for me today?"

Chapter 2
Tuesday

Harry stepped forward with hand outstretched. "I apologise, Gregory, for calling you out on this beautiful day, but we need you to declare this man dead and to ascertain the cause of death."

Doctor Ebsworth smiled. "I can always count on you, Harry, to call me when I have a waiting room full of patients and two babies due at the hospital today. Hello Joe. Next time Harry asks you to call me, tell him I'm out of town and unavailable. So, what have we got here?"

Harry pointed towards Sue. "Sue here is the lab assistant for the zoology department. When she came in here this morning she found all the rats from the cages running around and over this man's body on the floor, just as you see him here now. His torso and legs are covered with lard but the rats didn't eat the flesh. There were two whole cooked sausages stuck end on into his mouth but they have not been eaten or even chewed. I assume that they were placed there after death. We have not moved the body except to turn him on his side temporarily to remove a piece of cardboard taped to his back. There are no obvious wounds to the front or sides of the body but we have not yet done a thorough examination."

"Thanks Harry," replied the doctor. "I'll get you to help me with the preliminary examination."

He turned to Joe. "Could you go to the office and call David Hobbs from At Peace Funerals to come as soon as possible to take the body to the morgue. It will be much easier to examine the body thoroughly there on their table rather than in this mess on the floor."

"I'm new to the city, Gregory. As a matter of interest where is David's funeral parlour?" asked Joe.

"You travel up Dangar Street from the centre of town, up the hill past the teachers college, over the railway bridge and turn right onto

Uralla Road. It is just on your left, this side of The Armidale School, or TAS as it's locally known. David likes it there because he is close to the cemetery in Memorial Avenue."

Harry turned and pointed at Joe. "While you are over at the admin office in Booloominbah calling the funeral director, ask one of the senior staff to come here to identify this man."

Joe strolled out of the shed. Harry turned to see Sue had started to sweep the straw and other debris away from the cages.

"Stop, Sue!" he shouted. "Don't touch another thing in this room. In fact, it would be best if you returned to your laboratory and waited there in case we want to ask you more questions later. We must not disturb any evidence in this room. Could you go and ask the professor in charge of zoology to come here now. We want to ask him some questions. Tell him to wait at the door until we are ready to talk to him."

"That is Professor Gwyn O'Connor. He was in his office a while ago when I went to phone you, so I'll get him for you," replied Sue. As she walked out she smiled and added, "You might not understand him. He's Welsh with an accent so thick you can't get through it with a crowbar."

Gregory Ebsworth laughed. "She's right, you know. I know Gwyn. He's in Rotary with me. When he gives a talk the others tell him to speak bloody English, but he ploughs on as if they are not there. He keeps telling me that he was named after the Welsh king of the Otherworld and leader of the Wild Hunt. Now, Harry, help me take off this man's trousers and underpants."

As Harry bent down to grab the body, the doctor pointed at the man's face. "Hold it there, Harry," said Gregory. "I know this man. He visited me once briefly last year. He is a student here but I can't remember his name. Okay. Let's turn him onto his left side so we can examine his right side."

Ebsworth ran his hands through the man's hair and down the side of the face and neck. He lifted the right arm to examine both sides of it and the armpit before proceeding to the waist, hips, buttock and leg.

"Now onto his stomach, Harry."

That examination revealed no visible injuries on the back of the man's body.

"Now let's roll him over further and onto his right side, Harry."

The examination there revealed no external injuries.

"I can write a death certificate, Harry," said Gregory, "but I'll need to do an autopsy to determine the cause of death. Do you know anything about this man? Do you have any ideas on what might have been the cause of death? Did Sue say anything about him? Did the rats have anything to do with it?"

"Neither Joe nor I know this man and Sue said that she didn't know him either. She also thinks he might be a student but not in the science faculty. That's why we need someone from admin to identify him."

"What about the cause of death, Harry? Any thoughts?"

"Not really, Gregory," replied Harry. "It could be anything. With no obvious external injuries one might think that he could have died from a massive heart attack or a stroke. Just look at him. He's about twenty stone and the only exercise he probably ever did was open his mouth and shove food down his gut. He was a funeral waiting to happen. But the fact that he had a coloured pendant with a number painted on it around his neck, together with a written sign taped to his back and two sausages rammed into his mouth, means that someone else was involved in his death. The evidence is very clear that his death was not by natural causes or even by suicide. I now believe this is murder. We have a killer at large."

"You know, Harry, that the good citizens of Armidale won't like this," said Gregory. "This is a very conservative community with a strong religious culture influencing everything that goes on in this place. This is a small city but it has two cathedrals and numerous churches. Many of the settlers from here and across the New England region came from Scotland, who brought their strong stoic values and strict adherence to the rules, regulations and the Ten Commandments in the Bible with them. They have little tolerance for criminals. They will be on your back to get an early arrest and see the perpetrator hanged and for Armidale to retain its deserved image as a law-abiding city."

"Well, Gregory," laughed Harry, "you had best get yourself over to At Peace Funerals and do your autopsy as soon as possible to find the cause of death."

Gregory patted Harry on the back. "I will gladly do that for you, Harry, if you go to the hospital and deliver those two babies for me. Besides, because there are no external injuries, it is possible that death was caused by poisoning, in which case I will have to send stomach contents and other bodily samples to Sydney for testing."

Harry nodded. "Okay. After you finish your autopsy, Joe and I will drop by the parlour later today to collect them from you. We'll put them with the fingerprint samples and evidence bags from here and send them on the train tonight to Sydney. I'll contact Tony Jacobs, who is in charge of forensics, and ask him to pick them up from Central Railway Station in the morning for an urgent testing. Tony's a good man and has the experts there to do the job quickly."

Gregory stood tall and looked up at the ceiling. His right forefinger was resting on his nose and his thumb was locked under his chin while he thought. "It is important those analyses are done as quickly as possible before the chemical substances deteriorate. If it is food poisoning, we need quick results. Whether it was a self-administered overdose of drugs or poisons, or administered by another party, those substances deteriorate or are excreted from the body relatively quickly. In saliva or urine the time is short. In blood or hair samples it could be much longer, but the sooner we can do the testing the better."

"Let me examine his head and neck more thoroughly," said Gregory.

Gregory again ran his fingers around the victim's head, face and mouth again. "There are no breaks or bruises in the flesh or any sign of blood here. Let's roll him over."

The further examination found no obvious breakages of bones or lacerations to the back of the head or neck.

Harry stepped back from the body. "Gregory, we found a bit of vomit on the bottom of the sausage that were in the victim's mouth. Would that indicate that he died from something he swallowed?"

"Perhaps. But when I first arrived you said his mouth was filled with those sausages. Do you think he could have choked on them?"

"I thought about that," said Harry. "The sausages were not rammed deeply into his mouth. They weren't pushed down into his throat. I would say they were placed in his mouth after death. But if the sausages were the cause of death then they might have been full of poison and the victim had consumed some other sausages before collapsing on the floor."

"Could he have had an overdose by injection instead of ingestion?" asked Harry.

"I've found no puncture marks on the body."

"Could he have died from a massive heart attack or stroke brought on by whatever trauma happened with the other person?" asked Harry. "We know that there was another person involved because he couldn't have stuck the sign on his back and there was no lard on the palms of his hands."

"Let's just wait until I get him on the table at David's parlour and do a full autopsy."

"Okay," replied Harry. "But I will also send the two sausages off to Tony Jacobs with the other samples tonight."

Gregory walked to the washbasin but stopped. He stepped around the picnic table and two fold-up chairs. He looked disgusted.

"I wouldn't use that stinking towel or use that basin. There are probably more germs on that towel and basin than in the whole of this room, including on all those rats. I'll have another wash when I get to David's parlour. And I certainly wouldn't drink from those glasses on the table. They will be needed for evidence testing."

"It's already organised," said Harry. "Joe will include those glasses in the package for the SIB. They still have some liquid in them. Now, let's step back and think about what we know already about this situation. We have a dead male body here on the floor. There are no obvious signs of external injury from a blunt or sharp instrument or by any of the objects in this shed. We have not found any puncture marks from injections. There is no sign of a struggle or fight. The rats did not attack the body. This is a real mystery."

Gregory coughed and wiped his nose with an ironed and neatly folded blue handkerchief. "Have you thought, Harry, that death might have happened in another place and the body dumped here after the event?"

"I thought of that," replied Harry. "It is most unlikely. Look at the size of that man. He is well over twenty stone. It would take two or three strong men to carry him here. There are no signs that he was dragged or wheeled across the floor."

"So what you're saying, Harry, is that this man did not come here to commit suicide but that another person gave this young man some drug or poison that killed him. Then they put the pendant around his neck, stuck the sign to his back, rubbed lard over his skin, shoved the sausages into his mouth and then let the rats out of their cages."

"Yes, that is my theory at the moment but we won't know about the poisoning until we get back the results of the tests and autopsy."

There was a knock on the door frame and David Hobbs, the undertaker, walked in. He looked at the body on the floor. "Oh my God. Thanks a lot, you two. If I had to pick up that bloke by myself, I'd need Gregory here to deal with my heart attack and dislocated back. So, you two are going to help me get him into the bag and the wagon."

"Come on, David," said Harry. "Are you getting weak in your old age? I heard that you played representative rugby for New England in the front row."

"Mate, that was back before the war. I'm no spring chicken now. So you two get your sleeves rolled up and help me with this body."

There was another knock at the door. They turned to see a middle-aged woman dressed in a green, heavily pleated tartan skirt and a cream, thick Irish Aran sweater standing in the doorway. She looked at the body on the floor and screamed.

Chapter 3
Tuesday

Harry moved quickly towards the door and held the woman's arm to support her as she stumbled back out of the building. David held her other arm. Harry and David helped her inside the shed.

"Gregory, can you bring that stool near the door over here, please?" asked Harry.

When she was seated, David asked Gregory to steady her. "I just have to duck out to the hearse for a moment."

Harry moved in front of her but kept his hand on her shoulder and arm for further support. "Hello, I'm Detective Harry Taylor. Are you okay?"

"Yes," she replied. "It's just a shock seeing that man there like that."

"Could you please tell me your name and position at the university?"

"My name is Bonnie Munro," she said as she regained her composure. "I am a senior administrative officer at the university and I work out of Booloominbah—that old building over there. I supervise student enrolments and matters concerning student accommodation. I am also the point of contact in any student concerns or disputes."

"Thank you, Bonnie. I've been called out here to the university this morning because the laboratory assistant, Sue Ellis, found that man's body on the floor of the hut when she came in to do the regular clean. Sue does not know who the man is. She thinks he is a student but not in any of the sciences. Do you know who that man is? Is he a student here?"

Bonnie sobbed. She reached under the sleeve of her Aran sweater to get a handkerchief to blow her nose and wipe her eyes. She looked up slowly and pointed at the body. "That is Jonathon Petherby. He is studying for an arts degree—poor Jonathon. He was such a lovely lad but he had such a hard time. I feel so sorry for him. He didn't deserve anything like this after all he had been through."

"What do you mean—after all he'd been through? Had he been sick?" asked Harry.

"No," gasped Bonnie. "He didn't have any serious illness that I know of but he was the target of all the bully-boys here. As you can see, he was not the sporting type, but that was not his fault. Not everyone can be trim, taut and terrific and be sporting champions with medals and ribbons. But a lot of those so-called sporting heroes or wannabe heroes took it out on Jonathon because he had an eating problem and was so fat. Just look at him. How could he have run four hundred yards around the track like Marjorie Jackson or Shirley Strickland or played football like Keith Holman or Doug Ritchie or ridden a bike like Russell Mockridge? He was flat out walking to the dining table in the Bevery. The Bevery is the dining hall in that wooden building on the northern side of Booloominbah."

"Did any of the other students physically assault Jonathon?" asked Harry.

"I never saw any of them punching him, but I did see some of them poke him in the belly and laugh and call him 'Fatso' and 'Guzzle Guts'. I saw one student in the Bevery one day spit on the leftovers on his own plate and then pass it to Jonathon for him to eat. I reported him and he was suspended from lectures for a week."

After David Hobbs came back with the body bag and laid it next to the body, he looked towards Harry, Gregory and Bonnie. "Harry, I have seen this young fellow at church singing in the choir during funerals."

"What church, David?" asked Harry.

"Presbyterian. He always stood at the back of the choir."

Joe Simms arrived back at the hut. "While I was out, I also checked the time of the trains, Harry. The last one leaves here at midnight."

"Thanks Joe," said Harry. "That's great. Could you now stand behind Miss Munro to support her back on the stool."

David and Gregory stood back as Harry faced Bonnie again. Bonnie gave a sigh and turned up the collar of her blouse to lessen the chill from the south-westerly coming through the door. Harry turned to face her. "What else can you tell us about this young man, Bonnie?"

"He was in his second year of an arts degree. He didn't have a good year last year, failing two of his three subjects."

"What were they?" asked Joe.

Bonnie sighed again. "He passed psychology but failed philosophy and English, but it wasn't all his fault. What he had to put up with from the bullies had a lot to do with it. The university considered terminating his enrolment because his pass in psychology was only a bare pass-mark. But we in the office and a couple of the female students put in a special plea to let him continue his studies."

Gregory stepped forward. "I didn't remember his name at first, but now you mention these things, I remember that when he came to see me briefly last year he was in a very agitated state. I tried to help him but he left and didn't come back again. He demanded that I give him strong sedatives to help him sleep. I tried to explain that it was important to first discover what was causing his insomnia before I could prescribe any medication, but he became upset, got up and walked out, and I've never seen him since."

"Did he explain why he wasn't sleeping?" asked Harry.

"No. He didn't get around to that before he left. He obviously needed help but I wasn't going to prescribe medication without knowing more about his condition and whether other remedies were more appropriate."

Harry turned back to Bonnie. "Bonnie, I want you to tell me the names of the students who bullied Jonathon."

"I can't do that, sir," replied Bonnie. "That would be a breach of privacy."

Harry moved a little closer to Bonnie. He fixed his eyes on hers. "Bonnie, that man is dead. We believe that he was murdered. This is now an official police investigation. It is no longer a matter of privacy. It is a serious matter of finding the perpetrator before he commits another murder. How will you feel if that happens again because you have refused to give us vital information that might lead us to the killer? Who might be next?"

Bonnie took out her handkerchief again and dabbed at the tears rolling down her cheeks. "I don't have that authority, sir."

"Who does?" asked Harry.

"You'll have to ask Mr Arthur McBryde. He's the general manager of the university and he's in the main office."

Harry looked up. "Joe, please help Bonnie back to the office. While you are there ask McBryde to come here immediately. Tell him to bring the student file for Jonathon Petherby. Don't take no for an answer. Make certain it contains the details of his family. I also want the files on the bullies. Bonnie can give McBryde the names."

After Joe and Bonnie left, David Hobbs tapped Harry on the shoulder. "While we wait for Joe and McBryde, can you two help me bag the body?"

"Sure David," said Harry. "We don't need it here anymore. The sooner you two get over to the parlour, the sooner Gregory can get on with the autopsy and have the samples ready for the train tonight."

The three men had considerable difficulty getting the body into the bag before carrying it out to the hearse. When they finished, Gregory and David drove off in their separate vehicles to return to the funeral parlour.

Harry looked up to see Joe returning with a man dressed in a neat grey pinstripe suit. He was short with receding grey hair and a pencil-thin moustache. On arriving at the hut he stepped inside and introduced himself as Arthur McBryde. He carried a foolscap folder under his arm.

"Now, what's this all about?" he demanded. "I am a busy man and I don't like being ordered about by this young man, you or anyone else from outside this university."

Harry stared at the man, paused for twenty seconds before he picked up the stool Bonnie had been sitting on and placed it before the manager. With a wave of his hand, he invited him to sit. Harry remained silent for a moment as he stood in front of the manager. He leaned forward with hands clasped and forefingers pointing towards the manager.

"Mr McBryde, while you walked across from your office, did you stop to consider that you are alive and are able to go about your life as usual?"

"What are you talking about? Stop wasting my time. I'm not here to play games."

"That's the point, sir," replied Harry. "You are so lucky. You are alive. The hearse that just drove away had a dead man in the back. He can no longer play games or study or do the wonderful things in life like you. We have a murder on this property, for which you are the manager, and you think we are wasting your time with games. You have a choice.

You can talk to me here or I'll put you in the wagon and we'll continue this conversation down at the station. What's it to be?"

"I didn't know about any murder," snapped McBryde.

Harry looked up at Joe who, with a finger signal and a nod of his head, confirmed that he had talked to the man. Harry looked back to the manager.

"Detective Simms explained to you that we wanted the files on Jonathon Petherby and his bullies and the reason we wanted them. So, let's cut all the bureaucratic pomposity and get down to the facts. Where does Petherby come from?"

McBryde opened the file nervously. He would have liked to challenge Harry but he had enough animal instinct to know that the man in front of him was different and not one to be reckoned with. He pulled out a sheet and handed it to Harry.

"Thank you, Mr McBryde. That was not difficult, was it?"

Harry read down the page. He noted that Petherby's home address was Warwick-Killarney Road, Vermont, via Warwick in Queensland. His father's name was George and his mother was Agnes. Harry looked up at Joe.

"Joe, go back to the office. Take this sheet. Phone the police in Warwick. Inform them of our situation here. Ask them to go to the farm where his parents live and inform them of their son's death. It's better that they get that message face to face from a local who knows the family rather than from someone like us phoning from here. Get them to ask the parents if they can come to Armidale to identify their boy. Tell them to leave a message at the station and we will arrange a suitable time."

Just after Joe left, a smart looking gentleman, with short-cropped hair, blue flannel shirt, a woollen tie and tartan trews underneath an academic gown flapping in the breeze, strode confidently around the corner of the shed. He looked at the manager. "Good morning Arthur. What's going on here?"

McBryde looked up. "Good morning Hamish. This man is from the police. There has been an incident here this morning and we are assisting him with his inquiries."

The man looked at Harry. "Please excuse me. I didn't mean to interrupt. I'm Hamish Mackenzie. I'm a lecturer in psychology. I'll move on and get out of your way."

Harry raised his open palm in front of the man. "Mr Mackenzie, would you be available to talk to us tomorrow morning? As a lecturer of psychology you probably knew Jonathon Petherby, so my constable and I would like to know more about him."

"Certainly. I have a free period at ten in the morning. Where will I meet you?"

"Mr McBryde here will arrange a room for us."

As Mackenzie walked off, Harry turned back to McBryde. "Bonnie told us that Petherby was bullied by other students and you were asked to bring those files here. Do you have them?"

"I know nothing about this bullying but Bonnie and the other clerical staff advised me that the alleged perpetrators are Richard Osmanton, Eric James, Julius Shanks and Donald Wiley."

"Now Mr McBryde, I'll take these files with me and you will have those four men at Booloominbah tomorrow morning at nine ready for us to interview them. I want you to find four separate rooms or spaces for us. Is that clear?"

"These are private files and should not leave my office," replied the manager.

"This is a murder investigation and I can get a court order if necessary, but your reluctance to cooperate will be noted. Now what's it to be?"

"Okay, but can I have them back tomorrow morning?"

"Thank you, Mr McBryde. We are leaving now. Please have this room locked until further notice from me. Restrict access to yourself and Sue Ellis. Sue will need to be here to look after the rats."

Harry and Joe got back into the wagon and drove to the At Peace Parlour where they spent the remainder of the day.

Chapter 4
Wednesday

Harry woke early. He took a break from his usual early run as he had a lot on his mind with this new murder case. He put on his slippers and walked to the kitchen of his newly acquired dwelling in Taylor Street. He put on the jug for a cup of tea

Harry had been transferred to Armidale early last year after Danny Jones, the former superintendent at Lismore, was promoted to the position of chief superintendent in head office at Sydney to replace Allan Twain who was medically retired after a massive heart attack.

Danny Jones was well aware that the people in the New England region had been agitating for some time to secede from the state of New South Wales. The movement started after the First World War but subsided in the 1930s due to the Great Depression. Jones knew that from the end of World War II there was increasing pressure from the local politicians and wealthy elite to reignite interest in the idea.

Following discussions with the new police commissioner, Murray Fredericks, Danny Jones promoted and transferred key officers, including Harry Taylor, to the northern region. This was to show that Sydney still had their best interests at heart in the hope that they would remain in New South Wales. Danny remembered the good work Harry had done on difficult cases in Wagga Wagga and the Riverina.

After first arriving in Armidale, Harry boarded at the old Empire Hotel on the corner of Jesse and Beardy streets until he realised that it was unsuitable for him in his line of work. He took time remembering all the places in which he had lived after returning to the police force following his military service in World War II. There was the Shelbourne Hotel in Sydney, his uncle and aunt's place at Redfern, the Railway Hotel in Goonaburra, Eileen Matthews's garage at Stanmore and Macca and Ruth McKay's garage in Wagga Wagga.

Harry was aged thirty-three and unmarried but he thought it was about time that he owned his own house to have some independence, privacy and financial security. He had recently found an old weatherboard and tiled house for sale in Taylor Street. It was freshly painted dark green with white trim and had been kept in excellent condition by its former owners. It had only two bedrooms but there was a comfortable lounge room with an open fireplace, plus a kitchen, bathroom and laundry inside and a toilet down the backyard. The verandah extended across half the front and down the entire northern side. An awning of white-painted corrugated iron covered the triple window of the main bedroom fronting the street. There was a freshly painted white picket fence. The lawn and gardens were neatly maintained and there was a vegetable patch and a lemon tree near the toilet at the back. The fact that the street was named Taylor had not been a consideration for Harry finalising the purchase.

Harry had approached the Bank of New South Wales to arrange a loan to help pay for the house. The manager had been hesitant because Harry was unmarried. The manager considered that a man seeking to purchase a home needed a good woman to keep him sober, stable and dependable in making repayments on time. He was also worried that Harry was in a dangerous occupation and had moved four times in four years. In the manager's eyes that meant 'unstable', therefore not a good risk for a loan. It was only after Raymond Johnston, the local superintendent of police who was in the same Rotary Club as the bank manager, put in a good word for Harry that he got the loan. So there he was, the proud owner of his first house.

Harry had decided to sell his old ex-army Jeep and buy a more modern vehicle. On his way from Wagga Waga to Armidale he detoured via Sydney to search the car saleyards along Parramatta Road where he traded in his Jeep for a red 1946 MG TC sports car. Everyone he'd spoken to thought he was crazy buying a car with a canvas top and with no heater or demister for the cold winters in Armidale. He shrugged off the criticisms, put down the canvas hood and drove to Armidale with the summer breeze blowing through his hair.

After breakfast, Harry walked out from his new house, stepped into the MG and drove to the police station in Dangar Street. The air was crisp and the few people in the street walked with shoulders hunched forward and their arms hugging the front of their jackets to keep out the breeze.

At eight o'clock he walked to the main room where Superintendent Ray Johnston was to commence his weekly meeting. Ray was a tall, upright man with a well-earned reputation for honesty and hard work—a leader who demanded respect, loyalty and efficiency from his officers. Harry held him in high regard and was happy to be on his team.

Ray opened the meeting by asking Harry to inform the officers about the university murder case. Harry took his time outlining the details about the victim, the layout in the shed and his conversations with Sue Ellis, Bonnie Munro and Arthur McBryde. He praised Joe Simms for the coordination and dispatch of the samples to the SIB. He stated his intention to conduct a series of meetings with the manager, the four bullies and the psychology lecturer.

"There was a message here this morning telling me that the victim's family will be here tomorrow morning to view the body and answer questions about their son," said Harry.

Senior Crown Sergeant Ken Wright raised a hand. "Why would someone in Queensland send their son to the university here in Armidale? Why not go to Brisbane?"

"I don't know," replied Harry. "It could be that this university has such a great reputation, or that they wanted to get their son well away from home to make him stand on his own two feet, or that the climate here was cooler. The victim was obese and so a less humid environment was probably better for him."

"Well, that didn't do him much good, did it?" shouted big Lars van Dyke, the constable on general duties.

After a few more questions, Harry and Joe were excused from the meeting to return to the university.

Harry left the MG and went in the police wagon with Joe. Constables Jack Nelson and Charlie Hanwright went in the other wagon. Harry had already briefed them about the upcoming interviews with the bullies.

***

On arriving at the university, the four officers went directly to Arthur McBryde's office. Sitting outside the office in the hallway were four young men. Harry looked them up and down.

The first one sat slumped in the chair with his legs stretched across the corridor while he picked at his nails. He was about twelve stone in weight and fit with an arrogant scowl. His head was covered with unruly red hair and his clothes had never been touched by an iron.

The second was tall, fit and broad-shouldered with large hands and feet; the type of man one would select for the second row in the rugby team. The thick polo-neck sweater with food stains on the front added to his casual, don't-care image. He smoked a roll-your-own cigarette.

The third and fourth men were of average height and size and dressed in neat, clean clothing. The dark-haired one had a slick short-back-and-sides haircut while the other had a wiry mop of hair that had a mind of its own.

After meeting with McBryde, Harry took the red-headed man to the back verandah of Booloominbah and the other officers took one each of the other three. Harry watched as the man again slumped in his chair, legs spread out in front. The lad hunched his shoulders and folded his arms tightly across his chest. He tucked his chin against his left shoulder as if to protect it from a right hook. He kept his eyes on Harry who took his time to sit and look at his notes. Harry introduced himself.

"Do they call you Richard or Dick Osmanton?" he asked.

"What's that got to do with you? I haven't done anything wrong. Why am I here?"

"Well Richard, they tell me that you and your mates are the bully-boys around here. Would you like to comment on that?"

"Who said that? I'll deal with those bastards later."

Harry paused and moved a little forward towards the lad. "What do you mean? Are you four going to take them behind the building? Are you going do them over? How brave—four against one. Is that the way you treat people around here?"

"You're trying to put words into my mouth."

"Tell me about your friend Jonathon Petherby," said Harry.

"He's no friend of mine—the big fat slob. Someone said that he got knocked off. Good riddance, I say. The world will be better off without him."

"Where were you between five o'clock Monday afternoon and nine o'clock yesterday morning?"

"I don't have to tell you where I was. This is a free country. What I do is none of your business," said Osmanton.

"Let me make it clear to you, Richard. Jonathon Petherby was murdered sometime on Monday night or early Tuesday morning. It has been reported to me that you and your mates often bullied Jonathon and therefore you need to explain your movements in that period. If you refuse I'll take you to the station where you will stay until you cooperate with our investigations. If you are still in doubt you might like to seek legal advice."

"Okay, okay. The four of us went to Bruyn's Caledonian Hotel on Monday afternoon. After six o'clock closing we went into the back room where we had a few more drinks. We then went to the Greek café and had a toasted sandwich and a milkshake. After that we all drove back to the uni and went to bed."

"In whose car?"

"Mine."

"So, you were driving after quite a few drinks?"

"I was sober enough to drive."

Harry sat back in his chair, eyes still fixed on Osmanton. "Tell me about your bullying of Jonathon."

"Look, anything we did to him was all in fun. He knew he was a big fat slob and he enjoyed taking food from the plates of other students in the Bevery. We tried to get him up and walking or doing some exercises but he refused, and then sulked when we tried to get him going. We'd tap him on the shoulder or try to take his arm and lead him to the oval. One time we tried to take him in the car to the town pool to teach him how to swim, for his own safety, but he refused and burst into tears. He was his own worst enemy. I don't know who told you we were bullies but we didn't hurt him; I swear."

"Do you think you might have been a bit tough on him, considering his condition? How would you feel if us four officers took you out the back and worked you over?" asked Harry.

Osmanton dropped his head, looked down and took his time before answering. "When you put it that way, I suppose we were a bit tough on him. But we were only trying to help. I'm sorry now that someone killed him. He didn't deserve that."

Harry remained silent until Osmanton lifted his head and continued. "You see, me and my mates are all into sport and we get the benefit of being fit and healthy, so we can't see why others can't see the bloody obvious of being involved."

Harry pointed at him. "You have come from a privileged family and have been born with natural physical attributes. When you are a top athlete it's so easy to be critical of those less fortunate or less able. You'll walk out of this university with glowing results and champion ribbons and awards but that doesn't make you a decent human being. When you get out there in the real world after university and get smacked around by people more street smart than you, remember what happened to Jonathon. Would you like me to introduce you to Jonathon's mother and father tomorrow when they come here to identify their dead son so that you can tell them how you helped Jonathon?"

"No thanks."

"Did Jonathon have any close friends?"

Osmanton scratched his head for a moment before answering. "Yes, some of the students took pity on him, but it didn't do him any good."

"Who were they?" asked Harry.

"Jimmy Perryman, Rhonda Pierce, Fred Dickens and Sheila Doherty often sat down with him and tried to help."

"You may go now, but we might need to talk with you again. If I ever catch you or your mates drinking after hours in a hotel or driving under the influence, I'll throw the book at you."

Harry got up and walked inside to talk to the other officers. They walked out to the back verandah, away from the university staff. Charlie Hanwright spoke first.

"I took Donald Wiley, the dark-haired bloke. He was very nervous, not knowing why he was being interviewed. At first he thought we were going to book them for drinking after hours at the Caledonian Hotel. He pleaded with me not to tell his parents. He admitted that they teased Jonathon and had little respect for him, but claimed that they did not physically harm him."

Jack Nelson followed with his interview. "Julius Shanks was the one with all the curly, wrinkled hair. I suspect that he puts himself out there as the tough guy. He is arrogant with little tolerance for those less gifted than himself. Although, it's my opinion that he would be the least capable of the group, academically. He admitted to pinching and prodding Jonathon on occasions but claimed that they did it in jest. He said the same as Donald Wiley about their whereabouts on Monday night. He's a scumbag and needs bringing down a peg or two but I don't think he is a murderer or had anything to do with Jonathon's death."

Joe Simms followed. "I saw Eric James, the tall, broad-shouldered one. He's a big raw-boned country bloke who has been used to doing tough work on his father's property. He's very much into sport, although, I see him as being fairly immature socially and is more a follower of Osmanton rather than being a leader in his own right. His story confirmed what you blokes got from the others. He admitted to nudging Jonathon to get him moving plus tipping his plates of food into the garbage can, but nothing violent. I don't see him as someone causing permanent physical harm."

Harry recounted his conversation with Osmanton and summed up the interviews. "Thanks for your good work. While these four must remain on our list of persons of interest, I have serious doubts that these idiots killed Jonathon. I hope that this morning's interviews might have knocked some common sense into all of them and that they might treat others with a bit more respect from now on. Joe and I will stay here to interview the others. Jack and Charlie, you can go back to your other duties."

Chapter 5
Wednesday

Harry and Joe walked back to Arthur McBryde's office. The manager was sitting in his tall, upright leather chair behind a polished oak desk. The blotting pad in front of him had a clean sheet of paper inserted. A penholder and telephone were the only other objects on the desk. The wall to the right was covered with floor-to-ceiling bookshelves. All books with torn covers or with an untidy appearance had obviously been removed to some back room. There was an atmosphere of cold, clinical efficiency in the room. There were two upright wooden chairs on the other side of the desk. The manager invited Harry and Joe to sit.

Harry brought his chair closer to the desk and reached into his inside pocket. He took his time. He removed his pen and hard-covered notebook and placed them on the desk. He raised the cover so that McBryde could not see his notes. While Harry read the last couple of pages slowly and silently, McBryde's fingers fiddled nervously with his tie and the buttons on his waistcoat before he smoothed his pencil-thin moustache on each side. His eyes darted back and forth between Harry and Joe.

When Harry looked up, he fixed his unblinking eyes on the manager. "Mr McBryde, are you the person primarily responsible for the health and welfare of both staff and students in this university?"

Arthur McBryde blinked three times before answering. "Well yes," he stuttered. "I am the university manager."

"It has been reported to me," said Harry, "that the student Jonathon Petherby was regularly bullied at this university and that this fact was well known to both staff and students. It happened in the Bevery, the halls, the grounds and lecture theatres. This occurred last year and has continued this year. What did you do about that?"

McBryde's head jolted backwards as he stared at the ceiling. As his face lowered, his eyes were fixed on the penholder and he pointed the fingers of his right hand in that direction.

"You have to understand that the management of this university is a full-time job with many facets of responsibility. I have delegated the matter of student welfare to Mrs Munro. That is her responsibility."

Harry tapped his forefinger in front of the penholder on the desk. "Has Bonnie Munro ever discussed the bullying of Jonathon Petherby with you?"

McBryde shifted his visual attention to the telephone on the other side of the desk. "Yes, she did mention it to me once and I told her to deal with it."

"Did you ever follow up to check the progress of that action?"

McBryde took his time answering as he looked towards Harry. "If Mrs Munro had thought that necessary, she would have come back to me."

"Is it true that at least two of the students we interviewed this morning have been given awards for their sporting prowess and that you personally gave out those awards?"

"Yes. Richard Osmanton and Eric James have both received awards. They are outstanding athletes."

Harry slapped the desk. "And you gave them awards when you were fully aware that they were guilty of bullying Jonathon Petherby? Would you like to join me tomorrow morning when I meet with Jonathon's parents to explain the nature of his death?"

McBryde looked down. "No. That won't be necessary. I've already drafted a letter to be sent to them, extending the university's condolences on the unfortunate death of their son. My secretary will have that back to me shortly to have it in the mail this afternoon."

Harry stood and nodded to Joe to leave. "You are all heart, Mr McBryde. Thank goodness it was not your son who was murdered. We'll be leaving now, but I will be preparing a report on this matter for the vice-chancellor and the university board. Now please show us to another vacant room where we can interview other members of staff and some other students."

McBryde walked to the door and called to his secretary. "Mrs Jacobson, please show Detectives Taylor and Simms to the vacant room in the east wing."

Harry turned to Mrs Jacobson. "After we settle into the room could you ask Professor Gwyn O'Connor to meet us there. When he leaves, we would like to see Hamish Mackenzie, after which we would like to see four students together, if that is possible. They are Jimmy Perryman, Rhonda Pierce, Fred Dickens and Sheila Doherty. We have been told that they were close friends with Jonathon Petherby."

"Yes," replied Mrs Jacobson. "I'll arrange that if they are available."

"If they question the need to come," said Harry, "tell them of the urgency and importance of this inquiry."

"I certainly will. Please call me Yvonne." She confidently strode back to her office.

Ten minutes later, Doctor Gwyn O'Connor, the professor of zoology, came to the door.

"Come in, Professor," said Harry. "I am Detective Harry Taylor and this is Detective Joe Simms. Please take a seat. I assume that by now you are well aware of the death of Jonathon Petherby in the rat shed yesterday. Is there anything you or your staff know about Jonathon that might help us with our inquiries? Has he ever studied zoology or had anything to do with the laboratories or the rat shed? Do the people in the philosophy, psychology or English departments ever have anything to do with the experiments on the rats in that shed?"

The professor looked out the window. He tapped his right forefinger against his jawbone as he thought and nervously flicked the long strands of hair from his eyes.

"Please call me Gwyn. Let me think. I know he wasn't a student of zoology. He certainly had not been involved in any way with the study of those rats. He had not studied any of the sciences and, therefore, had no reason to be in any of our laboratories or that shed."

Joe Simms spoke up. "Did any of your staff know him?"

"Yes. Charles Snape, a zoology lecturer, remembered him being in the choir at his Presbyterian church. Others recognised him around the university. Let's face it, his grotesque shape did make him stand out in the crowd, but they had no dealings personally with him."

"Thanks Gwyn," said Harry. "If anything else comes to mind, please contact us at the station."

As the professor stood to leave, he turned. "Some of the staff said they witnessed Jonathon being bullied at the Bevery dining hut. They said that Jonathon was upset; although the actions of the bullies did not appear to be too physically severe."

After O'Connor left, Joe turned to Harry. "Petherby had no obvious physical injuries. That means that the killer, or killers if there was more than one, enticed him into the shed. What would make him follow people he didn't like into that shed when there was nothing in there of interest to him?"

Harry scratched his ear. "I know that we agreed that he most likely died in the shed but, on the off chance that he was drugged elsewhere, it would have taken more than one person to get him to the shed where he was placed on the floor before they released the rats."

"That means there were probably three or more of them; two holding him by the upper body and at least one holding the legs," replied Joe.

"That's right, Joe. Therefore, we must keep those bullies on our list of suspects," said Harry. "We must keep all options open."

"I had another thought," said Joe. "Could the killer have enticed Petherby into the shed to have a drink in a show of being friendly? When in the shed, the killer gave him a poisoned drink and he collapsed on the floor, dead, after which the killer let out the rats and left. But for that to happen, Petherby would have been desperate for friendship to accept an invitation to a rat shed for a drink."

"We are going to make a good detective out of you yet, Joe. Good work. For that to happen, Petherby would have only accepted if he was friendly with the other person or trusted him and therefore, that would not be the bullies."

Hamish Mackenzie came to the door. He strode confidently into the room and sat at the table. "Good morning, detectives. What can I do for you?"

Harry and Joe looked at a man very different to Gwyn O'Connor. He was in his mid-thirties and very fit for his age. Everything about him projected an image of confidence, energy and activity. He was dressed the same as yesterday in his tartan trews and academic gown.

Harry took out his notebook. "We have been informed that Jonathon Petherby studied psychology, philosophy and English last year. Could you tell us a bit about his progress and any other information that might help us in our inquiries about his death?"

"Certainly," replied Hamish. "He was in my psychology class last year. He barely passed. He failed English and philosophy. I recommended to our school that he not be permitted to continue this year but I was overruled by the bleeding hearts around here who wanted to give him another go."

"What was he like as a person?" asked Harry.

Hamish ran his fingers down the collar of his academic gown and smoothed any creases. "I saw him as an over-indulged, spoilt brat. He owned one of the few cars on campus and had tried to win friends by giving other students a lift. He bought packets of lollies and handed them out to everybody. The others took what they could get, then laughed at him behind his back. He even invited the lecturers to the Greek café and paid for their meal."

"Did you go?" asked Joe.

"No way. I don't stoop so low as to accept bribes. Some of the female students sympathised with him and so he responded kindly to them. They had tried to mother him but that only exaggerated his problem."

"What was his problem?" asked Harry.

Hamish sat bolt upright. "It's pretty bloody obvious. He was a big fat slob, too gross to get out of his own way. And he did nothing to overcome his condition. He was his own worst enemy."

Harry sat back and ran his hands through his hair. "Had he ever sought help or been given advice on how to deal with his weight?"

"As his psychology lecturer, I often talked to him in private. He had also been in the church choir with me, so I saw him outside the university."

"What sort of advice did you give him?" asked Joe.

"I told him that everyone became what they stuffed in their mouths. He had to eat less and only eat healthy food. You are what you eat. You two know that."

"You're the expert in this area, Hamish," said Harry. "Are psychological factors the cause of obesity?"

"There have been lots of studies in this area," replied Hamish. "There is strong evidence that mental health and physical health are strongly related."

"How is that so?" asked Joe.

"Stigmatisation, discrimination and the over-emphasis on body size and shape are key factors. While it could be argued that obesity is the result of the imbalance of bodily hormones, it is more likely that people over eat to calm themselves, to give themselves a reward, to alleviate sadness or guilt, or to reduce the stress of loneliness because others want nothing to do with them."

"I like my tucker, Hamish," said Joe, "but I'm not fat."

"But you keep yourself fit and burn up the calories. People like Jonathon use food as a panacea and rely on copious quantities of fatty and sugary food; and they don't burn off the calories. They can only overcome it if they change the emotional state that led to their excess."

"Thank you, Hamish. That makes a lot of sense and should help us to get a better understanding of this man and the background to his condition. Would you be available if we needed some psychological expertise in any future cases?"

"Certainly," replied Hamish. "I've always had an interest in the criminal mind and how victims are targeted and I'd love to help out whenever I can."

"Did you have any success in changing Jonathon's behaviour?" asked Harry.

"I'm in the Sydney University Regiment here at the university which is a unit of the Citizen Military Force. I tried to get him to join but he refused. I also tried to get him in the Highland Pipe Band where he could bang the drums and march. I told him to join the Scouts, play tennis, go for walks, learn to swim and join the bushwalking group. I told him to get off his arse and get active and to stop shoving all that rubbish down his throat. But you can't help someone who refuses to help themselves."

"Surely, you were not surprised that he didn't heed your advice?" said Harry.

Yvonne Jacobson came to the door. "Excuse me, Detective Taylor. There is a call from the station. You and Detective Simms are urgently required at an incident at a house on the road to Uralla. Sergeant Ken Wright is on the phone."

"Thanks Yvonne. Could you please inform the four students that we will see them tomorrow."

Ken told Harry that the incident involved a man who had physically assaulted a woman and her child. A witness claimed that the man could have been involved with the murder at the university because he was up on a manslaughter charge in Queensland and had always been very critical of people who went to universities.

***

Harry and Joe left the university and drove to a house in Hill Street, Uralla. When they arrived at the door they were met by a scruffily dressed man who told them to go away. He tried to close the door but Harry blocked it with his boot. The man tried to push Harry back away.

"Get out," he shouted, "we don't want anything. Get lost."

Harry forced the door open and introduced himself and Joe. He could hear a woman and some children crying and screaming inside the house. The man swung a punch at Harry who ducked, blocked the swinging arm and stabbed his right foot forward, catching the man in the kneecap with the edge of his boot. As the man fell forward, Harry rammed the man's head onto his lifted knee, squashing his nose out of shape. Joe helped Harry drag him into the lounge room and held him down in the chair.

As Harry turned to walk away, the man got up and swung a punch at Joe. Joe retaliated with a perfect short, straight left followed by a right hook that dropped him to the floor. Joe cuffed him.

Harry walked quickly to the hallway near the kitchen where the woman and children were cowering. The children were still crying. "Hello madam, I'm Detective Harry Taylor. There's no need to be afraid anymore. We have him in handcuffs. Could you please tell me your names?"

The woman wiped her eyes. "I'm Joan Somers and these are my children, Tom, John and Susan. That man there is Jack Gardiner. He boards here with me."

"Are you okay? Has that man hit you or the children?"

"When he came home, he slapped me around the face and punched me in the stomach but I kept the children behind me."

Joan Somers explained that she was a single mother and had taken in Gardiner as a boarder. She told Harry that he was an itinerant miner working mostly at Tingha, about sixty miles away. Whenever he was in Uralla, he treated her very badly with violence but she needed the money from his board and so took the punishment to feed her children.

She told Harry and Joe that Gardiner had beaten her and the kids last night after he came home from Tingha and the hotel and also this morning and threatened her that she would finish up like that bloke at the university.

"Do you have relatives or friends who can be here with you?"

"The Withers next door have been fabulous. They have always been so supportive, and Jack is not game to take on Charlie."

Harry walked back to the lounge room. "Keep an eye on him, Joe," said Harry. "I want to speak to the neighbours."

Harry walked to the house next door where he met Charlie and Mary Withers. He explained the reason for his visit. "Are you the couple who phoned the police station?"

"Yes," replied Charlie, "that mongrel next door went too far this morning."

"What can you tell me about this man?"

Charlie spoke first. "That bastard should be locked up for good for the way he treats poor Joan. He's always beating her up and she's too scared to tell anyone for fear of losing the rent. She's never got over the death of her husband who died in a truck accident two years ago, and I don't think she has any close relatives nearby."

Mary put up her hand. "I think Gardiner did that bloke in at the university. He told me that it was the best thing to happen to those lazy students. He said that they were all bludgers sponging off good workers like him. He said he was looking forward to another of them being done in."

Charlie coughed before speaking. "When I told him what a bastard he was for picking on women, he said he would do whatever he liked and anyone who disagreed would finish up like that student at the university, and he'd be pleased to see that happen. I think he did that kid in. He once told me over a beer or two that he was once charged with manslaughter in Queensland but got off because his mate, who was the only witness, took off for Western Australia."

Harry thanked the neighbours and returned to see Joan Somers.

Harry contacted Captain Jack Walsh from the Salvation Army to assist Joan and the children and then took Gardiner to the Sheriff's Cottage back in Armidale where he was put in a holding cell for those waiting to appear in court.

Chapter 6
Thursday

Harry drove to the courthouse and left some notes on the Uralla assault case for Bob Bertram, the prosecutor. He then walked around the corner to meet Joe at the Sheriff's Cottage where Jack Gardiner was being held.

As they entered the cell, Gardiner shouted at them, accused them of assault and threatened that he would get them when they least expected it.

Joe stepped forward. "That's the trouble with you bullies—you pick on little old ladies and children but you haven't got the guts to take on someone your own size and age in a fair fight."

"Hold back, Detective," said Harry. "Let me deal with this man."

He turned to Gardiner. "Where were you on Monday night and Tuesday morning?"

"I was in Tingha. I only came back yesterday."

"We'll check that with the mine owner. We were told that you came here from Queensland. Is that correct?"

"Yes."

"You'll go before the magistrate this morning. You most certainly will do time in gaol on numerous charges of assault causing actual bodily harm and one charge of resisting arrest. When you are released you will take a one-way ticket back to Queensland. If you ever cross the border this way again, I will put you back in the cell and throw away the key. Do you understand?"

Gardiner gave a grunt and hung his head.

"Let's get out of here, Joe. We have an important meeting with Mr and Mrs Petherby at the Imperial Hotel."

As they walked around the corner into Beardy Street, Joe posed a question. "Considering what Hamish Mackenzie said about Petherby yesterday, is it possible that the young bloke went to the shed and drank a poison like arsenic, or something similar, to commit suicide?"

"Good question, Joe, but I don't think so. I can't see why he would remove most of his clothes, cover his tummy and legs with lard and pull up his trouser legs before taking the poisoned drink. And why would he release all the rats before taking the poison? Besides, if he had a serious problem with being overweight, he would not want to be found half eaten by rats. And why would he shove cooked sausages into his mouth—as he was dying? Then there is the sign on his back and the two glasses and bottle of lemonade on the picnic table. It doesn't add up."

Harry looked up at the Imperial Hotel. He had always admired the old building with its highly ornamental features, its extensive cast-iron frieze work on the verandah, bull-nosed awnings and extravagant parapets. On entering the main door they were led to the back lounge where the Petherbys were waiting.

A fit tall, suntanned man aged about thirty stood up from his chair to greet the two detectives. He reached out with a strong calloused hand. "G'day, I'm Tom Petherby, and these are my parents, George and Agnes. I'm Jonathon's brother. My other brother is back home looking after the farm."

Harry did the introductions. He noted the strong contrast between Jonathon and his brother; a fit solidly built young man. The parents appeared to be in their late forties or early fifties. The father was five foot nine with the fitness of a man who had worked hard on the land all his life. His wife was plump but presented a kind and friendly face; though it was now flushed as she constantly wiped the tears from her eyes. Everyone found a seat.

Harry began. "I'd like to extend to you our deepest sympathies for your loss. Jonathon is at the At Peace Funerals parlour now and you will be most welcome there to view his body, if that is your wish. I would, however, like at least one of you to view the body to confirm it is your son."

Tom raised his arm. "I'll go and do that. Mum and Dad can stay here."

"Thanks Tom," said Harry. "You can go with Detective Simms while I have a talk with your parents," replied Harry.

As Joe and Tom left, Harry shifted to a chair closer to the parents. "Could we start by you telling me a bit about Jonathon? Take your time."

Agnes burst into tears. George leaned forward with his open hand pointing towards Harry. "I could never understand that boy. He wouldn't hurt a fly but he was too bloody lazy to get out of his own way. He was nothing like his brothers Tom and Brian. They have been two outstanding sons and I'm so proud of them. I couldn't do the farm work without them. Jonathon was his mother's son. He was not a Petherby. He took after Agnes's useless brother Jeremy, a good-for-nothing layabout. He spent more time eating than working."

Agnes screamed and rose out of the chair. Harry stood to take her by the shoulders. He let her cry on his shoulder before he helped her back to the chair. "Take your time, Mrs Petherby, and tell me about Jonathon."

She turned towards her husband. "You horrible man. How could you say that about your own son? You have hated him since he was a baby because he's not like you. Not everyone in this world is like you. Jonathon's problem started as a young boy when you treated him worse than you would treat an animal."

George snapped around and pointed at his wife. "He's a good-for-nothing layabout. His only exercise was shoving food down his throat. If he had got off his arse and did some real work he wouldn't have had a problem. He cost me a fortune buying him a car, paying for his board and university fees and then, when he was back on the farm, he ate us out of house and home. And what good have I got in return? He failed miserably last year but you pleaded with me to let him do it all again this year."

Agnes burst into tears again. Harry waited.

"Mrs Petherby, we know that your son was overweight, but can you tell me if there was any reason he ate so much? Was there a medical reason?"

She wiped her eyes again. "Jonathon was a plump baby and always liked his food. And he never liked sports like his brothers. Because of that he was always picked on and bullied by his classmates. And his horrible father treated him like rubbish. You just heard him. How would you like a father like that?"

She stood up from the lounge chair and left the room.

Harry looked at George. "Sometime later in the day you all might like to meet with David Hobbs from At Peace Funerals on Uralla Road to arrange the funeral of your son, either here or back at Warwick.

Whatever you might have thought about Jonathon, he was your son, and your wife is deeply traumatised by his passing. Give her the support and love she deserves. Not everyone in this world has been given the strength and interest in hard physical work you and your other two sons have."

"How did my son die?" asked George.

"At this stage we have not concluded our investigations but we will keep you informed when we have a definite cause of death."

Before leaving the hotel, Harry phoned the funeral parlour and left a message for Joe to meet him at the university.

***

On arriving at the Booloominbah building Harry asked Yvonne Jacobson which room was available to interview the friends of Jonathon. Yvonne directed him to the same room as yesterday.

Ten minutes later, four students entered the room.

"Come on in, please," said Harry. "Relax. Take a seat. By now you would have heard about what happened to Jonathon Petherby. I believe you all knew Jonathon, so I would like to ask you to give me any information that might assist us with our inquiries. Who would like to start?"

Sheila Doherty spoke first. "I feel so sorry for Jonathon. He never had a chance here. Those boys from the football team gave him hell. They are big nasty bullies but they get away with it because they are the star athletes in the university; and they work as a pack so that no one is game to take them on. They pushed and prodded Jonathon all the time and made jokes at his expense. He didn't have a chance. And look at what happened. I wouldn't put it past that mob to have been a part of what happened to him. I wouldn't trust them as far as I could kick them."

Jimmy Perryman raised his hand. "Because of the stress he was under, his results suffered and the lecturers didn't cut him any slack when they knew what he had to put up with. Mr Mackenzie is a wonderful person and a great lecturer but he is extremely demanding and will not tolerate any failures."

Rhonda Pierce sat forward. "The lecturers in the psychology department wanted to ban Jonathon from continuing his studies this year because of his poor results last year, but we went to the vice-chancellor and pleaded a case for him. I feel so shattered that we didn't do more to prevent his death."

"It's those bastards who bullied him who should have been the victims, not Jonathon," said Fred Dickens. "He didn't deserve that."

There was a knock on the door and Joe Simms entered. "Hi everyone. Keep going. I'll sit over here."

Harry did the introductions.

"Do any of you know Jonathon's family?" asked Harry.

Rhonda spoke first. "As far as I know, nobody else here comes from Warwick in Queensland. I met Jonathon's family once when they came to visit him. His mother was wonderful but I wouldn't trust his father. He was a grumpy old man. He was very abrupt with Jonathon for no reason. Jonathon would never talk about his family but he was never happy when they were here."

"Thank you very much for your help," said Harry. "Please give us a call if you think of anything else that might help. All the best in your studies."

***

Harry and Joe left in their separate vehicles and drove to St Paul's Presbyterian Church in Faulkner Street. It was an impressive building with dark manganese brick and white trim. As they walked in they admired the wonderful organ and the stained-glass windows. They found the minister, the Reverend Charles Aitken, near the pulpit. Harry explained the purpose of their visit.

The minister invited Harry and Joe to sit on the first-row pew while he stood in front of them. "It is so sad. Jonathon had several issues in his life. And it wasn't helped by his family, who I met this morning. Jonathon got much comfort here in the church and enjoyed the support of the choir. It was his chance to contribute to the religious community in Armidale. In this church he was treated as a real human being."

Harry thanked him for his comments. "Hamish Mackenzie, Gwyn O'Connor and David Hobbs all told us about Jonathon's involvement in the church."

"Yes. Hamish, in particular, is a very active member of our congregation and had a lot to do with Jonathon and would know him better than the others. Hamish was recently made an elder of the church.

He is in the choir and teaches at Sunday school. He is such a positive influence here and in the town. I treasure his contributions to the church even though he can be very demanding at times. I believe he tried to have a positive effect on Jonathon."

"In what way did he help Jonathon here at the church?"

"Hamish is an interesting character. On the one hand he is so generous with his time and support for other parishioners, including Jonathon, but on the other hand he can be somewhat intolerant of others who don't come up to his standards. He always tried to get Jonathon involved, especially with the choir, but without a lot of success."

Joe extended his open right hand towards the minister. "How did you and Hamish get on personally? We were thinking of consulting him on some police investigations that involved a psychological element. Do you think he would be the right type of person to assist us?"

Charles smiled. "Don't repeat this to any of my parishioners but, quite frankly, I find him tedious and boring. He's always trying to convince me that he knows more about religion than me. However, he has a wonderful grasp of psychology and could be of assistance to you."

After further discussion, Harry thanked the minister for his time and comments before he and Joe left to return to the station.

Chapter 7
Thursday

On arriving at the station, Harry and Joe were met by Senior Constable Pat Casey who reminded them that they were wanted at the court in half an hour for the Gardiner hearing.

Harry and Joe turned and walked to the main entrance in Beardy Street. The main courthouse was one of Armidale's oldest public buildings. It was built about 1860. It had a stunning facade and was a well-known landmark in the area. The large courtroom in the centre of the building was one of the most impressive in the country.

Bob Bertram, the prosecutor, met them in the foyer. "From your notes you left this morning," he said, "it appears to be a lay-down-misère case, but fill me in on anything else you see as important."

Harry removed his hat. "Gardiner is a low-life mongrel. He's an alcoholic and when he's had too much to drink he picks on Joan Somers and her kids. We have no evidence of sexual assault but I wouldn't put it past him. Mrs Somers is one of those poor women who get trapped by these types of men. She needs the money from Gardiner's board because she lost her husband in a truck accident about two years ago. She can't work because of the kids. She doesn't have the skills or training to get good employment during school hours. And she has no relatives nearby."

"I've asked her to be here today," said Bob. "But will she be okay to take the stand?"

"She's very fragile, physically and emotionally," replied Harry. "If you do put her up on the stand, go very carefully. She will crumble when she looks at Gardiner. She will be fearful of what he might do to her."

"What's this about him being involved with Petherby?"

"We were told that he had been charged with manslaughter in Queensland. We checked with the police there. There had been an accusation made, but there was no conclusive evidence and so he was not charged. He was found guilty of assault on a few occasions but he could not have killed Petherby because he was in Tingha at the time. Anything he might have said was more likely just him threatening to scare Mrs Somers."

"Okay, let's go in," said Bob as he strode off into the courtroom.

The court was brought to order as the magistrate, Gregory McMaster, arrived at the bench in front of the high arched windows. He called on Bob Bertram to present his case. Bob examined his witnesses: Harry, Joe, Joan's neighbours, Charlie and Mary Withers, and Captain Jack Walsh from the Salvation Army. Bob presented to the court photographs of the injuries sustained by Mrs Somers, but he did not ask her to testify.

The defender representing Gardiner, Kenneth Rumbold, commenced his case by accusing Harry and Joe of assault and showed photos of Gardiner's bruises as evidence.

The magistrate interrupted. "If you wish to bring charges against the police officers, Mr Rumbold, then do so by the normal procedures. Now proceed with your presentation."

Rumbold kept his presentation very brief and did not call Gardiner to the stand.

At the conclusion of the hearing, the magistrate determined that Gardiner was guilty of the charges of assault causing bodily harm, assaulting a police officer and resisting arrest. He sentenced Gardiner to three months in gaol with a further suspended sentence of six months, should he reoffend. He directed Gardiner to never approach Mrs Somers or the children ever again and remain beyond a ten-mile radius from their dwelling in Uralla.

Harry thanked Bob for his prosecution of the case and how he protected Joan Somers from in-court scrutiny. He talked to Joan and Jack Walsh for a while before he and Joe returned to the station.

***

As they walked in the door, Pat Casey asked them to report to Ray Johnston's office. They knocked on the superintendent's door and entered.

"At ease, officers," said Ray. "Take a seat and tell me about the Gardiner hearing and your progress with the university case."

Harry took his time describing the hearing and informed the superintendent that he was happy with the result. He added that he was confident that Jack Walsh would help Joan Somers.

"Where are we up to in the Petherby case?" asked Ray.

Harry spoke about Doctor Ebsworth conducting an autopsy and his meetings with McBryde, the four bullies, Mackenzie, O'Connor, the four sympathetic students and Petherby's family.

"Have you got any report back from Tony Jacobs yet?" asked Ray.

"No. They are always busy down there, but I'm hoping to get at least a preliminary report today or tomorrow."

"Do you have any clear motive yet for this kid's murder?"

"There is no evidence that Petherby ever threatened or attacked his tormentors," said Harry. "In fact, I'd say that would be the least likely reason for his death. I see him as having always been a victim rather than a perpetrator of mischief or lawbreaking. It is possible that, at some time, he lashed back at his tormentors, but that would have been only verbal. And I doubt that would have led to his death. He had always been the target of abuse from his father, maybe his brothers and his schoolmates too, but I can't yet find a definite reason why someone would take the next step to murder him. The lack of the killer's motive is one of the key problems."

"Could it be the father or brothers?"

"There is no evidence that they were in the Armidale district last Monday night or early Tuesday morning. The police at Warwick couldn't guarantee that the family were at home on that night or even if they were in the Warwick district. Despite his father's attitude towards Jonathon, I don't see him as a murderer. The brothers could have gained some extra inheritance if their brother was no longer alive after their father died, but my instinct is that they are hard-working farmers and were not involved in their brother's death."

Joe spoke up. "Yes sir. I'd agree with Harry. I had a father like that. But men like that shout and scream and threaten and abuse their kids until they are adults, but are too gutless to take it to the next step where they would murder their own son. They'll slap them around but they don't have the desire to kill their kids. They are a little like that bastard Gardiner we had in court this morning. They get their strength from using their power and control over others, especially those who depend on them for support. If the weak one is killed or leaves, the bully no longer has that power. They are all bloody cowards."

"Hold your language, Constable," said the superintendent. "We can get the message without swearing around here."

"My apologies, sir," Joe replied.

"There has to be some other motive behind this case," said Harry. "I can't see Petherby ever being a threat to anyone. He was so fat and weak physically that he wouldn't have hurt or damaged a fly in a fair fight. He couldn't fight his way out of a paper bag. From what others tell us he was not prone to verbal or other forms of anger. He got extremely distressed when bullied but didn't fight back."

"Could the killer have been jealous of Petherby's financial status?" asked Ray. "Despite the attitude of his father, Jonathon was quite well-off. And he was one of the few students who owned a car."

"Had anyone wanted to steal the car or take it for a joy-ride they could have done so easily," said Harry. "It's not that difficult to pick a lock and hot-wire the ignition."

"You sound like you are very experienced with these things, Harry," said Ray with a deep belly-laugh.

"In country towns, sir, people often lock their keys in the vehicle, or leave their keys at the pub or swimming hole, or forget where they put them. Everyone does it to get someone moving again. There would be lots of people around here who could do that."

Ray turned to Joe with a broad grin. "Keep an eye on Harry for me and report back any suspicious behaviour around vehicles."

They all burst out laughing.

"In Redfern we never locked our cars," said Joe, "because we knew that anyone could break in and take them. It was best to let them take it, have a joy-ride and, hopefully, leave it somewhere without broken windows or damaged locks."

Ray scratched his forehead and leaned back in his chair. "The thing I can't understand is why the killer put the pendant around Petherby's neck and stuck the sign to his back. And what does the number 1 represent? Is the killer telling us that this is the first of many murders?"

Harry stood to stretch his legs. "Those things were not put there by the victim. If the killer is sending a message, then who is the target of that message—the victim's family, the police, the community? Or is it the killer's way of working off his frustrations?"

"I have been on a few cases, and have heard of other murders," said Ray, "where the killer deliberately leaves a trail of evidence or clues to show the police that they have more control than them. They want to show that they are smarter than us. They must always feel that they are one step ahead, and they want to provoke the police in to doing something foolish. So, let's be careful of that as we continue."

"Thank you, sir," said Harry. "That makes a lot of sense. We'll keep it in mind."

Pat Casey came to the door to let Harry know that Tony Jacobs was on the phone. Harry went to the front desk. "What have you got for me, Tony?"

"I've put the report in a letter that I will send to you on tonight's train. It will be there in the morning," replied Tony.

"What is the guts of the report?"

"Regarding the fingerprints you sent us, most were matched to the staff from the zoology department, including many from those you labelled as 'Sue Ellis'. In order to identify the unmatched prints you would have to broaden your print-taking to eliminate others normally using that room."

"We could extend our fingerprinting to all the university staff and students using that shed but that could be a waste of time," said Harry, "because it is possible that the killer is not a member of the university."

"There were no prints on the bottle of lemonade or on one of the glass tumblers," replied Tony. "And the second tumbler had only Petherby's prints on it. Regarding the liquid residues, we found traces of phenobarbital in thc glass used by Petherby but none in the other one and none in the bottle of lemonade."

"Is phenobarbital a type of barbiturate?" asked Harry.

"Yes."

"Isn't that what vets use to put down dogs and cats?"

"That's right. It's also used as an anaesthetic."

"Was there any evidence that phenobarbital was present in Petherby's body?"

"Yes," replied Tony.

"Were the levels of phenobarbital in the body enough to cause death?" asked Harry.

"As you know, Harry, there are post-mortem changes. Blood tests are the most accurate method of testing for barbiturates. Residues of the barbiturates from the liver and urine can also last for some time. It is our estimation that the quantities in the victim's blood, liver and bladder were definitely of a level sufficient to cause death. Thankfully, you got the samples to us quickly, as phenobarbital lasts up to a week in the blood."

"Are you confident that the phenobarbital was the cause of death?"

"Yes, but, like any drug, it is the quantity that determines the impact," replied Tony, "no matter whether it was swallowed or injected."

Harry coughed. "Doctor Ebsworth and I examined the body thoroughly and found no puncture marks for injection."

"The traces in the blood, liver, stomach and bladder clearly indicate that the poison was ingested and was enough to cause death," said Tony.

"How much of the poison would be required to kill someone?" asked Harry.

"Most of the supplies in Australia come from European countries and is measured in grams and it would take between 5 to 10 grams to cause death."

"Would that change with the size of the victim?"

"Yes, but the concentration in the victim far exceeded that amount."

"Thanks Tony. Pass on my thanks to the team. Great work."

"Do you have more leads on the case yet?"

"No. It is very confusing. There's a lot more to the case than the blood, liver, bladder and stomach samples. Must go now, mate. Thanks again."

Harry went back to the superintendent's office to bring Ray and Joe up to date.

Harry pointed to Joe. "Later today I want you to contact every doctor, chemist, hospital and veterinarian here in Armidale and in Guyra, Uralla and Walcha. Check their records of supply and use of phenobarbital. Check if there are any supplies unaccounted for. This is a high priority."

Pat Casey came to the door. "Harry, we have just had a call from the Empire Hotel. A body has been discovered out the back of the hotel."

Chapter 8
Thursday

Harry and Joe parked the wagon in Jesse Street and walked around the corner to the Empire Hotel. They were met inside by Sheila and Billy Barnes, the publicans. Sheila was five foot ten, had curly red hair, freckles, broad shoulders and a no-nonsense stance. She stood with arms folded and a tea towel slung over her shoulder that clearly said that she was in charge of this establishment. Billy, with his florid complexion and puffy cheeks from too much drinking, stood back.

Harry needed no introduction, as he had stayed at the Empire Hotel briefly when he first arrived in Armidale last year. He introduced Joe.

"G'day Sheila, tell us what has happened here. Where is this body?"

"I went around the back of the pub to dump some rubbish at the back fence that borders the old Olympic Hall where the teachers college students live, and I saw a body face down in the old bath in the corner. I rushed back in to give you blokes a call."

"Do you know who the person is?"

"No. It was a man and he was face down in the water," replied Sheila. "His jacket was over his head. He weren't movin'. I didn't stop to take a better look. I just run here to get you blokes. It was the last thing on my mind to go and muck around with a dead body. I've got enough to do in here. That's your job."

"Has anyone else been around there since you saw him?"

"No bloody way. I got Billy to get Buster Smith to stand at the door to the laneway over there to stop anyone going out there."

"You're a gem, Sheila. Thanks a lot. We'll take over from here. Just keep everyone away."

"Hey Harry," said Sheila, "what's this I hear about you buying a house in Taylor Street? Who's the lucky girl?"

"Yes, Sheila," replied Harry with a laugh. "I moved in recently, but I'm there on my own. And I don't want you spreading rumours around the bar that anyone else is involved. Besides, you've still got Billy, so you're not available. And I wouldn't want anyone else in there with me."

"Just say the word, Harry, and I'll be packin' me bag in a flash."

Harry turned to go to the side door. "Come on, Joe, we've got work to do. Thanks Sheila."

Sheila called out. "Hey Harry, you might not know but, it is male bowerbirds that build the nests to attract the females. Let us know and we'll have the wedding reception here in the pub."

Harry laughed. "I'll keep that in mind, Sheila."

"I can line up any number of good Armidale girls for you. Just let me know."

"Dream on, Sheila. Good try," replied Harry.

"Thanks Buster," said Harry as he walked out the side door. "You best get back to the bar and have another drink before closing time. But close that door and don't let anyone out here. We'll take over here."

As Harry and Joe walked to the back fence they saw the area cluttered with rubbish: old boxes, bottles, rusty pipes, cardboard cartons and broken wooden kegs. Against the back fence was an old enamelled bath, half full of water, in which lay the body of a small man, face down. The head, shoulders and torso were in the water. The legs extended up over the end of the bath.

On an old box next to the bath were two almost empty beer glasses and an empty bottle of Resch's beer.

"You take notes, Joe, while I call out the details."

Harry put his hand in the water to check for a pulse at the neck, even though he saw it as a futile exercise. "Holy hell! That water is so cold. That shouldn't be so cold on a day like this, even at this time of the year. It feels like ice. Give me a hand to lift this bloke out of this bath."

The two of them lifted the body from the bath tub and laid it out on the gravel, face up. Harry checked for a pulse again.

"That was fairly easy, Joe," said Harry. "He's only small. He mustn't be much more than seven stone. Look at his very small hands and feet. Look at the small, shiny, patent-leather shoes. They certainly don't go with those ex-army camouflage trousers and the oversized bomber jacket he's wearing. His facial features are fine and sharp. And look here. In the inside pocket of his jacket there is a notebook with lists of names and amounts of money on the open page."

"He's about the size of a jockey," said Joe.

"By the look of the skin colour and the wrinkling on the hands, I'd say that this man has been here for some time," said Harry. "I'd guess that he might have been put here last night but was only found when Sheila came out here this afternoon. His teeth and gums are pink. The facial skin is discoloured and very wrinkled. That could have been the result of immersion in cold water. I reckon that bath had been filled with ice. It was still so cold here in the shade."

"Do you think, Harry, that this man might have been an SP bookie?" asked Joe as he flicked through the pages of the notebook. "This book reminds me of my uncle in Redfern who worked the local hotels and houses, especially on Saturdays, taking bets as small as sixpence from anyone wanting to gamble on the races at Randwick. He had a book just like this. It was surprising how many little old ladies would bet sixpence on the races even when they were on a pension. It was their only fun for the week."

"You could be right, Joe. Could he have ended up here like this because he didn't pay up on a big bet? There are a lot of big criminals messed up in the racing industry, and they don't take no for an answer. As I look at his face again, I think he's into racing and is often in the pubs around town."

"Let me take off that string and pouch tied around his neck," said Joe.

Joe took out his pocket knife and cut the string. It released a small purse full of pennies and halfpennies. "Does he have any money in his pockets, Harry?"

Harry searched the wet clothes but found no wallet or loose change.

"Joe, reach over and take off that other thing around his neck."

Joe removed a bootlace on which was secured a coloured metal pendant with the number 3 neatly marked on it.

"That's interesting," said Harry. "Petherby had the number 1 on the pendant around his neck. This man has the number 3. The shape and colours of the pendants are exactly the same. Does that mean that there is still a number 2 to come? Do we have a serial killer in the community?"

"There's something here under this man's jacket," said Joe.

Joe pulled back the front of the bomber jacket. Taped to the front of the man's shirt was a sheet of white cardboard with one clear black word written on it:

Charity

Joe tore off the tape and showed the sign to Harry. As he walked to the other side of the bath he noticed another sheet of cardboard nailed low on the wooden fence. Written in large letters by the same hand it read:

Be on guard
against
covetousness.

"I think at least we can say this man was murdered and that it was the same killer as with Petherby. Joe, go inside and ask Sheila, Billy or Buster to come out here and identify this bloke. While you are in there call David Hobbs from At Peace Funerals to come and collect the body. And phone Gregory Ebsworth and ask him to call at David's place later to conduct an autopsy. Let him know that the man is dead so he doesn't have to rush here right now."

Sheila and Buster came around the side of the hotel.

"Oh, bloody hell," shouted Sheila. "Somebody got to Splinter at last. It's a wonder it took so long."

"Who is this man, Sheila?" asked Harry.

"He's Splinter Winton. He's been the local SP bookie around here for the last few years. He took it up after he stopped riding."

"Do you know what his real first name is and where he lives?"

"Yes, he lives in the old boarding house down there in Donnelly Street. He's not married," said Sheila.

Buster stepped towards the body. "Yeah, that's him. He's been a bloody rip-off merchant around here for some time. I once met his old man from Tamworth. I think he called him Sam but I can't be sure."

"Did his father live in town at Tamworth or out on a property?"

"He owned a pub in Tamworth, and I think he still does. I heard that Splinter's father kicked him out of town after he took up SP betting in his father's pub. There was trouble with the local police and the old man didn't want to lose his licence."

Harry looked at Sheila. "You said that somebody got to Splinter at last. What did you mean?"

Sheila started to walk away from the body. "Splinter was a wheeler-dealer as well as the SP bookie around here. He took bets around the pubs on Saturday mornings. He was a cocky, loud-mouthed smart arse and many punters didn't like him. He would buy and sell anything if he could make a profit. He would also lend money to anyone at a high interest rate and would take back the goods if the borrower didn't pay the money on time."

"What sort of things did people want with the money? Are we talking cars or something like that?" asked Joe.

"Yeah, no," said Buster. "He would often lend money to the students from the teachers college and university, and when they didn't pay him back on time, he would take their watches or football boots or anything else they'd bought, which he then pawned. The poor kids had little money because most of them were on a piddling allowance and found it difficult to pay back. But he also robbed others in the city."

"Can you think of anyone who hated him so much they would want to kill him?"

Sheila coughed and laughed. "I wanted to kill the little bastard, many times. He wanted to set up in our bar every Saturday but we could've lost our licence. He also got cranky with some of our customers who had not paid up quickly enough. Some of our regulars started going over the road to Bruyn's Caledonian pub to get away from him."

"Sheila, you said he was a rider. Where was that?"

"He used to be a jockey. He rode mostly in Tamworth, but also on country tracks in the northern half of the state, from Newcastle up to the border. They say he would offer the other jockeys a handout if they opened up the field and let him through for a win. He was stood down a few times for illegal tactics. It's a wonder he lasted as long as he did."

"He came here after he had too many injuries and had to give the riding away," said Buster. "He worked at the Uralla pub for a while until he became established as the SP man around town in Armidale."

David Hobbs arrived along the passageway beside the hotel. "I'm going to start charging you coppers," he said with a laugh. "Janice and I are doing overtime every day because of you."

Harry tapped him on the chest. "If it weren't for us, David, you and Janice would be out on the street, so be thankful and shout Joe and I a beer when we go back inside."

"Well, you two best earn it by bagging that body there, picking it up and getting it into the hearse. Come on, get to it."

They all had a good laugh before they helped David load Splinter's body. Sheila and Buster returned inside. Harry and Joe took time to bag and label the beer bottle, glasses, signs, pendant, money pouch and notebook found at the site.

"It is important to keep those glasses separate," said Harry. "There could be evidence of poison in one of them."

***

Harry and Joe returned to the station to write up their reports.

"The thing that worries me, Harry," said Joe, "is that the murder must have taken place well after the pub closed at six o'clock last night and probably after the staff and owners had gone to bed. So how did they get around the back?"

"There is a gate off the main street leading into the passageway down to the back fence. It seems to me that the killer might have tempted Splinter down the back for a secret deal and he carried the signs, bottle of beer and glasses with him."

Chapter 9
Friday

Harry rose early, put on his shorts and sandshoes and ran along Dumaresq Street to the racecourse. The air was crisp but not cold. The magpies sitting on the light poles warbled their greeting. He went straight to the stables where three jockeys were saddling up for an early morning training gallop.

Harry introduced himself and informed the jockeys of the death of Splinter Winton. He invited the riders to sit on the bales of hay in the corner of the stables. Rowdy Dowd spoke first.

"Geez Harry, I thought you cops slept in until nine o'clock. You must be spyin' on us to get the good oil for t'morra's races at Tamworth."

Harry laughed. "No Rowdy. I go for a run most mornings. I've got to keep up with you blokes. When you do the wrong thing, I've got to catch you in the first fifty yards. Now what can you tell me about Splinter Winton?"

"We could go all day, Harry," said Spike Fletcher, "but we need to give these horses a run ready for tomorrow's races. Otherwise, old Birdbrain, the trainer who has just driven in over there, will put on one of his tantrums."

Sandy Erickson pulled down his beanie over his forehead and spoke up. "Splinter would 'ave sold his grandmother if he could have got a quid for her. He was a snifflin', miserable, wheelin'-dealin', little skunk. He'd rip ya orf as quick as a flash."

"How did he do that, Sandy?" asked Harry.

"Ya could never trust him. He'd tell ya one thing and then do the exact opposite if he could make an extra quid on the races. He'd tell ya that he was runnin' dead in this race with the favourite, and then go flat out and win the race. When he was a rider he would try to get us to rig the races and then have his mates lay the bets."

"They told me at the pub that a lot of people laid bets with him on Saturday every week," said Harry. "Many of them didn't like him but still used him for their bets."

"He used to look after the pensioners because they didn't win or lose much and they would get angry if anyone said a bad word against him," said Rowdy.

"He was a great mate of Johnny Lewis, the bookmaker," said Spike. "We all know that they rigged the races. Johnny would get his penciller, Shorty Peterson, to offer us a handful of notes to run dead on the favourite so that they could make a fortune on the other donkey."

"But didn't the stewards get on to that?" asked Harry.

Sandy coughed out the smoke from his roll-your-own cigarette. "Splinter and Johnny never got caught because they got their mates to do the dirty work and lay the bets at the last minute with the other bookmakers. If one of them got caught, Johnny would pay their fine and give them some extra cash to buy their missus a new dress. Everyone was happy. They'd already made a fortune on the other donkey."

Rowdy lit a cigarette. "It mostly happened on the smaller tracks like Moree, Scone, Murrurundi or Coffs Harbour where the horses were often entered in more than one race. If the horse was the favourite in the first race it would run dead. Those people who were in the know would then stack their money on the same horse in the fifth race at the last moment when the price was good, and it would win by a mile."

"Were any of you involved in this?" asked Harry with a broad grin.

Rowdy turned and spat at the ground and took a long puff on his cigarette. "Harry, you are lookin' at the three most honest jockeys on the face of this earth—cross me heart and spit. Fair dinkum, Harry. We know that you would throw the book at us if we got involved in dirty work like that on the track."

Harry chuckled. "It's so good to catch up with good honest blokes like you three. Thanks for your help. Which donkey should I put my money on tomorrow?"

"Keep your money in your pocket, Harry; it's a mug's game," said Sandy.

Harry looked across at the approaching trainer. "You had best get on those horses because old Birdbrain is coming over here. Thanks again."

Harry walked towards Jack Dodsworth, known to the jockeys as 'Birdbrain'. His small stature suggested that he was a former jockey. Harry introduced himself.

"Last night we found the body of Splinter Winton at the back of the Empire Hotel. What can you tell me about Splinter, Jack?"

The trainer looked up at Harry and tugged on the brim of his hat. "Bloody hell. Are you telling me that someone got to him at last? It's a bloody wonder that he lasted this long. Tell me who did it and I'll shout them to the best big nosh-up at the Imperial pub anytime. It's the best tucker in town."

"You obviously didn't like him. Tell me what he did to you."

"He and that bastard Lewis used to rig the races. I've had to sack some jockeys because they ran dead on some of my favourites without telling me. And I believe that some of the stewards were in on it too, so nothing was ever done about it."

"I take it that you won't be going to his funeral?" queried Harry.

"My bloody oath I will. I want to guarantee that he's gone," replied the trainer. "Now, I've got to get going. You've already wasted enough of our time."

***

Harry ran back to his house, cooked up a pan full of bacon, eggs, mushrooms and tomatoes before having a shower and getting dressed.

***

Harry drove to the station and went immediately to Ray Johnston's office. Joe joined him a few minutes later.

Ray asked them to fill him in on yesterday's death of Splinter Winton.

Harry began. "We were called to the Empire Hotel late yesterday and found the body of a man in a bathtub out the back. The man was identified as Splinter Winton, an SP bookie and ex-jockey. Some of the evidence suggests that he was murdered and that it was the same perpetrator who killed Jonathon Petherby. David Hobbs picked up the body and took it to his parlour. I went to the parlour last night to help

Gregory Ebsworth with the full examination of the body and autopsy. I sent off some samples to the SIB on the midnight train."

"So how is this case similar to the university murder in the rat shed?" asked Ray.

"We found another pendant around Splinter's neck which looked like it was made with the same metal and was the same size and colour. We also found written signs, one on the victim's front and one nearby, which appear to have been written in the same hand. And there was a beer bottle and two glasses."

"The numbers on the pendants were different," said Joe. "The Petherby pendant had the number 1 on it. This one around Winton's neck had number 3 on it. It's possible that we have a serial killer at large. Will there be a number 2?"

The superintendent sat back in his chair, fingers interlocked behind his neck. "Head office has called me, wanting to know what has happened and how we are progressing on this Petherby case."

"We are working overtime trying to put the pieces together," said Harry. "There were no serious injuries on Winton's body; no bruising, no scratches, no cuts, no puncture marks. In that regard it is also like the Petherby case."

"Do you have any evidence as to the cause of death? Could it be suicide?" asked Ray.

"Not as yet," replied Harry. "We will wait on the results from the SIB. Gregory Ebsworth and I are convinced that it was not suicide. The pendants and signs were similar for both bodies and therefore the same second party has been involved. Besides, Winton doesn't strike me as a character who would commit suicide."

"Did death occur at the back of the pub or was he brought there after being killed?"

"That bloke was so small," said Joe, "I could have picked him up under one arm and carried him around town. So he could have been dropped there after dark the other night without anyone seeing them."

"That's a possibility," replied Harry. "But why would anyone move a body there when the risk of being seen, even in the middle of the night, was high? Why wouldn't the killer just do the job at Splinter's place and leave him there? The bottle and glasses there suggest that they went there for a drink and that the murder most likely occurred there."

"Surely, it still comes down to the cause of death, doesn't it?" asked Ray.

"Yes, I agree, sir," replied Harry. "If the killer used the same method as on Petherby, we are looking at poisoning. There was some leftover froth and liquid that looked like beer in the bottoms of the glasses. They were sent to the SIB. I've asked Tony Jacobs to give it top priority."

"What I don't understand, sir," said Joe, "is why anyone would go to the back of the Empire pub to have a drink in the middle of the night amongst all that rubbish."

"You've got a good point, Joe," said Harry. "But from what everyone has said about Splinter, he'd go to Timbuctoo and further if he saw a chance to do a great deal and make a quid or two. If someone offered him a deal he couldn't refuse, he'd go there. The killer could have offered Splinter a drink to entice him to go outside the pub for a private deal but the drink was laced with poison."

Ray Johnston took a sip from his now cold cup of tea. "I've had a call from Ken Rudd, the senior reporter from *The Armidale Express.* He'll be here at nine-thirty. I want you to take that meeting, Harry. We need to work with the press and control the flow of information. We need to let the public know what has happened, but we want to stop any crazy theories and wild rumours."

"I'm also expecting a call from James Bolton from *The Daily Mirror,*" said Harry. "He's always the first to get onto a story like this. Don't be surprised if he's driven to Armidale and lands on our doorstep any moment. I had a lot to do with him at Goonaburra, Sydney and Wagga so, if he arrives, let me handle it. James is a super-egotist, so I always like to let him think that he has the upper hand and priority for an exclusive interview. In that way I can control what goes in the papers."

"What's your plan from here, Harry?"

"We'll talk to Lewis the bookmaker, and we'll do the rounds of the hotels to get their comments about Splinter. I'll talk to the newspapers and radio stations. I have already contacted Splinter's parents and I expect them here tomorrow or the next day."

"Okay you two, keep me informed," said Ray as he rose to get another cup of tea.

As Harry and Joe walked out, they were met in the corridor by the three constables, Merv Leech, Jack Nelson and Keith Blackmore.

Keith had just arrived back from traffic duty outside The Armidale School on Uralla Road. Harry stopped them.

"What can you lot tell me about Splinter Winton?"

"We could write a book on him," said Merv. "What do you want to know?"

"What dealings did we have with him here at the station in the past?"

Jack Nelson was first to answer. "Look, Harry, we don't have SP bookmaking high on our list of priorities. There are a lot of people in this place who get a lot of fun out of having a minor bet on a Saturday; especially the old pensioners and the blokes who have returned from the war. They deserve a bit of enjoyment. But Splinter was another story. He was a low-down skunk. He'd hand you a beer with one hand while he whipped your wallet out of your pocket with the other."

Keith added his comments. "I had him and his bully mates charged for bashing up a couple of university students because they were behind on their repayments to him."

"He got away with murder because he paid off those in charge," said Merv.

"I hope you're not talking about anyone here, Merv?" said Harry.

"Oh God no," replied Merv quickly. "Nobody here would have been stupid enough to risk their job by getting into bed with that mongrel. Thank God someone has done him in. Give them a medal."

"Thanks," said Harry before he and Joe walked out and around the corner into Beardy Street.

Harry looked up and saw both James Bolton from *The Daily Mirror* and Ken Rudd from *The Armidale Express* walking together across the street.

Chapter 10
Friday

Harry tapped Joe on the shoulder and pointed at the two men crossing the street.

"Those two reporters coming along here will want an exclusive interview with us. Let me handle it. Sit back and watch them try to get information from us. They'll promise to keep everything private until we give them the green light. Watch how they will try to get us to divulge everything we know even when we don't want to reveal many aspects of these cases at this stage. They'll start by being very friendly and want special access because of our long association, but don't be sucked in by that. They'll ask us if we can give them some background about the victims so that they fully understand the case, with a promise not to include the details in their reporting. But remember, Joe, that reporters are not your friends. Tell them only what you want them to know, not what they demand to know."

"Are they all like that?" asked Joe.

"The experienced ones are. Before you talk to reporters, think of two or three things you want to tell them and then, no matter what they ask for or demand, keep repeating those same few things. Here they are now."

Harry stepped forward and shook their hands. "G'day James. Great to see you again. I thought you would have been here yesterday. Hello Ken. What can we do for you?"

"Could we go somewhere to ask you about these murders?" asked James.

"Sure," replied Harry as he smiled. "Let's go into the Olympic Café here. "The drinks are on you, James."

The four of them sat in a booth in the café. Harry ordered a glass of water each for himself and Joe. The others didn't order.

"What can you tell us about this wild maniac running around the city killing the good citizens of this wonderful place? What sort of person are we looking at here, Harry?" asked James as he sat back with a serious look.

Harry sipped his water slowly. "Let's stick to the facts, James. There have been two deaths in the last week. One of them was at a shed used by the zoology department at the university and the other one was behind the Empire Hotel, just along from here in this street. Let's not encourage undue panic. Ask your readers to contact us if they saw anyone in the vicinity of the zoology department buildings on Monday night or early Tuesday morning or were here near the Empire Hotel on Wednesday night or early yesterday morning."

James tapped his pen on his notepad. "Harry, could you give us some background on these two victims? We heard that they were both bits of weirdos."

"James, you know that the personal details of the victims are a matter of privacy and I ask that you respect the families of those men in their time of grief."

"But come on, Harry, give us a bit of background, off the record. Help us understand what is going on here. What were these victims like? Is there a common link between them? Are the victims related or friends? Were the murders random? Why did the killer pick these individuals?"

"Please ask your readers to be on the alert and to contact us if they have any information that might assist us in our investigations."

"Come on, Harry," said James, "you can do better than that. You can trust us to keep mum on this until you give us the go ahead. Give us something to work on. The good citizens are waiting for us to give them the information so that they are better prepared if the killer is to strike again."

Ken Rudd stopped writing and looked at Harry. "Armidale is a very law-abiding city, Harry. These things don't normally happen here. I agree with James. We must give the locals all the information. People around here don't lock their doors. We must tell them what to do. I heard that the killer put numbers on the victims. Who might be the next number?"

"Thanks Ken. Those matters are a part of our ongoing investigations. Please ask your readers to contact us if they have any vital information. I guarantee that we will keep all discussions confidential if they want to talk with us."

James sat back so quickly that he banged his head against the wall. "Come on, Harry, that's cop talk for 'I'm not going to tell you anything'. Our readers need to know what the hell is going on here. What if one of them is to be the next victim? It could be Ken here. How will you feel if another person is murdered over the weekend and that it could have been prevented if you'd let us print the details with warnings?"

Harry leaned forward and took another long sip of water. "James, we don't need any sensationalist reporting from you or anyone else that might encourage the killer to strike again. You are an experienced reporter and you should know that killers often use reports in papers or on the radio to enhance their profile. Your fearmongering builds up their sense of power over the press, the police and the local population. You are encouraging their next move. The more you put in your publications, the more the killer knows our moves, and the better prepared he is to avoid detection. We need calm reporting so that people will be encouraged to give us information rather than wild theories based on emotion. Calm reporting, with good advice on how to lock doors, be vigilant and report any unusual activities, is what works best in these cases. Your overstated reporting gives the killer the notoriety he's looking for and that, in turn, gives him the encouragement to strike again to maintain his public profile."

Harry turned towards Ken. "Ken, you have probably lived here all your life and have your ear to the ground. You should know this place better than us. You know that news travels fast in a place like this and everyone will have an opinion about the victims, but much of that is based on personalities and not facts. What can you tell us about the two victims?"

Ken put down his pen and tapped the table nervously. "Well, most people in town knew Splinter Winton and, by now, they'll know of his death. He was the local SP bookie. He was quite a character. I didn't know Petherby from the university very well. When someone in the office described him, I remembered seeing him in the café sometimes. He was hard to miss because of his size and slow, waddling walk. I knew he owned a car. But I can't see him being associated with Splinter."

"Do you know anyone who would have held a grudge against either of them?"

"Splinter was a cranky little bastard. I've heard that he'd rip you off as quick as look at you, so I suppose some people would want to knock his block off; but not kill him."

"Thanks Ken," said Harry. "What about his mate Lewis?"

Ken chuffed. "They were as thick as thieves. I wouldn't trust either of them. They not only took bets on the horse races but they would go to the rugby league matches on Sundays and take bets. It is rumoured that they even convinced some teams to run dead against a weaker team. They also got the best goal-kicker to sometimes miss an easy kick for a payment after the match."

"Thanks. That's been very helpful. If you hear anything else give us a call. Now Joe and I have real work to do, so we will move on. You two stay and have a coffee."

As Harry and Joe walked across the road to Bruyn's Caledonian Hotel, Joe looked at Harry. "I now understand what you meant. Ken seems a nice bloke, but I wouldn't trust that other bloke from Sydney."

They were met at the bar by Mario Santini, the barman of Italian descent. Mario's family migrated to Australia in the 1930s and worked in the cane fields in northern Queensland. Mario's father earned enough money to buy up some large sugar-cane farms near Murwillumbah on the north coast of New South Wales. Mario preferred the easier work in cafés or in hotels to the hard work of cutting cane and ended up at the Caledonian as a barman. He was very popular with the customers and was happy to take their chiacking about being a garlic-stinking 'wog' or 'spag'."

"What can I do for you two wonderful gentlemen?" asked Mario as he greeted Harry and Joe.

Harry shook his hand. "Mario, what can you tell us about the two men who were murdered this week? Did they drink here?"

"Let's look at that big fat bloke first. He only came in here once or twice. He didn't drink much, only one or two beers. But he would go across the street to the café and a buy a couple of pies and stuff his mouth while the other students stayed here drinking."

"What about Splinter Winton?" asked Harry.

"He's bloody different. He came here with Johnny Lewis every Thursday afternoon and then he came here most Saturdays. He took a lot of bets in the morning and then he went to the other pubs."

Joe leaned on the bar. "But Mario, you know that SP betting is illegal?"

Mario gave out a big belly-laugh and stretched his arms together across the bar towards Joe. "Put the bloody cuffs on me, Joe, and take me over to the cell. I need a bloody break. The boss here works me days and bloody nights, seven days a week. I want a bloody holiday."

Harry laughed. "Okay Mario, relax. Don't think you're going to get free board and food with us. What can you tell us?"

"Come on, Joe," said Mario. "I even heard that you take a bloody bet every now and then. I heard that you laid a bet with Johnny Lewis for big Harry here. But Holy Mother of God, Joe, you're not going to stop the poor pensioners from having a little bet on Saturdays, are you? They can't afford to go to the track so they come here to bet sixpence on the donkeys. What's wrong with that, eh? What are you going to do? Lock 'em all up?"

Joe smiled, took the cuffs from his pocket and laid them on the bar. "You talk and I'll put them away."

Mario gesticulated in a very Italian manner. "You've got me, Joe. I'll go quietly. But fair dinkum, I'll keep my ears and eyes open and let you two know if I hear anything."

"Alright mate," said Joe, "I'll put the cuffs away. Thanks."

"Thanks Mario. Keep in touch," said Harry. "We'll move on now."

Harry and Joe walked to the Imperial Hotel. Christine Freeman, the receptionist, met them in the foyer. "How might I help you two?" she asked.

Harry introduced himself and Joe. "We'd like to talk to anybody here who might have known the victims of the two murders this week. It would probably be best to talk to the barman. He'd be most likely to have dealt with them if they drank here."

Christine remained standing between them and the entrance to the bar. "You can be absolutely certain that the barman would not know Winton. We banned him from coming into this hotel years ago; we do have standards here. This is not some cheap booze house or betting shop. I didn't know the other person."

"Thank you, Christine," said Harry as he took off his hat and started to step around her. "We appreciate your standards here but we will go to talk to the barman and some of the customers. Someone in

64

there might have the vital information that could help us solve these crimes."

Harry introduced himself and Joe to Wayne Seaman, the barman. For the next half-hour they talked to Wayne and the five drinkers at the bar. Nobody knew Petherby but everyone knew Splinter Winton, and the comments were much the same as they had heard from the Empire and Caledonian hotels. Harry thanked them all and asked them to get back to him if they had any other information. On the way out, Harry thanked Christine for her assistance.

***

For the next two hours Harry and Joe visited the New England Hotel on the corner of Dangar Street, the beautiful Art Deco Tattersalls in Beardy Street, the St Kilda on the corner of Rusden Street and the Wicklow in Marsh Street. There were lots of comments from the barmen and the customers but none of the information differed from what they already knew and had heard in the other hotels.

As they walked out from the Wicklow, Harry scratched his neck. "Nobody so far has shown us any connection between the two victims and they have not given us anything to lead to the killer. Many of these people expressed their concern that the killer might strike again and that they could be his next victims."

"I agree, Harry," replied Joe. "There is a lot of anxiety in town but I felt that they appreciated our willingness to visit them and seek their opinion and help."

"Let's get back to the station. We are not going to get any more out of these people. Let's see if any calls have come through."

***

On entering the station, Graham McInnes on the desk called out. "Hey Harry, while you were out, some sheila called Colleen called and asked for you to call her back. She said you had her number. She asked if you could give her a call tomorrow morning when she'd be back home."

Chapter 11
Saturday

Harry rose early and ran up the hill along Taylor Street to the football ovals behind the teachers college. The air was crisp but dry and the sunrise gave a fresh start to the day. There he completed ten laps before he ran back via Marsh Street.

Harry phoned Colleen McWhirter whom he'd first met at the agricultural show in Armidale soon after his posting last year. Colleen was a stunningly beautiful young woman, in a country style of way. She was tall, blond, slim and athletic, with a natural charm that won the hearts of everyone who knew her. She had a ready smile, a relaxed composure and could hold her own in conversation on most subjects with men and women of all ages.

Colleen was living with her parents on a farm about twelve miles out of town, off Rockvale Road. She was born in Armidale and went to Armidale High School. She completed her degree at the University of New England majoring with honours in zoology, botany and agricultural science. Her high grades earned her an immediate five-year appointment as an agronomist with the New South Wales Department of Agriculture at Bathurst. Harry poured milk on his cereal.

Two years ago, her brother Ken was killed in a truck accident at Guyra. On a foggy winter's night on Black Mountain, a heavy vehicle was driving on the wrong side and crashed into Ken's car. Colleen's mother Margaret pleaded with her to return home to help her father on their property because he was having difficulty with his knees after an accident on the wheat harvester.

Harry and Colleen had been seeing each other on a casual but regular basis since the agricultural show. Harry enjoyed visiting the McWhirter farm on his days off. It reminded him of his own family's property at Sandy Creek near Goonaburra. His father had been hoping to leave the Taylor property to Harry but then he ran off and joined the police force and later the army. Harry's father eventually decided it was best to leave the property to his two other sons who both loved farming.

Colleen reminded Harry of his first truelove at Sandy Creek. He tried to control his emotions as he remembered Elizabeth Brunton with whom he'd spent many special moments before he enlisted in the army. Had Harry stayed on his father's farm at Sandy Creek, it was almost certain they would've settled down to marital bliss, had many children and become model citizens in the district. But Harry was posted to the special Z Force commando unit that operated behind enemy lines in Borneo and New Guinea during the Second World War. Elizabeth often wrote to him. When she received no replies she was convinced he had been killed in action. So she married Jim, a teacher at the local school.

Harry had already decided that it would not have been fair on Elizabeth if he had taken her to the city and for her to adjust to his chaotic work schedule as a detective.

As Harry chewed the rind of bacon, dripping with the rich soft yellow yolk of a farm-fresh egg, he remembered another woman from Goonaburra. Shirley O'Farrell was the barmaid who nursed him when Harry suffered a recurrence of malaria and again after being assaulted by Zoltan the gypsy biker. Everyone in town expected Harry and Shirley to get married but Harry was too committed to his new position as detective. His long hours would have been unfair on a new wife. Since then, Shirley remarried and is well settled in Goonaburra with her young son from an earlier marriage.

When Harry moved to Sydney in late 1947 he rented the garage at the back of a Stanmore house owned by Eileen Matthews, a war widow with whom he had a brief intimate relationship. Again, Harry considered it unreasonable for him to ask any woman to marry him when he was a detective because of what the pressure his job would have had on their relationship.

When Harry was appointed to Wagga Wagga, he took up a casual relationship with Rita Flynn, the fingerprint expert attached to the Scientific Investigation Bureau in Sydney. When they were together their relationship was intense with no holds barred. As both were in the police force, they understood the pressures of the job. Their romantic relationship looked like becoming permanent until Rita commenced studies at Sydney University to become a forensic specialist. With Harry being three hundred miles away in Wagga for most of the time, and Rita being at night lectures when he was in Sydney, the relationship cooled. Since coming to Armidale, his relationship with Colleen had developed into something special.

When Harry heard Colleen's voice on the phone he said, "How's the best-looking girl on the east side of Armidale? I got your message to call. Is everything okay?"

"What do you mean—east side of Armidale? What about north, south and west?" she replied with a big laugh. "I was wondering, if you're not working today, would you like to come out to the farm? Mum's going to cook lunch for us. But on second thoughts, after your comment about the east, I'll tell Mum to hold the sweets."

Harry burst out laughing. "When I bring your mum a bunch of flowers, she'll give me sweets."

"Oh yes, here he goes with the old Taylor charm. You don't fool me, young Harry," replied Colleen. "Be here by noon or I'll throw your meal out to the pigpen."

"How's your dad? Does he need anything doing?"

"His legs are not good but he tries to keep going."

"I'm coming out now," replied Harry. "When I get there let me know what needs to be done. I can help."

Harry phoned the station and told Constable Jack Nelson that he would be at the McWhirter farm. He gave Jack the number to ring if anything urgent came up and asked him to contact Joe Simms and give him the same number. Harry got dressed in his work gear, jumped into the MG and drove to the farm.

***

Colleen met him at the door with a warm hug and kiss. When the two walked into the kitchen Harry passed a handful of flowers to Colleen's mother.

"Mum," shouted Colleen as she swept her arm in a wide arc, "throw them in the bin. Look at them. Harry comes in here with that miserable wilting bunch of flowers he picked out of the neighbour's garden to suck up to you in order to get you to give him a big helping of sweets. Don't fall for that, Mum."

Margaret walked over to Harry, gave him a kiss, held his arm and turned back to Colleen. "Now dear, don't be too hard on Harry; it's the thought that counts. Now you two go off and do what you have to do and be back here at lunchtime."

Colleen thumped Harry on the arm and pushed him towards the door. "Come on, you old smoothie, let's go and see Dad. He's out in the machinery shed."

When Harry got to the shed he saw that Colleen's father was in pain with his knees.

"G'day Stan," he said. "What's on your plate here today?"

"G'day Harry. I'm getting ready for the planting of the pasture crops. I've got to get the seeds and fertiliser ready and the planter greased up ready to go."

"What are you planting?"

"I'm doing lucerne in the bottom paddock and white clover and phalaris in the far paddock. I will do the lucerne first."

Harry looked at Colleen and smiled. "Well, I'll hook up the tractor to the seed drill while Colleen can lump the bags of seed and fertiliser and fill the bins."

Colleen burst out laughing. "Dad, have you got the shotgun in the shed or is it up at the house? I'm going to kill this rude bloke. He wouldn't know one end of a tractor from another."

"Listen here," chuffed Harry as he pointed to his left bicep. "I told you about our farm at Sandy Creek. It was tough country and I drove tractors at boarding school and worked my father's farm every holiday."

They all had a good laugh. "Okay Stan, you give the orders and show us where to start. Then you get back inside and rest those knees. Let's get as much done as possible while I'm here."

Colleen and Harry soon had the machinery filled with seed and fertiliser and ready to go. They worked all morning sowing the bottom paddock while Stan supervised from the truck and occasionally stopped them for a drink from the waterbag.

Harry and Colleen worked well as a team while they intermittently chiacked each other to relieve the boredom of driving a tractor around the paddock. There was also an occasional friendly hip bump and clod throwing. The energy flowed freely between them. They relaxed in each other's company.

At midday they all returned to the house where Margaret had a meal of roast lamb, baked vegetables and fresh mint followed by apple crumble and cream for dessert.

"What's all this about that terrible killer, Harry?" asked Margaret.

Harry spent most of the time during lunch briefing the McWhirters about the murders, but without the detail. He explained that it was an ongoing investigation. He tried to allay their fears about a killer on the loose. He tried to change the subject to the price of lambs at the saleyards, then to the lack of autumn rains, and finally to the upcoming CWA ball.

After lunch, Harry and Colleen returned to planting the pasture seeds. At three o'clock Stan drove the truck back to the paddock, got out, hobbled to the end of the freshly sown row and waited until the tractor came to a stop.

"Harry," he said, "you had best get up to the house as soon as possible. There's a phone call for you."

On arriving at the house, Harry took the phone. It was Joe Simms on the other end.

"Harry, we've got another body."

Chapter 12
Saturday

Harry pushed the accelerator of the MG to the floor as he drove along Rockvale Road towards town. Fifteen minutes later he turned left into Donnelly Street, drove to the end and parked his car on the bend behind a sleek new silver Jaguar XK120 sports car. He walked across the grass to the bank of Dumaresq Creek where Joe was waiting for him with Sergeant Eric Talbot and Constable Lars van Dyke. They pointed to a fully-clothed male human body lying face down under the arching branches of a large willow tree.

Most of the body was lying on the bank but the face, shoulders and arms were lying in the shallow water. Medium and small river stones were positioned on the neck and back.

"We decided, after checking that he was dead," said Joe, "to leave him here until you arrived so that you could see everything in its place as we found it. I went to the phone box over there and called you."

"Good work, Joe. Who found the body?"

Eric pointed across to Holmes Avenue. "Two young brothers were kicking a football around here and it ran down the bank to the willow tree. When they saw the body they ran home and told their mother. She is Mrs Stirling and she rang the station. I grabbed Lars and Joe and came here straight away. We phoned David Hobbs to let him know."

Harry pushed aside the thin branches hanging from the willow tree. He noticed a small, round folding table with two folding chairs on the bank. On the table were an almost empty champagne bottle and two wine glasses. Each glass had about an inch of liquid in it.

"Joe, I want the table, chairs, bottle and glasses tested for fingerprints and the remaining liquids sealed and sent to the SIB tonight. Also, check everything for stray hairs or stains, spilt liquids or food particles; anything you can find. I also want you to check all the furniture stores to see who stocks those folding tables and chairs. These chairs and the table are similar to the ones in the rat shed where Petherby was found. Ask if they remember who might have bought some lately."

"When we saw the champers bottle, Harry," said Lars, "we thought that was very unusual. I don't know any man around here who drinks or can afford champagne. All the men I know drink beer, rum or whisky. Champagne is for the rich sheilas. It's giggle juice to get them in the right mood for a good night out."

Eric pointed at the body. "I think that bloke in the water is that flash young bastard from the university who drives around in that Jaguar over there. I've had a few run-ins with him driving like a maniac around the streets to impress the girls. He was a real smart arse and couldn't care less when I'd fined him. I think he came from a rich family, and so to pay a few quid for a fine was nothing to him."

"Look at this bloke's gear," said Lars as he pointed at the body. "What a wank. Done up like a Christmas tree. This bloke had more money than common sense. He was definitely the owner of that Jaguar over there. I've booked him a few times as well. He was a pompous, arrogant little prick. I think his name is O'Sullivan. I'll duck over to the Jaguar and check if there is a licence or rego."

The others looked at the body in the shallow water. He wore a white tuxedo. His black pure wool trousers had satin stripes down the outside of the legs. The black patent-leather dancing pumps covered his white silk socks. The man was of medium height and average weight. The black hair showing at the back of his head was liberally coated with Brylcreem.

"Right," said Harry, "when we get back to the station, Eric, check all the records on this bloke. Now let's take a closer look. Take notes, Joe."

Lars returned with a licence and car keys. "It's definitely O'Sullivan."

"Thanks Lars. Now what do you three make of those stones on his back?" asked Harry.

"It's bloody obvious that he didn't commit suicide," replied Lars. "He couldn't have placed those stones there himself."

Eric scratched his cheek. "The stones were not placed there to hold him down. They are not heavy enough to do that. Even a child could dislodge them. They were obviously placed there after death."

"Is the killer trying to tell us something?" asked Harry.

Joe stepped into the water next to the body to take a closer look. "If it's the same killer as in the Petherby and Winton cases, we should find other similar signs. I'll lift his tuxedo."

As Joe removed all of the stones and raised the tail of the jacket he saw a cardboard sign taped to the back of the victim's shirt. It read in large letters:

Humility

Joe carefully removed the sign. "It's the same killer. This was written in the same hand as the others and on the same type of cardboard."

Harry stepped forward to the edge of the water and took hold of one of the man's arms. "Joe, take the other arm. Lars and Eric, you take his legs and we'll lift him out of the water and turn him on his back."

They carried the body away from the edge of the water and laid it face up on the grass. The victim was aged in the mid-twenties. He was wearing a white silk shirt with frills down the line of buttons and a bright-blue satin bow tie. His thin moustache had been trimmed to a fine line.

Joe lifted the bottom of the man's shirt to reveal another wet sheet of cardboard taped to the skin. On it was written:

Turn my eyes
away from
worthless
things.

Joe carefully removed the sign and placed it in an evidence bag. He then noticed a copper pendant with coloured enamel on one side. Joe reached around the man's neck and removed the leather bootlace holding the pendant. On it was the number 7. He placed it in the evidence bag.

"Well," said Harry, "it is definitely the same killer. All three pendants are the same size, shape and colouring. But why number 7?"

Lars placed his hands behind his head and looked skywards. "I can remember at church one day they talked about the number seven representing perfection because God created the heavens and the Earth in six days and, upon completion, God rested on the seventh day."

"Well, this bloke's seventh day has arrived. He ain't coming back here," said Joe. "But what about the other two victims? They were numbered 1 and 3."

Harry raised his finger. "When I went to Scripture lessons the number one only referred to God, and I don't understand how Jonathon Petherby could be seen as being like God because his pendant had the number 1 on it. We know he went to church and was in the choir but that doesn't seem to warrant a number one. I think the number three refers to the fact that everything in life is separated into a beginning, a middle and an end. We live our lives through birth, life and death but, how could that apply to Splinter Winton who had number 3 on his pendant?"

Joe chuffed. "That's it. This murderer has now completed all three of them."

"Hold it there a minute," said Eric. "I once had a girlfriend who was into numerology and horoscopes and all that stuff. She said that number one represented a fear of failure and risk; and that could apply to Petherby. Number three was associated with energy and communication but underneath, it was a very lonely number; a bit like Splinter. A number-seven-type person was always out there questioning but quickly became jaded, cynical and bored. How does that fit with this bloke?"

Lars laughed. "What number did your girlfriend give you, Eric?"

"She lived at number 13, so I left her," replied Eric as he cheerily slapped his hands against his thighs.

"Well, that was a lot of useless waffle," said Harry. "So, let's get on with the serious stuff."

"Where had this bloke been going all dressed up like that?" asked Joe.

"He could have been at the Red Cross ball at the Armidale Town Hall last night," said Eric. "There was a big crowd there. I was on duty early in the night but everything was under control. I didn't see him there."

"If he wasn't there," said Lars, "he could have been dressed up for a big dinner party at the Imperial Hotel to impress a girlfriend or his family. I've been told they put on a big nosh-up there, but it's not cheap."

Harry pointed to Eric. "When we get back to the station, check any information we have on him there. Find out his family details. Where do his parents live?"

David Hobbs drove his hearse across the grassed area and stopped next to the willow tree. "Harry," he said, "I appreciate the business—don't get me wrong—but if you keep this up I'll have to put on more staff. What have we got here?"

"Thanks for coming out on the weekend, David. If you can wait a minute while we finish our examination here, we'll help you get him in the wagon. Lars, help me get all his gear off. Joe, you take notes."

They stripped the man of all his clothes and Joe folded them before putting them in a canvas bag. Harry and Lars examined the body for marks, bruises, blood, open wounds and any other injuries. Other than a few scars, they found nothing.

"This fellow has led a fairly sheltered life," said David as he looked on while the others did their examination. "He's not overweight but he has led the good life. His hands look soft and his nails have been neatly manicured; so he's never done a hard day's work. In gear like that, and driving that Jag over there, I'd say he came from a life of privilege. I've seen him around town a few times and he was always preening himself like a bantam rooster waiting for the brainless chicks to rush him for a thrill ride in the car."

"Isn't it interesting," said Harry, "that in all three murders in the last week there were no signs of external injuries. There was nothing to suggest a fight or a brutal attack with any type of instrument. There was no bruising to their faces, arms, legs, backs or solar plexus to indicate an attack with fists or a blunt instrument causing death or unconsciousness."

Joe pointed to the face. "There has been no drainage of water from this man's mouth which suggests to me that he did not drown in the water. Remember that Splinter Winton also did not drown even though he was found in the water."

"This man, at his young age, surely didn't die of a stroke or heart attack when confronted by the killer." asked Harry.

"It does happen," replied David, "but this man is not overweight and has no signs of an unhealthy lifestyle. It does not rule out the possibility of a family history of such attacks, but we will not know that until we do the autopsy and get to the family and test that out."

"What's your best guess, Harry?" asked Lars.

"I don't like guessing, Lars, but I'd say we are looking more at poisoning as in the Petherby case. The SIB found fatal quantities of phenobarbital in his body. In his case he had drunk the poison from a glass left on the table. When we found Splinter at the back of the Empire pub there were two glasses left on a box next to the bath. Some of those glasses had liquid remains. I'm awaiting the results from the SIB on the Splinter glasses. In this case here, there is an almost empty bottle of champagne and two glasses on the table next to the fold-up chairs. We need to get the bottle and glasses and liquid on tonight's train so the SIB can test them. I believe it is our best lead at the moment."

David walked in front of Harry. "Are you saying, Harry, that each victim knew and trusted the killer enough to accept his invitation to have a drink?"

Lars turned. "If the relationship was so strong between the perpetrator and the victims, why would the killer poison them? There must be a very strong motive to take it that far. Is the killer envious of the victims? If the killer was envious of this man's possessions and wealth, with his fancy clothes and expensive car, then that would not have been the case with Petherby, and probably not even Splinter."

Harry, Joe, Eric and Lars did a final walk around the willow tree to check if they'd missed something. They got on their knees to check small twigs and other objects. The only item of interest was the champagne cork lying at the base of the tree trunk.

"Okay, let's help David load the body and we'll get back to the station," said Harry. "It's getting dark. Let's get the evidence for the SIB on the train for tonight. Be back at the station early in the morning. Joe, you go with Eric and drive the Jag back to the station. When you get it there, go over it with a fine-tooth comb; fingerprints and all."

"Don't let me catch you speeding, Joe," shouted Lars. "I'll throw the book at you."

Joe walked off with a broad grin and raised the middle finger on his right hand.

Chapter 13
Sunday

Serial killer loose.
Lock your doors

Armidale City rocked by crazed serial killer. Three citizens killed in the last week. Police up blind alleys. Who will be next?

James Bolton: Special Crime Reporter

Last Tuesday a violent killer struck at the University of New England. The body of a wonderful young student was found in the zoology department shed before the killer released the laboratory rats in that room to eat his flesh. Can you imagine such a horrible death?

That student was a dedicated, God-fearing member of the Presbyterian Church and sang in the choir. He was a studious, hard-working young man with never an evil thought. He came from a well-known and respected family from Warwick in Queensland. His parents are devastated by the news of his murder.

On Wednesday night or early Thursday morning the body of a well-known Armidale identity was found in an old bathtub behind the Empire Hotel.

Harry and Joe sat in the interview room at the police station. Joe sipped his cup of tea then banged the desk. "Bloody hell, Harry. Why do we even talk to those bastards? We should lock them up."

"What did I tell you, Joe? Reporters are not your friends."

"I could strangle all of them," replied Joe. "Who else is giving them information? Besides us, Eric, Lars and David Hobbs, who else knew about O'Sullivan?"

"It is always a problem for us when someone leaks information to the press. I don't think Eric or Lars or David would have spoken to them but I would not be surprised if the killer left an anonymous message with the newspaper himself in order to enhance his own importance. Some killers get a real thrill in seeing their exploits in the papers when the police don't have the answers. But don't forget about Mrs Stirling, the mother of the boys who found O'Sullivan's body at the creek. She could have talked to her friends and neighbours, and then the word would be out around town. But put all that aside and concentrate on what we are going to do today. Let's tidy up a few loose ends. We know from his licence that Eric found behind the sunshade of the Jaguar, that the man in the creek yesterday was Julian O'Sullivan and his address was a house in Mossman Street. Eric visited the premises and met Shirley Sayers, with whom O'Sullivan boarded in Armidale. She informed Eric that Julian's family came from a big property off the Narromine Road, south of Webbs Siding and west of Dubbo. Eric contacted O'Sullivan's parents last night. They said that they will be here sometime today."

"Do we see them first?" asked Joe.

"No. We'll start by going to Holmes Avenue and talk to Mrs Stirling and her boys. There was a note at the main desk this morning that Splinter Winton's family from Tamworth are coming here today. They will be at the station about lunchtime. So, let's go."

***

Harry and Joe took the wagon to Holmes Avenue and stopped in front of a neat cream weatherboard cottage. Along the front was a tidy verandah with two casual chairs. There was a single garage down the driveway at the back of the house. The detectives were met by an attractive woman in her late thirties. Harry did the introductions and explained the purpose of their visit.

"Please call me Merrilee. Come on in. I'll call the boys."

Harry shook the boys' hands and introduced Joe. "Please relax boys. I want to thank you for getting mum to call us when you saw that man yesterday. Can you please tell us what happened?"

John, the elder of the two at about ten years old, licked his lips and rubbed his hands down his thighs. He spoke first. "We were just kicking the footie around the park and the ball rolled down the bank to the willow tree."

"Were there any other people in the park?" asked Harry.

"We saw Mrs Black walking her dog but she was not near us. She lives up in Douglas Street. There was another old codger way over the other side but he was walking away from the park."

"Did you see that silver sports car parked on the road?" asked Joe.

Timothy, the younger brother, spoke up. "Yes, I wish we had one of those."

Merrilee Stirling burst out laughing. "A fat chance at that, Timmy. We're flat out paying for food, let alone a flash car."

"Have any of you seen that car before?" asked Harry.

John put up his hand. "Yes, it sometimes roars around the streets here, driving very fast around the corners and showing off. It nearly ran me over one day. There was a girl in the car and she was screaming as it drove past."

"Mrs Charlton, our next-door neighbour, said the man boarded in a house up the hill around Mossman Street. His car is parked out the front of that house," said Merrilee, "But other than that, we don't know anything about him."

Harry thanked them and he and Joe walked next door. Mrs Charlton confirmed that Julian O'Sullivan boarded with her friend Shirley Sayers in Mossman Street.

***

As Harry and Joe drove along Faulkner Street next to Central Park they noticed the congregation of St Paul's Presbyterian Church leaving the church. Harry stopped and waited until the congregation was leaving before getting out of the car.

"I'd like to talk to Reverand Aitken again about Petherby and ask him if he also knew the other two victims," said Harry.

Harry recognised Hamish Mackenzie, the lecturer from the university who they had met the other day. Harry and Joe walked through the front gate.

"Hello Hamish. Good to see you."

Hamish walked back into the church with Harry and Joe where they met the Reverend Charles Aitken. The four of them sat in the rear pews.

"Hello again, Reverend. I know we met the other day regarding Jonathon Petherby but can you tell us any more about him. And did you know Julian O'Sullivan, the man we found yesterday murdered in the park near Donnelly Street and Holmes Avenue?" asked Harry. "Have you thought of anything else that might help us in our investigations?"

The minister lowered his head and touched his forehead. He paused before answering. "Some members of the congregation this morning mentioned the death of Julian but I did not know him and he was not a member of the church. But we did include a special prayer in our service here today in memory of Jonathon. He was a wonderful young man but he had his demons. He and I spent many hours together. He spoke about his family and I gather he had problems there that led to his insecurity. I've never seen his parents."

"Can you think of anyone who would dislike him so much they would carry out such a horrible crime against him?" asked Joe.

"He was a gentle but troubled soul, but he wouldn't have hurt anyone. It was not in his nature. I can't see why the killer would have targeted him. He was obviously in the wrong place at the wrong time."

"What do you think, Hamish?" asked Harry.

"I agree with Charles, but Jonathon was his own worst enemy. He was just so lazy that he couldn't get out of his own way. He was a bit of a slob and a pig and ate and ate to overcome his misery. Had he got out and done something active he would not have had those problems."

"I think you are a bit harsh, Hamish," said Charles. "We can't all be like you and be involved in everything around the town. I still believe that Jonathon's problem was his upbringing and his difficult childhood."

"How did he get on with the other parishioners?" asked Joe.

The minister's face brightened. "They loved him; especially the ladies because he always took time to compliment them on the cakes and other food they brought to suppers and morning teas. They all wanted to mother him and he got much comfort from that. He didn't have much to do with the men except those in the choir, like Hamish."

"We tried to support him in the choir but, quite frankly, it was somewhat of a lost cause," said Hamish. "He had difficulty hitting the right notes. It was embarrassing, but we put up with it for his sake."

Harry thanked Charles and Hamish.

***

Harry and Joe drove to the station where they were introduced to Splinter Winton's family—his father Mick, mother Mary and sister Gwen—who had just arrived from Tamworth.

Mick was short and well dressed with a narrow-brimmed trilby hat pulled forwards and across his left eye. A cigarette was dangling from the right side of his mouth.

"I'm sorry we couldn't get here sooner," he said, "but we have the pub to run and our barman is off sick at the moment. Me and Gwen are the only ones serving."

Mary, also smoking a cigarette, spoke up in a very direct manner. "What the hell are you two doing to catch Splinter's killer? I heard you are sitting on your bums. There have been two others killed this week, and what have you done? When are you going to put a stop to all of this?"

"I can assure you, Mrs Winton, that we are working non-stop to catch this killer. Now, what can you tell us about Sam that might help us with our investigations? Did he ever work with you in the hotel in Tamworth?"

Gwen answered. "Splinter worked there some time ago but Dad had to move him on because it was getting too hot with him running the SP betting there."

Mick coughed on his cigarette. "Hold on there, Gwennie. Splinter left of his own accord. He used to do a bit of SP betting but he felt he needed to try his luck somewhere else, so he moved here to Armidale."

"Some people around here said that Sam was a jockey and was known to, on occasions, fix races. Would you like to comment?"

Mary puffed out smoke at a fast rate and banged the desk. "Tell me the names of the bastards who said that. I'll fix them up good and proper."

"Hold hard, Mary," shouted Mick. "Let me explain. In the racing industry, anyone who loses their money wants to blame the jockey or the trainer. Splinter was a good jockey but some owners thought their broken-down donkeys from out the other side of Bourke could come to town and beat well-trained horses from the big smoke. And when they didn't, they'd get angry. I know 'cause I was a jockey in my early days. Don't blame Splinter for that."

"Is there anyone you know who had it in for Splinter, either in Tamworth or here?" asked Harry. "Or anyone who would want to get back at him?"

"Give it a break," shouted Gwen. "Splinter was a cheeky devil but he was a likeable bloke who always tried to look after his customers. Don't blame him just because he did a bit of betting on the side. I know you coppers want an easy answer to wrap up a case but, if you try to blame Splinter, you'll have to deal with me first. Do you get that?"

"Let me assure you, Gwen," replied Harry, "that we fully understand that there are lots of old-age pensioners and part-time gamblers who get a lot of enjoyment out of having a little bet every weekend. That's not our problem. We are not interested in Splinter being an SP bookie unless some punter took to him in revenge for losing their money."

"I'm sorry, Detective," said Mary. "We don't mean to be critical. We know you have a lot on your mind with these murders but, we don't know of anyone who would want to harm Splinter. He might have been a cheeky little bugger but that doesn't excuse what happened to him. I'd say that the killer probably did him in to get his winnings."

"Thank you, Mary. You have been most helpful. David Hobbs from At Peace Funerals called me earlier to say he is ready to see you when you are ready. So, I'll let you go. If you have any further information, please leave a message here at the station."

***

After the Winton family left, Harry and Joe drove to the top end of Markham Street to meet with John Lewis, the local bookmaker.

Chapter 14
Sunday

The house owned by John Lewis was impressive. It was a triple-fronted dwelling built of dark manganese bricks. Two tall brick chimneys rose above a red corrugated roof. A long gravelled drive led to a double garage at the back. The solid brick fence had two white wrought-iron gates. The front garden was filled with roses reaching the end of their summer flush.

The door was opened by a well-dressed woman who introduced herself as Helen Lewis. She had just returned from church. She invited Harry and Joe into the lounge room which was filled with quality furnishings that showed the good taste of Helen.

"I'll get John for you," she said as she walked through to the back of the house.

A few minutes later, a tall man in his late forties walked in, wearing an old, torn football jersey, a pair of shorts with the waist pushed below his expanded belly and a stained pair of tennis shoes with laces undone. The man's clothes, his bent nose and cauliflower ears were the result of his early years packed in the thick of too many rugby scrums.

"G'day," he said as he walked over with hand outstretched. "I'm John Lewis. Please excuse my attire but it's Sunday and, after a big day at the Tamworth races yesterday, I need to relax. Now what can I do for you two?"

Harry introduced himself and Joe. "I believe that you are the expert on the racing industry around here and, as the leading bookmaker, you'd know everyone in that field. They tell me that you were great friends with Sam Winton. I believe he was known as 'Splinter'. Could you tell us what you know about him and whether he had any enemies?"

John sat in the lounge chair opposite Harry and Joe. He took a big puff on his ever-present cigarette and laughed as he blew out the smoke towards the ceiling.

"Hah, the little bastard. He was known as Splinter because he was always an irritating little prick—you know, like a splinter stuck up under your fingernail that you can't get out. He was always in your face wanting to know everything, but underneath he was a great little bloke. If I wanted a quid, he'd be the first to give me one."

Joe pointed his left hand towards Lewis. "Winton was an SP bookie. Didn't his activities cut in to your business as the official bookmaker in town?"

"Nah," was the reply. "Splinter did most of the pubs in town while I did all the racetracks north of Newcastle. I didn't cut into his work and he didn't touch mine. In fact, we helped each other. We always had a drink in the back room at the Caledonian every Thursday afternoon and went over the fields for the weekend. We went over all the race guides and comments from the so-called experts in the papers. We discussed the chances of every horse in Sydney, Melbourne and Brisbane and then looked at the regional races before we set our prices for the weekend. We gave each other tips we got from people we knew in the industry and kept that to ourselves. You get to know who's fair dinkum and who's not. It's the only way you survive in this game."

Harry shifted his position on the big lounge. "Talking about tips, we have received a tip that Splinter might have been involved in rigging races by paying off jockeys to run dead on the favourites. What can you tell us about that?"

John lurched forward with a raucous cough and spat the mucous into a stained handkerchief. He took another deep draw on his cigarette, wiped his mouth with the back of his hand and coughed again as he exhaled a cloud of blue smoke.

"Nah, you buggers have got it all wrong. Splinter wouldn't do that. If he did, the stewards and you blokes would have come down on him like a ton of bricks. If he couldn't have worked in the racing industry it would have killed him. He was with horses all his life."

"Then why would a number of people tell us that?" asked Joe.

"It's as obvious as the town hall in the main street or the nose on your face. Splinter was always in everyone's face and he pestered them until he got his answers. He was an annoying little bastard and so, when somebody's donkey didn't perform, they had to blame someone, and Splinter was an easy target."

"Who do you think had the best reason to kill Splinter?" asked Joe.

"Don't know. There were probably a lot who would have liked to give him a bit of a slap or two, but not to murder the poor little bastard."

"Have you ever been involved in fixing a race with Splinter?" asked Harry.

Lewis stood and took another long puff from his cigarette. "I'm going to ask you gentlemen to leave. Look, I want to help you blokes but I'm not going to be insulted in my own home."

Helen Lewis walked into the room with a tray of cups, saucers and cakes. Her husband turned sharply. "You can take that back to the kitchen, love. These blokes are leaving."

Harry and Joe walked out, got back into the wagon, drove to the end of the street, turned left and along to Mossman Street. They stopped at a well-maintained colonial weatherboard home with a verandah on three sides and a detached garage. They walked up the five steps to the front door and struck the brass triangle with the rod hanging from the chain. It reminded Harry of farming properties at Goonaburra. The door was opened by a middle-aged woman who introduced herself as Mrs Shirley Sayers. After introductions they moved to the lounge room.

"Thanks for seeing us, Shirley," said Harry. "What can you tell us about Julian O'Sullivan that might help us in our investigations?"

"Oh," said Shirley, "he was such a loveable young rascal. He has boarded with me here since the beginning of last year. I offered to put him up because I went to the local New England Girls School with Julian's mother Heather. She boarded but I lived here in Armidale. She often spent time with me on the weekends in this house that was my parents' home. She moved to Dubbo after marrying Peter O'Sullivan, but we kept in touch."

"Where did Julian go on the night of the murder?"

"He was going to the Red Cross ball at the town hall," replied Shirley. "He left here about seven o'clock."

"Was he taking anyone to the ball?" asked Harry.

"Not that I knew; but he didn't tell me everything."

"What was he like as a boarder?" asked Joe.

Shirley paused as she poured cups of tea. "Oh, he was a bit of a rogue but in the nicest way. In some ways he was quite lazy."

"How so?" asked Harry.

"Well, I am going to miss him so much but he was not easy to look after. He never picked up after himself. He would leave his clothes where he dropped them and he never helped around the house or in the garden. He wouldn't know how to fix a tap or do anything practical. He was not like that."

"Why would you keep him on as a boarder if he was like that?" asked Harry.

"You have to understand, Harry, that I joined the army during the war and met and married my husband Marlon who was an American soldier. He was killed at Guadalcanal, leaving me with a young child and no income. My son Carl is ten years old. He is down at the park playing with his friends. Peter and Heather O'Sullivan paid me well for looking after Julian. Peter came from a well-to-do grazing family and, with the increasing price of wool since the war, they could afford the best."

"What was Julian like as a person? Did he have any friends?" asked Harry.

Shirley sipped her tea before she answered. "He was exceptionally well mannered. He was brought up in the best social circles. He was a boarder at the private Kings School in Parramatta. He was always very well dressed in the best quality clothes bought mostly at David Jones' in Sydney, or more likely at Zink and Sons Tailors in Oxford Street. Julian often quoted their motto that was: 'Manners maketh man— but a Zink suit gives finish.'"

Joe turned to stretch his arm. "What about the flash car? Did you get to ride in it?"

Shirley laughed. "Yes, it's a bit over the top, but Julian could afford it. I did get a ride once but he drove too fast and it scared me, so I stuck to my old Riley coupé. He was also proud about his appearance. He never went out unless he was impeccably attired. He spent a lot of time in the bathroom—much to my disgust sometimes—grooming himself to the point where there was not a hair out of place. He would trim his moustache to perfection. He insisted that I had every item of clothing perfectly ironed and his shoes spit-polished."

"I would have made him do it himself," said Joe.

Harry swung quickly and grabbed Joe's arm. "That's enough, Joe. Apologise to Shirley. We are not here to make stupid comments like that. We are here to get the facts."

Joe pulled back, red-faced. "I'm sorry, Shirley. It's just that I was brought up in a different place."

Harry looked up. "Was there a touch of vanity about Julian? Was he trying to make others jealous? Was he constantly seeking praise? Was he trying to get others to think more highly of him with his ostentatious displays of wealth?"

Shirley sat back quickly. "No, no, I wouldn't say that. He was just being Julian. Yes, he was spoiled and he didn't work on the farm but, he was destined to become a famous scientist and so the family supported him all the way because they could."

"Did he have any very close friends or girlfriends?"

"He had lots of friends, and the girls flocked to get a ride in the Jaguar, but I wouldn't say he was especially close to any one of them. Let's face it, he was a young man out there sowing his oats. You boys know what that is all about. You're all the same; have a fling before settling down."

"I assume you have you been in touch with his parents?"

"Yes," replied Shirley. "They're on their way here today. I'm expecting them about lunchtime. I'll take them up to the funeral parlour and then we will come back here. They will stop here tonight."

"Could you ask them if they would be willing to talk with us later this afternoon, say at about four o'clock?"

"Certainly. I'm sure they will want to talk to you."

***

Back at the station Harry and Joe went to the interview room.

"What a jerk," said Joe as they walked in. "That O'Sullivan bloke was the greatest waste of oxygen around. He was so up himself. I'm surprised that someone didn't whack him before this. He just wanted to show he was from the upper wealthy class and above all of us who have to work our guts off to earn a living."

"Joe," responded Harry sternly, "you and I are not here to judge people on their social status or wealth. We have a job to catch his killer.

Treat our conversation with Shirley as a fact-finding mission, not some reason to hate people because they might be better off than you."

"But that's hard when I think what I've had to put up with all my life. And then I look at that jerk poncing around like a bantam rooster showing off and not having to do a hard day's work in his whole life."

"If you want a medal, Joe, put some baling wire through a bottle top and attach it to your top pocket. Now let's get on and consolidate our notes before we meet the family this afternoon."

***

At four o'clock Harry and Joe drove back to Mossman Street where they met Julian's family.

It took little time for Harry to assess the father, Peter, as an intelligent, confident, hard-working man capable of running a large-scale property. He was in command of his life and family. Heather, his wife, was still in shock at her son's death and found it difficult to stay in the room. Julian's brothers, Trevor and Brian, were more in the mould of their father than Julian. The men all wore tweed jackets, checked cotton shirts, jodhpurs and shiny boots.

Harry briefly outlined the circumstances of Julian's death. For the next hour they all sat around the lounge room discussing Julian—his studies and ambitions, his early childhood, schooling, friends, relations, girlfriends and the fact that he was so different from his brothers.

"Julian was different," said Peter, "but being different is not wrong. He was very ambitious in his own way and he was progressing towards becoming a scientist. And we supported him all the way."

Heather wiped tears from her eyes. "Julian was a premmie baby and had a hard time in early life."

"He was very lucky to have you as support," said Joe.

Peter stared at Joe. "It's not luck, son. We didn't get to where we are today sitting on our bums. We worked damned hard to get here and now we have the means to support our family and help them achieve their goals. That's what the real world is like."

Throughout the discussion no one could think of anyone who hated Julian enough to kill him, whether at Dubbo or at the university or in Armidale. They questioned why Julian might have been the victim of a random killer. Peter asked if it could have been the result of a robbery gone wrong. Harry mentioned that there was still cash in Julian's wallet.

After further discussion, Harry thanked Shirley and the family, and he and Joe left to return to the station.

***

Constable Mervyn Leech at the desk gave Harry a note.

Meet me at Armidale police station tomorrow morning at nine o'clock.
Superintendent Brian Ford.

Chapter 15
Monday

As Harry walked into the station he was handed an envelope that contained a note from Tony Jacobs from the SIB. He read it before going to Ray Johnston's office.

Harry
Regarding test results of Samuel Winton.
The samples from bodily organs confirmed that there was a very high intake of phenobarbital. That was the most likely cause of death. One of the drinking glasses submitted had a significant level of phenobarbital in the remaining liquid and on the glass, and the only fingerprints on that glass were that of the victim. Beer was detected in both glasses. The second glass had no traces of poison and no fingerprints. No poison was found in beer bottle.
Further details later.
Tony.

Harry and Joe walked to the meeting. They were introduced by Ray to Superintendent Brian Ford. Brian was attached to head office and was responsible for the coordination of major events across the state to ensure that resources were being applied to the prime cases as required. Harry knew of him more by reputation than personally or professionally, but they had met occasionally at Central Street headquarters. Harry had high respect for him as a no-nonsense, down-to-earth, sharp-thinking operator. After some idle chit-chat, Harry, Joe and Brian walked to the interview room. Ray remained in his office.

The superintendent started the conversation. "I'm here because we have three very difficult and complex cases here in Armidale. It looks as if you have a serial killer on the loose. I want you two to fill me in so that I can assess whether we need to bring in more resources to assist with your investigations. So, take your time and give me the details of what's happened."

Harry stood and walked to the blackboard. "Thanks sir. Let's start by Joe and I listing the main points about these three murders. Please ask any questions to clarify any details of any aspect of the murders."

Harry and Joe sparked off each other and wrote the following points on the blackboard:

- *Victims dying of phenobarbital*
- *Three murders by the same person*
- *Two drinking glasses at the scene*
- *Petherby and Winton—only one glass had poison*
- *No fingerprints on the other glasses*
- *Awaiting full results O'Sullivan case*
- *No obvious relationships between three victims*
- *No obvious similarities—appearance, background, interests*
- *No obvious external injuries*
- *Petherby and O'Sullivan—different subjects at university*
- *Winton—SP bookie; early life as jockey*
- *Similar oblong coloured pendant around neck of victims*
- *Each pendant had a different number: 1,3,7*
- *Cardboard sign taped to back; single written word*
- *Second written sign at each site*
- *Uncertain meanings of signs*
- *Locations differ: laboratory rat shed; bath at back of Empire pub; Dumaresq Creek*
- *Checked pharmacies, doctors, hospitals and veterinarians for phenobarbital stocks and sales.*

Brian Ford looked at the list for some time before speaking. "Have you found any losses of phenobarbital from doctors, vets or hospitals?"

"No, but we still have some to check."

"Okay, describe each of the victims to me; their character, family circumstances and interests."

"Let's take Jonathon Petherby first," said Harry. "He was in his early twenties, the son of well-off farmers from Killarney, near Warwick. He was studying English, psychology and philosophy at the university but had failed two subjects last year. He owned one of the few cars in the student body. He had money to spend, was spoiled and pampered by his mother, but barely tolerated by his father and brothers who were very active on the property."

Joe interrupted. "He was a big fat slob, too bloody lazy to get out of his own way. He was grossly overweight. He probably drove to town each afternoon to eat and drink before going back to the Bevery for a large evening meal. If he got off his backside and did some exercise, he wouldn't have had a problem."

"Hold it, Joe," said Harry. "We are not here to judge him. We want the facts. Yes, he was about twenty stone and he overate. As a result, it appears that he was bullied most of his life, including at university. We interviewed some of those bullies at the uni, and while they are still persons of interest, I doubt they are the perpetrators. He had always been a loner but some of the women and staff at the uni had sympathised with him."

"He tried to win friends by giving others a ride in his car or dishing out lollies and other rubbish, but it didn't work," said Joe. "His only outside interest was at the Presbyterian church and his involvement in the choir. The only thing he lifted was his big fat gut to get into the pews at church."

Harry walked away from the blackboard and looked out the window. "The interesting thing about these murders is that, despite the three victims being very different, all three must have had a close enough relationship with the murderer to have sat down and enjoyed a drink with him. In all three cases there were two glasses; one laced heavily with phenobarbital and the other one clear."

"That could be a telling point, Harry," said Brian Ford sitting back with hands clasped under his chin. "Now, what about the second victim?"

Harry referred to his notes. "Sam Winton, also known as Splinter, was about thirty and a former jockey. He came from a family heavily involved in the racing and hotel businesses. His parents own a hotel in Tamworth. When he retired from the saddle he took up SP bookmaking at his father's pub in Tamworth but his father kicked him out. He came to Armidale and became the main SP man in town."

Joe spoke up. "From what everyone tells us, Splinter was a wheeler-dealer, not only with the horses but with moneylending. He would buy and sell anything that would make him a quid. He even lent money to university and teachers college students and, when they didn't pay back in time, he would take their watches or anything else of value and pawn them. He was a miserable, cocky, smart-arsed, loud-mouthed wheeler-dealer. It's a wonder someone didn't do him in earlier on."

"Don't be too harsh, Joe," said Harry. "But you are right. And he was nothing like Petherby. And I can't see those two ever having anything to do with each other. Petherby had plenty of money but there is no evidence of him being involved in gambling."

"What about Winton's family?" asked the superintendent.

"We met with them," replied Harry. "There was a real love-hate relationship between them. We have to question whether they lived on the edge of the law. There are strong rumours that Winton and the bookmaker John Lewis were involved in race fixing, and I wouldn't be surprised if his parents were involved in that as well."

"Could Lewis be involved in all this?" asked Brian.

"He gave us the quick heave-ho from his house yesterday morning when we raised the race fixing with him," said Joe. "We hit a very sensitive nerve but, even if he had a fight with Splinter, I can't see him murdering Petherby or O'Sullivan as well."

"How was Lewis connected to Winton?"

"They were as thick as thieves. Lewis said that they met every Thursday at the pub to discuss all the weekend races and share information they got from other sources before they each set their prices for the weekend."

"Could something have gone wrong between them?"

"I don't think so," replied Harry.

"Okay, now tell me about the third victim," inquired the superintendent.

Joe answered. "Everything about that man O'Sullivan was in your face. He was a good-for-nothing ponce. He was brought up in a family of great wealth. He had an expectation of entitlement and privilege. He dressed in the most expensive clothes and stood out like a neon sign. He was so up himself. He went to the most expensive schools and had probably never done a decent day's work in his whole life. He was the type of bloke who would look down on anyone less well-off than himself."

"How did he get to be like that?" asked Brian.

Harry responded. "We understand that he was the third child in the family and was born premature. His mother saw him as an up-and-coming great world scientist. The family paid a high fee for him to be looked after in private accommodation. He never had to take any responsibility. He boarded with Shirley Sayers who said that he was spoiled by his parents."

"Who were his friends?" asked Brian.

Harry looked out the window. "I saw him as someone who sought recognition and honour by showing off his wealth. He drove selected girls around in his Jaguar XK120 as a show of privilege but he had no long-time friends. He attached an exaggerated importance to his external appearance. He was vain but lacked substance. I get the feeling that he was a person who wanted others to feel envious of him."

"The problem as I see it," said Brian, "is your point on the blackboard that says there doesn't seem to be any connection or similarities between the victims. Does that mean that the killer selected his victims by chance? Were they random killings? What would have drawn him to those men? And what is the meaning of the pendants and signs found on their bodies?"

Harry circled the words 'pendants' on the board. "They are a real mystery. The big question is how the killer enticed three different men from widely different backgrounds to sit down with him to have a drink, without any assault, restraint or injury. Had he regularly met them before at somewhere like a hotel or the races? Did he use natural charm? Or did he offer them an incentive to do so? We know two of them were university students, but Splinter wasn't and would never have stepped foot inside the grounds of the university except to collect a debt. Yet

Splinter was willing to sit down with the killer and have a drink at the back of the hotel so he must have been on friendly terms."

"Wouldn't the victims have known that their drink was laced with phenobarbital?" asked Brian.

"No," replied Harry. "I was talking to Jack Witherspoon last night. He's the drugs expert from the SIB. He told me that the drug comes in crystal form and is mixed with alcohol. It can be added to lemonade, or orange juice or sugar syrup to hide the taste that can be a bit unpleasant. The victim would be unaware of the poison. Large doses hasten the cessation of electrical impulses to the heart. It then proceeds to the liver and is excreted through urine. Post-mortem remnants are found in the stomach, blood and urine. There was no evidence of phenobarbital in the bottles of drinks which raises the question of how the killer added the poison to the victim's glass before or after pouring in the mixer such as the lemonade, beer or champagne. Could he have had something like a syringe with the exact quantity of poison up his sleeve to add to the victim's glass while the victim was distracted?"

Joe raised a finger. "Although it takes about five to ten grams to kill a human being, Tony said that there was a high intake of the poison in the victims. So the killer might not have given two hoots about the accurate amount needed for each victim according to their size and we don't know how much of the poison is in his possession. He could in fact have a bottle for each victim, and having finished off each one, throw away the remains from that bottle."

"Does phenobarbital come in a tablet form?" asked Brian.

"Jack Witherspoon told me that phenobarbital can be used as a sedative or anticonvulsant or for the treatment of partial and generalized seizures and the safe tablet dosages would range between thirty to one hundred milligrams a couple of times a day. He said in the Armidale cases it was more likely that the killer used the liquid form."

"Do we need to get some of the SIB team to you here in Armidale to assist your investigations?" asked Brian.

Harry thought for a moment. "I don't think that is necessary yet. We send samples on the midnight train each night and Tony Jacobs's team picks them up the following morning. And he gets the results back to us as soon as possible."

"Why are we so obsessed with the quantity needed to kill a man?" asked Joe. "We can't assume that the killer has medical or vet experience and knows the exact amount to use and we can't assume that the killer will keep the dregs of each bottle to use on the next victim. All we know is that he is using phenobarbital to poison the victims."

"Fair point Joe," said Harry.

"Before I go, Harry," said Brian, "tell me more about this upcoming court case you're involved in with former Criminal Branch members. What's it all about?"

"I got notice some time ago that I have to appear in Sydney on Thursday the 4th of May. Apparently, the wife and brother of an accountant who was murdered in Albury last year are suing the government for negligence. I've been told that the former CIB officers—Allan Twain together with Funnell, Lewis, Podger and Nolan—will be witnesses for the family. They even brought in Tomlinson who, before going on the desk at headquarters, was also in the CIB."

Brian added, "That lot have still got it in for you, Harry. Have you got legal support?"

"I've already briefed Fergus Whitelaw."

"My God, Harry, you must be desperate," said Brian. "I thought Fergus had been disbarred. It's a wonder he's still alive. Can't you do better than that?"

Harry smiled. "I know Fergus is despised by the legal fraternity and he constantly challenges judges and magistrates, but he has the best legal mind in the country. And even when he's drunk he can out-think most of them. I just have to get him to the court on time and sober."

"Do you think the old CIB officers might be behind these cases in Armidale?" asked Brian.

"I'm quite sure that Sherman and Cross, who are still in gaol, are not going to stop coming after me. And they have strong connections with the underworld. We believe that they were involved in arranging crimes carried out by some of the big gangsters in this state. I wouldn't put anything past them, including being involved with these cases here. They could easily get some of their criminal mates to randomly kill victims around here to cause confusion. It could explain the random nature of these killings because there is no other obvious connection between the victims."

"Didn't you work with them early on?" asked Brian.

"Yes," replied Harry. "Before the war I worked at the CIB but I was never considered by Sherman, Cross or Twain as being one of the team because I was never tempted to get involved with the corruption or bribery by those few."

"Have you any evidence that they're involved in the Armidale killings?"

"I have no clear evidence. I know that they want to take out their revenge on me but, arranging or even carrying out these bizarre murders seems too far-fetched."

"Okay Harry. For the moment let's leave it as it is. But if this killing spree continues, we will need to look into getting the forensics team up here."

Ray Johnston had just rejoined them. Brian Ford stood, shook the hands of Harry and Joe and walked with Ray back to his office.

A few minutes later, Graham McInnes from the desk walked in to tell them that two men claiming to be from the Racing Authority were waiting to see them.

Chapter 16
Monday

Harry walked out to be met by two well-dressed men in suits, ties and trilby hats. One carried a briefcase. The men introduced themselves as Charles Dakin and Laurence Simkins, senior stewards from the Racing Authority. Harry shook hands and invited them into the tea room where they met Joe.

"What can I do for you two gentlemen?" asked Harry.

Charles took off his hat and laid it on the table. "We have been investigating a small group of gamblers who we believe have been involved in race fixing. We believe that the main organisers are here in Armidale. It has come to our attention that one of those people was recently murdered here and, therefore, we have a direct interest in that investigation."

Harry made a quick assessment of their body language and immediately sensed that these two men were trying to insinuate themselves into the police investigation; not for the purpose of identifying the murderer but to assist them in finding out who was involved in the race fixing. They exuded a persona of power, self-importance and privilege.

"Tell me more."

"Our investigators have been following betting patterns in northern New South Wales and southern Queensland and there have been sudden betting plunges at the last minute on certain horses in races, suggesting the practice of race fixing. These events occur mainly in picnic races in the northern half of the state. Last weekend it occurred in races at Moree and Scone. When we checked the pattern of betting we found that the bookmaker least affected by the plunges was John Lewis from Armidale. He dropped his price on one particular horse just before the last-minute plunge while his punting mates immediately went and put stacks of money on that same horse at better than ten-to-one odds, before the other bookies had a chance to lower the odds. That same horse had failed miserably as the favourite in the second race on the same day but came back and easily won the seventh by twenty yards and made a fortune for the syndicate."

Harry spread his hands. "Well, how does that relate to our investigations?"

"Well," replied Charles, "Lewis was a great mate of Splinter Winton who was murdered last week. Winton was the local SP bookie here in Armidale and we believe he was involved in this race fixing. Maybe if the local police had done their job and locked up these illegal gamblers, all this mess wouldn't have happened."

Joe stood up and glared at the two men. "Would you two like to come along with me to the superintendent's office where he is about to have a meeting with other officers and tell them they have not been doing their jobs?"

Harry placed a hand on Joe's arm and spoke calmly. "We do not want to disturb the superintendent, Joe. We can handle this matter here."

Laurence Simkins sat back with a smirk. "We don't want to be upsetting the superintendent, do we? Now what can you tell us about Lewis and Winton?"

Without going into detail, Harry spent the next few minutes outlining the basic facts surrounding the murder of Winton and their interview with Lewis.

"Thank you, Detective," said Charles Dakin. "Everything you have said confirms our theory that Winton's murder was related to the race fixing that has been going on for too long in this region. Therefore, we will need to take control of aspects of this investigation. Some very influential people in the racing and gambling industries have powerful friends in the underworld and they don't like it when someone screws them for thousands. It is up to us to bring this matter to its conclusion as soon as possible."

"What do you mean?" asked Harry.

"We are under instructions from the top to take all necessary steps to bring this matter to a head. And if that means us being involved with the murder investigation, then so be it. So, we expect that you will give us every cooperation in our work."

"And what, in particular, do you want us to do?" asked Harry.

Simkins pointed both forefingers at the desk. "You will hand over your notebooks for us to examine."

"Well, that's not going to happen," said Harry as he pulled his book closer.

Simkins jabbed one finger at Harry. "You don't understand. We have directives right from the top. And I can assure you that the powers that be are not going to take no for an answer from you. You won't be able to deal with the pressure that will come your way if you don't cooperate."

Harry sat forward, stretched his arm across the desk and slapped his big open hand down hard in front of Simkins who immediately pushed back in his chair.

"What would you know about pressure? Look at me while I tell you about pressure. Pressure is being in a clearing in the jungle in the middle of Borneo and you are suddenly attacked by twenty Japanese soldiers hiding behind the trees. You have to stand in the open and rake the area with Bren-gun fire to keep the Japs down to protect your platoon long enough for them to cross the rope bridge to safety. Then you face a wild Jap soldier running at you with bayonet fixed, about to kill you. It is you or him. After killing him you have to cross the bridge and hope your mates can keep the enemy ducking from covering fire until you get across. That's what real pressure is. So, anything you try to throw at me will be like hitting me with an emu feather."

Dakin tapped the desk nervously. "Thank you for your war-hero tales, Harry. I'm sure that you could show me your medals later on. But you have to understand we come here with specific orders from right at the top of Parliament House in Sydney. You must also appreciate that the membership of our racing authorities in this country is led by the top legal authorities and business chiefs. They don't take no for an answer. So, hand over your books so we can get on our way."

Harry sat back and laughed. "Are they the same well-known identities who frequent the illegal gambling casino owned by Whispers Durante operating in Woolloomooloo on Friday and Saturday nights? And do they have access to the free call girls in the back rooms? Are they the same people who befriended the former head of the CIB, Fred Sherman, who was also a former guest of Durante's establishment? Fred's now doing time at Grafton gaol. Are you two also regular guests of Mr Durante? I must check the photos we took of the guests arriving at the casino two years ago."

"I don't know what you are talking about," snapped Dakin.

"Let me make it very clear to you two," said Harry. "We don't give over our notebooks to anyone; and I mean anyone. I can confirm that we are dealing with a serial killer and that one of the victims was Splinter Winton who was the local SP bookie. He associated with the bookmaker John Lewis. But the other victims had nothing to do with racing or race fixing so we can't assist you any longer. Please leave now."

Dakin stood and turned and pointed to Harry. "Don't think this is the end of this."

Harry laughed. "I'm sure you'll go back and tittle-tattle to all those important, powerful people. I'll have to be careful that my size-twelve boots don't fall off when my legs shake with fear from all that pressure that is going to come my way. Goodbye, and give my regards to Whispers Durante when you go to his illegal casino on Friday night. And make sure you give the girls a good tip after you pull up your pants."

Graham McInnes poked his head around the corner. "Harry and Joe, we want you over at the Wicklow Hotel. There is a bit of a ruckus there."

"Can't the uniformed officers deal with a fight at the pub? Why do they want us there?"

"Eric Talbot and Pat Casey are there but they said it had something to do with your case."

***

Harry and Joe drove to Marsh Street where they stopped out the front of the recently renovated Wicklow Hotel. The barman directed them to the back courtyard. Eric and Pat had one man sitting at the table in cuffs. Another man sat at the next table.

Eric pointed to the man in cuffs. "That man's name is Charlie McCoy. He says he comes from Sydney but he couldn't give us an exact address. The other man there is Stewart Miles and he lives here in Armidale. We all saw that report in the paper that the three victims were poisoned. Now Stewart claims that McCoy tried to poison him with a loaded drink—but he didn't drink it all. Stewart believes that McCoy is the serial killer who did in those other three victims."

Harry walked to the next table and introduced himself to Miles. "Now Stewart, tell us what happened. Take your time."

"That bastard tried to do me in."

"Slow down and tell me everything from the time you came to the hotel."

"Well, when I came in, I ordered my usual middy of old beer and I sat next to this bloke who was from out of town. We got talking. He seemed very friendly and was very interested in what goes on here in Armidale. He said he was interested in maybe moving out of the city and coming here to get some work. He said he was willing to do anything, like being a builder's labourer or work on a farm. He liked the idea of coming to the country where everyone is so friendly."

"What happened next?" asked Harry.

"Well, I suggested that I would get us a couple of pies and we could eat them with another couple of beers. He gave me a shilling to buy him a pie and said he'd get the beers. When I got back to the pub he had got the drinks and moved out to the courtyard at the back. That made me a bit suspicious because it was blowing a cold south-wester and I didn't have my coat with me."

"Go on. What happened next?"

"Well, we ate the pies while they were hot and it made me feel better, but when I took my first sip of that beer it tasted funny."

"What do you mean—funny?"

"Well, it had a bitter taste to it. And it was then that I realised why that bastard took me out to the courtyard where there was no one else around. I'm not a fool. I read about the poisoning of those other three blokes in the paper so I wasn't going to trust this bloke when the beer tasted sour. He was trying to poison me. He's the bloody killer. It was him who did in poor Splinter and those other two blokes."

"Where's the glass with your beer in it?" asked Harry as he looked around the yard.

"I got so angry that I threw it at him and then punched him to the ground. I smashed the top of the glass and was about to stab him with it when Curley Stratton came out of the dunny and stopped me. He called you blokes."

Harry looked at Charlie McCoy. He saw the shirt collar and jumper had beer stains down the front.

"Strip any wet clothes from that bloke," said Harry. "Find a bag or box from behind the bar or in the kitchen so we can send them off for examination. Pat, get another bag or box and gather as much of that broken glass as possible. Try to keep whatever liquid remains in the glass. Label them and have them ready to send off to the SIB. Joe, I want you to take Stewart's statement."

"What about me?" shouted Charlie. "I'm gunna freeze when you take my clothes off."

Harry walked over to the corner of the yard where he found two chaff bags. He gave them to Charlie, to wrap around his shoulders.

"Now Charlie," said Harry, "you had better start talking."

"I didn't do nothin'," he shouted. "I don't know what he's talkin' about. I just got the beers as we had agreed and came out here so we could eat our pies in peace."

"Why didn't you have your pies and beer inside where it was warm and out of the wind?"

"Well," said Charlie, "I'm a bit deaf from working on jackhammers in the mines for much of me working life and I find it hard to listen when there's lottsa people talkin' in a room. I find it easier outside in the open."

"Take everything out of your pockets," demanded Harry.

Charlie put on the table a dirty handkerchief, a set of keys, a packet of tobacco, cigarette papers, a pocket knife, an old Ronson cigarette lighter and some loose change.

"Stewart said you were coming here looking for work. Where's your other gear?"

"I booked into the Wicklow for tonight until I look around for board. My bag is in room seven upstairs."

Harry took the hotel key and went to room seven. Charlie's bag was filled with work clothes and shaving gear. There was nothing suspicious in the bag or room. Back downstairs, Harry took Eric, Pat and Joe aside.

"What have we got on this bloke?"

"Unless we get clear evidence of poison from those clothes and glasses, we have nothing," said Eric. "I know Stewart. He's a nice, decent bloke but, I think with this dust-up, he went too far. Those reports of poisoning in the newspapers have got everyone on edge. I think the other bloke was just trying to be friendly. There was still some beer froth in the glass Stewart threw at Charlie. I put in my finger and tasted it and it seemed normal to me. It just tasted like beer. But we won't know until we get the results back."

"I agree with Eric, Harry," said Pat. "The town is all on edge about these murders and everything unusual is seen as suspicious. I don't think there is anything here, but we can't take chances."

"Okay," said Harry. "I agree. I think Charlie is just a decent bloke looking for a job here. I see him as someone who came to the right place but at the wrong time."

Harry and Joe searched room seven again before taking Charlie McCoy back to the Sheriff's Cottage where they questioned him further before releasing him.

***

They walked back to the office and spent most of the day bringing their notes up to date.

Chapter 17
Tuesday

Harry had just returned from the dawn service for the Anzac Day ceremony at the memorial in Central Park when there was a knock on his front door. He turned and looked at the clock. It was six-thirty. He walked to the door to be greeted by Constable Keith Blackmore.

"Sorry to disturb you, Harry, on this important day but, when I was doing my early morning rounds on the bike, I noticed a tent pitched near the main pavilion at the showground. I drove in off Kennedy Street and around the main pavilion. As I got off the bike near the far wall there was this rotten smell that seemed to be coming from the direction of an old galvanised water trough on a stand against the building. When I got closer I saw the body of a man, naked to the waist, lying face down in the water in the trough. The skin was covered with black blotches. It looked as though it had been burned."

Harry scratched his hair and hitched his army pants. "Thanks Keith. Go and get Joe and take him to the showground. I'll meet you there in ten minutes."

Harry changed his trousers, grabbed his army-surplus battle jacket, hat and boots, slipped them on and walked out to the MG. He drove the few blocks to the showground. Keith arrived at the same time with Joe on the pillion seat.

Joe got off, rubbing his hands vigorously. "Bloody hell, Harry, Keith's trying to kill me. If he doesn't toss me off going around corners then I'll freeze to death on this bloody cold bike."

"Come on, Joe, you've had it too easy down there in Sydney in your nice heated houses," said Harry as he laughed. "You need to get some real country blood in your veins. Duck over the road to the racecourse and do a gallop around the track with those horses."

"No bloody way. Now why have you got me out here this early?"

"Well, Keith here has found another body for us. So let's go and look."

At the end of the pavilion building was a large, heavy-duty, galvanised-iron trough about six feet long, two feet wide and two feet deep. It sat on two large concrete blocks. There was a tap mounted on the wall above it. Harry recognised it as a drinking trough for the horses.

"Bloody hell," shouted Joe as he stepped back. "What's that bloody stink? That's so foul. That body must have been here a long time to stink that badly. That is the most awful stench."

"Calm down, Joe," said Harry. "That's not the body stinking. That smell is rotten egg gas. It comes from burning sulphur. Take a look on the ground in front of the trough. See that yellow powder scattered in the dust? That's sulphur. Get a paper bag and scrape up samples. There are some bags in the back of my car."

Keith pointed to the body. "Would that explain those black patches on that bloke's back? Has he been burned with that sulphur?"

"We won't know definitely until we do the chemical analysis but I'd say that is the most likely cause of those marks. This man might have been given the fire-and-brimstone treatment."

"What do you mean?" asked Joe about to go to the car for the paper bags.

"Brimstone means burning stones. It was often mentioned in ancient times in reference to the burning of sulphur. Apparently, the valley of the Dead Sea had lots of sulphur. When you burn sulphur it turns into sulphur dioxide and it stinks like the worst smell of rotten eggs. That's what you can smell here."

"I've never heard of brimstone," said Joe.

Harry smiled. "Did you go to sleep in church when the priest raved on about the fire and brimstone that God rained down on the towns of Sodom and Gomorrah? Didn't you read it in the Bible?"

"I never went to church, mate," said Joe. "On Sundays I went to the Police Citizens Boys Club for boxing lessons. I think Mum might have had a Bible. So, what's this sod almighty—or whatever it's called—got to do with this bloke here?"

"You don't know what you missed out on, Joe. That was always the best Scripture lesson I ever attended because there was some real action; a bit of blood and thunder. There is a story in the Old Testament about the two evil towns of Sodom and Gomorrah. The men in those towns had sex with each other. In God's eyes, that was a grave, unforgivable sin. He sent two angels disguised as men to investigate the sins in the towns. The angels hid in the house of a bloke called Lot, one of the few righteous men around, because the townsfolk wanted to have sex with the pure, uncorrupted angels. Lot offered his daughters in exchange for handing over the angels to the mob waiting outside. God saw this and determined that the people of the town must be punished. He sent down fire and brimstone. The brimstone was sulphur. God saved Lot and his family but his wife was turned into a pillar of salt."

"You're saying that God killed all those people because the men in the towns were a bunch of poofters?" asked Joe. "That's a bit rough, isn't it? But what has that got to do with this bloke in the trough?"

"Well," said Harry, "the killer might be sending another message. But before we get him out of the trough, look around and tell me what else you see."

Keith pointed to the corner of the building. "Over there is a small table with two empty glasses on it, and two stools. That looks like two empty Coke bottles on the ground near the table."

"Good work, Keith. It looks like the same killer has been here and it looks like there is about half an inch of liquid still in the glasses. We need to bag the glasses for prints, and the leftover drink, and then we'll send them all to the SIB today. He might have poisoned this man the same as the other three."

Joe pointed towards the oval. "Is that the tent you were talking about, Keith?"

The men walked over to the large two-man tent. The front flap was tied back. There were two sleeping bags inside, both unrolled. On top of a small methylated-spirits burner was a saucepan with remnants of cooked sausages and rissoles. Next to the stove was a paper bag filled with potatoes, carrots, a piece of pumpkin and pieces of cauliflower. Beside the left-hand sleeping bag was a Scout hat with a scarf and toggle. Behind the same bag was a neatly folded Scout shirt decorated with sewn-on badges. A pair of black boots lay under the side flap.

Harry turned to the others, lifted his hat and scratched his forehead. "Why would there be a single tent out here like this during the week?"

Keith waved his hand around. "We sometimes get travellers who pitch their tents here. They can use the washrooms in the pavilion and it saves paying for a room at the hotel. But this is different. Over the weekend the local Scout group had a camp here at the showground. You can see where the grass has been flattened in several places where the tents were set up. I rode past here a couple of times over the weekend and saw the set-up."

"Look in there," said Joe as he pointed at the narrow space between the sleeping bags. "There is something white."

He stooped and entered the tent and removed a sheet of cardboard. On it was written in clear bold letters:

***They will be consigned
to the fiery lake
of burning sulphur.***

"Right," said Harry as he turned to Keith, "I want you to go back to the station and phone David Hobbs and tell him what we have here. Joe and I will go up to examine the body in the trough."

As they arrived at the pavilion, Joe bent down to look under the trough. From behind the concrete blocks he took out a smaller piece of cardboard with just one word clearly written on it:

Chastity

"There is no doubt," said Harry, "that we have the same killer. Let's take this bloke's body out of the trough. Go inside, Joe, and get something to lay him on."

When Joe returned he had a large Union Jack flag and an old curtain. He laid them in front of the trough before he and Harry lifted the body straight out from the trough and laid it on the ground, face down.

"God, that stinks," shouted Joe. "Can't we carry him away from here?"

"Just put up with it, Joe, until we get a good look at this fellow. Look, there's a leather bootlace around his neck."

Harry cut the lace with his pocket knife and lifted it from the body and placed it on the curtain. He carefully wiped it clean with the edge of the flag.

"We got this just in time, Joe. Look at the back of this pendant that was attached to the bootlace. Something is already eating into the metal."

"What are you talking about, Harry?"

"When sulphur burns, it gives off sulphur dioxide gas, and when that dissolves in water it forms sulphuric acid which is very corrosive. That could be what is causing the effect on the back of the pendant. There is a lot of water in the trough, and hopefully the acid might not be too strong. It hasn't affected the coloured side of the pendant. Look, there is the number 2 clearly marked in the same way as the others."

"Could it be that those blotchy black marks on his skin were the result of the acid in the water? Or was it the result of burning sulphur?"

"We don't know, but we'll get Gregory Ebsworth to take samples for Tony Jacobs to test. But before we do anything else we must wash our hands in case there is acid in that water."

David Hobbs brought the hearse to a stop on the grass next to Harry and Joe.

"Don't tell me we have another one, Harry?" he asked in his slow casual drawl. "Well, let's get on with it and get him loaded."

"Before you do so David, I have to warn you that the body might have acid on it from that water trough. We found him in the trough there. Give us a hand to roll him over so we can look for any other evidence."

David walked over and slowly turned the victim's head on its side to look at his face. "I thought he looked a bit familiar. He's young Richard Gladstone."

"How did you know this bloke, David?" asked Harry as he took a better look at the face.

"He's a local boy. He lived with his parents on their small farm off Uralla Road, not far down from my parlour. You can recognise the house by the small painted sign on the white picket fence advertising the business of Richard's father, Chris Gladstone. He's a surveyor and a great bloke. He does big-time stuff for the government on projects around the state. He's often away from home. His mother Elaine is a primary school teacher at the Demonstration School and loved having Richard at home, especially when her husband was away on a job."

"What did this young bloke do, David?" asked Joe.

"He was at teachers college studying to be an infants teacher. He was a nice young bloke, about twenty years old. He was well-mannered and liked by his neighbours and friends."

"Are you close friends of the family?" asked Harry.

"In this business, Harry, we get to know almost everyone one way or another. But most people don't want to be seen as close friends of the undertaker. We understand that; it's part of the life we chose. We are friendly to everyone but close friends with only a few. The Gladstones are not that close, but I meet them at various functions and funerals. They are good people, and young Richard was involved in the Church of England Cathedral Choir and was a Sunday school teacher and a leader in the local Scouts."

"Then why would anyone want to do this to him?" asked Harry.

"Richard lived here in Armidale all his life. He went to the Dem School and then on to The Armidale School. From memory he did quite well academically at school but was never a sportsman and so he took a lot of bullying, especially at high school."

"Thanks David. Now let's turn him fully on his back and take off his pants, underwear, and socks. Let's look for any wounds."

As the man's underpants were removed, the three of them suddenly stepped back, staring at the body. There was a pink ribbon tied around his genitals.

Chapter 18
Tuesday

"Why the hell would the killer do that to him? Are they trying to tell us that this bloke is a poofter?" said Joe. "If he was a poofter, I would have expected the killer to have given him a good belting before he did him in, but then I'm not sure anymore."

"These things are not easy to work out," said Harry. "Let's not jump to conclusions before we do some more investigation."

David pointed to the body. "There doesn't seem to be any external injuries to the body on the front. And I didn't see any cuts or bruises to his back before we turned him over. I can see a small cut to his chin but that was not the cause of death and could have been made by a razor when he had a shave. Or his face could have scraped on the side of the tank as he was tossed into the water."

Harry scratched his forehead. "It seems that the killer must have known this young man because it appears that they sat down there and had a drink together. There are no signs of a fight or struggle. The young man was not wearing a shirt or singlet but we don't know if he took them off and placed them in the tent before having a drink, or if the killer took them off after death. We will bag those clothes, David, to test for fibres or other material."

"In Redfern, poofters were taken around the back and convinced to find another place to be," said Joe. "They were told to get back to Kings Cross where they belonged."

"Get used to it, Joe," said Harry. "This is not Redfern and you have to get used to dealing with these things as they occur, not as you would like them to be. Just talk to David here. He gets to see all types of cases, just like us. You could, of course, ask for a transfer to the fraud squad, but I can't see you sitting at a desk, going over books of accounts and bank sheets all day. You'd finish up punching the daylights out of the bank manager because he was out playing golf on Wednesday afternoons when you wanted him at the bank when you were investigating financial records."

"Are you finished here, Harry?" asked David. "I'd like to get this bloke back to the parlour. I'll call Gregory Ebsworth and arrange a time for him to do the autopsy."

"Sure David. Joe and I will give you a hand."

After he sent David on his way, Harry turned to Joe. "Joe, I want you to go through that tent. Check everything. Go through that duffle bag and note everything. I will cover the showground to check if there is anything else of importance."

***

Forty minutes later they came together at the tent and compared notes. Joe spoke first. "In the duffle bag were clothes, a Scout whistle, a cake of Sunlight soap and a razor. Then there was this brown paper parcel. It feels like a book. I haven't opened it yet so you can see it as it was in the bag."

"Open it, Joe," said Harry.

Joe untied the string and pulled back the brown paper. Inside was a new copy of May Gibbs's book *The Complete Adventures of Snugglepot and Cuddlepie*. Inside the cover was a short note:

To Joey, for being a good Cub. Richard.

Joe coughed. "Holy dooley. What's this bloke on about? Look at the cover of this book. It has two stark-naked babies with their bums pointing out at you on the front cover, and he was giving it to a young Cub. Here Harry, you take it. I've never seen this book before."

Harry laughed. "Don't worry, Joe. May Gibbs has written a lot of books for young children. She is a very talented illustrator and author. Most of her books are about the gumnut babies. Most kids I knew got them as a present or heard them read at school. They included all the Australian animals in the bush."

"But why would he be giving a book like that to a boy in the Cubs?" asked Joe.

"Good point, Joe," said Harry. "We must look into that."

Keith returned on his motorbike and walked towards Harry and Joe. "What do you want me to do, Harry?" asked Keith.

"Let's start by taking down this tent and packing it securely in a bag to be sent off to the SIB tonight with all of the other evidence from here."

Harry looked up and pointed to a shrub on the far corner of the building. "There's a garbage tin over there that I missed earlier. I'll take a look at that."

Harry returned soon after with a something wrapped in his handkerchief. It was a dark-brown glass bottle with a black lid. Printed in red writing on the white label was:

PHENOBARBITAL SODIUM 100g

"Wow," said Keith as he read the label. "There's probably enough in that bottle to kill a couple of horses. I'm very good friends with Rod Ironside, the local vet. I've been in his rooms when he has put down dogs. I've seen him take fluid from bottles like that with a syringe. I don't know how much he used but there didn't seem to be much in the syringe. I'll ask him next time I see him how much it would take to kill a man."

"That would be helpful, Keith. I'll also ask Gregory Ebsworth for his opinion. Could you now take the tent and its gear and the bags of evidence back to the station and get it packed, ready to put on the train tonight. Do you know who the Scoutmaster is?"

"Jack Robinson," replied Keith. "I know him well. He's in the same tennis club as me. He's also in the Highland Band. He's a top bloke and he does a marvellous job with the Scouts. He works in Richardson's store in the men's clothing section but he will be home today because of the Anzac Day holiday."

Harry nodded. "Thanks Keith. We'll catch up with Jack another day. But Joe and I will go to see Gladstone's parents now."

***

Harry and Joe drove through town but avoided Beardy and Dangar streets where the Anzac Day march had taken place. They heard the Armidale Highland Pipe Band still in full swing in the park after the procession. They crossed the railway bridge and turned onto Uralla Road until they came to a white-painted fence along the front of the Gladstone's property. At the end of the driveway they stopped in front of a relatively new dwelling with a two-storey section in the middle and an extension to both sides. Each side had a verandah. There were three chimneys above the blue-tiled roof. The house was surrounded by neat gardens and deciduous trees, some still in their autumn colours of reds and yellows. There were a few sheep grazing in the paddocks behind the house. The property was small but well maintained and, for a small acreage, was quite valuable. Harry knocked on the door. A woman still in her dressing gown half-opened the door.

"Good morning," said Harry. "I'm Detective Taylor and this is Detective Simms. May we come in? Is your husband at home?"

The woman looked embarrassed as she opened the door fully. "I'm sorry. I just got out of bed. I have a bad cold. I didn't even get to the Anzac Day parade. I'm Elaine Gladstone. Please come in. My husband is not here. He's a surveyor and is on a major project down at Muswellbrook in the mines."

When they had settled in the lounge room, Harry informed her of the death of her son and that he was most likely the victim of the serial killer. She screamed and covered her face with both hands. Her breathing convulsed and her body jerked as she sobbed. Harry moved to sit next to her on the large lounge and put his arm around her shoulder. He waited until her breathing slowed and her body relaxed. Joe went to the kitchen to get a glass of water for her.

"Where did this happen? How did he die?" she asked.

"At the showground," Harry replied.

Elaine took two deep breaths. "That's where the Scouts and Cubs were on a camp at the weekend. Richard was so excited to be there. I wasn't happy that he stayed there by himself last night. It was not safe. If only he'd taken notice of me, this wouldn't have happened."

Harry asked about Richard's involvement in the Scout camp. Richard's mother talked enthusiastically about Richard's involvement with the Scouts and said that Richard had stayed on at the park overnight to ensure everything was left in good order.

"Could you please give Detective Simms the phone number of the mine where your husband works? We will need to talk to him."

Elaine got up and walked to the bedroom, followed by Joe. She wrote the phone number on a piece of paper. Joe walked into the hallway, phoned the mine and left a message for Mr Gladstone to call home.

When Elaine returned she sipped the water and sat in the single lounge chair, her head bent forward.

"Could you tell me a little about Richard? What was he like? Who were his friends? What did he like to do?" asked Harry.

Elaine took her time before she replied. "He was such a wonderful son. He was my pride and joy. He didn't have a nasty bone in his whole body. He wouldn't hurt anyone. Why would anyone want to kill him?"

"We will know more when we get the results back from forensics," replied Harry.

"Tell me about his life with the Scouts," said Joe.

"He absolutely loved being in the Cubs and the Scouts. In the last two years he has been the leader of the Cubs and he adored all of the boys in that group."

"We noticed that he had a second sleeping bag in his tent," said Harry. "Do you know who that belonged to?"

"Richard always worried that some boys couldn't afford to buy the things necessary for camping so he purchased another sleeping bag. He told me he was going to let young Joey Ormond use his bag in the tent because his parents are not well-off."

"Where do the Ormonds live?" asked Harry.

"I think they live down on Odell Street," Elaine replied.

"In Richard's tent was a parcel that contained a copy of *Snugglepot and Cuddlepie* and a note addressed to Joey from Richard. Could you please tell us about that?" asked Harry.

Elaine put her hand to her mouth and gasped. "Oh, isn't that so beautiful. That's just what Richard would have done. Richard would have bought Joey a book because he didn't have many at home. And also, Richard used to babysit Joey."

"How old is Joey?" asked Joe.

"I think about eight."

"Did Richard babysit often?" asked Harry.

"Oh yes, he sat for a few families," replied Elaine. "The parents loved him because he was willing to babysit whenever they wanted to go out. And they were so thankful that they'd let him sleep over. They often sang his praises to us. It also helped him towards his ambition of becoming an infants teacher because he not only earned money but it gave him good experience with young children."

"What were his other interests?" asked Joe.

"We have always been regular members of St Peter's Anglican Cathedral and Richard was a member of the choir. He also taught at the Sunday school which, again, gave him great experience. He was a member of the Armidale Drama and Musical Society and had been very active in helping with the young people's pantomime each year. He also played in the Highland Pipe Band."

"How did he get on at school?" asked Joe.

Elaine paused. "He had his problems, but which kid doesn't? I think the other kids were jealous because he was at the top of his class. He was involved in music and acting rather than sport. The bullies picked on him and gave him a bad time but he rose above all that."

"Did that happen in primary as well as high school?" asked Joe.

"Yes, especially in the first year at high school. He was so happy to go to the local teachers college where he was accepted and recognised for his talents. And he got a high mark for his first practice teaching in the infants department at Ben Venue Primary School."

The phone in the hallway rang.

Chapter 19
Tuesday

Elaine walked down the hall. She was extremely distressed as she spoke on the phone. On returning to the lounge room she pointed to Harry.

"My husband wants to talk with you."

"Good day, Mr Gladstone," said Harry. "Please accept our sincere sympathies for the loss of your son."

"Well, your sympathies are not going to bring back my son, are they?" shouted Chris Gladstone. "How did you let this happen?"

"Excuse me, Mr Gladstone, but your son went to the showground over the weekend as part of the Scout camp. Surely, he did so with your knowledge and approval? He decided to stay on overnight to clean the camp area. I assumed that both you and your wife were well aware of his movements during the last few days."

"How the hell can I know everything when I'm down here at the mines working? What were you police doing letting a young man sleep by himself in the showgrounds when you knew that there was a killer at large around Armidale? This is not the last you'll hear about this from me."

"Mr Gladstone, your wife was well aware of Richard's intention to sleep over at the showgrounds, and Richard was an adult. He could make those decisions by himself. I suggest you discuss this matter with your wife."

"That's a bloody cop-out if ever I've heard one."

"Mr Gladstone, do you know of anyone who might have had a grudge against Richard, or someone with whom he might have had an argument or a fight?" asked Harry.

"Richard couldn't fight his way out of a paper bag. He was so wrapped up in his music and kids' stuff that he would have been an easy target for any bully."

"Can you tell me of any person who has bullied him recently?"

"He was bullied at school but I haven't heard of any incidents lately. But then that doesn't mean it didn't happen. Richard doesn't tell me anything anymore. I thought that's what you police are supposed to do; to deal with the bullies around town."

"I appreciate your concern, sir, but we can only deal with those matters if they are reported to us. And we can't be responsible for every decision within every family every day. Those decisions are yours as parents."

"I'll be home at the weekend and I'll expect you to have this bastard locked up by then."

"Could I suggest to you, sir, that you leave work now and come home today. Your wife needs your support now. She is very distressed with the loss of Richard."

"Thank you, but I'll decide when I come home. I must go now because the team needs my attention. We in the mines don't stop; not even for Anzac Day. And safety is our major priority."

Harry replaced the receiver and returned to the lounge room.

"Elaine, how did Richard get on with his father?" he asked.

Elaine sobbed into her handkerchief. "Chris could never understand Richard. He wanted a boy who was wrapped up in rugby, cricket and boxing like himself. He could not understand that Richard was more involved in the arts."

"But surely his dad was proud of his involvement in the Scouts?"

"No. He thought work with the Cubs was sissy stuff. Chris could never give praise for anything like that. Even when Chris went to the cathedral and heard Richard sing in the choir, he never even commented on Richard's participation. He would have preferred him to be in the boxing ring at the Police Citizens Boys Club, or doing judo or something like that."

"Who were Richard's close friends?" asked Joe.

"Richard was friendly with everyone but didn't have many close friends. He got on very well with Mary Faulkner at the teachers college. I don't think it was serious but they were in the choir and drama group together. She boards at Smith House with the other female students."

"And could you tell us of the other families where Richard did his babysitting?" asked Harry.

120

"He used to sit for Ruth and James Scott in Brown Street, but he hasn't been there lately. The other couple were Casandra and Geoff Lockhart in Mann Street. They swore by him."

"Have you got someone close by who can be with you now?" asked Harry.

"Yes, Clarise next door is a wonderful neighbour. I'll ask her to come in. Thank you."

***

Harry and Joe drove down Brown Street. Harry wanted to know why the Scotts no longer used Richard to babysit. They were met at the door by Ruth Scott, a woman in her late twenties. Two young boys, one five and the other just walking, clung to her skirt as she led Harry and Joe into the lounge room. Harry told her of Richard's death and the reason for their visit. One of her hands clung to the door handle for support. Her other hand covered her mouth in shock.

"Oh, my goodness. The poor boy. What a shock for the family. Do you have the killer?"

"Is your husband here, Ruth?"

"No. James is an electrician and he is working on a new house at Uralla today. He doesn't stop for the holiday."

"Could you please tell us what you thought of Richard Gladstone as a babysitter and why you didn't use him anymore?" asked Harry.

Ruth paused and turned her head towards the open window. "Look, I don't normally like to talk about these things. And I certainly don't want to speak ill of the dead. That is not the right thing to do. A couple of our friends have discussed their concerns with Richard with us but we don't want to talk about it."

"Take your time, Ruth. We appreciate your reluctance to talk about these things but we have a murder on our hands. And we need as much information about the victim to assist our inquiries. Let's start by you telling us how many times you hired Richard for babysitting."

Ruth found it difficult to look at Harry and Joe. She bent to adjust her shoelaces. "We had him here about eight times but we stopped using him about three months ago."

"Could you tell us why you stopped using him? Take your time."

Ruth rolled her handkerchief and twisted it back and forth around her fingers nervously. "We decided not to use him again. We found another sitter."

"Did you ever allow Richard to stop over at night when he was sitting?"

"Not at the beginning," she replied. "He would go home when we got back. But after a few sittings we felt that we could trust him to stay overnight. Our eldest son Jason liked him very much. And it helped Richard who didn't have to wait up every time we were late getting back. And we didn't have to rush home. He was so good with Jason and often brought him little presents like storybooks that he would read to him to get him to go to sleep. And sometimes there would be a chocolate if he was a good boy. On some weekends he asked if he could take Jason to the park to go on the swings. Jason loved Richard so much and we saw no harm in that. He didn't ask for payment on those days. Richard just got so much enjoyment out of playing with Jason."

"Why did you suddenly stop using him?" asked Harry.

Ruth got up and walked towards the kitchen, followed by the two boys. "I need a glass of water."

Harry turned to Joe. "Go with her, Joe, and look after Jason while she comes back here to answer that question."

Joe took Jason's hand. "Come on, mate. Let's go outside and show me your favourite toys. Have you got a car to show me?"

Ruth watched them go outside before she returned to the lounge room.

"Look," she said, "I didn't see it but, when we came home early one night about three months ago, James went into the boys' bedroom and found Richard in bed with Jason—and neither of them had any clothes on. He dragged Richard out of the bed and slammed him against the wall. I rushed in and pleaded for him not to hit Richard. James gave him a good lecture and threatened to kill him if he ever touched Jason again."

"Did he say 'I'll kill you'?"

"Oh my gosh, no," gushed Ruth as she stepped back in shock. "I didn't mean it that way. James is a very good man. There is no way he'd kill anyone. I know what you are thinking. It couldn't have been James who killed Richard because he was with me and the boys all weekend and last night after work. I can vouch for him being here."

"Ruth, calm down please. I'm not accusing your husband of anything. I just want to know what happened. Did you or James talk to Jason about that night?"

"James spoke to Jason the next morning. At first, Jason refused to talk. He said if he spoke about Richard, the big bad Banksia men would come and eat him up alive. James calmed him down and eventually got Jason to talk about it. It was then that Jason said that Richard was playing with his own penie and he wanted Jason to touch Richard there as well."

Harry leaned forward and took Ruth's hands to comfort her. "Did you or James think of reporting that to the police at that time?"

"No. We were so embarrassed that we didn't want anyone to know about it. And we didn't want to put young Jason through the ordeal of a police interrogation. It was enough for him to experience what Richard did and being threatened if he told anyone. We didn't want to put him under any more pressure."

"Thank you, Ruth," said Harry. "You have been very helpful. Do you know of other parents who used Richard as a babysitter?"

"Yes. Casandra and Geoff Lockhart in Mann Street as well as Barry and Jennifer Dodds at the top end of Taylor Street. Although, the Doddses didn't use him anymore. We thought about telling the other parents but decided that we might have gotten into trouble because we couldn't prove anything."

Harry stood up. "Thank you again, Ruth. Ask James to phone the station to make a time to talk to us. We'll leave now."

***

Harry and Joe drove to Mann Street where they stopped at the Lockhart household. Geoff Lockhart was an accountant and worked from his office at the front of his large brick house. They were met at the door by Geoff's wife Casandra who escorted them into the office. Harry explained the purpose of their visit and for the next half-hour Harry and Joe listened to the Lockhart's experiences with Richard Gladstone.

"Richard was one of the most delightful young men we have ever had anything to do with. He was so great with our children. He loved to play with them and he was pleased to do the babysitting at a moment's notice. That was so convenient to us because Geoff is often called out at all hours and we are expected to be at numerous functions in the district. Richard also took the kids to the pool and helped to teach them water safety. He didn't want payment for that. He loved to photograph them and the other children in the pool to show them their progress. What has happened to him is so terrible. We don't know what we will do now without his support for the kids. It'll be so hard to tell the boys. They are playing at the neighbours down the street."

***

Harry and Joe drove to Taylor Street where they visited the Dodds household. Jennifer Dodds met them and invited them in. Harry explained their visit and asked for her comments. She was shocked at the news but remained fairly composed. Her husband taught at The Armidale School where he took the English and history lessons but today was with the cadets in the Anzac Day march. When asked for her opinion of Richard, Jennifer was forthright in her reply.

"Yes, we used Richard as a babysitter a number of times on the recommendation of our accountant, Geoff Lockhart. Geoff and Casandra swore by him but, after a few times with us, my Barry got a bit suspicious. He saw a change in our son Albert in the way he reacted when Richard arrived to babysit. Instead of his usual happy, laughing self he went quiet and retreated to another room. We had no proof of anything nasty but we were not willing to take a chance. So we stopped having him as a sitter. Barry made some inquiries and said that some parents of Cubs had withdrawn their kids because they were not happy with the way Richard played with them and gave them little gifts. They didn't like how he kept taking their photos at the swimming pool. Some reckoned he was a bit queer."

Harry thanked Jennifer and asked if Barry could come to the station after he returned from the march to speak with them.

***

Harry and Joe drove back to the station.

"We'll call it a day, Joe," said Harry. "We'll start first thing tomorrow at the Ormond's house at eight o'clock. I will let them know we are coming. I want to talk to young Joey."

Chapter 20
Wednesday

At eight o'clock Harry arrived at an old weatherboard house on Odell Street. Joe was waiting in the wagon. Together they walked to the front door and were met by Rita and Greg Ormond, Joey's parents. Harry did the introductions and explained the purpose of their visit. The four of them moved through to the kitchen where they sat at the table.

"Thank you for seeing us this morning. You would have heard by now about the unfortunate murder of Richard Gladstone yesterday. We have been told that not only had Richard bought an extra sleeping bag for your son Joey but Richard had arranged for Joey to share his tent at the camp last weekend. Were you aware of that?" asked Harry.

Greg spoke first. "Yes, we were told of what happened to Richard. We were shocked by what happened to him. I work as a linesman with the PMG and we are not paid well but we wanted to give the kids every chance to be involved in things like the other kids have and we were happy for Richard to allow Jason to sleep in his tent and have a sleeping bag for him."

"How many children do you have?" asked Joe.

"Three; and another on the way. Joey is the oldest. He's eight. Then there is Mary who is five, and Freddie at eighteen months, and Rita is expecting another one in September. The kids are in the bedroom playing with their toys at the moment."

"Wow, you have a handful," said Joe.

Harry moved his open hand towards the parents. "So, did you give permission for Joey to sleep in Richard's tent at the Scout camp?"

Rita turned towards Harry. "Yes. Joey was so pleased to be in the Cubs. He loves being with his mates, and Richard had them doing lots of things every time they met. He always comes home very happy after each Cub meeting. We can't afford a tent and sleeping bag and so we were pleased when Richard offered to have a bag for Joey and let him sleep in his tent. Joey talked of nothing else for the last week."

Harry nodded. "In Richard's tent we found a parcel containing a book called *The Complete Adventures of Snugglepot and Cuddlepie* by May Gibbs. In it was a message that read: *To Joey, for being a good Cub. Richard.* Did you know about that?"

"Oh, wasn't that sweet of him," said Rita. "Richard had given Joey two other books to help his reading. They were *The Runaway Bunny* and *Mrs Piggy-Wiggle*. Richard was training to be an infants teacher and had said that reading is so important to Joey's development. He had been so helpful."

"Would you mind if I talked to Joey about the camp?" asked Harry. "One of you can stay here with him."

Greg stood. "I'll get Joey. You stay here, Rita, and I'll look after the other two in the bedroom."

As Joey walked into the kitchen he looked sheepish and shy but Rita tried to assure him that he didn't have to worry.

"Darling," she said as she smiled, "this is Detective Taylor and Detective Simms. They are policemen and they want to ask you some questions about the camp. You are not in trouble. Come here and sit with me."

Harry stood and shook Joey's hand. "Hello Joey. I used to be a Scout and Cub Leader and when I said 'dyb-dyb-dyb-dyb', what did the Cubs say?"

Joey paused. "We'll all do our best."

"Good boy, Joey. Can you tell us what you did at the camp on the weekend?"

"We had races and games and our team won the best flagpole test."

"Where did you sleep?"

"I was in the tent with Tommy and Barry Smithers. They are my friends here along the street."

"Someone said that you were going to sleep in the tent with the Cub Leader, Richard Gladstone."

"Richard had a sleeping bag there for me but Tommy, who is in the senior Scouts, told me not to sleep there. He made room for me between him and Barry. I was happy to be with them because they are my mates."

"Richard left a book for you. I'll get it to you in a few days," said Harry.

"He gave me some other books, but I haven't read them yet. Tommy told me to throw them away. They are too sissy."

"Thank you, Joey. You are a good boy. Go back to dad."

"I didn't know about that," said Rita. "I thought he was in the tent with Richard."

"Don't worry about that," replied Harry. "Don't blame Joey. He's just doing what boys will do. And he was happy with Tommy and Barry. I understand that you used Richard as a babysitter. Could you tell us about that? Were you and the children happy with his services?"

"Very much so," replied Rita. "The children loved it when Richard came. They loved playing games with him."

"Thanks so much. We'll leave you now. Keep in touch if anything comes to mind about Richard or the Cubs."

***

Harry and Joe drove in their separate vehicles to the main street. They walked into Richardson's Department Store where they found the Scoutmaster, Jack Robinson, working in the men's clothing department.

Jack was in his forties. He was well-dressed in charcoal-grey suit trousers, waistcoat and tie. A pair of silver cufflinks secured his sleeves at his wrists. His hair was short and slicked back with oil. A tape measure sat over his left shoulder, waiting for the next tailor-made fitting. Harry introduced himself and Joe and explained the purpose of their visit.

"Would it be possible for someone to take over from you for a while?" asked Harry. "We could go over the road to the Empire Café."

"Sure. I'll get Frank to take over. It's fairly quiet in here today."

After settling into the booth at the café, Harry started the conversation. "You would by now be well aware of what happened to Richard Gladstone. Can we start by you telling us what you know about Richard? And did anything suspicious happen over the weekend?"

Jack sipped a hot coffee. "You wouldn't find a more enthusiastic person on this earth. Richard was into everything. He was the Cub Leader, he sang in the cathedral and college choirs, he taught at Sunday school, he played the side drum in the Armidale Highland Pipe Band and he was studying to become an infants teacher."

"How was he with the young Cubs?" asked Joe.

"They loved him. He kept them busy and interested. I've never had anyone like him produce so many games and simple tests of skill to keep the young ones happy and active. He had a special way with kids. He would have been perfect as an infants teacher."

"Would I be right, Jack," asked Harry, "if I said that some of the Scouts looked on Richard as a bit of a sissy?"

Jack gave a chuckle. "Oh yes, but that's boys being boys. Richard was a bit effeminate in his mannerisms. I had to reprimand some of the senior scouts for saying that he was a poofter."

"Was there ever any incident that might have suggested that he was inclined that way?" asked Joe.

"No, never. If I'd had any doubts about him doing anything to harm those boys, I would have had him thrown out of the Scouts and I would have reported it to you people."

"Has anyone else outside of the Scouts mentioned this to you?" asked Harry.

"Look, you blokes know that anyone who doesn't fit the traditional mould of a man—who doesn't go to boxing lessons or doesn't play football and cricket—will always be a target for the critics. You've heard the old saying that you can't trust a man who doesn't smoke and drink and play footie? Well Richard was different. Unfortunately, he wasn't given enough credit for what he did for this community."

"Jack, you are also a member of the Armidale Pipe Band. How did Richard fit in there?" asked Harry.

"When he first asked to join, he wanted to play the tin whistle but we had to make it clear that we were strictly a pipe-and-drum band. So he took on the side drum. It took him some time to develop enough skill to be included in our main parades but I've never seen anyone so proud as when he first marched in his new tartan kilt down the main street in the Easter parade."

"How did the other band members take to him?" asked Joe.

"Oh, he copped a bit of chiacking, but he took it in good spirit. But that's no different to all of us. If you can't take it and laugh, you'll never fit in; and you won't last in an outfit like the band."

"Thank you, Jack. We won't keep you any longer," said Harry. "Thanks for everything you are doing for those boys."

***

Harry and Joe drove separately up Dangar Street to the teachers college. They were directed by the receptionist to a ground-floor lecture room filled with trainee infants teachers. They were met by Eric Clements, the history lecturer.

Harry explained the purpose of their visit and invited the students to talk about Richard, his friendships and his activities.

"Who in this group were his close friends?" asked Harry.

Mary Faulkner stood up, tears in her eyes. "I was in the drama group and the college choir with Richard. He was so talented. We did our second practice teaching at the Demonstration School earlier this year. We shared a class. I can tell you that the kids preferred him rather than me. He had them sitting up and hanging on his every word and game. He was a born infants teacher."

A tall young man at the back of the room put up his hand. "They tell me he was a rock spider, so I wouldn't put my kid in his class."

The comment startled Harry. He knew that this was prison talk for paedophiles. "Young man, would you mind stepping out into the corridor for a moment. What's your name?"

"Sure. My name is Norm."

Harry turned to Joe. "Joe, will you continue the talk with the others for a while."

Out in the corridor Harry faced Norm. "Thank you for talking to me away from the class, Norm," he said. "When you referred to Richard as a 'rock spider', what did you mean?"

"I thought you would know that. Well, a schoolmate of mine who did time in a gaol for kids once told me that a rock spider referred to a poofter, and they had to lock them up in a special cell to protect them from the other prisoners."

"Are you saying that Richard was a homosexual or a paedophile? Do you have proof of that?"

"I can't say for sure. I couldn't swear on the Bible that he fiddled with kids, but there was talk around the local footie teams and the pubs that he'd had it off with some of the kids in the Cubs. Some of the older blokes in the teams refused to let their kids join the Cubs because Gladstone was in charge of them."

"Thanks Norm. If you have definite proof of abuse of a kid then don't hesitate to contact us straight away. But if there is no proof to back up your claim, be careful what you say to others. Let's go back inside."

Back in the lecture room the students talked about Richard's talents and his involvement in the Cubs, choirs, drama group, band and Sunday school. There were a couple of snide comments from some of the men about the fact that Richard was not interested in sport except swimming.

"I found it a bit odd," said a student who identified himself as Charlie, "that he kept taking photos of young kids and babies at the local pool. He told me that he was thinking of producing a book of photos of kids and selling it. Quite frankly, I thought that was a bit queer."

"That's because you don't understand the beauty of nature," shouted Mary Faulkner, still in tears. "Some of you boys need to grow up."

"Thank you all," said Harry. "You have been very helpful. If you have any other information that might assist us in our investigation, please don't hesitate to contact us."

***

Harry and Joe returned to the station.

***

At five o'clock Graham McInnes from the desk came into the interview room. "We want you two around at Bruyn's Caledonian Hotel now. There's a ruckus on there. Pat Casey and Jack Nelson are on their way there now."

Chapter 21
Wednesday

Harry and Joe jogged around into the main street. On entering the bar at Bruyn's Hotel they saw about twelve men. Many of them had moved to either end of the bar, holding their glasses and puffing vigorously on their cigarettes while keeping out of the way. Some were shouting abuse or encouragement to one or two of the group who were pushing, wrestling or throwing punches at each other. Constable Jack Nelson put one of them in a headlock after Constable Pat Casey had been rabbit-punched in the back of the head.

Joe quickly rushed over to put cuffs on the man held by Jack. He kicked the man's left leg from underneath him and dumped him heavily on his backside onto the tiled floor in the corner.

"Now, don't you move until I say so," he said.

Harry stepped between the other fighters, trying to push them apart with both arms. There were seven men throwing punches or wrestling with each other. Harry shouted, "Right, back off. Settle down."

"Not before I knock that bastard's head off," said a big, scruffy and unshaven man dressed in an unironed, dirty blue drill shirt and stained boiler suit as he elbowed Harry aside.

Harry stepped quickly to the side and flicked his left foot out to catch the man's ankle, forcing that foot behind the other. The man went down heavily, firstly to his knees and then onto his face on the hard tiled floor. Harry turned and forced his size-twelve boot onto the back of the man's neck, holding him down firmly on the floor.

"Pat, put the cuffs on this oaf and we'll pull him over to the corner with the other bloke," he said.

Harry turned to see another big man in work gear throw a haymaker at Joe who had been trying to separate two men pushing each other against the bar. The man did not see the sharp right cross from Joe. It only travelled a very short distance but had the desired effect. The man sank to his knees. Jack put on the cuffs, rolled the man on his back and pulled him out of the way against the wall.

"Shit," gasped one of the drinkers back against the wall as he tried to keep away from the action. "That was so fast. Sandy was out to it before he hit the floor. Don't take that bloody cop on. He means business."

Harry turned quickly, conscious of another man over his left shoulder. He tensed but soon relaxed as he recognised him as Hamish Mackenzie, the lecturer from the university. Hamish put up both his open hands in defence and backed away from Harry.

"I'm not involved with this bunch, Detective," he said, eyes wide open with shock. "I just came in here to buy a bottle of Scotch whisky. What the hell is going on?"

Harry placed a hand on Hamish's shoulder and pointed towards the door leading into the back bar. "Would you go back to the ladies' lounge until we get this sorted out. I'd like to speak to you after that. Thanks."

As Harry turned, one man pushed another backwards over the bar with a chokehold. Harry grabbed the man's collar and pulled him away. The man steadied before throwing a wild punch at Harry. Harry ducked, blocking the blow with his raised left shoulder before ramming the knuckles of his right hand up under the man's rib cage into the solar plexus. As the man dropped his right arm, Harry, with a swift easy movement, bent it behind the man's back before throwing him over his right knee to the floor. Harry pinned the man to the floor with his right knee until he applied the cuffs.

As Harry stood and walked back to the bar, he blocked a man who was threatening another man at the bar. Chris Gladstone, who had returned from Muswellbrook the night before, introduced himself, apologised for being so rude the day before, and thanked Harry for intervening.

The other men backed away. One of them raised his arms so quickly that he spilled some beer from his glass. He looked at Harry. "Don't hit me. I've got nothing to do with all this, sir. I only came in here for a bloody drink. Shit! What's goin' on 'ere?"

Harry looked at the man. "It's okay, mate. It's not your fault. Why don't you and your mate go into the back lounge bar to have a quiet drink before closing time until we sort out the mess here."

Harry looked around the bar. The fighting had ceased. The regulars were still at one end of the bar or the other, trying to stay out of it. Some had already left the room. Harry walked to the bar and called to the barman who was cleaning up some broken glass.

"Hey Mario. Could you ask the rest of the drinkers to move to the lounge bar? That will give you and us space to clean up this mess. We'll leave those blokes on the floor there for a while. Could you tell us again what happened here?"

"It all started when Jimmy Scott accused Chris Gladstone of having a poofter son and so they got stuck into it. A couple of the other blokes joined in, some to fight Chris and some to help him. Another bloke got angry because his beer got spilled so he got into it as well. It was a bit of a mess before you blokes got here because it was difficult to see who was fighting who."

"Could we use the office to question some of the people here?"

Mario stood, a dustpan full of glass in his hand. "Sure Harry. Who do you want to talk to first?"

Harry pointed to Chris Gladstone still wiping his face with his hanky. "Chris, go to the office over there and take a seat. I'll be with you in a minute."

He turned back to the barman. "Mario, I'll talk to Jimmy Scott after Chris. Then could you come in before I take those other three idiots on the floor? After that, will you call Hamish Mackenzie from the back bar."

He turned to Pat and Jack. "Will you two look after those blokes on the floor? When we have finished with Chris, Jimmy and Mario, bring them in."

Harry and Joe walked to the office and sat opposite Chris Gladstone.

"In your own words, Chris, tell us what happened in there. Who started the fight?" asked Harry.

Chris wiped his mouth with the back of his hand. "It was that bloody Jimmy Scott. He came up to me at the bar while I was having a drink and shouted something about my son Richard. He threw a glass of beer in my face and started to punch me. So I got stuck into him because no one was going to accuse Richard of anything. Richard was different to most kids but he didn't do anything wrong."

"We have been told," said Joe, "that James found Richard in bed with his son Jason and that neither had any clothes on. Is that true?"

"That's a bloody lie. Richard wouldn't do anything to those kids. He loved them so much. He'd be the last person to hurt a kid or do anything wrong to them. Look, I know Richard was different. He didn't play football or cricket like the other boys, and he was more into drama, music, choirs and the Cubs, but that doesn't mean he would do anything to harm a child. Why can't kids like that be left alone to do the things they want to do? He did so much to help others but he never got credit for that. He got picked on because he was different."

"Go on home," said Harry. "You need to be there with your wife. She's suffering a lot. Richard meant so much to her. Stay away from here."

James Scott came into the room and sat with head down.

"Now tell us why you got into a fight with Chris," said Harry.

James folded his arms. "When I saw him at the bar, I couldn't help myself. I threw a beer at him and just let go and thumped him."

"Why didn't you go to his house and talk to him about it in private?"

"I don't know. Maybe I felt it worse because Chris is away a lot in the mines and wasn't here to keep Richard under control. How would you feel if it happened to your son?"

"We appreciate that you are upset, James, but having it out in the hotel is not the answer and your actions are only making it more difficult for us in our investigations into these murders. I'm taking no further action on this today but I'm warning you not to go anywhere near the Gladstone family. If you do this again, I'll book you for aggravated assault. Now tell us what you saw when you found Richard in bed with your son."

James described the bedroom scene and how he had dragged Richard out of the bed and threatened him.

"Why didn't you come to the police station and tell us about that incident?" asked Harry.

"I was too angry and embarrassed at the time and I didn't want my son to go through a police investigation."

"I understand," said Harry, "but now go home to be with your family. They need your support."

Harry asked James to send in Mario. Mario came in with a tea towel over his left shoulder.

"Tell us again what happened," said Harry.

"The first thing I saw was Jimmy Scott throwing a beer over Chris Gladstone and then it was on for young and old. Those two got stuck into it and then those other clowns got mixed up in the brawl. I decided to stay on my side of the bar and let them wear themselves out before I went to the other side. When there's a blue on, it's easier to sort it out after they punch each other to a standstill."

"Good thinking, Mario," said Harry. "Why did the others get involved when it was an argument between Gladstone and Scott?"

Mario laughed. "I couldn't say for sure but I know that Yappy, Bluey and Sandy are three boofheads who would rather have a fight than a feed. So when Scott and Gladstone got stuck into it, those three took the opportunity to throw some punches themselves. The others in the bar covered up or got out of the way. A couple tried to hold the boofheads back. That's when you lot got there."

"What else did you notice?" asked Harry.

"I wouldn't get into the ring with young Joe here," he replied. "Listen here, Joe. You can have free beer all afternoon if you just sit at the bar any Saturday or when there's a special event on. Is that a deal?"

Joe laughed. "That's kind of you, Mario, but no thanks. I've got enough on my plate doing my job here."

Harry pointed to the door. "Thanks Mario. Ask Pat and Jack to bring in those other three."

As the others walked in, Sandy Douglass nodded towards Joe. "I'm gunna get ya, ya bastard. Nobody hits me like that and gets away with it. Do ya hear me?"

Harry stood and pushed Sandy against the wall. "Now, you listen to me carefully. You are in enough trouble already so don't be so stupid to carry on like a dumb boofhead. Now stand there and listen."

"But he punched me when I wasn't lookin'."

Harry chuckled. "I can assure you that if you were standing still in front of the detective, with both eyes wide open and with your hands up around your ears ready for round one, you would still not have seen him hit you. So, stop being a stupid arse and don't get into these fights."

"We didn't start the fight," shouted Yappy. "So why have you got us in these cuffs?"

"So why did you get involved?" asked Harry.

"Well, that bastard Gladstone got stuck into our mate, Scotty, and we went in to help. Someone said that Chris's son is a poofter and we don't like poofters."

Harry looked up at Pat and Jack. "Take off their cuffs."

He turned to the three men. "I'm going to let you three go now with a warning. You will stay out of all hotels in Armidale for at least a week. If you get into fights like this again, I'll lock you up and throw away the key. Do you understand?"

"Yes," said Yappy. The others nodded begrudgingly.

As they walked out, Harry asked Pat to call in Hamish Mackenzie. Soon after, Hamish entered the office and sat at the desk.

"Thank you for waiting, Hamish. You probably heard about the death of young Richard Gladstone. What can you tell us about him?"

"I didn't know him well," replied Hamish. "He was in the C-of-E choir. I'm in the Presbyterian one; although, we saw each other at competitions. I'd also seen him in the Scouts. I used to be a Scoutmaster but left because there was not sufficient supervision of the young ones. I had my doubts about Richard. He got too close to some of those young Cubs. And Richard joined our pipe band last year. He was not good on the drums so we never let him go in competitions here or anywhere else. Our band travels across Australia for big competitions but we never let him go with us. He did not mix well with the others. Most of the players didn't like his effeminate ways."

"Do you know any of the men in that fight?" asked Joe.

"I only know Jimmy Scott. The people in the back lounge told me that he got into a fight with Chris Gladstone. I don't know him well. They say that he works down south in the mines. I've seen the others around but am not friends with any of them. I think they are all tradies."

"Hamish, it's been alleged that Richard Gladstone had sexual relations with some of the boys he babysat," said Harry. "You're a psychologist. Why would a talented young man like Richard behave like that when he had everything going for him in his chosen career?"

"I'm not aware of anything like that happening and I don't like dealing in rumours. But if Richard did anything like that to kids, that would have been a serious evil act and God would have punished him. It is as simple as that."

"Thanks Hamish," said Harry. "Enjoy your Scotch."

After Hamish left, Harry looked to Pat, Jack and Joe. "Thanks, you three. You did a marvellous job. Joe, will you teach me how to do that right cross? That was a cracker. Now, you three, get yourselves home. I'll see you in the morning at the station."

"Thanks Harry," they said in unison and walked out.

***

Harry walked back to the station, drove home in his MG, changed clothes and ran six laps of the oval at the showground.

Chapter 22
Thursday

When Harry arrived at the station he was informed that Ray Johnston had called a meeting of all on-duty officers. Harry went to the meeting room where Joe, Ken Wright, Merv Leech and Greg White were already waiting. Ray called the meeting to order.

"I've called you in here this morning to get your feedback about the spate of murders and about the brawl at Bruyn's yesterday. Let's start with the pub brawl. Over to you, Harry."

For the next few minutes Harry described the fight and the participants and how he, Joe, Pat and Jack handled the matter.

"Wasn't it Gladstone's son who was murdered at the showground?" asked Ken Wright.

"Yes," replied Harry. "That's how the fight started. Jimmy Scott told Chris Gladstone that Chris's son Richard had been naked in bed with Jimmy's son while babysitting, and his son was also naked. Jimmy threw a beer over Chris Gladstone who retaliated with a punch. Some other boofheads took advantage of the situation to get involved."

"Is that true about the naked babysitter, Harry?" asked Ken.

"Unfortunately, the Scotts didn't report it and so there was no medical examination of the boy to determine if sex took place. And it was too long ago to do it now. As Richard has been murdered, it won't serve any purpose now."

"Had we had clear evidence of sexual abuse of a child," said Joe, "we might at least have a motive for the murder."

"Are you implying, Joe, that Jimmy Scott might be the murderer?" asked Sergeant Greg White. "I know Jimmy, and I won't go along with that."

Joe nodded. "I don't think he is either, Greg, but when a parent finds out that the babysitter might have been having sex with their son, would that have given the parent a reason to assault the babysitter so badly that it might have resulted in death? Could that be motive enough?"

Eric Talbot put up his hand. "I have heard rumours that Gladstone was showing too much interest in little boys, especially at the pool but I have no evidence of any incident worth following up."

Lars van Dyke followed. "I've heard those same rumours but without any evidence to back it up I put it down to jealousy."

Harry tapped his forehead with his right middle and forefinger and then paused. "But that doesn't fit what we found at the showground and it doesn't explain the motives for the other three murders; unless someone can provide me with evidence of a group of paedophiles that included Jonathon Petherby, Splinter Winton and Julian O'Sullivan. Besides, there was no evidence of physical assault on Gladstone, only the burns from the sulphur."

"You're spot on, Harry," replied Greg. "Everything you have told us about these murders points to a single serial killer and, while we might have serious suspicions about this young bloke Gladstone, there is no evidence or suggestion that the other three were involved with kids. I didn't know Petherby or O'Sullivan but I'd put my house on Splinter not being involved with kids. He couldn't stand them."

"While he might not have got on with kids in his daily life," replied Joe, "that doesn't mean that he wouldn't have got his kicks from having sex with them; especially if he had the protection of anonymity. Let's face it, Splinter wouldn't have attracted too many women into bed, would he?"

"Come on, Joe," said Merv. "You're a bit tough on Splinter. If there is no evidence to point in that direction, I'd advise you to leave it alone."

Ray pointed at Greg. "Didn't you say yesterday that young Gladstone belonged to the Armidale Highland Pipe Band? You blow those god-awful bagpipes, don't you? Aren't you in the band? Did you know this kid?"

"Yes," replied Greg, "but not well. He was only fairly new in the band and still learning the drums. There was a lot of talk in the band about him being a queer but I never heard anything concrete about him offending with kids."

"Okay," said Ray, "let's stop it there and get back to duties. But I want you all to keep your ears to the ground and let Harry or Joe know of anything that might help their cases."

***

Harry and Joe drove in the wagon to St Peter's Anglican Cathedral in Dangar Street, opposite Central Park. It was a majestic blue-brick Gothic building at the centre of the city. They were met by Dean Alister Larkin who escorted them through to the deanery.

"What can I do for you gentlemen?" asked the dean. "I doubt that you are here for spiritual enlightenment."

Harry smiled. "Thanks for meeting with us, Alister. We are certainly looking for enlightenment, but not necessarily of the spiritual kind. We are here regarding young Richard Gladstone's murder. We have been told that he was a regular member of the cathedral choir and was a teacher here at the Sunday school. Could you please tell us about Richard and his work in the church?"

"Richard was an outstanding member of the congregation. He volunteered at almost every function we ran in the church like the fête or the Church of England ball and on every special day such as at Easter, Christmas, Mothering Sunday, Father's Day, Harvest Sunday and All Saints' Day. And yes, he was a regular in the choir and he taught at Sunday school."

"Were there any concerns with the way he handled the little folk at Sunday school?" asked Harry.

"No. Why would you ask?"

"Some people have expressed concerns about his touching of small children inappropriately, even on their private parts. Have you heard about this?"

Alister straightened his shoulders and spoke more precisely. "I had heard rumours but they were only rumours. And I have my doubts about those members of the congregation who spread those rumours. I believe that those people had the problem, not Richard. I told two of them to bring me the facts or forever hold their tongue. Nasty rumours like that are so unchristian."

"Thank you Alister," said Harry. "We must be on our way. There is so much to do."

"Yes," Alister replied. "I must go too. I have to arrange for Richard's funeral on Monday. No doubt I will see you two there."

***

Harry and Joe drove up Dangar Street to the teachers college. Reception directed them to the office of Eric Clements, the senior lecturer in history. Eric was an impressive figure in his academic gown. His dark hair was neatly combed but had an odd patch of white-to-grey hair on one side. He spoke in well-educated English. He was highly respected in the college and the Armidale community.

"We're sorry to bother you again after meeting with you and the students yesterday, but we would like to ask you some more questions about Richard Gladstone."

"By all means, gentlemen. Please take a seat. I'll be very willing to assist."

"Could you please tell us more about Richard and how he performed as a student teacher, and how he got on with the other students and the children in the classes he attended?"

Eric sat back and tucked his thumbs into the armpits of his waistcoat.

"You would have heard the differences of opinion from the students yesterday. Some, mostly women, liked him and got on well with him. They enjoyed his playful character and his willingness to participate in the drama plays and the choir. Most of the young men, and especially the rugby boys, treated him very differently. He was not one of them. He didn't like contact sports and he didn't go with them to the hotel for drinks. Because he lived at home he was not boarding in that terrible Olympic Hall or Minto Hotel where most of the men sleep and where they have built up an *esprit de corps.* He was always an outsider."

"It has been suggested to us that Richard might have had a special liking for young boys. Could you comment on that?" asked Harry.

"Ha. Here we go again," replied Eric bluntly as he moved forward and spread his arms across the desk. "Yes, I've heard that too. Are you asking if Richard was homosexual?"

"Yes," replied Harry.

"Richard had been called everything here, with 'poofter' being the most common term used. But there was no evidence put to me or anyone else on the academic staff that he was that way inclined. I'd spoken to Richard on two occasions to give him the opportunity to talk about his tendencies in private. He assured me that he had never been involved in such activities."

"But surely he wouldn't tell you if he was that way," replied Joe, "because homosexual acts are illegal in this country? Surely he wouldn't have openly admitted to a serious crime to you or anyone else?"

"Quite frankly, Joe, I couldn't care less. I might be different from others around here but I believe that some people are born that way. It happens in the animal world and it happens with humans. My only concern is that teachers must never take advantage of children in their care. That is where the law needs to be strengthened. We teachers act *in loco parentis*. It means that we act in the place of a parent and, therefore, any such act would be considered professional incest. I gave Richard some good, sound advice about those things and I believe he understood the consequences of erring on those matters."

"I'm sure he would have bowed to your wisdom in regard to children in his classes while he was teaching," replied Joe, "but what about the children in homes where he babysat? Do you think he might have been tempted when the parents weren't at home?"

Eric nodded. "Fair point, Joe. But I believe Richard was so committed to becoming a teacher that he would not have placed himself in a situation that would have threatened his career, no matter what the circumstances. I believe you need to be looking at another motive for his murder."

"Thank you, Eric," said Harry. "You have been very helpful. We'll be going now."

***

Harry and Joe drove back to the station. As they entered, they were met by Ken Rudd from *The Armidale Express* and James Bolton from The *Daily Mirror* who were sitting in the cramped space next to the reception desk.

"What can we do for you two gentlemen?" asked Harry as he shook both their hands in greeting. "Come on through to the interview room."

As they sat at the table, James asked the first question. "Thanks for meeting with us, Harry and Joe. We know you are very busy, and we don't want to waste your valuable time, but we need to let the public out there know what is happening with these murders. The whole country is on edge. This is now a national news item. We are even getting calls from overseas asking about the murders. People are afraid to leave their homes. The only ones benefiting from these killings are the locksmiths. They are running out of supplies."

Ken raised his hand. "Harry, we know you came from the country, and you know that country folks don't lock their doors, but that's now changed. I had locks put on my house yesterday. There's no way that killer can get into my house now. I need to protect my wife and kids."

"Thank you, James and Ken," said Harry. "We appreciate the public's concern but we are working overtime trying to get this killer and we would appreciate if you would keep your reporting to the facts and not wild theories as in your last articles."

James interrupted. "Are you certain that the same person did all four murders?"

"Yes. The evidence points that way."

"What is the evidence that proves it is the same person?" asked Ken.

"We won't go into detail now as those matters are part of our ongoing inquiries. You two could help us by asking the public to contact us if they suspect anything that might be connected to these murders."

The discussion continued for another twenty minutes after which Harry stressed the need to get on with their investigations.

After the reporters left, Joe expressed his disgust with the reporters.

"Always keep to yourself a few specific details that are only known to the police and the killer," said Harry. "After the reporters run their articles in the papers, and the local radio station repeats the messages on their hourly news broadcasts, we are going to be deluged with people ringing in. Many of those calls will be hoaxes or someone trying to get back at others they don't like. However, if we are interrogating someone and they slip up and mention pendants, signs or phenobarbital then we will know they have something of importance.

Let's spend the rest of today going over all the details of the four murders."

Chapter 23
Friday

Early in the morning, Harry rushed out from his house to put up the hood on his MG sports car. It had started to rain. The wind from the south-west was chilly and the bad weather was settling in for the day. It was one of those days when most people in Armidale lit their wood fires to warm the house. The wet autumn leaves on the many nearby trees hung in despair. Back inside the house, Harry took a call from Graham McInnes from the station desk.

"I've just had a call from Taipan Charlie Young from the snake farm on Bundarra Road. He said that he found the body of a man in one of the snake pits. He said he checked the body and the bloke was definitely dead."

"Call Joe and tell him I'll be at his door to pick him up in five minutes."

***

As Joe got into Harry's car he asked, "Who's this Taipan Charlie bloke? Is he a Chinese kung fu expert? Or is he an Indian snake charmer?"

"No," replied Harry. "He is a dinkum Aussie who is well known around the New England district as a snake catcher and he keeps live snakes in enclosures on his property. Anyone can go there and look at them. And he gives talks to school kids and university students about reptiles and how to deal with them in the bush or at home."

"But why the name 'Taipan'?"

"Taipan was born on a farm outside Bundarra and was used to wild snakes coming onto the property. He took a keen interest in them even as a kid. He left home after school and travelled to North Queensland where he worked as a sugar-cane cutter and earned good money. He would have seen snakes almost every day in the plantations. It was there that his interest in snakes grew and he studied their habits, and with one in particular, the deadly taipan. The taipan is the most venomous snake in the world. Charlie became quite an expert. During the war he got a job south of Darwin clearing jungle to construct emergency air strips, and his interest and knowledge of snakes developed further in that environment."

"But you can't make a living looking at snakes," said Joe.

"Taipan has a farm where he raises sheep and cattle," replied Harry, "but he also is well known as a snake catcher. So when someone calls him he catches the snakes for a fee and takes them away. He has become one of the best experts on snakes in Australia. He also works closely with the Commonwealth Serum Laboratories in Parkville in Melbourne. They have developed a serum to counter the bites from tiger snakes and they are trying to develop antivenom for other deadly snakes. Charlie is now trying to milk the venom from other snakes such as the taipan and sending it to the CSL laboratory down south to help them."

"Well, there's no way I'm going near any snakes, Harry; especially those deadly ones," said Joe. "I don't know how anybody could even touch those slimy devils. You'd have to have a death wish to play with snakes."

"Oh, come on, Joe," said Harry as he chuckled, "all you have to do is outstare them. I will give you some advice: never blink when you are up close. The moment they see your eyelids move they'll have you for breakfast."

Joe thumped Harry on the shoulder. "Yeah? Come on, Harry. Now you're pulling my leg. But where does he keep all those snakes?"

"They roam around the farm during the day eating all the mice and then he tucks them into the bed in the spare room each night."

"Now I really know you're pulling my leg."

"Well, here we are. You can see for yourself," said Harry as he pulled off the road onto the property.

He drove past the house to the sheds at the back where he saw Taipan Charlie standing in the doorway.

"G'day Charlie," said Harry as he shook his hand. "What have you got for us?"

"G'day Harry. I was away from the farm yesterday and when I got back here this morning I did a quick check and found a body in one of the snake pits. Who's your mate here?"

"This is Joe Simms. He wants you to take him into the snake tanks. He wants to talk to the snakes up close. He wants to look them in the eye. Joe never had them in Redfern where he came from."

Joe took two slow steps towards Charlie and shook his hand, half-expecting a snake to emerge from Charlie's sleeve. "No. I'll stand back and look. You and Harry can do whatever needs to be done."

"Come with me, Joe, and I'll show you my collection," said Charlie.

Charlie walked away from the shed towards some trees where there were four large circular enclosures, with each measuring fifteen feet across and about four feet high. They were made by cutting two water tanks in half around the corrugations and placing each section on top of the ground. Inside each of the four sections were logs, small ponds and boulders. Charlie climbed over the side of the nearest tank.

"Where are all the snakes?" asked Joe.

"They are under those logs and stones," said Charlie. "It's a bit too cool yet. They'll come out when the sun warms the ground. They are not warm-blooded and so they need the sun to warm them up. In a month or two they'll start to hibernate."

"I'll just stand back here," said Joe.

"Don't feel afraid, Joe. Most of them are still asleep but I'll get one from under the log here. I won't let him eat you."

Charlie found the tail of one snake, lifted it slowly and held it up for Joe to see. Joe, with arms lifted, stepped quickly away from the side of the tank. "I'm not going anywhere near that snake."

Harry walked over to the next section and leaned over the side to see if any snakes had emerged into the sunlight. He spotted a piece of white cardboard attached to the inner wall of the pit. He walked around and pulled off the tape that held it in place. The sign read:

The desire kills him,
for his hands
refuse to labour.

Harry looked at it and called Joe over. "It certainly seems like the same killer is involved here. This writing is the same as the others. Treat it gently, Joe, in case there are fingerprints. Let's have a look in the other tanks."

As they walked to the third tank, Charlie pointed into the enclosure. Harry and Joe looked over the wall. Lying face up on the ground was the body of a young man. He was wearing an opened sheepskin jacket over a partly unbuttoned blue shirt and singlet, and a black Irish flat cap. The legs of his trousers were pulled up to the knees, and his feet were covered with blue woollen socks and riding boots. On his hairy upper chest lay an enamelled copper pendant with the number 6 clearly marked on it. There were no signs of injuries to his face, upper chest or lower legs. The man looked at peace.

"Right," said Harry as he pointed to Joe. "We need to get him out of there. Just hop in there, Joe, and lift him up so I can pull him over the top of the wall."

Joe jumped back from the enclosure. "No bloody way are you going to get me in there. Leave him there for the snakes to eat."

Harry and Charlie laughed loudly. As Harry lifted his leg over the tank wall he turned to Joe who was now standing at least ten feet back. "If I don't get out alive, will you phone my parents? They'll want to arrange the funeral."

Harry and Charlie lifted the body high and lowered it to the ground outside the pit. As they climbed out, Joe came forward to look again into the pit. "You're tricking me. There are no snakes in there."

Charlie placed his hand on Joe's shoulder. "They are certainly there but I told them to stay in bed until breakfast time at nine o'clock. If they come out early they know I'll smack their tails and they won't get breakfast."

Joe stepped back. "Yeah, sure. Now whistle Dixie and I'll know you're telling big fibs."

"Okay," said Harry. "Let's examine this man. Do you recognise him, Charlie?"

"I've seen him quite a few times. He was one of the university students who came out here to study reptiles. The uni brings the zoology students here because we have snakes, goannas, lizards and turtles. This bloke was also one of the students who came back on the weekends sometimes to help me. He never said much and kept to himself. He

148

seemed to be up himself a bit and I noticed that the other students left him alone to work by himself."

Joe pulled back the front of the man's jacket to undo the remaining buttons on the shirt. As he did so he saw a piece of white cardboard. It was taped to his singlet. One word was clearly written on it:

Diligence

"This is definitely the same killer," said Harry. "Both pieces of cardboard and the writing are exactly the same as those found in the other cases. And that pendant around his neck looks like it is made from the same metal, with the same colouring and numbering, and tied by the same leather bootlace."

Joe pointed across to the large stringy-bark tree next to the far tank pit. "There looks to be a blanket on the ground over there. I'll go and check."

Harry turned to Charlie. "Would you mind going back to the house and phoning David Hobbs at the funeral parlour and Doctor Gregory Ebsworth? Joe and I will stay here and look for more evidence."

"Look over there under the tree," said Joe. "There are two large beer glasses next to that blanket. There looks to be some liquid in them."

Harry walked closer to Joe. "They didn't eat all their sandwiches. On that plate there are the remains of a sandwich next to that beer bottle."

Harry grabbed Joe's arm to stop him from going closer. "Look down there, Joe. There are boot prints in the soft earth. They could be the victim's or from the killer or anyone who might have visited the farm. There is some plaster of Paris in a small bag in the boot of my car. Get it and take some moulds. Then take off the boots from the victim and bag them. When we get back to the station, we will take prints from the boots and compare them with the plaster casts."

"Look at those prints, Harry," said Joe, pointing to the ground. "They are two different sizes. That man we took out of the pit had fairly small boots so the larger print is more likely to belong to the killer."

"Or it could belong to Charlie or one of the students from the university or one of the hundreds of visitors who come here to see the snakes. But you have a good point. Let's take off one of the victim's boots now and test it against these depressions. And when Charlie comes back from the house, we'll test his boots."

Joe walked back to the victim and took off one of the boots. When he placed it lightly over the prints in the soft earth it matched the size of one of the smaller prints.

"His shoe says it is a size seven," said Joe.

When Charlie returned he placed his boot beside both the larger and smaller depressions. It was obvious that his size twelves were far too big to have formed either of those prints.

"I'd guess," said Joe, "that the larger of the prints is about a size nine."

They continued to search the area until, sometime later, they saw both David's hearse and Gregory's car come through the gate.

Chapter 24
Friday

"Hey Charlie," shouted David as he got out of the hearse. "I brought a biscuit tin as a coffin because I thought that it was one of your favourite snakes we are burying."

Charlie laughed. "Thanks David—but no, it's not for the snakes. But you best measure up Joe here because he's going to help me clean out the pits and handfeed the taipans. If one bites him we need to bury him quickly before the rot sets in and upsets the other snakes."

"There's no way you're going to get me in those pens," shouted Joe as he stepped back a couple of paces.

Gregory smiled. "Don't worry, Joe, I've got my tourniquet with me, but try to get it to bite you on the lower leg or hand. It's easier to apply the tourniquet there."

Joe shook his head. "You're all the bloody same. And Harry told me to stare at the snake but not blink."

Charlie tapped him on the shoulder. "Better still, Joe, while you're looking at the taipan, poke out your tongue and it will see that you have a much bigger one than him and he will back off."

Charlie stepped over the side wall of the tank and took hold of the tail of a snake that had just emerged into the sun from under a log. He held it at arm's length while he used a long hook to control and lift the neck. He walked back to the side of the enclosure.

"Come on, Joe, don't be scared. I'll hold its head. I've got him. I won't let him hurt you. You can touch him along its back. You're in the country now so you'll come across snakes around here often. Get to know how to handle them and you'll be fine from then on."

"What type is it?" asked Joe.

"It's an eastern brown. It's the third most venomous one in the world."

Joe stepped cautiously towards Charlie and touched the snake before jumping back. "That felt queer. The skin wasn't slimy."

"Okay," said Harry. "Enough fun and games. Let's get on with the job."

He led David and Gregory over to the body. Gregory leaned down, felt the man's skin, turned the head from side to side and checked the bare upper chest and lower legs. He pulled back the man's cap.

"I know this man. He and his parents are patients of mine."

"Who is he, and where does he live?" asked Harry.

"He's Jerome Slaughter. He lived on a farm with his mum, dad and two sisters out along Rockvale Road, about twelve miles out of town."

"That must be out near the McWhirter's property," said Harry.

"Yes," replied Gregory. "They live on the adjoining farm."

"After I visit the Slaughter's farm," said Harry, "I'll drop into the McWhirters next door and see what Colleen and her family know about this man."

Harry and Joe helped Gregory remove the shirt and trousers.

"Well, you didn't need me to tell you he was dead," said Gregory with a smile. "But there are no obvious injuries to the body so I'll need to do an autopsy back at the parlour to determine the cause of death. Do you have any ideas, Harry?"

Harry turned and pointed. "Over there beside that tree we found an empty bottle and two glasses next to a blanket. There was enough fluid left in them to send off to the SIB but we will need to send stomach, blood and tissue samples as well. We suspect that the killer might have used the same method of giving the victim a drink laced with poison."

"It surprises me," said Charlie, "that with all the publicity about these murders in the newspapers and on the radio, that people would not be suspicious about someone bringing them out here yesterday or last night next to the snake pits. That doesn't make sense to me."

Harry nodded. "You're right, Charlie. So we must be looking at some connection between the victim and his killer. They must have been on friendly terms and so much so that the victim would never have suspected any foul play by the perpetrator. And the victim, or both the victim and murderer, must have had an interest in reptiles and knew the layout of the property."

"And they must have known that I never lock the gate," said Charlie. "With all these snakes here I don't need to."

Joe pointed at Charlie. "You said that you had seen him before and he was a university student with an interest in reptiles. That might be the clue. It could be possible that the victim and killer are both from the university."

"He was here with that zoology professor."

Harry nodded. "That would be Gwyn O'Connor. We met him about a week ago in relation to the Jonathon Petherby case."

"Does that mean that all of these murders are linked to the zoology department at the university?" asked David.

Joe stepped forward, hands on hips. "Petherby, O'Sullivan and now Slaughter were at the university, but Petherby was not studying zoology or any science subject. Gladstone was at the teachers college and Winton was an SP bookie. I don't see the connection."

"I'll be leaving now," said David. "I have to get this bloke back to the parlour. Some of us have to work. Here, give me a hand, Joe."

"I'll see you at the parlour later in the day, David," said Gregory. "I'll go and open the surgery."

Joe helped David bag the body and load it into the hearse, after which David and Gregory drove off.

Harry turned to Charlie. "The killer and the victim would probably have driven out here to your place yesterday when it was daylight and warmer. When did you last check the pens?"

"As I already mentioned, Harry, I was away yesterday. The telephonist at the exchange gave me a call yesterday afternoon when I got back to the house and passed on a message for me to go out to two farms on Ebor Road. When I got there the two farmers told me that they hadn't phoned the exchange. The calls were fake but I stopped there to look over the two properties for the farmers for free. I then went to stay with my old mate Freddy McVeigh for the night and I didn't get back until this morning. I checked the pits yesterday morning before I left and again this morning when I got back. So, I didn't see the body until a couple of hours ago."

"That means that the killer made the fake call to the exchange," said Harry.

"What about your dog over there, Charlie?" asked Joe. "Surely it would have barked if the strangers came onto the property."

Charlie chuckled. "Struth mate. Old Mollie is fifteen years old and mostly sleeps inside, and she's nearly as deaf as me. But she was with me in the truck yesterday. Let's face it, mate, I don't need savage dogs to protect this property. Most people won't come within miles of here because we have all these snakes. And the signs at the gate are enough to keep people away. But if anyone who's been here before comes back uninvited, they obviously know the layout and where the snakes are kept, and know they are safe because the snakes are confined to the pits."

Harry nodded in agreement. "Which makes our job harder because you have had hundreds of school kids, university students and visitors over the last few years."

"Let's eliminate the school kids," said Joe. "I can't see them involved in this murder; and certainly not with the other victims as well. Because we have a serial killer of local victims it is more likely that the killer is a local and someone known to the victims."

"Good point, Joe," said Harry. "Now let Charlie get on with his work while you and I do a thorough search around the area."

For the next hour Harry and Joe walked the property from the farm gate through to the house, sheds and across the paddock to the trees and snake pits. They took plaster casts of tyre marks and footprints in the soft soil. As they walked away from the tree where the picnic blanket was found, Joe pointed to the tall grass in front of them.

"There are some fresh food scraps here," he said.

He bent over to pick up a half-eaten lamington, two Monte Carlo biscuits and three Melting Moment biscuits that had been half-dipped in chocolate and filled with orange cream. He placed them carefully in a paper bag.

"The poor bloke didn't have a chance to finish these goodies before he died," said Joe.

Harry slapped his thigh. "I find it difficult to think that anybody would come out here at night to look at snakes and have a picnic of lamingtons, biscuits, sandwiches and a bottle of beer. Therefore they must have come here in the afternoon, knowing that Charlie was out."

"And what relationship was there between the two of them?" asked Joe. "They obviously knew each other; otherwise, the victim wouldn't have come out here even in the afternoon to meet with a stranger."

"Maybe the killer was friendly with young Slaughter and knew he regularly came here at a certain time to study the snakes and he followed him here. To be friendly the killer brought the food and drinks."

Harry walked across to a black stump. He picked up a reddish-brown bottle with a black lid and a white label.

"It's the same as the last case, Joe. It's clearly marked 'PHENOBARBITAL'. Is he being careless in leaving the bottle? Or is he sending us a signal? Or was he rushed and threw it away before leaving? It looks to be three quarters full."

"I'd say he deliberately left it as a message for us," said Joe. "But it doesn't tell us anything about him or his relationship with the victim."

"What about the other common factors with all of these cases, Joe?" asked Harry. "The others all happened at night and none of the victims had any injuries. They were not bashed unconscious before being carried to the sites where they were found. There were bottles, glasses and poison as well as signs and numbered pendants. Is there a common interest? What is the relationship between the victims and the killer?"

"Or are we talking about random killings?" asked Joe.

"Okay," said Harry. "Let's get this stuff back to the station. I want you to get it packed up ready to send on the train to the SIB tonight. Then go out to David's funeral parlour and get any samples and reports from him and Gregory to send as well. I will go out to the Slaughter's farm and tell the parents about their son.

****

Harry drove Joe back to the station before turning around to go to the Slaughter's farm. He drove the MG through the forest along Rockvale Road before the country opened up to rolling paddocks with wire fences, tall grass, dams and distant farm houses. He drove into the Slaughter's property where he was met by four barking dogs as he emerged from the car. He gave them a pat and they followed him to the door of the house. A woman in her forties wearing a neat floral-printed dress opened the door. Harry introduced himself and was led into the kitchen where he met a suntanned man who greeted him with a firm farmer's handshake.

Living in the house were Harrison and Violet Slaughter and their two daughters, Leanne and Hilda, who came into the kitchen soon after. Harry took his time informing them of the death of their son and brother.

"When was the last time you saw Jerome?" he asked.

Violet wiped the tears from her eyes. "He went to the university yesterday morning for lectures. He said that he would be late home because he was going to meet a friend yesterday afternoon. We weren't worried because he has his old Riley car to get home. It wasn't until this morning that I realised that he hadn't come home. I thought that he might have stayed at a girlfriend's place."

"Tell me about Jerome and his interests," said Harry.

Violet's face lit up and she smiled. "He was such a darling boy. He was so talented and bright and caring. He topped his subjects at school and we got him a second-hand car as a present for doing so well."

"You mean you got him a car out of the money your parents left you," said Harrison.

"Well, he deserved it," shouted Jerome's mother.

"Oh, come on, Mum," said Leanne as she wiped the tears from her eyes. "We know he was your favourite. You spoiled him rotten to the point that he didn't do anything around here or for anyone else. He was a boring, self-centred, lazy, good-for-nothing layabout. Hilda and I did more work around here than him; and you always let him get away with it."

Violet burst into tears. "But you never had to suffer what he went through. He had whooping cough as a baby and lots of other problems, but he pulled through and would have become a brilliant scientist in the future. Don't you be so hard on him."

"Leanne is right, Violet," said Harrison. "Jerome was so lazy he wouldn't work in an iron lung. He was so self-centred that he not only ignored me and the girls but even walked away from the church. You mentioned his girlfriend. He never had a real girlfriend for any longer than a few weeks. They liked to ride in his car but laughed at him behind his back. He didn't know how to love anyone else. He loved himself so much."

Violet let out a scream and ran outside.

Harry turned to Harrison and the girls. "Do you know anyone who would hate Jerome so much that they would want to kill him?"

Hilda blew her nose and held her handkerchief over her mouth. "Jerome had very few real friends. He was bright and studied a lot but he was so focused on his studies that he had little time for others; unless it was in the academic world. I can't see anyone at uni who would do that to him. He wasn't into sport and he was bullied at school; but not to that extent."

"What was he studying?"

"He was very much into science and zoology," said Leanne. "Lately he had taken a serious interest in the study of reptiles. He wanted to specialise in that field while applying his scientific knowledge."

"Did he show that interest here on the farm?"

Harrison turned and thumped his hand on the table. "Not on this farm he didn't. As a kid he used to run a mile if he saw a snake. The girls did more than him. He was apathy with a capital A."

"Was he a drinker or smoker?" asked Harry.

"He would have an occasional beer with us here on the farm," replied his mother as she came back into the house. "But he never drank to excess."

"How often did he visit the snake farm?"

Leanne answered. "Very little in the beginning of his studies but far more often lately as his interest in reptiles grew."

Harry rose. "Thank you very much. Please contact me at the station if you have any more information that might help us in our investigations."

He drove to the neighbouring farm of the McWhirters.

Chapter 25
Friday

As Harry walked in the door, Colleen came forward to give him a big hug and kiss. "And what have we done to deserve the pleasure of your visit today?" she asked with a broad grin.

Harry looked up at the ceiling with an impish expression. "Well, I came out to talk with your mother and father."

Colleen stepped back and thumped him on the arm. "So, you didn't come to see me?"

Harry took her by the arm and turned her towards the kitchen. "It'll be okay for you to sit in while I talk to your parents, so long as you behave yourself."

As Colleen walked past Harry into the kitchen, she gave him the hip which pushed him into the doorjamb. She turned to her parents having a cup of tea at the table.

"Harry's not staying. He's got work to do at the station. And please don't offer him a cuppa. He hasn't got time for that."

Colleen burst out laughing as she grabbed Harry's arm and pushed him onto the chair at the table. "Now what do you want, tea or coffee?"

Harry put his forefinger up to his nose and looked up as if thinking about the choice. "I'll have coffee with milk and two spoons of sugar stirred five times clockwise and once anticlockwise, and with a big slice of your mum's fruit cake on a plate, please."

Colleen clipped him behind the ear. "You'll get a mug of dirty water from the dam and an Arnott's Milk Arrowroot biscuit riddled with weevils."

Stan sat back laughing. "Well Harry, you did ask for that one, mate. Now, is this a social visit or something more serious because, this is in your work time?"

Harry took a bite of the fruit cake that Colleen put in front of him. "You live next door to the Slaughters," he said. "This morning we found young Jerome's body out at Taipan Charlie's snake farm. What can you tell me about him?"

"What happened to him?" asked Colleen's mother Margaret.

Harry gave them a brief outline of the circumstances surrounding Jerome's death at Charlie's farm.

Stan stood and walked across the room to stand with his back to the fuel stove and warmed his hands behind him. "I hate to speak ill of the dead but he was about as useless as using a piece of string to tow the tractor out of a bog."

"Don't be too harsh on him, Stan," said Margaret. "Remember he had a lot of sickness as a child."

"He had whooping cough as a baby and a few other kids' sicknesses," replied Stan, "but that's no excuse for being a good-for-nothing, worthless piece of mummy's boy. All the kids got those sicknesses but they got on with their lives. He sat around whimpering like a mongrel dog."

Colleen took a sip of her tea. "We must go over to the farm later on to give Violet support. Jerome was thoroughly spoiled by his mother who took pity on him, and he played on it all his life. She bought him the Riley car because he didn't like catching the bus into town. He hated sport and therefore didn't mix with us other kids as we were growing up. And he refused to go to church because he got bored. He was more interested in turtles than having serious relations with girls and rarely went to the dances. He was very negative and critical."

"What about his sisters?" asked Harry.

"Leanne and Hilda are great girls. Leanne was in the same class as me at Ben Venue Primary School. Both the girls were older than Jerome. They were always very active in school, on the farm and in the community. Jerome was the opposite to them. He was always so self-centred, apathetic and despondent. He sought sympathy by putting on the image that he was having difficulty putting one foot in front of the other; anything to get out of work."

"What happened when he wouldn't do what the other kids were doing?" asked Harry.

Colleen laughed. "He'd put on a tantrum until his mother gave in and he got his way. And then he would go away and sulk in the corner and criticise everyone else."

"How old was he?"

"I think he was nineteen or twenty. He was about three years younger than Hilda."

"Did he have any talents?" asked Harry.

"Oh, he was very intelligent," replied Colleen. "He was near the top of his class at school every year and I've been told he was doing well at university. He had specialised in science and zoology."

"Thank you," said Harry. "I must be going now."

"See what I mean, Mum?" said Colleen as she laughed. "He only came in here for the coffee and your cake. Now he'll run away without even a how-do-you-do."

Margaret gave Harry a peck on the cheek. "You can come anytime, Harry."

Colleen walked him to the door. "Are we going to the dance tonight?"

He stopped with his hand on the half-opened door. "Drop around to my place and we'll go together from there."

***

Harry drove back to the station, picked up Joe and proceeded to the university. They walked to the science block where they met the professor of zoology, Gwyn O'Connor, in his study. They were invited to sit in the comfortable chairs near the window. The professor stared out the window for a moment before turning back to Harry. His long, wispy strands of hair blew across his face, necessitating their frequent flicking away from his eyes.

Harry explained the reason for their visit. The professor sat back in shock. "Oh my God. He was one of my best students. What a loss. How are his parents?"

"As Jerome was a top student of yours, you might like to share your thoughts about him?" said Harry.

The professor continued to stare across the lawn towards the distant trees. "Jerome was a difficult student but one with hidden talents."

160

"In what way was he difficult?" asked Joe.

"He was always late with his assignments and would have up his sleeve a plethora of excuses including regular notes from his mother explaining Jerome's medical conditions."

"How did he get away with it?"

"I gave him some leeway because he was so highly intelligent and had a special relationship with animals; especially reptiles."

"Was he familiar with Taipan Charlie's farm and his collection of reptiles?" asked Joe.

"Yes. We had regular visits there and Jerome told me that he went out there occasionally by himself or with other students."

"How did he get on with the other students and lecturers?"

"The others thought he was a bit up himself; too aloof. He found it difficult to form friendships and so they just ignored him or gave him cheek to stir him up. Some girls would occasionally ask for a ride in his car but they had no intention of ever having a relationship."

"What else did he study?" asked Harry.

"When he arrived at university he was unsure what to study so he did biochemistry and psychology last year. He dropped psychology this year to concentrate on the sciences. He decided his future lay with the biological sciences. It was his real strength. His heart was never into psychology."

"I just saw Hamish Mackenzie walk past. He might have taught Jerome last year in psychology. We must see him at some point. Thank you very much, Gwyn. You have been most helpful."

"Do you want to see him now?" asked Joe.

"No," replied Harry. "We need to get back to the station."

***

Harry and Joe spent the next couple of hours working at the police station. At the end of the day they took the evidence and samples from the crime scene and autopsy of Jerome Slaughter to the railway station ready for the midnight train to Sydney.

***

At six-thirty an old Bedford truck stopped in front of Harry's house in Taylor Street. Colleen emerged from the cabin, dressed in a smart sleeveless, pleated, white chiffon dress with small red polka dots. A wide red band pulled her waist in tightly. A string of white pearls and a pair of white, strapped, high-heeled shoes completed her outfit. As Harry opened the front door he found Colleen absolutely stunning. He gave her a long hug and a peck on both cheeks. He was afraid to hug too tightly for fear that he might crack the perfect image embracing him.

"Well, are you going to invite me in or are we going to stand here in the doorway for the world to see?" she asked.

Harry laughed, put his arm around her waist and led her to the lounge room.

After small talk for five minutes, Colleen looked into Harry's eyes. "Are we going to the dance or are you cooking up a storm for me here?"

"I'm going to get my coat," he replied. "I've booked a table at the Imperial Hotel for dinner and then we'll go to the town hall for the dance."

***

They drove in the MG to the hotel where they were escorted to the dining room.

Harry had pre-ordered a bottle of Mateus Rosé. The waiter removed the cork and poured two glasses. Harry ordered a rump steak while Colleen had lamb cutlets with vegetables. They followed with a pineapple upside-down cake served with rich cream for dessert. After draining the last of the wine, they left and walked to the town hall where they danced all night to the swing jazz of the big brass band. The quickstep was followed by the barn dance, the Pride of Erin and Gypsy Tap, before the supper was served.

After supper they danced until midnight when the lights were turned down low and the band played *Blue Moon* for the final jazz waltz. Harry and Colleen were lost in the romance of the occasion. They moved as one in perfect rhythm around the dance floor, admired by the mothers and grandmothers who sat on the chairs around the hall as they watched all the young people.

On leaving the dance hall the two of them walked to the MG. Harry drove to the top of the hill next to the teachers college where they watched the stars and the lights of the city until Colleen shivered with the cool night air. They drove back to the house.

Colleen walked to the bedroom where she removed her coat, earrings, dress and shoes. Harry followed and pulled back the bedcovers. Without another word they slipped under the doona where they remained all night.

Chapter 26
Saturday

Harry rose early, ran to the showground and completed his ten laps around the oval. The air was clear and crisp. The birds gave him their usual welcoming calls. He felt invigorated. If it wasn't for the recent murders he would have been in seventh heaven. He jogged back to his house.

When Harry entered the bathroom he found Colleen in the hot bath water with a big sponge held to her chest. He bent over to kiss her on the forehead. He felt her hands slide smoothly under his arms but, with a quick jerk, she pulled him fully clothed into the bath. Twenty minutes later, and with the water going cold, they emerged, dried each other and got dressed.

Harry walked to the kitchen, turned on the electric jug and put on the bacon and eggs for breakfast. For the next hour they sat and talked about everything in general but nothing special. They enjoyed each other's company. The early morning sun warmed the room, and the smell of freshly ground coffee and cooked bacon created a homely atmosphere.

"I'll have to go soon," said Harry. "Joe and I have to go over some matters with our cases," said Harry. "You can stay here or go to the shops before they close, but I have booked a table for us at Nick's Café for lunch at twelve."

"That fits in well," replied Colleen. "I have to pick up some parts for the shearing shed from the farm machinery people on the highway and some bales of lucerne further down. I'll meet you at Nick's at noon."

***

Harry picked up Joe and they drove to the station. They worked on summarising their notes on the Jerome Slaughter murder and listing all the things they still needed to do. At ten o'clock Pat Casey came in from the desk and informed them that they were needed urgently at the St Kilda Hotel on the corner of Rusden and Marsh streets.

"The publican's wife said they are holding a bloke there who might be a suspect in the murders," said Pat. "He's kicking up a fuss so they want you there immediately."

"Thanks Pat. We'll be there as soon as possible. Give us two minutes to get ready."

Harry and Joe sprinted around to the hotel. When they got there the owner, Steve Irvine, was kneeling on the shoulders of a man spread-eagled on the bar-room floor. Shorty Hadley, a local character, was holding the man's legs. Shorty was so named because he was a six-foot-four-inches tall, raw-boned timber cutter. No one ever argued with Shorty.

"Okay," said Harry. "Let him up. We'll take over from here."

"We'll stand here with you, Harry," said Shorty. "We think this bastard is the killer you're looking for; and he ain't gettin' away this time. We'll make certain of that."

Harry led the man into the back lounge bar where there were no customers this early in the morning and sat him down. Steve and Shorty followed him. Joe stood behind the chair.

Harry turned to Steve. "Now tell me about this bloke and why you think he's the killer."

Steve's face was flushed as he pointed at the man. "He booked into the hotel on Thursday afternoon. He said he had broken down and had to wait for his truck to be fixed. Yesterday morning after my wife finished cleaning the rooms she said that this bloke's bed had not been slept in at all on Thursday night. That was when that young bloke was killed at Taipan Charlie's farm. We didn't see him all day yesterday and, when we confronted him this morning when he came in the back door at ten o'clock fully dressed and late for breakfast, he refused to tell us where he'd been. He got bloody cranky when I asked him. When I stepped around the bar to get the truth from him he swung a punch at me. Lucky for me I ducked in time. It was then that Shorty grabbed him around his shoulders and dumped him on his bum. I got my wife to ring the station. He's as guilty as hell and I bet he did in Splinter Winton and those other blokes as well. Lock the bastard up, Harry. And I can tell you that he also booked in here the Monday before last. That was the night that young bloke from the university was killed in the rat house."

"Thanks Steve and Shorty. You can leave him with us now."

After the others left, Harry sat in a hard chair in front of the man. "Now, you best start talking. Who are you? And why are you in Armidale?"

"I don't have to tell you anything. I haven't done anything wrong. Those two bastards need to be locked up for assaulting me. But I bet you won't do that because they are your mates here in this town. You're going to pick on any stranger to blame so you can big-note yourselves in the papers. I know how you cops work."

Harry leaned forward. "We can do this here or we can do it at the station. You make up your mind. Now I'll repeat the questions. Who are you? Where do you come from? And why are you in Armidale?"

The man coughed and wiped his mouth and nose with the back of his hand. "I live in Newcastle and I do truck deliveries between Sydney and Brisbane. I'm here because my truck broke down and they didn't have the right parts. They had to wait on a delivery from Sydney."

"Get out your licence papers," commanded Harry.

"I don't have them. They are in the glove box of the truck and that's down at Armidale Motors."

Harry turned to Joe. "I hope they're working on a Saturday, but give them a call and check on that licence."

Joe left the room.

Harry turned back. "Now tell me where you were last Monday week and last Thursday night."

The man looked to the ceiling. "On that Monday I met this girl in the bar here and we had a few drinks. She invited me back to her place and we spent the night there. When my truck broke down on Thursday I booked in here and I met up with her again and I went to her place. That was the reason my bed here was not slept in."

"What's her name? And where does she live?"

"Her name is Mary and she lives around the corner from here."

Harry continued to ask questions to tease out details about Mary and where she lived.

Ten minutes later Joe came back in. "Clarrie was on duty at the garage and he confirmed that he was working on this bloke's truck. He said he will be finished in half an hour. The name on the licence paper is

166

Laurence Playford and he lives in Stockton, a suburb of Newcastle. I phoned the station down there. The sergeant knows him and said he has a wife and two kids and has never been any trouble."

"Go to the bar and ask Steve about a woman called Mary who was drinking with this bloke that Monday and Thursday he was booked in here."

Sometime later Joe returned. "Steve confirmed that Mary is the local town bike and regularly picks up strangers at the bar. So I went around the corner to her place and she confirmed that this bloke spent those two nights with her all night. She said he was nice and generous."

Harry stood up and told the man to get going down to the garage. "I'd suggest you stay away from Armidale and away from Mary for a while, or at least until this matter of the murders is cleared up. People around here are on edge. Pick up your truck and get going. I don't want to see you here again for a while. And give a thought to your wife and kids."

Harry and Joe walked to the main bar where they explained to Steve and Shorty that Laurence Playford was not their man. Harry thanked them for their vigilance and good work but cautioned them about using violence against anyone who looks suspicious.

"Would you two like a drink on the house?" asked Steve.

"No thanks, Steve. It's far too early," shouted Harry as he walked to the door. "Joe is on duty and I have an important lunch date that I must get to now."

Joe walked back to the station. Harry walked to the main street and turned into Beardy Street. He saw Colleen up ahead carrying a parcel. He quickened his pace to catch up. They walked together towards Nick's Café. As they approached, Harry noticed two men, one on either side of the café entrance, slightly blocking the doorway. They were dressed similarly in blue drill shirts with long sleeves rolled up to the elbows. Their blue jeans were well worn and their boots were dirty. Both were unshaven. One had tattoos on both arms. Harry noticed that they both kept glancing nervously towards him and Colleen and then quickly away. Harry felt a heightened anticipation that something was not normal.

As they reached the entrance, Harry turned to one and then the other man. "Excuse us, gentlemen, we are going inside for lunch."

The man on the right suddenly pushed Colleen, making her fall on the pavement. "Get out of the way, bitch. Let me get at this bastard."

As Harry turned, the same man punched him hard in the chest. "That's from our mate, Sherman. You do remember who the 'Tank' is, don't you? You put our mates in Long Bay and Grafton and now you're gunna pay for that. Nobody does that to the Tank and Joe Cross and gets away with it."

Harry instinctively backed off but remained between himself and Colleen who was trying to get up off the footpath. He ducked a glancing blow from the other man before blocking a second punch from the first assailant. As that man came forward and tried to take Harry in a bear hug, Harry jabbed his knuckles directly into the man's Adam's apple. As the man staggered away choking, Harry gave him a karate chop to the collar bone. He took both sides of the man's head and rammed it down hard onto his raised knee, smashing the man's nose and knocking him unconscious.

Harry turned to hear the other man screaming and falling to the footpath holding his knee. While lying on the footpath, Colleen had swung her long leg in a wide arc and collected the side of the man's knee, bringing him down. Harry stepped across and stamped on the man's wrist, increasing the volume of the man's screams.

Harry bent over to lift Colleen back to her feet. He noticed her holding her left arm away from her body. She had a pained look. "Let me look at that wrist," said Harry.

"No," she replied. "It's okay. It's just bruised a bit."

"No, it's not," said Harry. "That looks broken. We'll get Gregory to come and look at it."

Nick, the owner, came out. "I've just called the station, Harry. They said they will be here in a moment."

"Thanks Nick," Harry replied. "Could you also call Gregory Ebsworth to see if he is available to look at Colleen's wrist here? I think it might be broken. If she goes inside with you, could you give her a cup of tea? I'll wait out here until the others come."

The police wagon pulled up in front of the café and out stepped Joe Simms and Pat Casey.

"Do you know these blokes, Harry?" asked Pat.

"I don't know them but they said that they were sent by Fred Sherman and Joe Cross to do me over. You will remember that Fred and

Joe headed the corrupt CIB two years ago and that I led the investigation that put them away for life. Well, I've been half-expecting them to try to get back at me. And they had so many criminal mates that I would never know where the attack would come from. But at least we can put their mates here inside with them. They can compare notes for a few more years."

Harry walked over to the assailants and cuffed both. One was just regaining consciousness. "Give me your names and addresses."

"We don't have to tell you anything you mongrel. You wait till Fred hears about this."

"You're right. You don't have to tell me anything, but you'll stay in the cell until you do. It's up to you," replied Harry.

Pat walked over and removed the wallets from their back pockets. "This one's name is Michael Simpson. The other one is John Buttsworth."

"I should have remembered," said Harry. "You two were mixed up with Whispers Durante at Kings Cross. You two are better known as Speedy and Cruiser and we know you were connected with Fred Sherman and Joe Cross. Lock them up, Pat."

"It could be just coincidence, Harry, but these blokes would have been here when Jerome Slaughter was killed," said Pat. "Is it possible that Sherman and Cross are organising these killings here in Armidale to get back at you by making you look incompetent in not solving these crimes quickly?"

"Well, they certainly have no shortage of criminal friends around the state who would be willing to do their dirty work; and they would be well compensated for doing it. They already have their old mates from the CIB lined up to have a go at me at the hearing next week in Sydney over that Albury case. It would be so easy for Sherman and Cross to have a criminal do a killing and then disappear before the body was discovered. The death of Splinter might be one done by them."

Pat responded. "That's right, Harry. No one would take notice of a person who only came to Armidale once. And because each of the victims was killed by the same type of poison then that would lead us to believe that it was the same killer each time and that he probably was living locally."

"A good theory, Pat," replied Harry, "but if the victims did not know the killers they would not have been inclined to go with them for a casual drink. And then there's the signs and the pendants which are too personal and complicated for a group of simple-minded crims to organise perfectly each time. But I will still keep all the ex-CIB and their criminal mates as persons of interest and I will ask Chief Superintendent Danny Jones to organise an undercover man to be planted in the gaol with Sherman and Cross."

After Joe and Pat took away the prisoners, Harry went inside the café with Colleen to have a wonderful lunch of Nick's famous fish and chips. Nick did not charge them for the lunch.

***

Late in the afternoon Harry and Colleen saw Doctor Gregory Ebsworth. Harry had a couple of deep bruises but no broken bones. Colleen had a severely sprained wrist that the doctor bandaged. They retired to Harry's house for a quiet evening together.

Chapter 27
Sunday

Harry and Colleen sat across from each other at the breakfast table. Colleen unfolded the *Sunday Truth* and read the following article out loud.

Attempt on life of local detective

James Bolton: Special Crime Reporter

There has been an attempt on the life of Detective Harry Taylor, the senior detective in charge of the Armidale serial-killer investigations.

Yesterday, in broad daylight outside the popular Nick's Café in Armidale's main street, two well-known criminals attacked Detective Taylor and a female friend, causing serious injuries.

Reliable sources reported that the two assailants have a criminal record, and have spent time in gaol and were close associates of two well-known inmates, Fred Sherman and Joe Cross. Sherman is the disgraced former leader of the Criminal Investigation Branch, and Cross was his senior detective. Both were found guilty of corruption and murder in Sydney. For the last two years they have been serving the early part of their sentences in Long Bay, Goulburn and Grafton gaols. Detective Taylor led the investigation that put those corrupt officers behind bars where they belong.

Reliable information points to Sherman and Cross planning to get back at Taylor by using their numerous criminal contacts in and out of gaol to do the dirty work for them.

The good citizens and local police in Armidale want answers. Are Sherman and Cross guilty of arranging the serial murders in their beautiful city as revenge against Taylor?

Come on, Mr Commissioner, what is head office doing to assist the local police get to the bottom of these murders? How long before we have another murder?

We will keep you, the public, up to date on these murders. Keep reading the Sunday Truth *and* The Daily Mirror *for the only accurate news bulletins.*

"That's interesting," said Harry. "We were only talking about that yesterday afternoon. We were wondering if Sherman and Cross have had something to do with the local murders but the evidence so far does not support it. It points to someone local. Those two are desperate to get back at me for putting them away two years ago but they picked two dumb idiots to do it. If they'd had enough common sense, they could have knocked me off at night in my own home and been back down the coast before dawn. Nobody here would have known. The police would have been chasing locals as the possible offenders."

Colleen folded the paper. "How could Sherman and Cross be involved when they are in gaol?"

"When those two were in charge of the CIB, they had close connections with some of the worst criminals in the country. They worked with some of those criminals to pull off major crimes such as bank robberies. They had close connections with the big four crime bosses in Sydney. Those two and their mates would be very happy to get back at me for putting them away, and money is not a problem."

Colleen put the paper in her bag. "I'll take the paper home with me and read it after finishing my chores."

"When we finish breakfast," said Harry, "I must go because I'm going to use the library today to research serial killers."

"But the library isn't open on Sundays," replied Colleen.

"That's right, but Sarah Connors, the librarian, has made special arrangements to let me in today."

"Ha. And what will you and Sarah be researching together by yourselves all alone behind the bookshelves?" asked Colleen with a laugh.

Harry laughed too. "Sarah is going to church with her husband and children so it will be just me there."

"That's okay then," replied Colleen. "I'll have to get the truck and parts back to Dad, so I'll catch up with you later in the week."

"Are you okay to drive with that sore wrist?" asked Harry.

"Sure. I bandaged it again, and we Armidale girls are tough."

She bent over and kissed Harry on the forehead. "Next time, give me good warning when your old friends come around for lunch."

***

At ten o'clock Sarah let Harry into the library and pointed to the section dealing with true crime. He hoped to uncover any common threads linking the murderers with their victims. Were there any characteristics of the killers or patterns of behaviour that were similar to the current murders in Armidale? The first books he found dealt with English serial killers. He took brief notes on each of them.

The first was Jonathan Balls, an Englishman who poisoned at least twenty-two people—almost all of them close family members—in the village of Happisburgh from 1824 to 1845.

The next was John Bishop with the London Burkers, a gang of body-snatchers. They murdered victims to sell to anatomists by luring them to their homes before being drugged.

In February 1886 Mary Ann Britland went to a nearby chemist and, claiming to have had some mice infest her home, bought some packets of rat poison that contained both strychnine and arsenic. She poisoned her daughter, husband and the wife of her lover.

In the 1880s George Chapman poisoned three mistresses.

Mary Ann Cotton was believed to have been a serial killer who killed three of her four husbands for their life insurance payouts, and eleven of her thirteen children. She poisoned them with arsenic.

Another poisoner was Thomas Neill Cream, also known as the 'Lambeth Poisoner', who was a Scottish-Canadian medical doctor. He killed up to ten people in three countries, targeting mostly lower-class women, sex workers and pregnant women seeking abortions. He was convicted and hanged on the 15th of November, 1892.

Amelia Hobley, popularly known as the 'Ogress of Reading', murdered infants in her care over a thirty-year period. She adopted unwanted infants in exchange for money. She initially cared for the children, in addition to having two of her own. She murdered the children she adopted, strangling at least some of them, and disposed of the bodies to avoid attention.

There were the William Burke and William Hare murders where sixteen murders were committed over a period of about ten months during 1828 in Edinburgh, Scotland. The corpses were sold for dissection and anatomy lectures.

There was the case of Jack the Ripper who typically targeted women working as prostitutes who lived and worked in the slums of the East End of London. Their throats were cut prior to abdominal mutilations.

Harry went to the toilet and had a glass of water before returning to investigate Australian serial killers.

In late 1825 British convict Thomas Jefferies murdered six people in Tasmania. Jefferies's killings included those he robbed, a baby and a policeman. He was also a violent sexual offender and accused of cannibalism.

Robert Francis Burns was an Irish-Australian murderer and serial killer. After Burns's death the hangman made a sensational claim that the prisoner had stated to him that he had murdered eight people—five in Victoria and three in New South Wales.

During the war, Eddie Leonski, a United States Army soldier, killed three women in Melbourne in 1942.

John Lynch was an Irish-born Australian killer who confessed to the killing of ten people between 1836 and 1842. He even killed a farmer and took possession of his property. He and his family had a long criminal history in Ireland.

In the late 1800s John and Sarah Jane Makin adopted Australian infants. The couple answered a series of advertisements from unmarried mothers seeking adoption of their babies for a payment. The remains of fifteen bodies were found by police in the backyard.

Arnold Karl Sodeman, also known as the 'School-Girl Strangler', targeted children. He confessed to four killings before being hanged at Pentridge Prison, Victoria in 1936.

Another killer was Martha Needle who poisoned her husband, three children and her prospective brother-in-law and was hanged in 1894.

Harry also read about people like Squizzy Taylor and the razor gang wars of the 1930s, and the turf wars between the famous brothel madams Tilly Devine and Kate Leigh from the Darlinghurst and Woolloomooloo areas of Sydney, but dismissed them as not related to the style of killings in Armidale.

After hours of concentration, Harry stood and wiped his eyes, his mind confused with the variety of serial killers, their methods and the sheer terror they brought to their victims and families. He took his time to walk around the library to clear his mind, after which he ate two apples he had brought from home.

As he sat again he focused on looking for any patterns or common elements within the mass of information he'd found within the many books that could help him with his own cases.

Towards the end of the day Harry took out his notebook and listed the main points:

- Some killers were driven by visions or voices of God or the Devil
- Some saw it as their duty to eliminate people who were considered as below acceptable standards
- Some were driven by strong impulses of lust even when the act of killing itself was not motivated by sexual urges
- Most of the killers derived great pleasure from controlling and dominating victims
- Most murders took place close to the home of the killer
- There could be any one or several motivations that induced the killer into action such as cultural,

biological, psychological, environmental and sociological

- Serial killers were mostly well prepared
- They organised the selection of the victim, isolation from the group and control of the murder scene
- They planned how to kill, how to dispose of the body and how to dispose of the evidence
- Most killers were between twenty and forty years of age
- They mostly acted alone
- There was at least one common trait among the victims of each killer such as gender, occupation, interests, location, race, lifestyle, age or economic status
- There could be a strong spiritual commitment to their actions
- Some just do it for the excitement or sexual gratification
- Most killers displayed a sadistic tendency and a strong urgency to complete the task of killing

By the time Harry completed his summary he felt completely exhausted. He questioned how relevant this research had been as it related to the murders here in Armidale. If nothing else, it gave him a better understanding of the various motives of serial killers.

For the next hour Harry searched through a Bible he took from the shelf and tried to find quotes similar or the same as the writings on the pieces of cardboard found at the site of each murder.

It was late into the afternoon. He thought about going home, opening a bottle of beer, getting into the bath and relaxing. He returned the books to their shelves and walked from the library.

***

Harry drove back home where he opened a bottle of beer, kicked off his boots and was soon asleep on the lounge.

Chapter 28
Monday

Superintendent Ray Johnston brought the meeting to order. "Before we commence, Harry, I have to inform you that I have just received a telegram from the commissioner. He is aware that you have to be in Sydney this Thursday for the hearing involving the Albury matter. You are to catch the train tomorrow and be in the commissioner's office Wednesday morning at nine o'clock. He and Superintendent Ford want to discuss the serial murders and the attack on you at the weekend."

"Thank you, sir," replied Harry, "but I'd prefer to drive down to Sydney tomorrow night because I still have work to do here before I go. And I'm not that fond of train travel anyway; especially at night. So with your permission, sir, I'll take my own car."

"Okay Harry. Now, can you bring us all up to date on the serial murders and the incident at Nick's Café on Saturday?"

For the next half-hour Harry went through the circumstances of the murder of Jerome Slaughter at Taipan Charlie's snake farm and his conversations with the McWhirters and Jerome's parents.

Ken Wright called out with a broad grin. "Hey Harry, did you go to the McWhirters to get information about Slaughter or was it to see the fair Colleen?"

Harry laughed. "You know me, Ken; I have my mind on the job at all times."

Ken pointed both forefingers towards Harry. "How is Colleen after she was attacked by those goons at the café?"

"She's coming on fine," replied Harry. "The McWhirters are neighbours of the Slaughters. Now, let's get back to the murders. I want to take you through my work yesterday in the library when I researched the history of serial killers both in the UK and Australia. I'm not certain that the research has added anything to what we already know but I was looking for patterns and behaviours to compare with these killings here in Armidale. I'll write the summary here on the blackboard and you tell me if something catches your attention."

Harry took time transferring his notes to the blackboard.

"The problem with the Armidale murders," said Eric Talbot, "is that the victims are quite different. It's not like they are all prostitutes or from the same family or from the same age or social group. The only common threads we have at the moment is that they are all locals and were all killed by poisoning."

"Yes Eric," replied Harry. "And the poison in the early cases was phenobarbital. But I want you to keep that information to yourselves."

"Where could the killer get enough phenobarbital if he wasn't a doctor?" asked Ray.

"Doctors, pharmacists and vets are the only ones who would stock enough of this poison to carry out all these murders. Doctors use it in small doses to treat or prevent seizures. It can also be used short term as a sedative. In small doses, under careful supervision, doctors and vets use it as a relaxant. In larger doses it will kill. Veterinarians use it to put down animals; mainly dogs and cats. Both doctors and vets have to keep accurate records of their supplies but I'm sure that some criminals could acquire enough on the black market or from break-and-enters into pharmacies or vet clinics. There is no record of that happening here yet. We have checked all pharmacies, vets, doctors and hospitals here and in Uralla, Walcha and Guyra. All supplies have been accounted for."

"All of the murders were in this district," said Graham McInnes. "That suggests that the killer is also a local. But the difficulty is that we have no record of anyone who we would suspect of carrying out such serious crimes."

Lars van Dyke pointed at the blackboard. "Forget what's up there on the board. I think this bloke is a blow-in who carries out these killings randomly on any unsuspecting victim. I think he's a nut-case or a religious freak from out of town. We need to do a more thorough check on every one who was booked into the hotels in the last two weeks."

"I would disagree with that," said Joe. "In all five cases the killer sat down with the victim and had a drink. To do that it is almost certain that the killer was well known to the victims to the point of them being happy to sit and talk while they had their drinks. There were no signs that the victims were bound or injured or forced to eat or swallow the poison."

"In addition to that," said Harry, "the locations of the murders suggest that the killer and victims were comfortable being in those odd places, even at night. There was Petherby in the rat shed, Winton behind the pub, O'Sullivan in the park, Gladstone behind the showground pavilion, and Slaughter at the snake farm. The evidence shows that each of the victims were there voluntarily with the killer when they were poisoned."

"Has anyone seen caravans or tents around town or on the outskirts lately?" asked Ray.

Graham lifted a finger. "There was a camp out along the Ebor Road but that was a PMG gang doing repairs to the telephone lines. There's always a couple of truckies who park in the rest area on the highway at night, but most of those are regulars doing the Sydney-to-Brisbane run."

Merv Leech put up his hand. "In each of the murders there have been two glasses left at the scene; one for the killer and one for the victim. That suggests the killer works alone."

"The problem," said Jack Nelson, "is that I can't see the common connection between the victims except that four of them were students; three at the uni and one at the teachers college. There's no evidence that those students were friends or socialised together. And why would Splinter Winton be associated with them unless he gave them loans? I can't see any connection or common interest."

Charlie Hanwright stood and pointed to the list on the board. "It says there that some killers are motivated by lust and some for sexual gratification. Have you seen any evidence, Harry, that the killer had any sexual relations with the victims prior to their deaths or that the killer or victims were part of a group who got together for shared sex? For example, did they all go to the same brothel, or to any brothel?"

"No," replied Harry. "The autopsies have shown no evidence of that. But that doesn't mean that the killer didn't get sexual gratification before, during or after the killings. While that might be a factor in these cases, I think there has to be another motive for the killer."

Keith Blackmore coughed. "From your research you have told us that many serial killers target their victims because they consider that they are below acceptable standards. Would that include things that are socially unacceptable like prostitution? Could that be the case here?"

"I thought about that, Keith," replied Harry, "but I can't see the evidence. A lot of people don't like betting, and it is illegal, but I can't see Splinter being murdered just because he was the local SP bookie. The four others were students. O'Sullivan was booked a few times for speeding. There were rumours about Gladstone being homosexual and maybe fiddling with boys he babysat. But there is nothing else to go on. Three of them came from families that are comfortably well-off and there's no history of other family members being involved in crimes or even misdemeanours."

Ken Wright tapped the table. "You mentioned, Harry, that killers are often led by spiritual visions and are driven by the command of God or the Devil. Is there any evidence that these killings could be like that?"

"It's a good point you raise, Ken, and there is the evidence of the signs on the bodies and at the sites of all the murders. The sayings on those signs definitely have a religious tone to them. Those sayings come straight from the Bible. It doesn't mean that the victims were all good church-goers but it does point to the killer trying to get across a religious or spiritual message. Winton was guilty of minor offences of illegal gambling, loan-sharking, and didn't go to church, but his death was not an accident. Gladstone was a regular church-goer, was in the choir and taught at Sunday school, but there is no evidence that he was leaning towards a religious cult. I was involved in a case two years ago in Wagga Wagga where a weird cult set up on the banks of the Murrumbidgee River. We had a lot of trouble with them and finally gaoled the leader, but I don't see any similarity to the cases here."

"Isn't it young Gladstone's funeral today?" asked Ken.

"Yes," replied Harry, "but I can't get to it. Joe will go to look over the attendees."

When there were no further questions, Harry sat back at the table. "Thanks everyone. It's good to get your opinions. With regard to the assault on me and my friend Colleen on Saturday, I can assure you that the perpetrators were organised by Fred Sherman and Joe Cross from gaol. The attackers would have been on a good payout from the big crime bosses in Sydney to do me over. Both Fred and Joe were closely associated with many high-profile criminals when they were in charge of the CIB, and were very close to the big four crime figures in Sydney. As
180

I explained to Colleen the other day, they organised major crimes like bank robberies and the murders of well-known criminals who were becoming too competitive for the big boys. The two who assaulted us are still in the holding cells next door and I expect a hearing when I get back from Sydney. Now I must go to the university."

***

On arriving at the university, Harry and Joe went to the zoology building where they met with Sue Ellis, the laboratory assistant.

"Thanks for meeting with us again, Sue," said Harry. "Can you tell us what you know of Jerome Slaughter who was killed the other night at the snake farm?"

Sue gasped. "That was terrible. We had Jonathon Petherby killed in our rat shed, and now Jerome, one of best science students, is murdered."

"How did you find Jerome as a person and as a student?" asked Joe.

"He had one great love: he was obsessed with reptiles. He once told me that reptiles were much better than humans. He could never understand why people shot snakes. He would befriend the lizards and handfeed them."

"How did he get on with the other students?"

"He was a bit of a loner. He didn't mix with the others. He didn't play sport and didn't join in social events with them. Others looked on him as lazy, boring, self-centred, apathetic and always critical of others. When he whinged about something they all got up and walked away from him. They couldn't stand his grizzling; especially when they saw him as someone too lazy to get out of his own way. I found him so frustrating in the lab because he would walk out every time and leave his mess for me to clean up. I wasn't here as his nursemaid but that is the way he looked upon us staff."

"How did the lecturers react to him?" asked Harry.

"Most of them felt the same. They got sick of his lateness in doing his assignments and giving ridiculous excuses."

"But he was still doing zoology, wasn't he?"

"Yes. He did well in his biochemistry exam. Gwyn O'Connor felt sorry for him and wanted to keep him on because of his love of reptiles. He wanted to give him every chance to succeed."

"Thanks for your help, Sue. We must go now."

***

Harry dropped Joe back at the station and drove home. He phoned Doug, the publican at the Shelbourne Hotel in Sydney, and asked him to leave a key in the usual place as he expected to be late arriving on Tuesday night.

Chapter 29
Tuesday

Harry got out of bed slowly. There were no eggs or bacon in the refrigerator and the milk had turned sour so he was restricted to three pieces of stale bread and cheese for breakfast. He toasted the bread, scraped the remains of the butter from the dish and cut the cheese. It was not a good start to the day.

***

He picked up Joe from the station and headed for the university. Upon arrival at the zoology laboratory, Harry and Joe found second-year students doing dissection work on Norwegian rats. Joe put his hand over his nose as he smelt the fumes from the formalin that was used to preserve the rats. Gwyn O'Connor introduced them to the class.

"Hello everyone," said Harry. "Most of you knew Jerome Slaughter in this class last year and this year. Please share with us your thoughts about Jerome. Who were his friends? And do you know of anyone who might have hated him enough to murder him?"

A young man at the back put up his hand. "His closest friends were snakes and lizards."

There were ripples of giggles around the room.

Gwyn O'Connor scowled at the student. "That was uncalled for, Mark. Please, show some respect."

"I'm sorry, sir," replied Mark. "What I meant to say was that Jerome didn't mix with other students because he was so absorbed in his study of reptiles. He told me once that those snakes had more personality than me and the other blokes in the group. He didn't play sport or go to the dances or other social events. He was happy to give girls a ride in his car if they asked, especially on cold days, but he wasn't really interested in people."

The young woman in the front row spoke. "I think Jerome must have had a spoilt upbringing because he was so lazy. He always had his head down low. He looked so despondent and bored. For him to say hello was a real struggle."

Another student continued. "To me he was so self-centred. He expected everyone else to do the preparation and cleaning up. He always seemed depressed. He was so apathetic that he was too tired to get out of his own way. He told me once that sport was the greatest waste of oxygen of any human activity."

"He always looked bored and depressed," said another student. "I suggested that he join a church group or a choir or volunteer for the St John Ambulance, but he laughed and said that those people were all wankers and all they wanted was to big-note themselves."

An older student from the back of the room stood up. "I think Jerome must have had a weird upbringing. It appears, on one hand, that he was thoroughly spoiled to the point that he didn't have to take responsibility for anything. And on the other hand, I believe that he was not loved by his parents or other members of the family. That's the reason why he fell in love with reptiles. He was so despondent and listless. I believe that was the result of the lack of real love or friendship in his life."

"Did he ever have one particular girlfriend before he developed his interest in snakes?" asked Joe.

A quietly spoken girl in the front put up her hand. "I was never a girlfriend but I tried to befriend Jerome to try to bring him out of himself. We often met in the library doing research but he was more interested in the books than having a real conversation with me. I gave it away as a lost cause. I felt he was uncomfortable being with me."

"Did he have any enemies? Or was he treated badly by the bullies in this place?" asked Harry.

"He had an easy answer for all the bullies," said the girl who'd spoken. "He just walked quietly away leaving them shouting into the wind. He never fought back or even spoke to them. When they got no reaction from him, they gave up."

"Thank you, everyone," said Harry. "That gives us a much better understanding of Jerome. All the best in your studies. I'm just so glad I wasn't born a Norwegian rat."

Harry and Joe walked to the next building where they found Hamish Mackenzie in his office. They were introduced to another man sitting in one of the chairs at the large desk.

"I want you to meet Aled Prosser," said Hamish. "He is a qualified psychiatrist from Wales, which probably says a lot about his behaviour. He then saw the light and switched to the field of psychology. He migrated here this year and was appointed to our staff."

Aled laughed. "The truth is that the university pleaded with me to come here because the psychology department was suffering collectively from serious mental illnesses. My job is to treat them with dignity without the rest of the community knowing of their plight."

"How can we help you, Harry?" asked Hamish.

"I'm glad you are both here because we have a serial murderer at large and three of the five victims are university students. Firstly, I thought you might know some of those students but, more importantly, you might help us get into the mind of the murderer. What makes a person become a serial killer? What goes through their mind? What drives them to commit multiple murders?"

Hamish pointed at Aled and grinned. "Aled should know because the Welsh are all a bit that way. Just watch what happens in the scrums when they play rugby against Scotland."

"I haven't had much direct experience with serial killers," said Aled, "but I did a lot of work in gaols and learned a lot from the prisoners; especially murderers. Serial killers are different from most other killers. They seem to have a strong urge to plan for and commit murder, and they get great satisfaction from doing it. They do it because they desperately want to do it."

"What drives them to do it?" asked Joe.

"The necessary psychological preconditions usually arise during early childhood; especially in an abusive home environment. The situation is worsened if it is the mother who rejects and torments them. The child lives in a constant state of fear, guilt, shame and blame but is too young to know the reasons why. As an unconscious counter to this torturous emotional state, they direct their pain outwards and inflict an even more intense and destructive form of pathological behaviour onto others. The person is thus changed from the abused into the abuser and their newly acquired sense of personal power is wielded in punishing those whom they judge unworthy in some way, just as they were considered unworthy by their own parents."

Hamish sipped his glass of water. "I would say that there is another affected group that could become serial killers: those suffering from a serious mental illness that developed later in life. It doesn't stop them from organising the murders, but they rarely follow through."

Aled burst out laughing. "Get out your cuffs, Harry. Your perpetrator is sitting right there in front of you. Lock him up now."

Hamish picked up the blotting pad from the desk and threw it at Aled. "He's the one you should lock up, Harry. King John of England should have killed all those Welsh peasants in the thirteenth century when he had the chance in the war at that time."

"What do you two think of the theory that serial killers are driven by lust or that they get some sexual satisfaction from the act of killing?" asked Harry.

"Good question, Harry," said Aled. "Studies show a few different patterns of behaviour in this regard. Some repeat murderers are compelled to kill by a sexual urge, but not all derive the sexual satisfaction that they hoped they would have had from taking another life. That is, the urge and the satisfaction are not necessarily connected and the emotional response can be a hit-or-miss experience with each victim. But these types of people will continue to be driven by their sexual urges and their desire for fulfilment, regardless of the actual result and regardless of whether sexual penetration takes place or not. Then there are others who are motivated to kill for completely non-sexual reasons but are pleasantly surprised by the sexual gratification that comes either at the point of death or just afterwards. Depending on how strong the association is between the act of killing and the heightened sexual response they experienced during the first or first few murders will determine if that killer forms an addiction to that mode of behaviour."

"I'd say, Harry," said Hamish as he broke into the conversation, "that narcissism could be a factor. Narcissists have a high sense of their own importance and they react against the slightest criticism. Their self-righteousness combined with their lack of empathy can cause them to carry out some pretty extreme acts against others."

Aled burst out laughing and pointed at Hamish. "There you have the perfect type. Look at him. Hamish is the perfect example of an anal-retentive, narcissistic, obsessively-compulsive, intolerant perfectionist who would love to kill everyone who does not fit into his narrow boundaries of exemplary behaviour. I never turn my back for fear that he will stab me."

Hamish turned and threw a psychology textbook at Aled. "Killing all the Welsh would be judged as justifiable homicide, Harry. It was God's one big mistake to let them be born and be in the community of the human race."

"Could serial killers have multiple motives?" asked Joe.

"Definitely," replied Hamish. "And the motive or incentive could change from one victim to the next. It could be greed for one murder and desire for monetary gain for others. Some murderers take a dislike to a certain group of people based on that person's race, nationality, creed, gender, age or looks because they might see them as a threat."

"You see, Harry?" chortled Aled. "You see what Hamish is doing? He wants to kill off all of us Welshmen. But what he didn't mention was that Wales thrashed Scotland in the last rugby test. Look at Hamish's dropped lower lip. It is a clear sign that anger is a strong motivation for serial killers."

Hamish threw another textbook at Aled. "I'm guilty, Harry, but don't lock me up until I have done away with every Welshman."

"Is it true," asked Joe, "that serial killers are well organised and are less inclined to act on impulse?"

Aled stood and walked around the room as he flicked his long hair from his forehead. "Yes Joe. The killer will usually study the victim well in advance of their murder—their lifestyle, habits, routines, interests, acquaintances and the like—so that they will know the best time to strike. And one of the best ways to do this is to form a relationship with the victim to not only gather information directly but to gain the victim's trust. That might be through casual conversations, social outings, gifts or other methods. Having won their trust, this creates the situation where the victim lets down their guard and allows the opportunity for the killer to get in close to the victim. The killer will also determine the particular motive for each victim's death, select the most appropriate location and method of killing for each individual, and decide how to dispose of the body."

Hamish added, "It can be difficult for you police if the killer is aware of investigative methods and forensic analysis techniques and they use that knowledge to avoid detection and mislead. For example, we know from the news reports that poisoning was the most likely method in your cases, so the killer would already know before the actual murder where to source the poison, the effects of different quantities, what the symptoms are and the time required for the drug to take effect, and what residual evidence remains in the body after death. I have also read that some killers enjoy leaving clues for the detectives to follow."

"That's very interesting," said Harry.

"What happens to killers after the event?" asked Joe. "How do they feel after the act?"

"The murderers I interviewed in gaol," said Aled, "told me that they often felt deeply depressed after the event; not from physical exhaustion but from the fact that the killing did not satisfy their strong urges or fulfil their desires or meet their expectations, whatever those were. The lack of satisfaction from the killing caused their depression."

"How do murderers hide themselves in society, knowing what they've done?" asked Harry as he pointed to Aled.

"They are good at compartmentalising different aspects of their personality or behaviour, essentially living two separate lives," replied Aled. "Killers often lead what, to the general public, appear to be normal lives. They are seen to have regular relationships, are gainfully employed, are socially involved in the community and, to many people, look like model citizens. That makes it very difficult to identify the murderers behind their masks."

Aled walked towards Hamish and placed his hands on Hamish's shoulders. "Look at this shining light of Armidale society, involved as he is in the church, choir, Scouts and band, as well as his great work here at the university. But he could be your serial killer hiding in plain sight of all of us. I'll hold him down while you get the cuffs on."

Hamish laughed as he jumped up and pushed Aled away. "I'm about to become the next killer, Harry. I'm going to throttle this Welshman. The world will be better off without him."

Harry and Joe stood. "Thanks," said Harry. "All of that has been very valuable information. We hope that we can call on both of you again. We'll leave you two to pack down in the scrum."

***

Harry and Joe drove back to the station and walked into the meeting room to have a cup of tea. They had only taken one sip when Ray Johnston entered the room.

"At ease, men. We know that you have to be in court on Thursday, Harry. Tell us a bit more about it."

Harry sat back in the chair. "The wife and brother of the Albury accountant who was murdered two years ago are suing the New South Wales Government—and the police service in particular—for misfeasance. The hearing will be conducted in the Central Court next to headquarters on Thursday morning at ten o'clock. I received a summons some time back. As I was the leading detective on that case, I have to be there."

"What the hell is misfeasance?" asked Joe.

Ray coughed. "Misfeasance is a failure of an officer to carry out their public obligations in accordance with common law or by regular procedures. It permits an individual to recover the loss or damage suffered after an officer acted maliciously and was likely to harm the complainant."

Harry continued. "These people from Albury are saying that I failed in my duty to catch the killer after the death of the earlier victims. They are saying that, by failing in my duty to catch the killer earlier, I was responsible for the death of their relative. They are now claiming damages from the government for the losses to their family and business from my incompetence."

"Why is this happening now?" asked Joe.

Harry pushed back in the chair. "I guess that it has taken this long for the old CIB team to come up with a strategy to get back at me, and they might have been encouraged to do so because of the recent publicity about the Armidale murders. I'll drive to Sydney this afternoon and I'll meet with the commissioner tomorrow before going to the SIB to bring them up to date with our cases in Armidale. I'll stay at the Shelbourne tonight and tomorrow night and attend court on Thursday."

"This is serious, Harry," said Ray. "One of my sources informed me that other officers such as former Chief Superintendent Twain, Sergeant Jack Tomlinson, ex-Crown Sergeant Dick Funnell, Reg Lewis, Chicka Podger and Merv Nolan will also be called."

"Yes, I was made aware of that. I'll be depending on my good friend Fergus Whitelaw, if I can get him out of the pub," said Harry. "He might look like what the cat dragged in, and he doesn't work with any law firm, but he will love taking that lot apart."

"You have more confidence in him than me," replied Ray.

"With your permission, sir, I've got a few things to do before going."

"By all means. All the best," replied Ray.

Harry phoned Fergus from the station to confirm their early meeting on Thursday morning at their regular café in George Street.

He left Armidale at lunchtime.

Chapter 30
Wednesday

Harry walked into the Central Street headquarters of the police force. He went to the main desk where he was greeted by Matt Jackson.

"Hi Matt," he said. "Good to see you again. I thought you were out at the Penrith station. Are you relieving Jack Tomlinson?"

"G'day Harry," replied Matt. "No. I'm working here now full time. Jack was transferred back to the main station at Wollongong."

"I bet he wasn't happy about that. I'm here to see the commissioner at nine."

"He's waiting for you. I'll buzz to say you're here."

The commissioner's office was large with a solid cedar desk and high office chair backing onto the window, three large cedar bookcases, two tall cabinets, three filing cabinets and a large table surrounded by eight chairs. Commissioner Murray Fredericks was sitting in the main office chair and Superintendent Brian Ford in the nearest chair next to the desk. They both stood and shook Harry's hand.

"Take a seat, Harry," said the commissioner. "We've asked you in here today because of our growing concern about these serial murders at Armidale. And we also want to hear your side of the story about that incident last Saturday. Let's start by you telling us about the attack on you."

Harry briefly described the attack on him and Colleen.

"Is Colleen a close friend of yours or was she an innocent bystander?" asked Brian Ford.

"She is a friend of mine and we were going to the café for a meal when the goons attacked me. To get at me they pushed Colleen to the ground, spraining her wrist."

"Now, what's this supposed connection with Fred Sherman and Joe Cross?" asked the commissioner.

"The two assailants were Speedy Simpson and Cruiser Buttsworth and they used to do a lot of standover jobs for Whispers Durante around Kings Cross. They recently did time for armed robbery and have been in and out of various gaols. They made it clear to me last Saturday that they were sent by Sherman and Cross to do me over."

"We'll need to keep them apart and shove them in other prisons away from those other two," said Brian Ford.

Harry nodded his approval. "As you are aware, Sherman and Cross have so many contacts in the criminal world that there will always be a danger of others trying to get at me. We all know that when they were in the CIB they used to organise some of the well-known criminals to do jobs for them. At least I won't have to worry about those other two blokes. I've just got to be on the lookout for the next ones."

Brian sat back. "I'll get my assistant to identify and locate any criminals who have a history with Sherman and Cross. We will build an intelligence profile on each of them and put a trace on their movements. We'll let you know if any are likely to move towards you, Harry."

"Thanks sir. That would be most helpful."

Commissioner Fredericks stood and walked to the window. He rubbed his hip to relieve the pain of a former injury. "Now fill us in, Harry, on where you are up to with this serial killer. You will appreciate that we are coming under a lot of political and media pressure to get these murders solved. We need a quick resolution. Brian will see that you get any assistance."

For the next half-hour Harry outlined the details of each of the five murders.

"It appears, Harry, that the victims had very little or nothing to do with each other, even the three who were studying at the university," remarked Brian.

"Yes, that's right," replied Harry. "Of the three university students, one lived at home and the others lived in private, offsite accommodation rather than on-campus. There's no evidence that they associated with each other at the university or in the city. Gladstone was at the teachers college but lived at home on a farm on the outskirts of town. Winton, the SP bookie, lived in a boarding house in town and had nothing to do with the others."

"So, what is the link between the victims?" asked the commissioner. "Or are these homicides just random?"

"That is the unanswered question," replied Harry. "If we knew that, we would be closer to a solution. A couple of them were involved with their church but they were from different denominations. Four of them were students but studying different subjects. And there is no connection through sport or community activities. Gladstone was in the Church of England choir, the Armidale Highland Pipe Band, the Boy Scouts and taught at Sunday school. Petherby sang in the Presbyterian Church choir but, other than that, none of the others were involved in those activities."

"Tell us about those numbers on the pendants around their necks and the cardboard signs. Were they on all five victims?" asked Brian.

"The pendants and signs were prepared by the same person and, together with the method of poisoning, it clearly indicates that it is the same killer in all cases."

"Do these pendants and signs give you any clues, Harry?"

"I really don't know yet but we have to ask whether the killer is trying to send us or the victims or their families a message, especially regarding the signs. In his own odd way, is he trying to tell us why he has committed these horrible crimes? The difficulty for us is that the numbers are not sequential and do not indicate the reason for the succession of killings so far. The apparent random numbers are confusing."

The commissioner sat back at the desk. "Have you been able to make head or tail of the signs?"

"For each victim there were two pieces of cardboard. On each of the smaller pieces was a single word: humility, temperance, diligence, chastity and diligence. The longer statements found on the larger sheets are from the Bible. This suggests to me that there is a strong underlying religious belief motivating the killer to commit these murders."

"Is it possible that he is driven more by visions brought on by psychiatric problems?" asked Brian. "Are we dealing with a real out-of-control nut-case?"

"There has to be a mental illness behind any string of murders of this nature, but I believe this man is very much in control. He knows what he is doing. Although the numbers are not in sequence, he seems to plan every move. Convincing the victim to arrive at a particular location where the killer has set up the table, chairs, bottles and glasses in advance has required careful organisation. But it might be that the detailed planning will bring him down in the end. He might leave that vital clue that will bring him down."

"Are you getting cooperation from the team up there?" asked Murray Fredericks.

"Oh yes, sir. Everyone at the station has been very supportive. Superintendent Johnston is a good leader and is behind Joe and me in our work. Joe is learning on the job but he'll make a good detective, and he puts in one hundred per cent every day."

Brian Ford wrote a name on a piece of paper and handed it to Harry.

"We have added a psychiatrist to Tony Jacobs's SIB team: Doctor Luke Dearing. We feel that he will be a valued member of the team; especially when dealing with these types of cases and those involving child offences and domestic crimes. I suggest you talk to Tony about this. And I want you to take some other members of Tony's team to Armidale. It's best that they work where these murders have taken place, not back here in their labs. I've already mentioned this to Tony and he is expecting you to see him before you go back to Armidale. Also, I'm sending you one of our brightest young detectives, Mary Rutledge. She might be of some help to you during your investigations. I believe that she worked well with you last time, so I will get her to travel together with the forensics group. Let me know if you need any more support up there. We must get to the bottom of this as soon as possible."

"Thank you, sir," replied Harry. "I intend to go to Redfern to see the team after I leave here."

"Thanks Harry," said the commissioner. "You may go now. But keep in touch with Brian here so we know what's happening."

***

When Harry entered the headquarters of the Scientific Investigation Bureau at Redfern, he ran into Rita Flynn, the fingerprint expert and his former romantic interest. She took Harry by both arms and blocked his path.

"So where did Mr Detective Taylor stay last night?" she said as she looked directly into his eyes.

"Hello Rita. I stayed at the Shelbourne last night. I didn't get in till late."

"Hey, you know there is always a bed for you at my place? That was never an excuse whenever you came to Sydney before, was it? You do still know your way to my place at Maroubra, don't you?"

"I apologise, Rita. I've heard so little from you in the last year and I thought you had lost interest; and I know you are now very much involved in your university studies. I've often rung at night but got no answer. I thought you might have struck up another relationship with some charming lecturer at the university. How are your studies going?"

Rita gave Harry a gentle slap on each cheek before she put her hands firmly on each side of his head and pulled it closer to her face. "Don't use my studies as an excuse, Harry. But I'll forgive you, because I have spies in Armidale and I've heard about young Colleen. You've made a good choice there. And if you do anything to hurt her you'll have to deal with me. Do you get my message loud and clear?"

Harry smiled and bent over to give Rita a kiss on the forehead. "Thanks, Rita, for being so understanding. And I'll promise not to do anything to hurt Colleen."

Rita laughed, stepped aside and walked arm in arm with Harry to the meeting room. As they walked in, there was a cheer from the squad. Tony Jacobs stood to shake Harry's hand.

"Take a seat, mate. You know everyone except Doctor Luke Dearing over there."

Harry reached across and shook hands with Luke. "Hello Luke. Brian Ford told me all about you and I'm sure you will be of great assistance up at Armidale on these cases."

Tony sat. "Take your time, Harry, and tell us all about these murders you have up there."

Harry walked to one of the blackboards and wrote the names of the five victims across the top. He noted the main points surrounding their murders under each name. On a second blackboard he listed some of the key characteristics of serial killers that he had found from his research in the library last Sunday.

For the next hour Harry answered questions from the team. They were similar to the ones from Murray Fredericks and Brian Ford earlier in the morning.

At the next break in questions, Tony spoke. "The commissioner and chief superintendent have asked me to send some of my team to Armidale to assist you and Joe with these cases. Brian said he is also sending Detective Mary Rutledge up with my team. So, what do you need from us?"

"Thanks Tony," replied Harry. "These murders are not straightforward. The victims are quite different and I can't put my finger on the psychological influences driving this man to commit these murders. So, I would very much value Luke Dearing's contribution. If you could also spare Rita Flynn, Jack Witherspoon and Ian Weaver, I would be very grateful because their combined expertise with prints, drugs and pathology would be very helpful."

"What about me?" called Archie Ingram as he chuckled. "I need to get away from Tony for a while; and I like Armidale."

"I can spare Rita, Jack and Luke but Ian is busy on another job and can't go. When do you want them, Harry?" asked Tony.

"As soon as possible. Let me know when they are coming and I'll book them into a hotel."

"Okay, Harry. I'll make their travel arrangements and will phone you with the details," replied Tony.

Harry stood and turned to the group. "We'll be very grateful for the help from the team. You know how much I value you all. I'll go now because I have to get organised for tomorrow."

Rita walked him to the door and gave him a kiss and a hug. "I'm looking forward to meeting Colleen."

Chapter 31
Thursday

Harry sat in the booth in the café in George Street. Soon after nine o'clock Fergus Whitelaw walked in with the stub of a roll-your-own cigarette hanging from his lip while he rolled another with both hands. His unironed shirt matched the wrinkles in his suit and loosely knotted tie. His shoes were dirty and worn. He threw his black bag containing his gown and wig into the corner of the bench seat, sat and sipped the mug of black coffee that Harry had pre-ordered for him.

"Bloody hell, Harry," snorted Fergus as he blew great clouds of smoke across the table. "Why have you been stirring up the ants' nests again? Stop banging the bloody ground to get them angry. Those bull ants have sharp nippers, and they can hurt."

Harry laughed. "The trouble is, Fergus, that you and I are too much alike. We don't like seeing injustice and we hate termites eating away at the foundations laid down by the good, honest workers."

"Talking about good officers," said Fergus, "I notice from my brief that there are some witnesses to be called with names like Twain, Tomlinson, Funnell, Lewis, Podger and Nolan. Aren't some of them the same characters who were against you in that case we had here two years ago?"

"Yes," replied Harry. "Twain was the chief superintendent who took me off the case when we were investigating several murders around Wagga in 1948. Twain appointed Lewis, Podger and Nolan from the CIB to take over my investigation, but you will remember that they stuffed it up, destroyed all our files, and I was reinstated. They also hated my guts because I was the lead detective responsible for sending their old CIB mates, Fred Sherman and Joe Cross, to gaol. As we left the courtroom, Lewis told me that he and his mates would get back at me for what I'd done. He told me to watch my back because they had friends."

"Who are the other two turkeys?"

"Dick Funnell was the crown sergeant at Wagga and Jack Tomlinson was on the main desk at headquarters. Both of them were in the CIB before the war and were friends of Twain, Sherman and Cross. Funnell has since retired and Tomlinson was transferred back to desk duties at Wollongong by the new chief superintendent."

"Did I read lately that there was an attack on you in Armidale?" asked Fergus. "If you're such a sucker for punishment why don't you just go out on the weekend and stick your head into a rugby league scrum opposite that tough cop Bumper Farrell who still plays prop for the Newtown Blues? If the rumours are correct he'll rearrange your face and chew off your ear. And he's also that tough detective in charge of the 21st Division at Kings Cross. It couldn't be worse than what we have here. Better still, you should ask Bumper to be on your side and he'll bang those clowns' heads together in no time. It'd be all over in five minutes."

Fergus blew another cloud of smoke across his coffee mug.

"Yes. Two criminal mates of Sherman and Cross recently attacked me in Armidale but I got the better of them. The difficulty is knowing who else will come around the corner or whether those two thugs were involved in the recent killings in Armidale—but enough of that. Before we go in can you just give me an overview of this misfeasance accusation as a refresher, because my mind has been on other things of late?"

Fergus scratched his unshaven face and sipped his coffee. "This tort has been part of English law for hundreds of years but, until recently, has rarely been used. In simple terms it means that you, as a government officer, were knowingly negligent in the performance of your duties and that your actions caused harm or damage to the Webbers. The plaintiffs are Mrs Webber and her brother-in-law and they are suing the government for compensatory damages over their financial losses suffered directly from your actions, or lack thereof."

"But I don't see that I was negligent in dealing with Webber's murder in Albury."

"Harry, Harry, Harry. I thought you were brighter than that," replied Fergus as he sipped his coffee and blew smoke into the mug. "It's got nothing to do with your investigation. We are surrounded by taipans and death adders. Look at the line-up of witnesses. All the police officers are friends of Sherman and Cross. After our hearing two years ago,

Lewis, Podger and Nolan were found guilty of gross negligence in dealing with Mrs Rose MacQuoid and the destruction of all your files regarding the Wagga serial killer. I smell a rat. I suspect that this is a conspiracy of ex-CIB members to get back at you. In the hope of getting compensation from the government for the death of Webber, his wife and brother have been convinced by these clowns to become the plaintiffs. I think they are the innocent pawns in this exercise. These bastards are using those poor people for their own devious purpose."

"But how do we prove our case?" asked Harry.

"It's not up to us to prove our case; they will have to prove their case. And to do so they will have to prove that you exercised your power knowing that it was illegal and that it resulted in a loss to the plaintiffs. They must prove that you did it with intent, without due respect for the plaintiff, and with reckless indifference to the lawful authority you had in carrying out your duties. It is not just negligence. It relates to a dishonest exercise of power. For them to successfully argue their case they will have to prove that your failure to act resulted in a loss to the plaintiffs. Leave it to me, Harry. Get me another coffee."

"How will the hearing proceed?" asked Harry.

"I don't know," replied Fergus. "These cases are so rare. The magistrate might take the approach of being like a mediator trying to reach an agreement between the parties, or he might adopt a more formal approach."

"Do you want something to eat, Fergus?"

Fergus stubbed out his cigarette. "God no. I'd rather have good cups of strong healthy coffee grown in the pure environment of the rainforests of South America. And I'll light my pipe with these magic tobacco leaves to calm my nerves. It'll get me through the day until dinner which I'll wash down with a good whisky made with the pure mountain waters of the Scottish Highlands. I want to live a good, clean, healthy life. Loosen up, Harry."

"Hey Fergus," said Harry as he sniffed the air after Fergus lit his pipe. "That is a sweet-smelling tobacco, the best I've ever smelled."

Fergus chuffed. "I have my favourite tobacconist in George Street and he keeps some special imported blends. I mix two of my favourites. One is called Bishops Choice and the other is Three Nuns."

"You are disgusting, Fergus, but I like you," replied Harry. "Now let's get into court."

***

As they entered the courtroom, Fergus introduced Harry to Timothy Cochran, the lawyer representing the Webbers. Harry nodded to Andrew Webber's wife Monica and his brother Kevin who were sitting on the other side of the room. Harry sat next to Fergus but turned when he heard noise from the back of the courtroom and noticed the ex-police officers enter and sit in the back row. Reg Lewis stabbed two fingers sharply towards his own eyes then turned them directly towards Harry. Harry responded with a smile and a mock salute. Fergus pulled a wrinkled handkerchief from his pocket and, with a loud snort, cleared his nose, which brought frowns to the others in the courtroom. A few minutes later, the magistrate, His Worship Stephen Lawford, entered from a door behind the bench, nodded to the standing gathering and sat.

Fergus and Tim Cochran rose to introduce themselves to the court.

"Before we start proceedings," said Stephen Lawford, "I want to clarify the nature of misfeasance and how we will conduct this hearing. Briefly, misfeasance in public office is a rarely used tort. It is a remedy for when harm has been caused by acts or omissions by a public officer who, in bad faith, either knew they were abusing their power or was recklessly indifferent to the limits of their power. Misfeasance is tried under civil law and not criminal law. I will listen to the claims from the plaintiffs and their witnesses after which the defendant and his witnesses may give their response. At any stage the proceedings will conclude if the two sides come to a settlement agreeable to me."

"Your Worship," said Fergus, "let's stop all the hullabaloo and nonsense that normally goes on in these hearings. Let's stop wasting the public's time and expense. These allegations are ridiculous and I ask that you throw this whole matter out of court now."

"Sit down now, Mr Whitelaw," shouted the magistrate. "This is not some boozy barbeque gathering in your backyard where you can dictate to your mates what will happen. This is a court of law and we will follow the proper procedures."

Fergus coughed loudly. "Thank you for the lesson on legal proceedings, but we don't have to defend this nonsense and, as there is no substance to the charges, I ask that you dismiss these matters now."

"What is your point, Mr Whitelaw?" demanded the magistrate.

"Your Worship, the plaintiffs, Mrs Monica Webber and Mr Kevin Webber, have travelled a long way from Albury. They are respectable people but they are relying on the evidence of that bunch of turkeys sitting at the back of the court."

"Mr Whitelaw," shouted the magistrate. "You will treat witnesses in this court with respect. Now stop wasting my time."

"That's the point, Your Worship. I want to save the court's time. This is a civil case, not criminal, but the witnesses at the back of the room are not here to support the Webbers. They are here to do damage to my client. Let's pay respect to the Webbers and listen to their case and then move on."

"This is a most unusual request, Mr Whitelaw. Have you discussed this with your client? And does he agree with your suggestion?"

Harry rose. "Your Worship, I wish to inform the court that I agree with Mr Whitelaw's request."

Timothy Cochran rose. "Your Worship, I find this request beyond all reason. Mr Whitelaw has no right to determine who appears as witnesses."

The magistrate turned to Timothy Cochran. "I agree. We will proceed with this hearing in the regular way. Call the plaintiffs."

Monica Webber was called to the stand. Timothy Cochran took her through her evidence, with his questions clearly geared to find fault in Harry's conduct of the investigation into the Wagga murders and the death of her husband. He teased out the details of the financial and reputational damage to the family and their accountancy business. Much mention was made of Andrew Webber's outstanding achievements in the sporting arena and his contributions to the welfare of the Albury community. It was a heart-rending presentation and achieved the result of gaining the attention of the magistrate.

When Fergus rose to cross-examine Monica, he was very courteous and gentle with his few questions.

"Was Detective Taylor thorough in his interviews with you?"

"Yes."

"Did he ever threaten you or your family?"

"No, he never threatened us," replied Mrs Webber, "but we claim that his inability to bring the killer to justice, when that person had already killed three other people before he murdered my husband, caused serious damage to our family and the business. We claim that Detective Taylor's slackness in investigating the earlier cases allowed the murderer to remain at large which led to him murdering my Andrew."

"As you did not know Detective Taylor before the murder of your husband, and you had no access to files relating to the earlier cases, how did you come to the conclusion that he was deliberately inefficient in carrying out his earlier investigations?"

"We were informed that he was removed from the case by Chief Superintendent Twain, and the detectives who took over the case informed us of Detective Taylor's inefficiency. They also recommended that we take action against Detective Taylor for damages caused by his inability in not catching the killer earlier. They said that Detective Taylor's tardiness allowed the killer to continue his killing spree which led to the death of my dear husband. They also told us about his ineptitude in conducting similar investigations into the multiple murders that occurred at Goonaburra in 1947."

Fergus turned sharply and pointed towards Lewis, Podger, Twain and Nolan sitting at the back of the court. "Are those men who are sitting in the back row the men who told you those lies about Detective Senior Sergeant Taylor?"

"Yes. They were so understanding and helpful to me, my family and to Andrew's family. I couldn't have asked for more from them. They were so helpful in advising us how to take the action here today."

"Are you aware that in this very court two years ago, Lewis, Podger and Nolan were found guilty of destroying all the relevant files of Detectives Taylor and McNulty on those cases as well as forcing another woman, by physical assault and intimidation, to falsely admit to killing the earlier victims?"

"But Mr Twain told us that he had to remove Detective Taylor from the position because of his inefficiency and the mistakes he made in the earlier cases. He also told me that I might have a case for compensation and that he was the chief superintendent, the third-highest-ranking officer at the time, and a true gentleman. And that he would support our claim."

"Thank you, Mrs Webber. No further questions."

Timothy Cochran took Kevin Webber through his testimony with emphasis on the financial and reputational damage to his accountancy firm from the death of his brother. He echoed the main points presented earlier by Andrew's wife, Monica.

During cross-examination, Fergus ignored the accountancy firm and concentrated on what the three disgraced detectives and Allan Twain had told Kevin about Harry's inefficiency and their advice to the Webbers to proceed with the current hearing.

Following that testimony, the magistrate called a halt to proceedings for lunch, with a recommencement scheduled for one o'clock.

Fergus and Harry were joined at the café by Tony, Mary, Jack, Luke and Rita who all came as support for Harry.

Chapter 32
Thursday

His Worship, Mr Lawford, brought the court to order and called upon Timothy Cochran to call his next witness. Ex-Chief Superintendent Allan Twain entered the witness box. To establish Twain's credibility as a witness, Timothy took him through his career history and his role as chief super during the war years, concentrating on his leadership of the Criminal Investigation Branch. Twain was in his element, explaining the difficulties he had coping with the volume of crime with a drastically reduced staff and the proud work done by his senior detectives in keeping the country safe. He took time outlining the serious criminals brought to justice in those difficult times.

"Why did you remove Detective Taylor from his investigation of the Riverina murders?"

Twain looked across at Harry.

"Detective Taylor had been a very dedicated and competent police officer. When he worked with me at the CIB before the war, I recognised him as a man with potential. He was very raw, but he was willing to listen and learn from the more experienced officers such as myself and Detectives Sherman and Cross who had proven track records in dealing with the worst criminals in this country."

"What changed that forced you to move him from the CIB?"

"It is well known that Detective Taylor joined the army and served his country with distinction but he was wounded in action. He returned to the police service in 1947 but he was not the same person. I believe that the after-effects of the war, including bouts of malaria and his wounding, led to him losing confidence in making clear decisions when investigating serious crimes."

"Which cases were affected?"

"At Goonaburra in 1947, he took far too long in dealing with a serial killer and he was distracted by the fact that he knew the killer personally. But I gave him some slack because of his experiences during the war and his illness."

"Did he improve after that?"

"I transferred him back to duties in the city where I could keep an eye on him. But I found that he was extremely envious of other officers who had stayed in the CIB and carried the burden of responsibilities here on the home front while he was away playing soldiers overseas."

"Is it right that he was later transferred to a country appointment?" asked Timothy Cochran.

"Yes," replied Allan Twain. "I felt he was not coping with the pressures of city life and the intensity of working in the big crime scene with the worst criminals. So I appointed him to the quieter environment of country Wagga Wagga."

"How did he cope in that environment?"

"Initially he went well, but then I had to question his performance. His investigation of the murders in the religious cult was not up to standard. It came to my notice that his love life was getting more attention than his work, and his drinking sessions at the Kapooka army base officers' mess were not of the standard expected of senior officers in the police force. It was a poor example to the good citizens of Wagga Wagga who had to abide by the law. Nobody should be above the law."

"Why was he removed from the serial murder cases two years ago when he was investigating the death of Andrew Webber, the husband and brother of my clients?"

"He should have wrapped up that investigation well before that murder happened and, had he done his job properly, Andrew Webber would still be alive today. Whether it was the after-effects of his war experiences or his love life or the effects of his drinking, I cannot say, but I had to remove him from those cases."

"Thank you, Mr Twain. I have no further questions."

Fergus rose slowly, looking up at the shaft of light coming in the high window, as if looking for divine inspiration, but knowing that it was never coming his way. He wiped the sleeve of his gown across his nose before spreading his arms wide, resembling a bat in flight. He brought his hands together in a loud clap and pointed both hands at Twain.

"You never went to the war, did you Mr Twain? You were always envious of Detective Taylor because he came back a hero with distinguished service and medals."

Twain banged the rail beside him. "I and other officers stayed back to do the dirty work to keep this country safe, but we didn't get recognition for that. We didn't need medals for the work we did. We did it to protect the citizens from the worst criminals who were taking advantage of a reduced force."

"You mentioned Detective Taylor's love life. Had you been spying on him through his bedroom window? Had you been sneaking looks as he cuddles and kisses his companions under the sheets? Had you had cameras installed to check on his love life? Did he do it out in the forest to avoid your scrutiny? Was it illegal to have romantic relationships in the police force? Did you have romantic relationships while in the police force?"

Timothy Cochran rose. "Objection, Your Worship. Relevance?"

The magistrate stared at Fergus. "Get on with it, counsellor. We don't want any amateur dramatics in this courtroom."

"Thank you, Your Worship. But it was Mr Twain who raised the issue of Detective Taylor's love life affecting his performance. I ask Mr Twain again to tell us what aspect of Detective Taylor's love life affected his performance. Was he so exhausted after his love-making that he couldn't put one foot after the other? Did Mr Twain personally observe that love-making to assess the level of exhaustion? What evidence did he have to come to that conclusion?"

Twain coughed into his handkerchief. "It was reported to me that Detective Taylor was swimming in the nude with his mistress in view of all the Wagga public."

"You are well aware, Mr Twain, that this matter has been dealt with before. Detective Taylor and Miss Flynn—who happens to be sitting at the back of this courtroom today and is a highly respected member of the police forensics team—were doing extensive investigations on the banks of the Murrumbidgee River, well away from the town, in temperatures of over 110 degrees in the shade. After many hours working in that heat they stripped to their underclothes and swam in the river to cool off. I have been assured that their underclothes covered much more of their body than the skimpy bathers that you used to wear as a lifesaver at Bondi Beach. Maybe, Your Worship, we could have a demonstration in court to prove my point?"

"Get on with it, Mr Whitelaw," snapped the magistrate.

"Mr Twain, you also mentioned Detective Taylor's excessive drinking. How much did he consume? On how many occasions? Did he drive a vehicle while intoxicated? Was he ever charged with such an offence? Which of your officers observed those drinking sessions? Are they in court today? Was he ever charged and convicted of those offences? If so, could you please present to this court the case files dealing with those charges?"

Twain looked down at his shiny boots. "I was informed that the other officers took pity on Detective Taylor because of the stress and wounds he suffered during the war and didn't proceed to charge him."

"You are telling this court that the other officers were negligent in their duty? They should have been the ones removed from their duties. Please name those officers now. Are they in this courtroom today?"

"Objection," shouted Timothy Cochran as he jumped to his feet.

The magistrate slapped his hand on the bench. "Enough, Mr Whitelaw."

"Thank you, Your Worship. I have no further questions of this witness."

Reg Lewis was called to the stand. Cochran took him through his extensive police career, with emphasis on his major cases with the CIB.

"Mr Lewis, could you please tell this court what you found when you took over the Riverina serial-murder case from Detective Taylor?"

"Let me make it very clear," replied Lewis. "I had the utmost respect for Detective Taylor when he worked with us in the CIB before the war but after he returned I noticed a distinct reduction in his drive and efficiency. It was as if his heart wasn't in it anymore. It was also reported to me that he had significantly increased his consumption of alcohol and became more interested in his women friends in Goonaburra, Sydney and Wagga Wagga. I tried to understand his situation because of the effects of his war service. But in the real world, criminals don't wait for officers to get treatment and get back on their feet before carrying out their crimes. If you can't do your job you have to step aside and let others do it, before the good citizens suffer more anguish and loss at home."

"What was the state of the investigation when you arrived in Wagga?"

Lewis took his time answering and never looked at Harry. "It was in a mess. There were no files. We had to begin from scratch. Detectives Taylor and McNulty were not up to dealing with cases like that. They hadn't the experience to do the job, and that resulted in the murderer continuing to kill innocent people including Mr Webber. His death was preventable."

"Thank you, Mr Lewis. I have no more questions."

Timothy Cochran sat down.

Fergus jumped to his feet, clapped his hands and stared at Lewis. "Is it true, Mr Lewis, that you worked extensively with Senior Detectives Sherman and Cross at the CIB?"

"Yes. They were outstanding officers and well recognised as the greatest crime-fighters in this country."

"But, as you very well know, they are now serving time in Grafton and Long Bay gaols for corruption and other serious crimes. Did you ever share in the bribes that they received from the well-known criminals in the city, and especially from the Kings Cross precinct?"

"No. Definitely not."

"Wasn't it you and your friends who frequently visited the illegal casino run by the well-known Whispers Durante at Kings Cross?"

"No."

"My sources tell me that you took advantage of the free prostitutes offered to you when you went to the casino."

"Definitely not. I find your accusation offensive, and I ask Your Worship to stop this line of questioning."

The magistrate leaned forward with a scowl. "Mr Whitelaw, I won't warn you again."

"Thank you, Your Worship, but I was merely trying to establish if this witness had any credibility to give evidence on this case. It has come to my notice that a person looking like this witness was filmed upstairs in Mr Whispers Durante's illegal casino, having sex with a prostitute. It is well known in the criminal world that Mr Durante offers girls to high-ranking police officers, senior law officers and politicians. If any charges of illegality are ever made against Mr Durante, he has threatened to release the films of those freely offered encounters starring the aforementioned prominent members of society. Maybe we could call a recess to see if I could borrow one of those films to play to the court."

"You'll do nothing of the sort," shouted the magistrate. "Now get on with your questioning."

"Mr Lewis, wasn't it you and your two lackeys—who are sitting at the back of this courtroom—who were found guilty of destroying all the Riverina serial murder files of Detectives Taylor and McNulty?"

"The files were not destroyed. They were stolen from a police vehicle."

"Mr Lewis, wouldn't you agree that criminals are not that stupid as to steal police files unless they were affected by those files? Who do you think would have benefited from their destruction or loss?"

"I have no idea. It could have been by accident."

"Is it not true that your officer mate, Mr Podger, who is sitting at the back there, choked a female witness into falsely confessing that she not only killed her husband but was also guilty of murdering the other victims in that case?"

"She admitted to those murders freely. It was established later that she was not of sound mind."

"There is no reason for me to bring out the court records, Mr Lewis. You and Podger and Nolan were found guilty here two years ago and you were removed from that case. Since then, you and your other mates of Sherman and Cross have been planning to get back at Detective Taylor. Were you, Podger or Nolan involved in organising the attack by two well-known criminal friends of Sherman and Cross against Detective Taylor recently in Armidale?"

"I don't know what you are talking about," replied Lewis with a snarl.

"That is very interesting, Mr Lewis. On the nights before and after that attack on Detective Taylor in Armidale, the Empire Hotel registered the names of Rogers and Lewitson as guests, and the manager's description of those two visitors exactly match that of you and Detective Podger. How do you explain that?"

"I know nothing of that. I have never been to Armidale."

"Isn't it true that you, Podger and your other mates were also involved with Sherman and Cross in the recent murders in Armidale?"

Timothy Cochran leapt to his feet but the magistrate put up his hand. "Mr Whitelaw, you will retract that question. I won't warn you again."

Fergus threw up his hands in anguish. "Don't you read the papers, Mr Lewis? The trouble with you, Mr Lewis, is that you and your mates, with your hatred of Detective Taylor, have conspired to convince Mr and Mrs Webber to act as pawns for you to bring on these ridiculous charges for your own gain because Detective Taylor exposed your crimes. The ones we should be sorry for are these two innocent people here from Albury who have done nothing wrong and who are still suffering from the loss of their wonderful Andrew. You are a blot on the good record of the New South Wales Police Force."

Fergus walked across to Timothy Cochran and whispered in his ear.

The magistrate slapped his hand on the bench. "Mr Whitelaw, resume your seat."

Fergus turned to face the bench. "Your Worship, I ask that you call a break in proceedings. Mr Cochran and I request a meeting with you in your chambers before continuing."

"The court will recess for thirty minutes."

***

On the resumption of proceedings the magistrate addressed the court. "Following my meeting with Mr Cochran and Mr Whitelaw, I have decided to terminate this case. I wish to make it clear to Mr and Mrs Webber that the court extends its sincere sympathy for your loss but there is no evidence that the actions of Detective Taylor had anything to do with the murder of Andrew."

There was stunned silence in the room.

The magistrate continued. "This court recognises that Mr and Mrs Webber brought this action by acting honestly on the advice of the former members of the CIB present in court today. I find that those officers acted dishonestly in convincing the Webbers to proceed. Their deliberate misrepresentation was aimed at causing harm to Detective Senior Sergeant Taylor and they used Mr and Mrs Webber to advance their cause."

The magistrate looked directly at Monica and Kevin Webber.

"I believe you deserve an apology and recompense from those officers, but that is for another time and place. This case is hereby dismissed. I demand the following people remain behind in court with Mr Cochran. They are Messrs Twain, Lewis, Podger, Nolan, Funnell and Tomlinson."

***

Harry, Fergus, Tony Jacobs and the rest of the SIB team retired to the Adams Hotel for a counter lunch and a few drinks.

Harry put his arm around Fergus's shoulder. "Now Fergus, tell us what really happened between you, the magistrate and Cochran."

Fergus took a long drag on his cigarette, coughed three times, sipped his whisky and wiped his mouth before answering. "Well, I informed the two of them that I have been an occasional visitor to the illegal casino run by Whispers Durante at Kings Cross and, while there, I had seen Fred Sherman, Joe Cross, Allan Twain, Reg Lewis, Chicka Podger and Merv Nolan, as well as judges and lawyers and prominent members of parliament, mixing freely with well-known criminal identities."

"Wow," gasped Harry. "That put the cat among the pigeons. How did they react?"

"When I told them that my very good friends at the *Sunday Truth* were pressuring me to give them all the details so they could do a front-page exposé about this case and those involved, Timothy Cochran agreed not to proceed," said Fergus.

"Were Lawford or Cochran involved?" asked Tony.

"My lips are sealed," replied Fergus as he took another long draw on his cigarette.

After two drinks, Harry left the group and the bar and headed for his MG.

***

He arrived home in Armidale at nine o'clock.

Chapter 33
Friday

Harry's body was stiff from the round trip to Sydney and his brain was still tired from the court case. So he ran ten laps around the oval in the brisk early morning air of Armidale to refresh himself. He was finding it difficult to remove the thoughts of the court hearing from his mind. He felt sorry for Monica and Kevin Webber who had been duped by the corrupt officers into believing they had a good case against Harry. As they left court yesterday, Harry attempted to console Monica and Kevin Webber but they were not in a mood to talk with anyone outside their immediate family.

Harry also found it difficult to comprehend why senior officers would go so far as to crucify a fellow officer. Harry could understand the bastardisation he experienced at boarding school because the bullies were other immature pubescent boys. But he now had to come to terms with the fact that senior officers in the police force were involved with serious crimes such as corruption, armed assault and murder and had established strong relationships with the top criminals. If they could do this in Sydney, could they also be involved with the recent killings around Armidale?

Harry's mind was still too tired to think too deeply, so he surmised that some combination of good and evil exists in every person, including those in the police force. He concluded that greed was likely a very strong motivation. Worse still, those police had the desire to exercise their power over more and more people, abusing their positions of authority.

Harry had a quick breakfast of toast and orange marmalade.

***

Harry drove to the station where he met with the two senior officers, Ray Johnston and Ken Wright.

"What happened to Twain and the other officers?" asked Ken.

"Tony Jacobs phoned me early this morning," replied Harry. "He said that Matt Jackson from the desk at headquarters had phoned him. He said that the magistrate contacted the commissioner and recommended the sacking of the ex-CIB officers involved in this case. He also said that the magistrate and the commissioner should approach the government with a view to setting up a Royal Commission to investigate the link between corrupt officers and well-known criminals."

"Wow," said Ken. "They are serious. And about time."

"Tony also heard that Jack Tomlinson handed in his resignation," said Harry. "My guess is that Lewis, Podger and Nolan would be determined to fight on if they were charged. I don't know about Funnell."

"Well, now that matter is out of the way you'll have a clear path to get on with the current cases here," said Ray. "You can be sure of our support for you and Joe. Just tell us when you need anything."

"Thanks Sir," replied Harry, "that means a lot. But I still have to be alert for the next move by those mongrels. Lewis, Podger, Nolan, Twain and their mates Sherman and Cross are not going to give up because of the case yesterday or because of any charges that might be laid against them. In fact, it will make them even more determined to get back at me. I just have to watch my back. Next time they will be more careful in their planning; and they won't be sending goons like Simpson and Buttsworth to knock me over."

Harry walked to the tea room where he had to answer numerous questions from Joe and the other officers. At nine-thirty Graham McInnes came into the room from the desk to announce that a woman called Mrs Van Brouwer called to say her husband had not arrived home last night and had not opened his store this morning.

"I checked with the hospital and the other officers," said Graham, "and there were no reports of any accident or incident involving a Mr Van Brouwer. I put out a notice to all officers to keep a lookout for this man."

***

Harry and Joe drove to College Street where they knocked on the door of a neat weatherboard house with a verandah on three sides. The door was opened by a woman in her early forties. She introduced herself as Mrs Peta van Brouwer. Two young girls about the ages of ten and eight were peeking around a door further down the corridor. Mrs Van Brouwer was dressed in a plain white blouse, cream cardigan and grey woollen skirt. She was tall and painfully thin with a pale complexion and sad deep-set eyes. Her hair was thin and wispy. Her make-up couldn't cover the bruises on her neck and hands.

Harry and Joe were invited into the lounge room filled with high-quality furniture and they sensed an atmosphere of orderliness and discipline.

Harry asked the first question. "When did you last see your husband?"

"My husband Jan left here at five-thirty yesterday morning. He leaves precisely at that time every morning to go to the shop to prepare the food items for sale during the day. He owns a delicatessen in Rusden Street, around the corner from the old Minto Hotel. On Mondays to Fridays he remains at the shop until seven o'clock at night after which he comes home for dinner. On Saturdays he leaves at the same time in the morning but is home by one o'clock for lunch."

"When did you realise that there was something wrong?" asked Joe.

"Jan phoned me at seven o'clock last night to say that a man who was a regular customer, who he knew at church, had come in and wanted to talk with him. He told me the man was always very friendly and that they were going to enjoy a glass of schnapps and good conversation. He told me not to wait up."

"Did he come home last night and then leave early this morning before you woke up?" asked Harry.

"No. He never came home. And it is always my duty to get up early to prepare his breakfast before he leaves and to have his bag packed with the day's cash."

"Could he have stayed in the shop overnight?"

"When Mrs Vera McDonald, the shop assistant, arrived at seven this morning she couldn't get into the shop. She doesn't have a key and depends on Jan being there early to open up. The door was locked, the lights in the shop were not on and nobody answered her knocking. She
214

went around the back but could not see Jan through the window, so she went to the telephone box and called me."

"Did you go to the shop and open up?" asked Harry.

"I don't have a set of keys. Jan is the only one with keys. He doesn't trust anyone else."

"Did your girls hear or see anything of their father last night or this morning?"

"No. I've kept them home from school today until we sort out what happened to Jan."

"Is there someone to look after them?" asked Harry. "I want you to come to the shop with us."

"I'll ask Mrs Tanner next door. She has always been such a help since we moved here."

"I detect a strong South African twang in your speech," said Harry. "How long have you been here?"

"Yes. We came from Pretoria. We were unhappy with what was happening there so we came to Australia two years ago. We started first in Melbourne but decided to move to a good country town early this year. When the opportunity to buy the shop here came up, Jan grabbed it."

After Mrs Van Brouwer took the girls next door she climbed into the wagon with Harry and Joe.

***

Upon arriving at the shop they met Vera McDonald who was waiting nervously on the footpath. She expressed her concern that Jan was not at the shop. She pointed to the red and black BMW 340 sedan in the laneway beside the shop.

"Mr Van Brouwer's car is still parked where he normally parks it but he hasn't opened the front door or unlocked the back door for me to help him get the shop ready."

Harry asked Joe to go to the phone box and call Snowy Smith, the locksmith, to come and open the shop. Harry peered through the front window.

Harry put his hands up to the front window and spoke to Mrs McDonald. "I can see the front counter with what looks to be a refrigerated glass cabinet filled with a range of food items and there appears to be a walk passage to the left leading behind the counter to a door. Over to the right in front of the counter I can see two small tables and chairs. On top of the counter to the right there is a milkshake machine. On the wall there are photographs of the wild animals from South Africa and men on safari with high-powered guns. Everything in there looks in order."

"That door to the left goes to the back room," said Mrs McDonald.

While they waited for the locksmith, Harry asked Mrs McDonald about her work in the shop.

"I was so pleased to get the job but it hasn't been easy. Mr Van Brouwer is always so insistent about being here on time every day. If I am a minute late, he docks an hour off my wages. That's why I thought he must be sick this morning or had an accident for him to be late. Then I saw his car and thought he must have gone for a walk, which would be most unusual. He is a very disciplined man and he does not tolerate a change to routines. He gets very angry if things aren't perfect. I've had to do a lot of learning about African foods and have often made mistakes. He sometimes gets so angry with me, even in front of the customers, but I just keep quiet and put up with it. I need this job."

Ten minutes later Snowy Smith arrived with Joe. He studied the locks.

"Yes. I remember putting these locks on the front and back doors earlier this year. There are multiple locks of the best quality on each door. Mr Van Brouwer didn't want anyone getting into this shop. I thought he must be hiding boxes of valuable diamonds he had brought from South Africa. I tried to tell him that we live in a quiet country town with little crime, but he insisted on the best."

Mrs Van Brouwer nodded. "You have to understand that we came from South Africa where there were lots of crime and break-ins and we needed security."

Snowy worked on the locks for ten minutes before opening the front door.

Harry pointed to Joe. "Get the fingerprint kit from the wagon. Before anyone else goes in, dust both the handles and locks on the front and back doors. I'll go in to check if the owner is here."

Harry checked both sides of the counter inside the front of the shop. Nothing seemed out of place. He walked through to the back room. It was a large room. On one wall were two large ovens. On the other wall were two large commercial refrigerators. On the next wall were high cupboards. Another door led to storerooms stacked with tinned and packaged food items and equipment. Harry walked towards a large bench of solid pine in the centre of the room. On top were two small glasses with a small amount of liquid in each. Next to the glasses was a small plate with some biscuit crumbs and remnants of cheese. In front of the bench were two stools and a half-empty bottle of schnapps. Shiny pots, pans and cooking implements hung from the bottom of the wall cupboards. Everything appeared to be in its correct position. There was no sign of the owner.

After Joe had taken prints from the inside of the back door, Harry called to Snowy to work on the back door deadlocks to allow him to have access to the backyard. He returned to the front to talk to the two women. "Mrs McDonald, have you ever had complaints from customers or was anyone angry with Mr Van Brouwer?"

"I hate to say this in front of Mrs Van Brouwer—because she is such a beautiful person who has always treated me with the utmost respect—but her husband is very strict and he often berates me in front of customers if I get one thing out of place. He flies into temper outbursts if things aren't done exactly as he wants them. I am the third woman to work here this year because the other two left in tears after being abused by him. My friend Mary, who worked here, warned me. I needed a job because I lost my dear Dougie who was killed on the Kokoda Track in New Guinea, and I have three kids to look after so I put up with his abuse."

"I notice in the refrigerated glass case there are lots of foods that I don't recognise. What are those things?" asked Harry.

Mrs McDonald pointed to various items. "That is biltong. Next to that are boerewors, the South African sausages; skilpadjies, which is lamb's liver wrapped in netvet; and those pastries are Hertzoggies."

"How did you get along explaining these to the customers?"

"It was difficult at first. Some of our customers are from South Africa and they love coming in here, and others gradually grew to enjoy coming in here to try the exotic foods. But I often get into trouble for not knowing every detail about every product. I am good with the traditional products in a delicatessen but not with the new African ones."

"Thank you, Mrs McDonald, you have been very helpful. Would you two ladies move outside until we look around. Don't touch anything. After we have looked through these premises, Detective Simms will take your fingerprints so we can eliminate them from any others we find."

Harry asked Joe to follow him out the back. The yard was not large but had a gate opening on to a side lane. The ground was covered by paving stones neatly arranged in a hexagonal pattern. There were no weeds anywhere. To the right was a toilet. Joe opened the door to check. There was nobody in there.

"It is pristine clean in there," said Joe as he retreated from the cubicle. "There are no stains or mess but I'll check everything for prints."

Towards the rear of the yard was an incinerator beside a shed. It was clean with no ashes left in the fire-box and no rubbish ready for burning. To the left of the incinerator were two pallets ready for the carrier to pick up. To the right was a forty-four-gallon drum fitted with a removable lid that was closed by a leaver-locking ring clamp. It was different from regular petrol or diesel drums which have a small screw cap on top.

"This looks interesting, Joe," said Harry. "This could be a drum used for salting food or for pickling gherkins. Help me take off this clamp and let's look to see what's in here."

As they undid the clamp and removed the lid, Harry and Joe jumped back.

"Bloody hell!" shouted Joe as he raised both hands to his face. "What the hell is all that?"

Chapter 34
Friday

Harry placed the lid and clamp carefully against the side of the drum. He and Joe leaned over the drum to get a better look.

"Oh my God," said Harry. "That is a man's decapitated head floating in the liquid. It could be Van Brouwer but I don't know him, so we'll need verification."

"Look," said Joe as he moved to the right to reduce the reflections of the sunlight off the surface of the liquid. "That looks like a leg, and it's also cut off. We'll have to get Mrs Van Brouwer out here to verify if this is her husband."

"No Joe. Definitely not. She mustn't see this. If it is her husband, it would be too much of a shock. There are other ways to identify him. Besides, we can wait until David Hobbs cleans up the body and has it on the table at the parlour. We could ask Mrs Van Brouwer to come to the funeral parlour after that to identify him by showing her just his face."

"As I look deeper into the drum," said Joe, "it appears that all this man's limbs and head have been cut off. This killer is mad. He has a serious illness. How can we deal with a nut-case like this?"

"That's for us to work out, Joe."

As Harry moved to the left for a better look, his foot touched the lid and clamp which rolled to the side of the drum and clanged on the paving stones with sharp rattling bangs.

"Look," said Joe. "There are signs stuck on here."

Two pieces of white cardboard were affixed to the underside of the lid with tape. On the smaller one was written:

Patience

and

Respect

The larger second sheet had the following words:

***Put your sword
back in its place.***

"This is definitely the work of our serial killer," said Harry. "Those signs have been handwritten in the same manner and on the same type of cardboard as the others. It is some sort of message he is leaving, but it is difficult to know what is in his mind as he goes about these killings."

"Who is he leaving them for—us or his family?" asked Joe.

"Let's start by getting the ladies out of here and secure this backyard," said Harry. "Nobody is to enter any part of this property without my permission. We'll let Mrs McDonald go home and we'll take Mrs Van Brouwer home. When we get there, I want you to go next door to her neighbour who is minding the children and ask if she can stay with her. I don't want her and the kids there by themselves. She seems too frail to deal with this alone. We need to bring back photos of her husband so that we can check if this bloke in the drum is him."

Harry turned and noticed the shed door had been jemmied and was slightly ajar. He opened the blade of his pocket knife and used it to fully open the door. Inside were drums of kerosene for the heater, diesel for the generator, brooms, dustpans, tools and some gallon tins of preserved prunes, peaches and apricots on shelves.

"Look," said Joe as he pointed to the bottom shelf. "Those clothes have been neatly folded as if freshly ironed. And those boots are so clean and neatly arranged. The apron folded neatly next to them has *Safari Delicatessen* printed on the front. I'm guessing that they belong to the owner."

Harry stepped forward with his handkerchief wrapped around his right hand. "I'll look to see if the shop keys are in the pocket of the trousers. Yes, here they are. If they fit the locks then they will belong to Mr Van Brouwer."

Harry tested the lock on the back door. They worked. "This will save Snowy cutting another set for Mrs Van Brouwer."

"Isn't it interesting that the killer took his time to arrange the victim's clothes so neatly in the shed?" said Joe as he pointed to the lower shelf. "Could he be a bit bonkers in the head? It seems that he has a fixation with order and discipline. He is obsessed. I bet he was made to wash his hands five times before he came to the table for breakfast or dinner. Everything is perfectly arranged. Could this be a reaction to active duty during the war, Harry? I've heard about all these old blokes from the First World War who suffered from shell shock. Could he be like that?"

"I can see what you are getting at, Joe, but I doubt this man served in any war. Returned soldiers usually don't want to see any more killing. They've seen too much already and they develop a deep respect for life."

"I see what you mean," replied Joe.

"What is more interesting is that that man out there in the drum was dismembered, but there is no sign of blood on those clothes or in this backyard or in the shop; not even on the drum or lid. If that was done here, that is what I would call obsessive-compulsive cleanliness to the nth degree. But I still want you to dust everything inside and out for fingerprints. He might have made at least one mistake."

"What next Harry?" asked Joe.

"When we finish examining these premises, I'll lock up this place and I'll return to the station. We want every officer out there looking for this killer. I'll also call the commissioner and chief super at headquarters to let them know of this latest body."

Joe turned. "I'll ask Mrs McDonald if she wants a lift home on the way to taking Mrs Van Brouwer back to her neighbour's place."

"Good idea Joe. After you drop all of us off, call into the hardware store. I want you to buy some small and large tarpaulins, buckets with sealed tops, bottles with screw-top lids for sealing liquids and large rubber gloves, even if you have to get the ones the welders use. I'll call Gregory Ebsworth and David Hobbs. And I'll pick up the cameras from the station."

Harry and Joe walked back to the front of the shop and sat with the two women. Harry leaned forward and took hold of Mrs Van Brouwer's hands. Her thin fingers were so frail.

"We're finished here for the time being, Peta. Detective Simms will drive you home now. And he will ask your neighbour Mrs Tanner to stay with you and the girls while we continue with our investigation."

Mrs McDonald put up her hand. "I'll go with Mrs Van Brouwer and stay with her and the girls. I can't do anything here."

"Thank you, Mrs McDonald," said Harry. "You are so kind. You can come with us in the police wagon."

Before they left, Harry and Joe locked the back gate and rear door to prevent entry from the side lane. Harry used the shop phone to contact Graham McInnes at the police station to arrange for a constable to be sent around to the shop to ensure nobody entered the site. They removed the side of a cardboard box and wrote a notice that the shop was closed until further notice. They placed the notice on a chair against the front window.

***

Joe dropped Harry at the police station then proceeded to the Van Brouwer house in College Street where he dropped off Peta and Vera and picked up photos of Jan.

***

Harry met with Ray Johnston and Ken Wright to fill them in on the current situation.

Ray turned to Ken. "Ken, I want you to call a meeting of all officers at midday to inform them of the latest developments and for them to change their programs to include searches of all areas in the district with a view to finding any evidence of the serial killer. Get them to check the register of visitors at every hotel from Guyra through Armidale and on to Uralla, Walcha and Tamworth. They are to question anyone who might have information that might lead to their capturing. Question any strangers in town."

Harry phoned the commissioner to alert him to the current situation. He then phoned Tony Jacobs.

"Tony, we have another murder on our hands. How soon can you get the team up here to Armidale? We need them as soon as possible."

Harry briefed Tony on the latest case so that he could alert the team before they came to Armidale.

Tony replied. "Sorry mate. I've only just had their travel plans confirmed now. Jack and Rita will be arriving late tonight in the wagon with the gear, while Luke and Mary are coming in by plane tomorrow morning."

***

Harry drove to the delicatessen where Joe was waiting for him to unlock. They unloaded the hardware items from Joe's wagon at the back gate in the side lane.

"Help me lay out these tarps, Joe. I want the big one near that drum and the smaller ones spread out near the shed. We'll also need the buckets close to the drum. Put on a pair of those long rubber gloves and pull them up to your elbows. As we get the body parts out, try not to get any liquid in your gloves. Remember the trough of water where we found Gladstone. That had acid in it. As we remove each part we'll bucket some of the liquid to get to the limbs at the bottom of the drum. Keep samples of the liquid in those sealed buckets for later examination."

Harry pulled on some gloves and gently lifted the severed head from the drum and laid it on the large tarp. The skin was pale and wrinkled on the forehead. Around the mouth, below the walrus moustache, the skin had a faint bluish tone.

Harry pointed at the cut edge on the neck. "That cut is so neat. There was no struggle when that was done. There are no other injuries to the face or head. Obviously, he was dead or at least unconscious before dismemberment. There is no tearing of the flesh and no rough edges. Whoever did this used a very sharp scalpel or razor-edged knife. Look at the vertebrae on either side of that cut. They have little damage. That really is such a neat job. The person who did this has the skills of a butcher or a surgeon or a veterinarian or someone skilled in the dissection of animal bodies."

"What about those people in the zoology department at the university, Harry?" asked Joe. "They were all dissecting rats when we went there and they might also do dissections on larger animals. What do you think?"

"It's a good thought, Joe, but I think this person is more skilled and experienced than those students."

"But it could be an experienced zoology lecturer who has been dissecting animals most of his adult life. Remember that three of the victims have been university students."

Joe bucketed some of the liquid from the drum, allowing an arm to come to the top.

Harry removed it from the drum and laid it onto the tarp. "Look at the skin. There is not much wrinkling on the hand and there is little discolouration, which indicates that it has not been long in the liquid."

They repeated the process until the other arm, both legs and main body had been removed and laid out on the tarp. They had difficulty getting the torso out from the drum without spilling the liquid over themselves.

As Joe bucketed the rest of the liquid from the drum, he called to Harry. "Look here at the bottom. There is another coloured pendant attached to what looks like a leather bootlace."

Harry took a wooden garden stake from the side of the shed and lifted the article out of the drum. He turned it over in his glove.

"That one looks the same size as the others," said Joe. "It feels like the same type of metal and has similar colouring but this one has the number 5 marked on it."

"Okay," said Harry. "This just confirms we have the same killer. However, I'm still interested in the skilled way the killer dismembered the body. Did he bring his own equipment? Did he use what was here in the shop? You look around here, Joe, and I'll search inside the shop."

Harry searched through all the cupboards and drawers in the kitchen area but found only cutlery knives, a serrated bread knife and small vegetable knives, none of which could have separated a man's head from his body. When he looked up at the far end of the overhead cupboard, he found a thick leather belt to which was attached a solid butcher's cylindrical knife holder containing five knives hanging from a hook at the end of the cupboard. Harry took a clean tea towel from the counter and removed the knives from the holder. As he placed them on the bench, he noticed a small piece of white cardboard attached by string to the handle of one of the knives.

On it was written:

This is the one
you're looking for.

Harry called to Joe. "Come in here quick. This killer is getting so cocksure of himself that he is now deliberately leaving clues for us. This probably is the knife he used for the dismemberment. It is a butcher's boning knife. This large size is the type used by the slaughtermen in abattoirs to cut up the carcasses ready for display and sale in butchers' shops. Are we now looking at someone like that as our killer?"

"How will we check that, Harry?" asked Joe.

"The big towns have their own abattoirs but in most of the small towns the killing and preparation is done by the local butcher. This could have been done at the saleyards or on one of the local farms where the livestock come from. It won't be easy to trace. Even if it was done here, there are no immediate neighbours on any side of the shop who might have been disturbed."

"If you like, I'll check up on regional abattoirs when we get back to the station," said Joe.

Both David Hobbs and Gregory Ebsworth arrived independently at the front of the shop. There were muted greetings all round. Harry explained the situation and led them to the backyard to view the body.

"I don't have to waste time on this one, Harry," said Gregory. "He's certainly dead, and by the looks of him, by dismemberment."

"We can't be sure of that," said Harry. "He could have been poisoned to death before being cut up. I found two glasses and a half-empty bottle of schnapps. The killer could have used the same method as in the other cases where he poisoned them with phenobarbital. But you won't have to do the testing because I'll have all the SIB team here by tomorrow morning. So, hold off on the cause of death until they do their examination."

"Thanks Harry," replied Gregory. "I'll hold the death certificate until you give me the green light. I must fly now. I have to do an operation on a farmer who lost some fingers in the chaff cutter."

Harry and Joe helped David wrap the body parts in the tarps and loaded them into the hearse. It was an unpleasant task, but they did it with little fuss or talk.

Harry approached the cabin of the hearse as David was about to leave. "Could you do your best at laying out the body parts to make it look like they are in one piece, and arrange it so that everything is covered except for the face? I will be bringing this man's wife to the parlour later. Joe already has photographs of her husband. When she gets there just show his face for identification. Thanks mate."

***

Harry and Joe returned to the station before Joe went off to talk to the butchers in town and check the abattoirs. Harry arranged accommodation at Bruyn's Caledonian Hotel for Tony's team and prepared the initial reports on the day's activities.

Chapter 35
Saturday

After breakfast, Harry drove to Bruyn's Caledonian Hotel to meet Rita and Jack. He found them in the breakfast room. They looked tired after the drive from Sydney yesterday. Rita stood and gave Harry a big hug and kiss.

"This latest case looks very serious, my friend. How are you coping? Are you getting support from the local team?" she asked.

Harry shook Jack's hand and they all sat down. Harry poured himself a cup of tea from the pot on the table. "It's been tough but all of the officers are great. Superintendent Ray Johnston and Senior Crown Sergeant Ken Wright have both been very supportive. My sidekick, Joe Simms, is still a bit raw but he gives me one hundred per cent effort and support."

"I remember you had problems with a couple of officers in Wagga," said Rita.

"Yes," replied Harry. "Dick Funnell was ex-CIB and mates with Sherman and Cross. I hope he gets his comeuppance in court one day. It's nothing like that here."

"What do you want to do with us, Harry?" asked Jack.

"After breakfast I'll take you to the station to meet Ray and Ken. We'll set the team up in a spare room in the Sheriff's Cottage across the way. It's not big but we'll be mostly out in the field. We have prisoners in one cell but we can use the other one."

Jack burst out laughing. "What are you going to charge me with, Harry?"

"Gross insolence and insubordination," replied Harry as he pointed at Jack.

The three of them sat back and had a good laugh.

"We have always worked well together on other cases and I'm so pleased to have you here," said Harry.

Harry tapped the table. "The others fly in at ten. After we book them into the hotel, we'll take you all to the delicatessen where the latest murder took place. After that we'll meet back at the station to plan our strategy."

When Jack went to the toilet, Rita put her hand on Harry's shoulder. "How's the fair Colleen? Are you doing the right thing by that girl as I asked? I hope it is not just another wild fling?"

Harry blushed. "Colleen and I are still seeing each other. In fact, you might get a chance to meet her. She's coming into town tonight. I've asked her to come and have dinner with the team. You can buy the bottle of wine, Rita."

Rita punched him on the arm. "Right, mate. You wait until I have a good talk with Colleen. I think she and I will get along just fine. And if I have to buy the wine, so be it."

Rita gave Harry another hug.

***

Following breakfast, the three of them went to the police station where Harry introduced them to Ray and Ken. Ray had called a special briefing meeting to introduce Rita and Jack to the local officers. Following that meeting they walked to the Sheriff's Cottage to set up in the limited space.

***

At ten o'clock Harry picked up Mary and Luke from the airport and drove them to the Sheriff's Cottage. He spoke to the whole team.

"At this stage, we won't discuss all of the cases. We will go immediately to the delicatessen where the last murder took place. I want you to cover that scene while it is still relatively fresh. We'll follow that with a visit to the funeral parlour to examine the body. Then we'll meet to go over the details of all six cases. Bring all of your gear and let's get started."

***

Harry and Joe took two wagons and drove the team to Rusden Street. After a quick walk through the shop and the backyard, Rita called to Harry.

"I want all of you except myself and Jack out of here now. We need an open go to collect samples without you lot polluting the crime scene further. We'll let you know when we are done."

"Why do you want us out? Why can't we help?" asked Harry.

"We are looking for blood stains but we need to take samples of dust from all areas. So we don't want it polluted by you or your boots, hair or clothes."

Joe pointed to the floor. "This place is so clean you could eat your breakfast off it."

Rita became agitated. "Get out, Joe, and the rest of you with him. You'd be surprised what can be found in dust—fibres, dried blood, small particles of food, hair, skin and powder from ballistics. Go up to the morgue and examine the body or whatever else you need to do, but get out of here."

"Okay," said Harry. "Luke and Mary, you come with me to the funeral parlour. And Joe, you stay here to make sure nobody enters these premises."

"Before you go, Harry," said Rita, "where can we get our hands on a decent microscope?"

"All in hand," replied Harry. "I've already lined one up in the science building at the university tomorrow. I'll leave Joe here in case you or Jack want anything. I'll take Luke and Mary to the parlour now."

***

When they arrived at the funeral parlour, Harry asked David Hobbs to wheel out the gurney with the body parts. Mary stepped back, stunned, but then took out her notebook and started to record the details. Luke put on some rubber gloves and stepped calmly towards the gurney. He examined each body part carefully.

"What do you think, Luke?" asked Harry. "What type of person would take so much care dismembering a body? All the cuts are so neat and clean."

"In most of the murders I've been involved in, death mostly resulted from violent assault using guns, sharp weapons such as a knife, blunt instruments, fists or boots. But look at this corpse. Other than the cuts to dismember the body, I can't see any other external wounds."

Mary tapped her pen on her notebook cover. "If the dismemberment took place at the deli, I can't fathom why a criminal would be so stupid to stay behind after the victim is dead to carefully dismember the body and clinically clean the site before leaving. The extra time taken to complete those tasks would increase his chances of being caught. We'll see if Jack and Rita find any blood."

"This is not your average dumb or impulsive murderer," said Luke. "I believe that this person is mentally unstable. But it also suggests at least that this person is capable of exacting plans and their precise execution. Without talking with this person or knowing them, it is difficult to make a clinical diagnosis regarding any specific psychological disorders. There has been a lot of recent medical research into disorders such as schizophrenia but we don't know enough about that condition yet to judge it as causative in cases like these."

"Can we say what type of person we are dealing with?" asked Mary.

"I'm only guessing at this stage, but I'd say that this person probably had a strict and maybe brutal upbringing that was dominated by regimentation, rules and regulations and severe penalties for disobedience. His mother or father could have suffered from alternating extreme high and low emotional states or mood swings which were taken out on the children. In such an environment, some children become so conditioned to that way of surviving that they obey the rules and regulations without question. At the same time, they become very intolerant of others who don't meet those same standards. They mimic the behaviour of their parents but in a controlled way. In continuing with that behaviour, they experience a sense of real power over others. And eventually some discover that their most rewarding sense of power comes from the act of murder."

"Does that mean, Luke, that we are looking for a reclusive person who sees others as irresponsible and below their level?" asked Harry.

"Some could go that way but many see themselves more as saviours of the human race by eradicating undesirables so that the good people are protected from them. Many join community organisations, especially those involving young people, and are often seen as upstanding citizens for their contributions to society. The problem for you now,
230

Harry, is how you find the one person who is the killer among the many types of similar people in Armidale. How do you pick them?"

"You're only giving me problems, Luke, not solutions."

Luke grinned. "I can give you patterns of behaviour but you are the detective, Harry. That's why they pay you that big salary."

"Ha ha. Thanks a lot."

"However," said Luke, "we are probably looking for a narcissistic type who is a perfectionist, is anal retentive, acts compulsively, harbours a deep-seated intolerance and hatred of others who do not come up to their own standards, and who won't listen to advice. Those character traits might have developed in households where there was no love and where physical violence was common."

"Are such people also deeply religious?" asked Mary.

"Good question, Mary. Religious motivation for murder is certainly not uncommon, despite one of the Ten Commandments strictly forbidding such acts. But you can get some over-zealous types who believe they are on a mission from God to literally and practically cleanse the world of sinners, going on a self-righteous rampage of murder. But unless the killer is interviewed or confesses, it is impossible to know whether their faith began in childhood or was developed as an adult, whether they belonged to a traditional church or some breakaway religious group, or exactly what drove them to take such an extreme step to achieve their goal. I might add that this doesn't just apply to Christian denominations; any religion can produce people who can justify the death of innocents by their beliefs. And if you mix piousness with a mental illness then all manner of heinous crimes are possible. Such extreme behaviour is often seen in the various cults around the world and could be worth looking at."

***

At four o'clock Harry took Mary and Luke back to the delicatessen and checked on Joe, Rita and Jack.

"Okay, stop what you are doing. We'll take you all back to the hotel to unpack, get freshened up and I'll see you in the lounge bar at five."

They locked the shop and secured the site.

***

At five-thirty Colleen came into the hotel lounge bar and gave Harry a hug and kiss. Harry did the introductions.

"I'm sorry, Harry, but I don't feel like going to the dance or the pictures tonight. I've just come from the saleyards and I'm in my work gear. Could we give it a miss tonight?"

"Sure, I feel the same. We have been flat out on the latest case all day. Join us for dinner here. You don't have to change. Rita is buying the drinks tonight."

Rita stood up, picked up her glass and threatened to throw the contents over Harry. "Now you listen here, young Harry. If you're not nice to me I'll go back to Sydney and leave the team without a real expert. Now what's it to be?"

"Okay, okay, I give in," said Harry as he feigned shock and horror. "I'll buy the bottle tonight."

Colleen smiled. "Okay, I'll stay, but I must go to the ladies' room to freshen up. I won't be long. Order me a gin and tonic, Harry."

Rita put down her glass. "I'll go with you, Colleen. You can show me the way."

The two of them walked out of the room as Harry watched them chat like old friends. He was uneasy not knowing what Rita would say to Colleen about their earlier relationship, or if she would say anything at all. It was fifteen minutes before they returned to the lounge.

After a couple more drinks and a three-course meal, the team retired to their rooms.

***

Colleen drove her truck and Harry picked up the MG from the station and drove back to his house.

As they slipped into bed together, Harry asked "What did you two girls talk about in the powder room? You were gone for ages."

Colleen smiled, put her arm across Harry's chest and pulled him closer. "Wouldn't you like to know?"

Chapter 36
Sunday

Harry and Colleen ran laps around the oval but Colleen didn't enjoy running like Harry did. She would rather go to the racecourse and ride horses. They returned to the house, showered together, dressed and ate a breakfast of bacon and eggs.

"I have to get going," said Colleen. "Dad and I have to fix the fences in the bottom paddock. The big red bull knocked over the old posts the other day."

"Yes," replied Harry. "It might be Sunday but there's no rest for the wicked. I'll have all the team out again on the job with me today."

Colleen stood in front of Harry, pushed the hair back from his face and looked him in the eyes. "You will be missing one of your team this morning. Rita is coming out to the property with me. She wants to see what happens on the farm."

Harry pushed back. "No way. I need her here on the job. I don't care if it's Sunday."

"Stop and think about it. Rita comes from the city. She's never been on a farm. And if she is going to understand this area where these murders are taking place, she needs to see what the country looks like and what us farm people do for a living. For example, she can't understand why we never lock our houses, sheds or trucks around here, or why we trust our neighbours and others in town. I promise to have her back by ten."

"Okay, but bring her to the physics lab at the university. I want her to start analysing those samples."

Colleen smiled. "Whatever you say; you're the boss."

She gave Harry a kiss and drove off in the truck. Harry sat for a while listening to the radio for news of the latest murder. He heard that the commissioner had sent a special team to Armidale to chase down this killer. Harry continued to listen as details of the impending war in Korea dominated most of the news. Last month, North Korean leader Kim Il-Sung got permission and support from Soviet leader Joseph Stalin to invade South Korea, with the Chinese Government supporting the North. The United States president Dwight Eisenhower had convinced the United Nations to form a combined force to support the South Korean Government. Australia committed our troops to the UN-led force but Harry worried that the Australian Government would call up experienced soldiers to fight the Communists as part of the United Nations force. He had witnessed enough killing.

****

Harry drove to the hotel where he met Joe, and together they took Luke, Mary and Jack to the university. They walked to the physics department building and were introduced to Felix Schmidt, the professor.

"Jack, when Colleen brings Rita to the uni at ten," said Harry, "somebody will bring her here and you two can work together on the samples from the delicatessen and from Gregory's autopsy of Brouwer. I'll check back at lunchtime."

Felix led Jack through to one of the laboratories to use the equipment already assembled for him.

Harry and Joe took Luke and Mary to the rat shed of the zoology department. "I want you two to see the site of the first murder."

Mary Rutledge walked around the room and observed the rats in their cages. "They have very good specimens here. I studied zoology in Sydney and we did lots of dissection work. I remember grabbing the biggest rat on my first attempt, thinking it would be the easiest to work on, but found that it had so much fat inside the body that it was difficult to tease out the individual organs; especially the fine Fallopian tubes. However, enough of that. Harry, what was it like when you saw the body?"

Harry described the scene in the shed.

"Did you know this man Petherby?" asked Luke. "Did he have many friends or enemies? Did he have a girlfriend?"

Harry turned to face Luke. " No. He didn't have a girlfriend, and he didn't have any real friends. He was bullied because he was so overweight, which led to his isolation. He tried to get the uni students to like him by giving them sweets and rides in his car, but most people only looked on him with pity and sympathy. Nobody remembered him being abusive or threatening or even angry."

Luke walked around with his head down as he thought. "The big question, therefore, is why was this man murdered when, from what you say, he was not a threat to anyone? He didn't abuse or assault anyone. And he was not a romantic competitor against other men. Is it possible that he was the wrong person in the wrong place at the wrong time?"

"I don't think so," said Harry. "I believe that the killer knew this young man and, in his mind, had a good reason to kill him. This was not an impulsive event. It was not an accident. The evidence suggests that the killer planned to meet this young man here in this shed. It appears that the killer came prepared with drinks and that they probably sat down and discussed something of interest to the victim. The two glasses, with only one containing the poison, were left over there. There was no sign of a struggle or fight. There were no weapons found. The body had no cuts or bruises. It all points to the killer inviting Petherby to this room to enjoy a friendly chat and a drink, during which time he handed the victim a glass containing the poison. Before leaving, the killer released the rats, even though we were told later that rats do not eat human flesh."

"Therefore the killer and the victim must have known each other," said Mary.

"You're right, Mary," said Luke. "It has got to be a strong family relationship or through some organisation or social group such as the Church or something here in the university. Could they have been in the same class? Did they belong to some club here or in the wider Armidale community?"

"Could they have been close neighbours? Or even lovers?" asked Mary.

"Wow. That puts a different light on it. That's certainly possible," replied Luke. "But why wouldn't they have had their drink and talk in the comfort of their own home, away from prying eyes? Why would you want to come to this stinking place to socialise? It doesn't make sense. There has to be a deeper underlying reason driving this man to kill so many people."

"And," said Mary, "the killer must have had sufficient charisma or have been very persuasive for the victim to accept his invitation to a place like this for a drink and a chat. Why here and not at the university dining room or the pub? So, we are not looking for your everyday, hard-nosed, brutal criminal; nothing like the usual murderers we have to deal with. This person could be Mr Personality Plus and very attractive to the victim."

"Good point, Mary," said Luke. "He could be the type of person who would be least suspected by his family, friends, workmates or neighbours of being a nasty criminal capable of taking people's lives."

Mary tapped her nodding forehead and pointed to the ceiling as if acknowledging inspiration from above. "You have told us, Harry, that the victims were poisoned by phenobarbital. You also mentioned that there were multi-coloured pendants with numbers marked on them tied around the victims' necks and cardboard signs were stuck to the body or fixtures. Could this confirm Luke's earlier ideas that this man may be trying to eradicate undesirable people or rid the world of sinners? If so, the difficulty is that the victims are all so different in every way—other than the fact that some are students—and that they have little to do with each other in their daily lives."

"Spot on, Mary," replied Harry as he scratched his head. "If you and Luke are right, the big question is whether he has finished or there are to be more killings? Let's look at the numbers on the coloured pendants we have so far. Petherby had number 1 but the next victim, Splinter Winton, was number 3. O'Sullivan was number 7. Richard Gladstone was number 2. Jerome Slaughter was number 6. And Brouwer's pendant that we found at the bottom of the barrel was number 5. Does that mean we still have victim number 4 to come? If so, this amplifies the urgency to identify the killer before he strikes again."

There was a tap at the door. Harry looked around to see Hamish Mackenzie and Aled Prosser at the door.

"Hello Harry," said Hamish. "We heard noises in here and decided to check who was working here on a Sunday or, whether someone was up to mischief. We'll leave now. We don't want to disturb you now that we've seen that all is under control."

Harry walked towards the door. "Come in, you two. Let me introduce you to some of my team. You know Joe, and this is Mary from headquarters and Luke from forensics. Luke is a qualified psychiatrist so he'll understand your language. But why are you two here on a Sunday instead of out there on the golf course or at church?"

Hamish nodded. "We are planning the activities for the live-in practical workshop for the third-year psychology students which we will hold shortly at the fitness camp at Lennox Head down on the coast. The students will do daily surveys of the local populations from Ballina to Byron Bay on a range of critical social issues."

Aled threw up his hands mockingly and laughed. "What he really means, Harry, is that he wants to go to Lennox Head to surf all day and barbeque and grog-on all night on the beach and he'll try to tell us that he is carrying out serious investigations. He'll finish up producing an academic paper to be published in the professional journals detailing the emotional differences between women who wear traditional lisle cotton stockings and those lucky enough to have silk ones, or, whether women are more scared of spiders and snakes than men. Maybe you can understand him, Luke, but we in the psych faculty here call him the Fairy Floss Man."

Hamish threw a mock punch towards Aled.

Harry pointed at Luke. "You might like to have a break and talk to these two while Mary, Joe and I continue here. You can give us a translation later over a drink at dinner."

After the others left, Mary turned to Harry. "You obviously know those two."

"Yes," replied Harry, "but we've only met briefly a few times."

"How do you find them?"

"They are like chalk and cheese. Hamish appears so rigid and disciplined in his thinking and his attitude towards others. Aled, on the other hand, is more liberal. I believe that Aled is streets ahead of Hamish in intellect, and Hamish is very jealous of that. He is always arguing with Aled to try to prove him wrong, while Aled sits back, laughs and pokes holes in his arguments to stir him up."

***

After Harry, Joe and Mary finished in the rat shed, they drove to College Street to pick up Peta van Brouwer and take her to the funeral parlour. Harry had phoned David Hobbs earlier to arrange the body under sheets with only the face showing. Upon arriving at the parlour Mary took Peta's arm to support her.

"When we go into the room, Peta," said Harry, "I want you to look at the face of the man on the table and tell us if that is Jan. We need a definite identification."

When Peta looked at the face she screamed and fell on the floor. David handed her a glass of water. Mary and Harry lifted her slowly and walked her back into the lounge room where they settled her in a deep lounge chair. Peta sobbed uncontrollably for ten minutes. In between sobs she said that the man on the table was her husband Jan.

"What will I tell the children? What will I do with the shop? I don't know why we ever came here. I want to get out of here."

After some time, Harry, Mary and Joe took Peta back home where they arranged for Mrs Tanner next door to be with her. Mrs Tanner said that she would sleep at Peta's place to give her comfort through the night.

***

Back at the hotel there was little talk. The team was very tired and everyone wanted to get to their rooms as soon as possible after dinner. As Harry was walking out to go home, Rita took him aside.

"Let me say something to you privately, Harry. Those precious jewels you have hidden between your legs are in serious danger of being crushed and extracted if you ever do anything to upset that wonderful Colleen. She and I had a great time at the farm. You will do the right thing by her or you'll have me to deal with. Is that perfectly clear, Mr Wonderful?"

"Aye, aye, Captain," said Harry as he snapped his heels together. "But I don't need orders to do that. She is so special and I'm glad that I have your approval. Thanks for being so honest."

Rita gave him a big hug before going upstairs.

Chapter 37
Monday

When Harry arrived at the hotel, the team were finishing breakfast. Joe arrived soon after in the wagon. Harry poured himself a mug of tea and sat at the table.

"What have you got for us today, Harry?" asked Mary.

"I'll get Joe to drop Rita and Jack back at the university to complete their testing. The professor has allocated a room for them. I'll take you and Luke to the various crime scenes where the other murders took place so that you can see them with your own eyes. You might pick up things that we missed. We must quickly find the links to establish the motives behind these murders to prevent any more from happening."

Harry turned towards Luke. "How did your talk with Hamish and Aled go yesterday? We were interested in their opinions as psychologists. Hamish also knew two of the victims. Jonathon Petherby—the lad found in the rat shed—was in the Presbyterian church choir with Hamish, and Richard Gladstone—who was killed at the showground where we'll visit later on—was in the Armidale Pipe Band with Hamish."

Luke took a sip of his tea before answering. "They are a weird couple. Aled floats on whatever breeze is blowing at the time; he's a free spirit. On the other hand, Hamish is regimented to the nth degree. They get on well together, maybe because opposites attract. We talked about the student victims but they added nothing to what we already know. Aled seemed to think the killer has a definite plan to exterminate a select few who do not measure up to his strict standards, whereas Hamish thought the killer murdered his victims at random as his psychiatric condition fluctuated. He supported that idea by the fact that none of the victims seemed to have a close relationship with the others. So, I doubt that my talk with them could add to our findings so far."

"These are not random killings. There has to be a connection," said Jack. "They have all been killed by poisoning from phenobarbital administered in the same way, with no evidence of assault before the event. The only obvious physical violence was with this last case where the victim was dismembered after death. Why was Brouwer treated differently to the others? Why didn't the killer dismember the other victims? These have been well-planned events and I believe the killer has been systematic in choosing his victims. Our difficulty is finding the motive. What did those victims do or say to warrant being killed?"

"Good point, Jack," said Harry. "I want everyone to keep that in mind as we continue our investigations. Let's go. We have work to do."

***

Joe drove Rita and Jack back to the university and returned to the Empire Hotel where the others had gathered to investigate the site where Splinter Winton was murdered. They stood around the old bath out the back of the hotel where the body was found.

"What's over the fence, Harry?" asked Mary.

"That's the old Olympic dance hall that is now being used to accommodate teachers college students. Half of them are in the hall and the others are in the old Minto Hotel behind that. I doubt that the killer would have come over that fence or retreated that way. As you can see, the fence is quite high. I believe they accessed the back of the hotel through the gate leading from the main street."

"The big question in my mind," said Luke, "is how the killer enticed the victim to come out here amongst this rubbish to sit down for a quiet drink and chin-wag in the cold air. Could it be that they wanted to discuss some important matter in private away from the others? Was it before or after closing time of six o'clock? Was anyone else left in the pub at that time?"

"We know that the murder took place well after 6 o'clock closing time at the pub, but we can only speculate on why they were here out the back," replied Harry.

"Didn't you say, Harry," asked Mary, "that Splinter came from Tamworth where he was a jockey and his father owned a hotel? Could the killer have known and been friends with Splinter or had major issues with him back in those days?"

240

"Good point. It's worth considering. There might have been a friendship back in those days but I can't see how that might be connected to the other cases."

"The thing that worries me," said Joe, "is that Splinter Winton was nothing like the other victims. Four of the others were students and Brouwer was a business owner. Splinter was a good-for-nothing former jockey; a layabout involved in illegal SP bookmaking. I can't see any connection with the other victims. I doubt that his SP betting on races would have been a reason to have him killed but, if someone had been badly ripped off by Splinter when he rigged races, and especially if it was one of the big crims involved in racing, they might have wanted to make him disappear. I can only think that the killer had lost a motza betting on the races with Splinter and this was his way of getting back at him. But that doesn't explain the other murders and why the friendly drink at the back of the pub at night? To me, he's the odd one out."

***

The four of them drove to the banks of Dumaresq Creek near Holmes Avenue and Donnelly Street. Harry walked them across the grass to the bank where Sergeant Eric Talbot and Constable Lars van Dyke first saw the body of Julian O'Sullivan. He pointed to the spot under the overarching branches of the large willow tree where the body had been positioned face down in the water. Harry showed them the location where the small, round folding table with two folding chairs were when they discovered the body. And he told them where the almost empty champagne bottle and two wine glasses were placed, with each glass containing about an inch of liquid.

"Those river stones on the bank are the ones that were placed on the victim's back and neck covered by the water," said Harry. "They were not heavy enough to hold down a conscious, living man so they must have been placed there after death. Although his head was in the water, death was not by drowning. It resulted from the poisoned drink."

"The stones on the back might have some symbolic meaning but it's difficult to tell at this stage," replied Luke.

Joe burst out laughing. "I think you psychologists are all mad. Where I come from, if you don't like someone you whack him; and if he dies you go to gaol."

"But in these cases, Joe," said Harry, "we don't know why the killer wanted to whack them. And Armidale is nothing like your Redfern or Kings Cross."

"If the triangle of stones was important to the killer they could have represented something like the sacred trinity, but I doubt it," said Luke, "or they could symbolize the integration of body, mind, and spirit or they could be powerful symbols of transformation, protection, and spiritual ascension. So far we have not been able to get into the killer's mind to find what is driving him to act like this. Without any supporting evidence I doubt that this is important to our investigations."

Mary stopped writing in her notebook. "You mentioned that O'Sullivan was wearing a tuxedo and he was driving a brand-new Jaguar XK120 sports car. That puts him well above the financial status of the other victims. You couldn't find someone more different in every way to Splinter Winton. And the other victims were mostly poor by comparison. How do we explain that?"

"I can't," replied Harry. "But his fancy clothes were explained by the Red Cross ball on at the town hall that night which O'Sullivan was planning to attend. We always have a police presence at those functions but O'Sullivan was not seen, and no reports of strangers inside or outside the hall were made. The fact that his car was parked so far away from the town hall suggests that he met with someone before arriving at the ball. However, our inquiries so far have not identified any friend of O'Sullivan who attended the same event whose whereabouts could not be verified before or after the ball. Now, let's go to the showground."

***

On arriving at the pavilion, Harry took the team to the end wall where the old galvanised water trough stood on a concrete stand against the building.

"It was in this trough that we found the body of Richard Gladstone. We found yellow powder on the ground near the trough and there was a stinking rotten-egg smell indicating the presence of sulphur. We could see that the victim's back had been burned and, because of the smell, I guessed that it might have been from sulphuric acid. The subsequent analysis by the SIB confirmed our early suspicions."

"How was this death similar to the others?" asked Luke.

"Over there at the corner of the building were two stools next to a small table with two beer glasses on it," replied Harry. "A numbered pendant was found around the victim's neck and similar cardboard signs were found onsite. But most importantly, we found the first bottle of phenobarbital in a bin over there. It was obvious that the killer and victim knew each other and that the victim was happy to sit there and have a drink with the killer. There was no sign of physical violence before death."

"Why did it happen at this location?" asked Mary.

"There had been a Scout camp held here at the showground over the weekend. There was a large two-man tent left on the ground over there after all the others had gone home. It belonged to Richard Gladstone. Inside were two sleeping bags and a duffle bag acting as a pillow; a small methylated-spirits burner and some pans with leftover sausages and rissoles; a Scout hat, scarf, toggle and shirt, and a pair of boots."

"You mentioned two sleeping bags," said Mary. "Was there any evidence that the killer slept in the tent with the victim? Could they have been a homosexual couple who stayed on for you know what after the others left? Could something have gone wrong? Could the couple have had a fight that resulted in murder?"

"No," replied Harry. "We have clear evidence that one of the Cubs was supposed to sleep in that tent with Gladstone during the camp, but some of the older Scouts convinced him to move into their tent for protection. There have been rumours that Gladstone might have been homosexual and he was found in bed naked with a boy he was babysitting."

"If I had been there and found out that he was having it off with one of the boys," said Joe, "I'd have killed him myself."

"We have no evidence of that, Joe. That doesn't mean that it didn't happen, but many victims of child sexual assault will never talk about it because they feel so much blame, hurt, guilt and shame and the perpetrators often threaten them with extreme punishment if they ever mention it."

"None of the other victims were known paedophiles," said Luke. "All these things are worth considering but we must concentrate on finding a common motive for all the murders."

"Okay everybody," said Harry. "Let's get over to Taipan Charlie's snake farm where Jerome Slaughter was found dead."

***

On the way to the farm, Mary asked "What's his real name?"

"Charlie Young," replied Harry, "but everyone just knows him as Taipan Charlie because of his work with snakes and other reptiles. He is the best anywhere around. He owns the snake farm off Bundarra Road and it was him who found the body of Jerome in one of the snake pits."

After the team emerged from the cars, Harry did the introductions. Mary was nervous shaking Taipan's hand. She didn't like snakes. Harry walked them to the third tank. He described the victim's position in the snake pit, the clothes he was wearing, and that there were no obvious signs of injuries to the face, chest or lower legs. The autopsy revealed no evidence of snake bites. He pointed to the spot where the phenobarbital bottle was found.

"He looked at peace lying in the snake pit," said Harry. "And over there beside that tree was a blanket, a bottle and two glasses and some leftover food. There was enough remaining fluid to confirm the presence of phenobarbital in the victim's glass. That was supported by evidence from the stomach, blood and tissue samples. It appears that the killer and victim sat on that blanket for a friendly picnic."

"The bleeding obvious," said Luke, "is that the killer was friends with or a very close associate of each and every one of the victims. It's not everyone who will sit down out here in the middle of a snake farm to have a drink with someone else during the day or night unless that person was well known to them."

"We know that Jerome was a loner," said Joe, "but could he have been happy that someone he knew came to the snake farm to share his interest in the reptiles and have a drink?"

"Thanks Joe. It probably depends on how well the killer knew Jerome at the university or elsewhere, but we'll keep that in mind," replied Harry.

"Could you tell me more about Jerome, Harry?" said Mary.

"Jerome lived out on a farm off Rockvale Road. He was thoroughly spoiled by his parents and two sisters. His parents bought him a nice Riley car for topping his class. He studied zoology at the university. He was seen by his parents as the next brilliant scientist. Outside his study of reptiles, he was interested in world affairs. One of the students told me that Jerome looked on world politics as resembling communities of snakes each competing for the limited supply of frogs and other good eats."

"I don't know about you, Harry, but I'm saturated with information about these cases and it is getting late in the day," said Luke. "Could we go back to the hotel before dinner?"

"Sure. Joe will pick up Rita and Jack and I'll take you and Mary back now, and then we'll all meet for dinner at six."

Chapter 38
Tuesday

When Harry arrived at the hotel, the other team members had just walked out of the dining room. Joe arrived at the same time. Each of them looked more relaxed after a good night's sleep.

"Let's move into the back lounge where we can talk, away from the other guests," said Harry as he took a bite from the piece of toast he picked up from the table.

"The one thing we didn't discuss yesterday, Harry," said Jack, "was the matter of the signs found at the sites of all murders. Could you tell us more about them?"

"Sure," replied Harry. "At each site there were two white cardboard sheets, one bigger than the other. The smaller one was about six to eight inches square whereas the larger one was twice as big. The messages on all of them were written in black Indian ink. The smaller ones had only one or two words whereas the larger one had a longer message."

Harry took a few moments to write something in his notebook then placed it on the table for the others to see. "Can any of you make something out of them?"

Temperance - Petherby
Charity - Winton
Humility - O'Sullivan
Chastity - Gladstone
Diligence - Slaughter
Patience & Respect - Brouwer

"To me," said Luke, "these words look like key words that a priest or minister might list as important ideals that he should cover in his weekly sermon for the Sunday service."

"With the exception of Brouwer," said Rita, "there was only one word for each victim. Why would Petherby have the word Temperance on him? What has temperance got to do with him? Why would Winton have the word Charity on him? There's no evidence that he was charitable. In fact, he was the opposite."

"Maybe that's the point, Rita," said Mary. "The killer might be sending messages and warnings to the police and others. He might be saying that for Petherby there was a need for more moderation in actions, thoughts and feelings or a need for less indulgence of the appetites. He is probably preaching abstinence from excessive food, drugs or alcohol. Let's face it, from what you have told us, Harry, Petherby was a big fat slob who wouldn't get off his backside to pick up anything except his food and drink. He needed to be more temperate in his life choices."

Harry nodded. "That's fairly blunt, Mary, but I think you have a good point."

"Was this preacher-man killer trying to tell Splinter Winton that he had spent most of his life robbing others and he needed to be more charitable?" asked Jack. "What do you think, Luke? You're the psychiatrist."

"Well, there is one thing definite," replied Luke. "Splinter won't be doing anything like that ever again; neither robbing nor being charitable. But I agree with Mary's point. Each message seems to have been directed to that particular victim, not all of them together."

"What about the others?" asked Harry.

Joe tapped the side of his chair. "I agree with Luke. The more I get to know about the victims the more I think each word is appropriate for that particular person. Look at our most recent case. He was a pig-headed, impatient, arrogant bully. The message for him was to be more patient and respectful and stop abusing others."

Mary put up her hand. "Everything we know about Slaughter is that he was a spoilt brat who was too lazy to get off his bum to do anything. So why did the killer write *Diligence* on the sheet of cardboard? He must have seen a different side in him."

"Okay," said Harry. "The consensus is that the words on the small cardboard pieces are targeted at the lifestyles of the individual victims and might be inspired by religion. But the big question now is whether the perpetrator is heavily involved in the Church or whether he is totally opposed to religion in general, or any denomination in particular. Could it be that he has had a very bad experience with someone in the Church?"

"Are you saying that the perpetrator is a deeply religious man out of his mind?" asked Jack. "Could he be a leader or member of a cult with a mission to rid the world of those who don't follow the Word of God? Or could he have been the victim of a paedophile priest?"

"We don't know," said Luke. "Any of those situations could be correct. It wouldn't be the first time that someone has gone over the edge and killed. We must be open-minded."

"I have a question about the numbered pendants," said Joe. "They have not been in sequence. If this man is so well organised and sticks to a plan, wouldn't you expect him to tick them off, 1, 2, 3 and so on, in order?"

"Not necessarily," replied Harry. "Let's sit back and consider it from the perpetrator's situation. He could have planned all of these murders well in advance but the opportunity to murder each victim might not have occurred in the same sequential order as the plan. As each opportunity arose he could have taken the phenobarbital, selected numbered pendant, chairs, table, drink bottle, glasses and printed signs to that particular site. He would have had to be certain that the location would remain undisturbed for the duration of the meeting. I believe that he took advantage of the opportunity that came along each and every time. It appears, therefore, that the killer had a prepared list with each potential victim numbered in advance. He had already produced the coloured pendants with the numbers marked on them. As each opportunity arose he selected the particular numbered pendant that had been allocated to that victim on the list."

"So, we still have number 4 to go," said Rita. "The problem is that we don't know the next characteristic that the killer will be targeting, and thus we have no idea who the victim could be."

Mary got up quickly, pushing over her chair behind her. She turned and slapped the wall. "The bloody trouble is that we are chasing our tails. We are running around in circles. This is so frustrating. The victims are all so different. The only common factors are the phenobarbital and the killer and we don't know who that person is yet or where they got the poison. There is still another victim to come and we have no clue who they are and we seem helpless to act to prevent that death. That's what makes me mad."

248

Mario Santini, the barman, came to the door from the dining room. "Hey Harry, there's a call for you in the office. It's the police station."

Ken Wright was on the phone. "You best get over here as soon as possible, Harry. A man called Dusty Spackman has just walked into the station and has admitted to being the serial killer. We are holding him in the cell at the Sheriff's Cottage."

***

Harry and the team walked the couple of blocks to the Sheriff's Cottage. On the way, Harry asked Joe and Luke to be in the cell with him but gave them instructions to only observe the prisoner. He asked the others to sit outside the cell but not to intervene.

On entering the cell, Harry introduced himself and Joe and Luke to the prisoner. Harry sat opposite the prisoner. Joe and Luke stood against the wall to the side.

"What is your name? And where do you live?"

"What are those bastards doin' out there?" said the prisoner as his head jerked from side to side. He jabbed his closed fist nervously towards the officers he could see through the glass panel on the door.

Harry didn't answer for a while as he watched the man's movements. The man had an intense stare with a sudden sharp blink about every five seconds. His upper body was never still. His shoulders jerked as they moved nervously from side to side and front to back. At first Harry thought that the man had been a boxer who had suffered too many hits to the head, but he didn't have the physique of a fighter nor the scarring around the eyes and ears. His nose had never taken a hard punch.

It dawned on Harry that this man might be suffering from shell shock. Harry had witnessed it in Port Moresby with soldiers returning from the Kokoda Track where they had been under constant attack for months. He had to step in sometimes to protect some soldiers from unsympathetic officers who wanted to charge the men with cowardice in the face of the enemy for walking away from the front. It could have resulted in long gaol terms or the firing squad.

"Those police officers outside the cell are here with me," Harry said sympathetically. "They are not going to hurt you. I promise you that. Now tell me your name and where you live?"

"Me name is Dusty and I live over there," he said as he pointed over Harry's shoulder in a north-easterly direction.

"What's your surname? And which street do you live in?"

The man's head twitched side to side a few times more before he answered. "Me name is Dusty Spackman and I live with Sheila and Bob down on Donnelly Street. You know, because ya mate Mervy-boy lives a coupla doors down the street."

Harry remembered that Constable Merv Leech lived in that street and that Sheila and Bob were most likely the Sealys who also lived close by.

"Why did you come into the police station this morning, Dusty?"

There was a long pause while Dusty dropped his head and moved it sharply from side to side as if looking for something he dropped on the floor. Harry waited for more than a minute until Dusty looked up and stared at the barred window.

"Well, ya know those blokes who 'ave been killed? Well, I did it."

Harry paused. Joe moved forward towards Dusty but Harry put up his hand to caution him not to move or speak. He tore a page from his notebook and wrote:

Get Merv Leech here ASAP

He handed it to Joe and turned back to Dusty.

"How did you go about killing those men, Dusty? Take your time."

"I don't 'ave ta tell ya that. What a stupid question. You know 'ow I got rid of those bastards. You've been there and seen 'em after I dun 'em in."

"Why did you want to kill them, Dusty?"

"Because they treated me like shit."

"Let's look at Splinter Winton first. What did he do to you?" asked Harry.

Dusty banged the cuffs on the table. "He took me money every week and wouldn't give it back to me. Never, never, never. Well, I showed 'im who's boss now, didn't I? I don't git much doing a few odd jobs and so when he took me money I didn't 'ave enough for even a few drinks. The bastard ain't gunna rob me no more, is he?"

"Do you like a drink, Dusty?" asked Harry.

"Yeah, but I can only afford to buy a bottle of that tutti-frutti sweet sherry rubbish every now and then. It's gut-rot but I can't afford anything else because Splinter ripped me orf."

"Now tell me again how you killed him?" asked Harry, using up his patience.

"Are you dumb? Ya know how I did it. Why do ya keep askin'? Well, I'll tell ya. I followed 'im out of the pub and whacked 'im behind 'is 'ead with a piece of four-by-two and he fell in the old bath. If the whack didn't finish 'im orf then he would 'ave drowned."

"What did you do then?"

"I went through 'is pockets and took 'is money. I went back in the pub and bought a bottle of good rum."

"But wasn't the hotel closed at that time?"

"They know me so they let me in the back door to get me bottle."

"Did you check if he was dead?"

"Yeah. He wasn't movin'. When I lifted 'is 'ead, he was bleedin' a lot where I whacked 'im. But I did leave 'im me pendant that Mum gave me when I come back from the war. I put it around 'is neck as a constant reminder of who did 'im in."

Joe returned with Merv Leech. Harry stood and met them outside the cell door.

"Do you know a Dusty Spackman, Merv? He says that he knows you and you live in the same street."

"Poor old Dusty. What's he up to now?" asked Merv.

"He came in here this morning and admitted killing all six of the victims."

"That's not possible, Harry," replied Merv. "He is suffering from shell shock from his time in New Guinea. He can't work full-time anymore. He does a bit of gardening for a few neighbours. He cuts my lawn when he feels like it but that's only about once a month, and I pay him a few shillings to buy some drinks. He wouldn't be strong enough to lift any of the victims. He could never have dragged Gladstone into that trough. He wouldn't know how to dismember Brouwer. He couldn't have pulled Petherby's body across the floor of the rat shed. And he certainly couldn't have dragged and lifted Slaughter's body into the snake pit."

"Why do you think he is telling us he is the killer?" asked Harry.

"I'm not a medical expert, Harry," replied Merv, "but I think Dusty is mentally sick from his time fighting in the war. He has very bad spells. Sometimes he is screaming loudly at night out in the front yard. I think he believes he's still out there at the front fighting the Japs. He's not a killer. He's just a sick old man."

"Did you ever tell him about the cases?" asked Harry.

"He asked me about the murders one day because he heard about them on the radio."

"Did you ever mention the pendants around the victims' necks and the position of Splinter Winton's body in the bath?"

"I can't remember. I might have. But he wouldn't remember anyhow."

Harry poked his forefinger into Merv's chest. "How many times have I got to tell you that you don't tell anyone the details of our cases? When the public knows the details, we get a rush of loonies wanting to admit to the murders to get publicity or notoriety. And that is a waste of our valuable time which is better spent on finding the real killer. We also get copycats which add to the cases we have to deal with. Don't ever do that again; not even to people like Dusty. Now, I'm going to release Dusty into your care. Get him to a doctor. Check that he takes his medication. Look after him and don't let him in here again. Do you get my message?"

"Okay Harry. I'm sorry. I won't do that again."

"Now I want you to look after Dusty. Get him home. See if Doctor Ebsworth can see him and give him some medication."

Harry walked back into the cell and released Dusty. He was so pleased to see Merv and went off happily with him.

Harry suggested that the others should go with him to Nick's Café for coffee where he could fully fill them in on Dusty.

Chapter 39
Tuesday

Harry and the team sat at the back of Nick's Café. There were no other customers. They discussed the morning's events, especially the session with Dusty Spackman.

"I feel so sorry for veterans like Dusty," said Harry. "Men like him went through the worst of the war in the toughest jungle conditions on the Kokoda Track, fighting against one of the most experienced armies in the world, with six Japanese soldiers to each Australian. Many of them were conscripted against their will from civilian life, had little training and had limited supplies. People like Dusty get almost no support from the government now. In those jungle conditions, your body and mind get exhausted from being hyper-alert, with a tension caused by the suppression of the mode of flight or fight. There are limits to how long you can maintain that intensity before your body and mind break. Some might take a few days while others might last three months or longer. The army tried to rotate soldiers but they had few replacements."

"You are so right, Harry," said Luke. "I did some work after the war at Broughton Hall Psychiatric Clinic which is next to Callan Park Mental Hospital in Sydney. Those men need medical help, not condemnation. What can you do here, Harry?"

"I'll get Merv to keep an eye on him in the street and I'll get Gregory Ebsworth to assess him so he can get more benefits or be referred to an institution. Now let's move on," said Harry.

Rita looked at Luke. "I've always had a question in my mind about the level of responsibility you can prove in court against an alleged perpetrator who is suffering from a severe mental illness over which he has no control. I know you are not a lawyer, Luke, but if Dusty is schizophrenic, and he was the actual serial killer we're looking for, do you think he could he be judged legally responsible for the murders?"

"Good question, Rita," replied Luke. "We had such cases at Callan Park. It depended on the judge in each case. There were many such cases where the perpetrator was committed to a mental institution where they spent the remainder of their life. Others were sent to prison like any other criminal. For example, scientific progress in understanding schizophrenia has been very slow, long and arduous and we have no cures at this stage."

Mary broke in. "To change the subject, I'm still confused about the numbered pendants around the necks of the victims. On Sunday and after breakfast this morning, we were talking about the randomness of the numbers and the fact that there appears to be one number missing, that being number 4. Why would that be so?"

Luke stretched his arm across the bench towards Mary. "That depends on who you talk to or what you have read. The idea of numbers being related to death stretches back a long way. Horace, an ancient Roman poet, listed various virtues and nine sins to avoid. Around the early 1300s another Italian poet named Dante Alighieri got kicked out of the city of Florence, but in his anger he started to examine the concepts of hell, purgatory and heaven. He wrote an epic poem called *The Divine Comedy*. It is probably the most respected poem ever written. It was a landmark in Italian literature and led to a profound vision of man's destiny after death. In the first two parts of the poem, Dante explains the journey through an inferno into hell and then purgatory. He follows man down through nine circles into the pit of hell, with each circle representing a specific group of sins that have been committed. In every circle man is surrounded by demons and mythical beasts that punish the people who have committed those sins. The circles are concentric, representing a gradual increase in wickedness the deeper he goes. The worst sinners finish at the centre of the earth where Satan is waiting. If our murderer is using Horace's or Dante's ideas of the nine circles of sin, then there are three numbers still to go. They would be 4, 8 and 9."

Mary raised her finger. "But when I was brought up in the Catholic Church we were threatened with severe punishment if we were guilty of any of the seven deadly sins."

"You are right, Mary," said Luke. "Well before Dante, Pope Gregory in the sixth century outlined the seven deadly sins. If the killer is following that system, there is still one victim to go, not three as I just mentioned."

"Why did that bloke call it *The Divine Comedy*?" asked Joe. "To me, sins, demons, beasts, death and going to hell are no laughing matter. I certainly won't be going to the Saturday flicks to see the film about that comedy. I like to have a good laugh."

The team sat back and roared laughing. Joe's comment eased the seriousness of the discussion.

"Right," said Harry as he tried to get their minds back on track. "From what Luke has said, the numbers might have an underlying religious or spiritual background, but if so, there is confusion between whether the killer is fixated by the nine levels leading to hell as per Dante, or by the seven deadly sins dictated by Pope Gregory. Or could there be a different system? Does the killer see a relationship between a particular number and each victim or to an event where that number was so important? That's the mystery."

Luke sat back and pushed the hair behind his ears with both hands. He stretched and looked up to the ceiling. "I am a psychiatrist, not a psychic. The information I just gave you was only a guess as I tried to make sense of the numbers and signs left by the murderer, seeing as we have few other leads at the moment. It might have nothing to do with such things. So without knowing the identity of the alleged perpetrator we can't say for sure what is driving him to act in this way."

Harry looked up to see James Bolton from *The Daily Mirror* and Ken Rudd from *The Armidale Express* come through the door and approach the group. Harry tapped the bench top. "Let me handle this."

"Hello Harry," said James. "Could we have a chat?"

"Sure James. Good to see you again. Hello Ken. Drag up two of those chairs."

Harry introduced them to the team. "How can we help you two?"

"You'd have to admit, Harry," said James sternly, "that the public deserve better than this? You now have six murders and you are no closer to finding the killer than you were three weeks ago."

"Thank you for that observation, James," replied Harry as he tried to remain as calm as possible. "I must apologise that we didn't seek your expert opinion and assistance well before this. Let's face it, you are the most experienced crime reporter in the country. How would you go about finding the killer? Tell the team here what they should be doing. I'm sure that they will respect your experience in this area."

James snorted with contempt. "Listen to me, Harry. I'm not the detective on this case. That's your job."

Harry leaned forward towards James and stared at him. "And I'm not the reporter so why don't you do your job and let us do ours? Sitting here in front of you are members of the most highly skilled forensic team in Australia. We have been going over every shred of evidence since the first murder. If you believe that they are not doing a good job, I suggest you tell them to their faces what strategies they should have implemented to solve these cases. If you are not willing or able to do that then I suggest that you sit back and listen. So, to help you do your job, let me fill you in on our current situation. Get your pens ready. We believe these murders have been committed by the same person who was known to all the victims, one way or another. He probably lives in this region but we can't be certain. We believe the killer is intelligent and well organised. Each event has been carefully planned to the nth degree; these are not random events. We know he is known to the victims, but whether or not they are close in their relationships is uncertain. It is unlikely that all the victims knew one another. We don't know if the killer will strike again and, if so, what type of person he might have in his sights. It could be you, James. He might have been offended by one of your articles. In fact, killers in the past have sometimes threatened reporters who don't get their facts right. It is their one chance at glory so they don't like it when some reporter doesn't get the facts right as they see them, or paints a very bad picture of the perpetrator."

"Okay, okay, Harry. I get the message. I apologise. So, what do you want Ken and I to do?"

"I want you to alert the public that the killer is probably a citizen of the New England district and probably known to many people living in this city. He could be a next-door neighbour. He might be involved in community groups or events. To the average person he could appear to be a regular upstanding citizen. Tell the people to lock their doors and their vehicles. People here don't normally do that, but we are now in a difficult time with this man on the loose. Ask people to carefully select those with whom they have a drink. In each of the cases so far the killer has invited the victim to sit down at a folding table and chairs to have a drink. Ask anyone who receives such an invitation to immediately leave and contact us."

"Thanks Harry. That gives Ken and I something to work on. Now can you tell us something about the numbers that the killer uses? Someone said he works by numbers."

"Forget about that, James. After the first two murders, people have been asking how many more might take place. Take no notice of it."

Ken tapped his pen on his forehead. "All the victims are men. Do you think he has a hatred of men? Is he someone who was bullied in his young days or maybe sexually assaulted by men?"

"Good question, Ken, but until we find him we won't know. Now, you'll have to excuse us. We have work to do looking for this man. If you have any more questions or get any responses from your articles I'd be pleased to work with you. We'd be very thankful for your help and support."

The team shuffled out of the café.

Jack tapped Harry on the shoulder. "Well done, mate. You handled that pair very well."

"Where to now, Harry?" asked Rita.

"I'd suggest that you, Jack and Mary return to the office and start comparing notes and preparing a summary for our next meeting. I want Joe and Luke to accompany me to visit Mrs Van Brouwer."

***

All of them walked back to the Sherif's Cottage where Harry got the wagon and drove Joe and Luke to College Street. They were invited into the lounge room by Peta van Brouwer.

"Peta, could you please tell us why you and your family left South Africa to come to Australia?" asked Harry.

"Jan was a very successful manager for a large food supply company. He ran a very tight ship but he did it his way. He was responsible for the northern and eastern zones in the country but he often clashed with the owner in Cape Town. He was demoted to sub-manager and transferred to head office. I think the owner wanted to keep an eye on him. They clashed every day until he got the sack. He was very resentful about his treatment and, without consulting me or the family, he arranged the move to Australia. We went along with the move because we were increasingly concerned with the lack of security there."

"Do you ever work in the delicatessen?"

"Oh, God no. I could not have stood taking orders all day, every day. It was bad enough when Jan was home. He was never satisfied. And because of his treatment in South Africa, he was very bitter."

Harry raised his hand to his face. "Would you mind telling us how you got those bruises to your hands and neck?"

Peta dropped her head and looked at the floor. Her hands lifted to cover the dark areas on her hands and neck. She paused before answering. "It's nothing. I'm clumsy. I keep turning around too quickly and banging into doors and the corners of cupboards."

Harry reached across and touched her on the arm. "Peta, it is alright to talk about it here. He is no longer with us. Did he hit you?"

"I'd prefer not to talk about it," replied Peta.

"That's okay. How did he treat the girls?"

"He was very strict. He believed in military-type discipline. He had been in the Active Citizen Force in South Africa which was like the Territorial Force they had in England, but he was not involved in the main war."

"How did he get along with the staff in the shop?"

"He had already sacked two this year. Mrs McDonald has only been there a couple of weeks but Jan had not made any comments about her."

"What will happen to the shop?"

Peta threw up her hands. "I can't run it. Jan wouldn't let me in on the running of the business so I'll sell it and go back to my family in South Africa. The girls would like that."

"On the day that Jan went missing you told me that he'd received a phone call the night before from a friendly member of your church. What church does your family attend?"

"St Paul's Presbyterian."

Harry stood. "We won't keep you any longer. Thank you for giving us your time."

***

Harry, Joe and Luke drove to the Presbyterian church and met with Charles Aitken, the minister. They sat in his office. Harry opened the conversation.

"Could you tell us about Jan van Brouwer?"

Charles paused, looked at the stained-glass window in his office and nodded. "When he arrived in Armidale I saw him as a highly intelligent, professional gentleman deeply committed to the Christian faith. He had been with the Lutherans but left after disputes with them. He volunteered here on Sundays when called upon. I initially had him tagged as a potential church elder."

"Why didn't you proceed along those lines?" asked Luke.

"He got offside with too many parishioners, and especially those in charge of events."

"What about Peta, his wife?" asked Harry.

"Now there is a different story. She is such a darling but I was concerned about her welfare. I counselled her on numerous occasions. I suspected that he treated her badly but I believe that she was so scared of him that she found difficulty in talking about it. We supported her as best we could under the circumstances but, without clear evidence of abuse, it was hard to take it further. But be assured, Harry, that we will do our best to support her and the girls as they adjust to their new lives without Jan. I might even ask Hamish Mackenzie, one of our parishioners to help her. He is a trained psychologist. You have met him before."

"Yes," said Harry, "we have been tapping into Hamish and Aled Prosser's expertise to assist us with our investigations."

"I have met Aled, but I know Hamish very well because he is a wonderful contributor to the church community. I can call on him at any time to help with any function. But he is a complex person, not liked by all the parishioners. He is very strict and demanding of others. What you probably don't know is that Hamish commenced training for the ministry but gave that away. His ancestors in the Highlands of Scotland were very much involved in the breakaway Presbyterian Free Church movement. They separated because they believed that the church wasn't strict enough."

"That's interesting," said Harry. "Does he now accept the church in its current form?"

"Not always," said Charles. "We often have long discussions and arguments about religion and philosophy. In his doctoral studies, Hamish specialised on early philosophers and their impact on religion."

"Thank you, Charles. You have been most helpful. Keep in touch."

***

Harry took Luke and Joe back to the station to meet up with the others.

Chapter 40
Wednesday

A cold south-westerly wind with a sprinkle greeted Harry as he walked out of the house. He changed the direction of his run. He jogged up the steep hill in Taylor Street, into Kentucky Street, behind the teachers college, along past the railway station, down Margaret Street and back via Donnelly Street to home. After a hot shower and a hearty breakfast, he was ready to meet the team.

***

At eight o'clock Ray Johnston called a meeting of all officers. "Good morning, team. I've called you here this morning to give Harry's team an opportunity to bring you up to date on the six murders we have now. You can feed any information directly back to them. The team has been very busy since we all came together last Saturday and all of you have been involved in a district-wide search for clues that could lead to the arrest of this killer. I want to thank all of you for your diligence in assisting the team. Now, over to you, Harry."

"Let me start with a caution. Under no circumstances are you to give out vital information about these cases to anyone who is not with the police. I appreciate that your friends, families and neighbours will want to pump you on every detail of these cases but you must remain firm. Tell them only what we want them to know, not what they want to know. The reason for this strategy is to stop the loonies and people who dislike the police from phoning in to claim that they did it, or know who did. Multiple murder cases like these bring those people out of the woodwork and we then waste valuable time chasing up on their stories when we should be working on these cases."

"What shouldn't we mention, Harry?" asked Charlie Hanwright as he adjusted his motorbike leggings.

"Thanks, Charlie. Don't mention things like the numbered pendants that have been placed on the victims' necks, or especially the fact that all of the victims have been poisoned with phenobarbital. Don't give out any details about the locations where the murders occurred. Don't divulge what was written on those pieces of cardboard. And under no circumstances mention the dismemberment of Brouwer's body. While the population gets more anxious about their safety we have to remain calm and focused."

Keith Blackmore raised his hand. "But if someone knew about the pendants, and saw a person making them, wouldn't that help if they told us?"

"I take your point, Keith, but if we tell them everything, we'll get numerous accusations against people who are involved in legitimate arts and crafts and we'll be running around chasing our tails. We know that doctors, vets, hospitals and chemists have access to phenobarbital but we do not want everyone telling us that they are suspicious about some of those people without other evidence. We have checked all the possible supplies of the poison in the region but all stocks have been accounted for. We have also checked all the supplies of those chairs, tables and glasses but can find no supplier in the region. Only the killer knows every detail, and when that person mentions a detail unknown to the general public, we will have that vital connection to let us move in to arrest."

"I think you are being a bit obsessive about this, Harry," said Lars van Dyke.

"You might be right, Lars, but yesterday a man called Dusty Spackman walked into this station claiming that he was the killer. We spent a lot of time dealing with that when we should have been out in the field trying to catch the real culprit. Poor Dusty is suffering from shell shock, but he couldn't give us any positive detail except for the pendant, and that was only because Merv told him about that. I've spoken to Merv and I don't want that to happen again. If we give everyone the details we will be dealing with people like Dusty or others who want to accuse their enemies of being the killer."

"The pendants you showed us look well made, but I haven't seen anything like that in jewellery shops," said Ken Wright.

"Good point," replied Harry. "I checked with a friend in Sydney who was in a lapidary club and made costume jewellery. She also did enamelling which is a process of applying a thin coat of coloured powdered glass to a metal like copper, then heating both to a high temperature, either in a kiln or with a blowtorch, so the glass melts and fuses to the metal. I'd say that the ones found on the victims here are not

top quality but have probably been made in a similar fashion by an experienced amateur."

"Are the numbers stuck on after firing?" asked Ray.

"No. I think the killer uses a special enamel powder after the initial firing to paint the number and then fire it again."

"That's interesting," said Pat Casey. "I've heard about a local lapidary club here in Armidale. I think they meet here and at Uralla just up the road. There are lots of good gemstone areas in the New England region; especially from here to Inverell. In fact, some of the best sapphires are found in this district. Last year I went to one of their shows and they had all sorts of jewellery, including enamelled copper pieces. At the time my wife was more interested in them than me."

"There are also some art and craft clubs in town and they have kilns for their pottery," said Jack Nelson. "We should look into them to see who uses the kilns."

"Good point, Jack, but the killer might be using a blowtorch to do the enamelling in the privacy of his own workshop. I doubt that he would do it publicly at a club, but I'll get Joe to take Jack Witherspoon and look into those clubs and talk to the members."

Mary Rutledge stopped writing notes and spoke up. "Harry, you keep referring to the killer as 'he'. Couldn't it be a woman?"

"Thanks Mary. I have worked on the basis that it would be difficult for most women to physically lift most adult men, especially when we look at victims like Jonathon Petherby who was well over twenty stone in weight. I also can't see most women getting involved dismembering a human body like Brouwer and cleaning up the mess afterwards."

Sergeant Greg White walked back into the room after a visit to the toilet. Rita Flynn stood up and walked towards him. She leaned forward with her weight on her left foot, crouched slightly and suddenly sprang up and rammed her shoulder under Greg's ribs. She wrapped her arms around the back of his buttocks and lifted him up onto her shoulder. She turned and carried Greg back to his chair. As Greg was about to complain, Rita bent down, placed her hands on each side of his face and gave him a kiss and a hug. The room was at first stunned but then broke into laughter.

"My apologies, Greg," said Rita. "You just happened to walk in at the wrong time. I was just showing Harry and the others that women do have the strength to lift adult males and carry them. But mate, can you cut out the lamingtons and cream buns at morning tea?"

Mary stood and clapped loudly. "Well, Harry, what about that?"

"Okay, okay, I get what you're saying. A strong, fit woman could do it but I stick with the point that the most likely perpetrator is a man because, in the case of Petherby, the victim was about six to eight stone heavier than Greg. Now, let's get on with it. Have you got anything else to report?"

There was much discussion but nothing concrete came from it. Lars summed it up. "There is a lot of anxiety out there and a lot of rumours. And some people are making comments to get back at others, but there are no leads to work on."

"Let's have a break," said Harry, "and when we resume, we can have some lamingtons I got at the bakery this morning on the way to work."

Greg looked at Harry. "Can I have some?"

"Don't ask me," replied Harry as he laughed. "You'll have to get permission from Rita. And she'll probably make you do ten laps around the block or ten rounds in the ring before you can have one."

Rita walked across and put her arm around Greg's shoulders. "Come on, mate, we'll share one."

***

After the break they resumed their seats and Harry called for attention. "I want you to keep your ears to the ground. You never know when someone will innocently say something that might lead us to the killer. Tell me what the people in town are saying."

Ken Wright started. "I'm in the Rotary Club. Most of the members are business owners and professionals. They are worried about the effect of these cases on business and the reputation of Armidale. They want it over and done with as soon as possible."

Constable Graham McInnes spoke next. "I'm in the Apex Club. Our members are much younger than Ken's group. There's much talk about the cases because some members knew some of the victims. Much of what they are saying is the same as what other people who knew the victims have said. At Friday night's meeting, some members commented on Brouwer. They said his produce was first class but his manner was rude and abrupt. They said that he was intolerant of customers who didn't understand South African food. My friend Sam said he witnessed him abusing Mrs McDonald behind the counter because she made a mistake with the change. Most of the members believe that it must be someone from out of town. They couldn't think of anyone here who would commit these crimes."

"Okay, thanks for that. Now let's change direction a little," said Harry. "Let's look again at the victims. I know we have talked about them before but we need to concentrate on them again. Is there anything you people might have found out that we haven't discussed before? Can any of you see a common link between the victims? Do you know of anyone who might be known to all the victims? Have any of you in here been friends with any of the victims or known them or their friends or neighbours? What can you tell the team about them? Let's start with Petherby."

There was silence. After a while Joe spoke. "We know he came from out of town as a student but he never fitted in, even at the university. I don't see that being a reason to kill him, even by those blokes who bullied him. His biggest crime was eating half the food in the Bevery at the university every day. But we already knew all that."

"What about Winton?" asked Harry.

There was a sudden gaggle of voices around the table.

"Hold on, everyone. One at a time. You start, Greg," said Harry as he pointed to Sergeant Greg White.

"I had a few run-ins with Splinter. He was a sneaky little rat who would take your money in a flash. I charged him once for SP betting but he just paid the fine and started again that same day. I'm not against SP betting but I object to race fixing and, had I got the evidence on him, I would have thrown him in the cell and left him there. The trouble is that everyone in the racing industry knows it goes on, but nobody is talking. I suspect his death was related to his betting and greed. Some people who talked to me said they hated Splinter because he stole back goods because they didn't pay back the money to him quickly enough. In some cases he punched some of them to get to their wallets but I don't see that as a reason for them to kill him and there was no evidence of physical violence."

"Thanks Greg, but if the killer was so angry with Splinter, how could he get him outside behind the Empire pub for a drink? We have already mentioned the possibility of race fixing. Did you find out any other reason? Did he offer Splinter some other deal he couldn't resist? What about O'Sullivan?"

"I didn't know him personally but he was a pumped-up, arrogant, spoilt brat and a snob," said Mervyn Leech. "He was so intolerant of anybody with less wealth than him. He only mixed with the rich graziers. He went to the most expensive private schools and was given the XK120 Jaguar. I got much pleasure in booking him twice for speeding. When I pulled him over he was quite rude to me. I wanted to do him in myself there and then, but held back. But he didn't care. He just paid it. Someone said that Sandy Coyle once had a fight with him and knocked him to the ground. I checked and Sandy was out of town on the night O'Sullivan was killed."

"Okay, now tell me about Gladstone," said Harry.

Sergeant Eric Talbot nodded. "I would never have been friends with him but I'd been keeping my eye on him for some time. There had been rumours that he was fiddling with young boys in the Cubs and at Sunday school. As there was no proof, I put it down to people being jealous of his popularity with kids, and I've had nobody mention any other reason why he was killed."

"I'd been looking at him also," said Lars van Dyke. "But like Eric, I questioned a number of people but there was no proof of any misdemeanour or crime."

"Then what about Jerome Slaughter?" asked Harry.

There was silence until Greg White spoke again. "Nobody I talked to knew anything about him. He was a university student and, from what everyone has said, he was so wrapped in his studies that he didn't mix with others; not even in his own class. Why he was a victim is a mystery. Maybe it was a mistake on behalf of the killer."

Harry paced slowly across the front of the room. "Is there anyone you know of who has had a close association with all the victims?"

Eric Talbot lifted his hand for attention. "It's hard to think of one person who would be friends with all the victims or even be close enough to sit down and have a drink with them. We have three university students and one teachers college student. There is a link there, but Winton and Brouwer are nothing like them."

"Lots of people might have had some sort of connection to all the students," said Harry. "Some of the lecturers knew or lectured to them. Hamish and another lecturer were in the band with Gladstone and competed in choral competitions against him. Many of the students would have come across them in lectures or at the Bevery or in social groups. Can any of you help with that?"

Lars coughed. "Some people who attend church and are also involved with other groups in the region like sport or the band, choral or history groups might have known a number of the victims. Then there are people like teachers, shop assistants, doctors, café staff, mechanics at the garages and many others who would know some or all those victims."

The discussion continued for some time. Little was added to what was already known but it was important to confirm the details with all the local officers and the Sydney team together.

Harry thanked the group for their cooperation and Ray Johnston closed the meeting. Harry asked his team to stay a while.

"Joe, I want you and Jack to go out and find members of the art and craft and lapidary groups who might have worked with kilns or know somebody who might do copper enamelling. We'll see you back at the hotel at five for refreshments."

"What do you want us to do, Harry?" asked Mary.

"I want the rest of you to stay here and get on with your analyses. By the end of the day, I want to know what you believe should be done that we haven't done so far. I want your clear advice by tomorrow morning. I'll see you at five."

Chapter 41
Thursday

Harry was still in bed when the phone woke him. The clock beside the bed registered six-thirty. Harry lifted the handpiece and heard the stern voice of Graham McInnes who was on early morning desk duty at the station.

"I'm sorry to wake you at this time, Harry, but I just got a call from the university to say that the body of a young man in military uniform has been found tied to the large wheel of the old bullock wagon off the main drive."

"Who called you?" asked Harry.

"It was the night janitor, Frank Upton. He was driving out to go home after his shift then went back to the office to call us and said he would stay next to the body until you get there."

"Thanks Graham. Call Bruyn's Hotel and tell the team I'll be there to pick them up in ten minutes. I'll call Joe to be at the hotel as well."

Harry had a quick birdbath in the basin before putting on the first pair of trousers and shirt he could put his hands on; then his boots, socks and a thick duffle coat. The air was brisk. He was out the door in ten minutes.

He wasn't expecting a warm reception when he arrived at the hotel—and he didn't get one.

"I haven't had time to shower or put on my make-up," shouted Rita as she came down the stairs.

"What about breakfast?" said Jack indignantly. "I never do anything before breakfast. Come on, Harry. It won't take long to have some cereal and toast at least."

"I don't start work without my coffee; and I want it hot, black and sweet," said Mary. "After that, I'm all yours, Harry. You can do whatever you want with me."

"Wow, Harry," said Luke. "That's an invitation and a half. Look, we others will go back to bed and leave you and Mary together for a while."

The team broke into laughter.

"Okay," said Harry. "I'll organise with Mario and the cook here at the hotel to prepare some food to be delivered to us at the university so we can get on with the job while we eat. Now, let's go."

***

As they drove towards Booloominbah, the main administrative building at the university, they saw the old bullock wagon set on the grassed area off to the left of the drive.

"Why would you have an old broken-down bullock wagon here on the campus of a university, Harry?" asked Mary.

"It's a long story, Mary. This land was a part of the original estate of the White family back in the 1800s. Frederick and Sarah White owned a lot of property in the Hunter region but Sarah found the cooler climate in Armidale during the summer months helped with her health problems. After travelling back and forth for years, they relocated the whole family here about 1880 when it was announced that the new railway line would pass through the town. Frederick bought numerous blocks of land to the north-west of Armidale. Later on, this part of the property was donated by the family to establish the campus for what would become the University of New England. The wagon over there was one used by the Whites to carry goods and chattels from the Hunter to here."

When they stopped the vehicles, Harry could see that the wheel on which the body was tied had been detached from the wagon and was lying on the grass.

"Look how the body is spread-eagled across the wheel. Is there something symbolic about that position?" asked Mary.

Harry immediately walked across to check if there was any sign of life. There was none. He invited Frank Upton to talk to the team.

"Thanks, Frank, for letting us know so quickly. The man tied to that wagon wheel is in army dress uniform. Do you know who he is and why he is dressed like that?"

"I don't know him personally," replied Frank, "but there was an army parade here last night. It was the Sydney University Regiment company."

"Why would they call it by that name when they are here in Armidale?" asked Rita. "That doesn't make sense. This is not Sydney."

"This university is still technically a college of the University of Sydney and the army unit here is a branch of the Sydney battalion. Two years ago the Citizen Military Forces were started up again after the war and the SUR was reformed as an infantry battalion, with a company raised again here at the university."

"Thanks Frank. Before you leave the campus, could you go back to the office and call David Hobbs from the funeral parlour as well as Doctor Ebsworth and ask them to come here as soon as convenient."

Harry asked the team to stand back and take note of the scene in front of them.

"Why is that back wheel much bigger than the front wheels?" asked Mary.

Harry pointed to the detached rear wheel. "The rear axle was fixed but the front axle had to be on a swivel for turning and therefore the wheels had to be smaller to turn under the tray. The back wheel is bigger in diameter than the height of the victim. I'd guess it is at least six feet, six inches across."

"Look over there at the rear of the wagon," said Jack. "There is a small round table and two chairs."

"They are the same type of chairs and table as the others," replied Harry.

"There are also two glasses and a bottle of what looks like Scotch whisky. Isn't that the same as for the other cases, Harry?" asked Jack.

"Yes, but in the other cases it was beer or other alcohol, or lemonade in the case of Petherby. Before we move to the wagon or the table and chairs, I want you all to spread out along the gutter of the driveway. Be careful because there might be footprints in the soft soil. After we finish on the roadside, walk slowly towards the wagon and then move around the ends and across the back. Stop if you see anything. Let's go."

Mary called out. "Look at the soft earth gutter here at the edge of the lawn. There are numerous footprints and tyre marks."

Harry asked Joe to get the plaster of Paris out of the wagon to take casts.

"There are more footprints here to the left of the driveway," shouted Jack.

Harry walked along the road towards Jack. "These look different to the ones Mary found but they might not even belong to the killer or the victim. They could have been made by any one of hundreds of students or staff, or visitors. We will at least be able to eliminate the victim because he still has his army boots on."

Luke pointed towards the table. "There are some depressions around the table and chairs, Harry, but the grass there is too soft to get plaster casts from them."

"Okay," said Harry. "Now I want all of you around on the road side of the wagon to view the body. Take note of everything."

"There are no obvious physical injuries to his face and hands. His clothes are neat and tidy," said Joe.

"Look at the grass between the table and the wheel," said Luke. "It looks like drag marks. I'd say he collapsed at the table and was dragged over to the wheel."

"If he died at the table and was then dragged to the wheel, why would the killer tie him to the wheel?" asked Mary.

Luke pointed to the wheel. "The time taken to drag the body from the table across to the wheel increased the risk of the killer being caught. I've been reading this man as being smarter than that."

"Look," said Rita as she bent over and pointed at the body, "there's an edge of cardboard showing just under the front flap of his tunic."

Harry stepped forward, took his handkerchief from his pocket and gently removed the small cardboard sign. He laid it on the grass. It read:

Humility

"Joe, help me untie these rope knots because I want to look to see if there's anything underneath him."

After the ropes were removed from around the man's wrists and ankles, Joe grabbed hold of the left shoulder and hip and gently rolled the body over on its side to reveal a second piece of cardboard taped to the wheel. Harry removed the sheet and laid it on the grass. It read:

Never be wise
in your own sight.

"Wow, that is a bit too profound for me," said Jack. "What do you think, Luke?"

"I'm finding it difficult getting into this killer's mind," replied Luke as he scratched his hip. "I've read that phrase somewhere before and I think it means to stop looking at yourself and thinking that you are the smartest person on this earth."

"Do you mean, Luke, that this bloke is a smart arse and is up himself?" asked Joe.

"To put it crudely, Joe, I think you have hit the nail on the head. And the word 'Humility' seems to me to be a message from the killer for this man to think more of others instead of his own pride."

Harry pointed at the man's shoulders. "This man is a one-pip officer in the army."

"What does that mean, Harry?" asked Mary.

"He's a new officer. A university company like this one would have a major in charge, then a captain and one or two lieutenants. This man has only one pip on each shoulder meaning that he is a second or lowest-order lieutenant."

"What now, Harry?" asked Luke.

"I want Rita and Jack to start by taking prints from the victim and take samples of saliva and hair and anything else of importance at this site. Then go over the table, chairs, glasses and bottle for prints and samples. Joe and I will check this bloke's clothes and body. Mary and Luke, I want you to check over the whole wagon and underneath and then move outwards from the wagon in circles to look for anything that might relate to this incident."

"I'm not climbing up on that wagon, Harry," said Mary. "I could fall through those rotten timbers and break my neck."

"Do what you can, but don't take unnecessary risks. I can't be sure but I doubt that there's anything of importance on top, so concentrate more underneath and the surrounds."

"What about that car parked on the other side of the road?" asked Joe.

They all turned around. There was a shiny 1940 bright-blue Ford Deluxe car with white-rimmed tyres parked on the grass under a tree on the other side of the road.

"Before anyone touches that car," said Harry, "I want Rita and Jack to go over it for prints and the collection of dust, fibres, hairs, stains or papers. Check in the glove box or behind the sunshade for a registration or licence. Luke and Mary, you continue around the wagon."

Ten minutes later, Rita and Jack walked back to the old wagon. "The car was unlocked so we looked inside," said Rita. "We found a licence and registration in the glove box. The owner is Stephen John Parker. His address is Bundarra Road, Armidale. His date of birth is the 25th of February, 1925. If this is him it makes him twenty-five years old. That would be about the age of this fellow. It could be his car. There are manila folders on the back seat filled with handwritten and printed notes about locust plagues, the problems of excess run-off from irrigation schemes, and the problem of eradicating Paterson's curse weeds from cereal crop farms."

"Thanks Rita. Good work. A person of that age could certainly be a second lieutenant and the notes suggest that he is studying or lecturing in agriculture. I'll follow that up with the university."

When Harry turned back to the body, Joe stood up and handed him two small objects. "I found these in his jacket side pocket, Harry. They were in a small box that looked new."

"Good work, Joe. Those are star insignias, or what we commonly call pips, and are worn on the shoulders by lieutenants in the army. I would guess that this man has just been promoted to first lieutenant and, therefore, he would be entitled to wear an extra pip on each shoulder."

"What do you want me to do now, Harry?" asked Joe.

"Pick up those ropes that held the body and bag them. They might have blood or other fibres on them. When you finish, we will lift him away from that wheel, undo his clothes and check the body for any injuries."

Together they laid out the body on the grass, undid the jacket and the buttons on the shirt to check for signs of any injuries. Harry pulled up the top of the singlet to check the chest area. Joe pushed up the trouser legs but found no bruises or cuts. They looked up and saw both David Hobbs in his hearse and Gregory Ebsworth coming up the drive.

Chapter 42
Thursday

"This is becoming a bit of a habit, Harry," said Gregory unsmilingly. "My patients are complaining that they can't get an appointment with me because I'm so busy dealing with the dead, and they want to be looked after while they're still alive. Will the government pay me extra for each of my patients who leave me to go down the road to Doctor Downes?"

Harry patted Gregory on the shoulder. "I don't sleep at night because I'm worrying about where you will get a few extra pennies to buy a bowl of porridge to keep you and the family from poverty's door. I rang Captain Jack Walsh from the Salvation Army to call around to your place today to see if he could help."

Gregory relaxed and smiled. "Alright, alright," he said. "I should have known I'd get no sympathy from you lot who get paid a fortune out of the money the government rips off from us hard-working people who pay our taxes."

Gregory walked towards the victim, bent over, checked for a pulse and looked over the exposed body parts.

"I know this man. He's Stephen Parker. He lives with his family on a property off Bundarra Road. I know the parents. He's certainly dead. On first viewing there doesn't appear to be any external injuries."

Joe stood up. "Look at this. We have another metal pendant with a number. It was tied around his neck. This one is number 8."

All the team quickly moved in to look at the enamelled metal pendant.

"That's interesting," said Luke. "Do you remember on Tuesday we were talking about the sequence of numbers and whether they could be related to Dante's nine circles to hell or Pope Gregory's seven deadly sins? If this one is number 8, does that mean we forget about the Pope's deadly sins and we have 9 and 4 from Dante's list still to go? Or is this just pure coincidence?"

"Hold hard," said Mary. "How many people have even heard of Dante's *Divine Comedy*? Wake up. I don't think it has anything to do with these murders, and the more we concentrate on these theories the more we are distracted from finding the truth."

Jack put both hands behind his neck and pulled his head forward while thinking. "It could be as simple as this killer, having produced a collection of numbered pendants, probably as a hobby, just selects one at random for each victim. He might have dozens of these pendants. The next victim might get number 20. We mustn't get bogged down in speculative theories. Let's get back to the facts."

"Thanks Mary. Good point, Jack," said Harry. "I want Mary and Joe to remove the rest of the victim's clothes and examine the body for injuries and help Gregory complete his examination. The rest of you will do circles outward from the wagon to check again if there are any other items of interest."

Twenty minutes later, Gregory approached Harry. "There are no external injuries; not even any bruising or cuts. And certainly nothing that would cause death by an external physical assault. When we get him back to the parlour I'll do an autopsy and examine the stomach contents and take samples of the saliva, liver, blood and kidneys. With your approval, Rita and Jack might like to be there to help."

"Sure, they can go back in the hearse with David," replied Harry.

Jack and Joe helped David bag the body and loaded it into the hearse. David drove off with Rita and Jack, closely followed by Gregory. Harry, Luke, Joe and Mary continued to examine the surrounds of the old wagon.

"Rita said that one glass and the whisky bottle had no prints on them, and the table and the chair on that side also had been wiped clean," said Luke. "This man has been so careful not to leave any trace of himself. He must be aware that the extra time taken to clean the site of any evidence increases the risk of someone seeing him at the scene of the crime, especially out in the open like this."

"How do you read this killer now, Luke?" asked Mary.

Luke took his time to think before he answered. "I see him as an anal-retentive type. He is probably extremely fastidious, stingy, obstinate and preoccupied with obsessive order, control and attention to detail.

276

Think about the amount of planning that this person has done to organise each and every one of these murders systematically, without anyone knowing. Such people are very disciplined and often gravitate to groups that are orderly and structured. They are extremely meticulous. In youth they are usually drawn to groups like the Scouts and later, maybe to the Church or armed forces where there are clear distinctions between good and evil and in an environment of discipline."

"Are you saying that they are obsessive and compulsive?" asked Mary.

"They can be," said Luke. "They can be obsessed with cleanliness such as repetitive hand-washing. They usually have high levels of anxiety which they sometimes try to hide through humour. And they are often suspicious, intolerant and critical of others who don't meet their standards."

Harry nodded. "Is it true, Luke, that some of those people retreat from society and isolate themselves because they become so frustrated by others not meeting their strict standards?"

"Yes. As I mentioned before, a few do act like that, but then there are others who resort to publicly lecturing those who ignore their advice and demands. They can become very frustrated and demanding. Some might put themselves in positions where they feel that they can help change society for the better. In that way they feel they can change people's behaviour towards matching their own strict standards. But the exact type of person we are dealing with here is only a guess."

"Okay," said Harry. "I think we have done enough here for the moment. People will be soon arriving at the university and we need to cordon off this area. When we go along to the administration block, Joe, I want you to stay here and get some rope and signs from the car and secure this area from the public."

"What then, Harry?" asked Mary.

"We'll get the details of this man from Records. Is he a student or lecturer? He could also be someone from town who has joined this army company here. After that I want to talk to the officers commanding the SUR unit who would have been here last night." Harry, Mary and Luke walked to Booloominbah and went to the office of Bonnie Munro, the senior administrative officer and informed Bonnie of the murder of Stephen Parker.

"Oh my goodness," gasped Bonnie. "I wondered what was going on when I passed you people in the driveway when I came to work."

Harry asked for and was soon handed the student record card of Stephen Parker.

"Bonnie, can you tell me which property on Bundarra Road belongs to the Parker family? asked Harry.

"You can't miss it," replied Bonnie as she wiped her nose and eyes with a linen handkerchief. "I know the family. This is so sad. Their property fronts onto Bundarra Road. At the gate there is a yellow forty-four-gallon drum on its side with the property name of *Dumbarton* painted on the lid. It is the name of the city in Scotland where the family came from."

"Tell me a bit about Stephen."

"Well," said Bonnie, "half the girls here would love to have been his girlfriend. He was tall, handsome, drove a nice car and came from a well-to-do family. He was captain of the rugby and swimming teams and, for many people, he was Mr Popularity. He was a little older than the other students in his year because he worked on the property for a few years before commencing his studies."

"What was he studying?"

"He was doing agriculture. He was in his third year and doing honours. He was naturally gifted intellectually and it looked likely that he would have won the medal in the science faculty at the end of this year."

"Now Bonnie, I detect a certain tone in your voice which tells me that you know more than the basic details about this man. You said you know the family. What was Stephen really like?"

Bonnie sat back in her chair, clasped her hands under her chin and smiled. "He was a spoilt brat. As the only son of a rich grazing family, he played the part to the hilt. He was a high achiever but skited about it all the time; a typical show-off. He was pompous, arrogant and intolerant of others less able than himself."

"But surely, Bonnie, if he was captain of the rugby and swimming teams, he must have been respected by the other students?"

"He was captain because he scored more tries than the others; he was the fastest freestyle and backstroke swimmer; and he was the one who kept telling the others what to do. The others just let him take over.

They were happy because they were winning, not because they liked or respected him."

"Can you give me the names of the officers in charge of the Sydney University Regiment that paraded here last night?"

"Yes. Paul Rundell is the major commanding the unit. He's a senior lecturer in the agriculture department. Hamish Mackenzie, who you have already met, is the captain and second in command. And Richard Watkins, the young history lecturer, is the first lieutenant."

"Thanks for your help, Bonnie. We must get out to the property to inform Stephen's parents of his death. Could you alert those three officers that we would like to talk to them later?"

***

Harry drove Mary and Luke along Bundarra Road and turned into the property near where the bridge crossed Saumarez Creek. The distinct letter box showed the way. The driveway was bordered by tall Lombardy poplar trees with the last remnants of golden leaves hanging on. The large brick house with a wide bull-nosed verandah was a relatively new construction. To the right were a large machinery shed and an older shearing shed with holding paddocks.

They were greeted at the door by a tall, elegant woman dressed in a tartan skirt and Aran sweater with diamond patterns. She introduced herself as Muriel Parker, invited them into the sitting room and then went to call her husband Scotty. When they had all settled into the comfortable chairs Harry explained the purpose of their visit.

There was immediate shock. Muriel Parker raised her open hands to each side of her face and closed her eyes as the tears flowed. Scotty Parker stood quickly and walked around the room, trying to gather his thoughts while he slapped his hands together before stubbing out a cigarette in the nearby ashtray. Both were speechless for some time.

"Oh my God," whispered Muriel after a while. "My beautiful son, taken from me in the prime of his life. Why would God punish us like that? Stephen had the world at his feet, and now that has been taken away from him. Why God? Why? Why? Why?"

Scotty sat down in the long lounge. "Do you know who did this to my son?"

Harry leaned forward. "No. We suspect that he might have been victim to the same serial killer we've been searching for recently."

"How was he killed?" asked Muriel.

"The cause of death is uncertain at this stage. That is part of our ongoing investigation. However, from an initial examination, it looks like he did not die in pain."

"Thank goodness for that. Where exactly in the university did it happen?" asked Scotty.

"It happened beside the entrance road to the university after the army parade last night."

"But last night was special because he was to receive his second pips to become a first lieutenant. It was a big night for him," said Scotty.

"Stephen was a one-off," said Muriel. "He always topped his classes at school. He was school captain at the Demonstration School. He went to Farrer Agricultural High School at Tamworth where he topped the classes, was school captain and captain of the football and swimming teams. He passed the Leaving Certificate with first-class honours."

Scotty coughed to get attention. "After school he helped me here on the property for three years to get practical experience with farming. Because he was on the farm he didn't have to enlist in the army. In the last three years he studied agricultural science and passed with distinctions. He was going on to do honours before going out as an agronomist. He was also captain of the rugby and swimming teams at the uni. Maybe somebody took a dislike to him because of jealousy? He's had to face that all his life. The other students didn't like it when they couldn't keep up with him. He was a genius in every sense of the word. He was a victim of the tall poppy syndrome."

"He'd even been thinking of doing vet science as a second degree to broaden his options when he graduated university," said Muriel.

"The circumstances surrounding his death suggest that Stephen knew his killer and might have been friends. Do you know of anybody who might have been a close associate or friend who would want to kill him?" asked Harry.

"Absolutely not," shouted Scotty. "Some of his mates might have been envious of him but they wouldn't go to that extent. No, no, no. Definitely not."

"What about neighbours?"

"He used to be very friendly with Anthony McAuliffe next door but not so much now," replied Scotty.

"When can we see the body?" asked Muriel.

"We have to carry out an autopsy and that should be completed today," replied Harry. "I'll get David Hobbs from At Peace Funerals to call you when you can see Stephen. We'll have to keep the car and his clothes for a few days to complete our examinations. We have our top scientific investigation team here this week to help with the analyses."

"Who were his closest friends?" asked Mary.

"He was great mates with the blokes in the rugby and swimming teams," replied Scotty. "He was friends with everyone. But I must say that he had only a few very close friends, and they tended to be in the same school doing the advanced studies with him. Quite frankly, he was so busy he didn't have time for many friends. But he was a person who others looked up to. He was a natural leader. He was not backwards in taking charge and telling people what to do and how to do it."

"Did he have a regular girlfriend?" asked Luke.

Muriel spread her hand towards Luke. "There were many girls who wanted to be his friend, but I can tell you straight that most of them didn't have a brain in their head and were totally unsuitable for my Stephen. They were a bunch of flippity-flops looking for a good time at Stephen's expense; but he could see through all of them."

Harry stood. "I'm sorry to have been the bearer of bad news but please contact me if you remember anything that might help us find Stephen's killer. We must be off now."

***

As Harry, Mary and Luke drove down the main street back to the station, Harry caught a glimpse of a man whose face looked familiar. The man walked into the entrance of Richardson's store.

Chapter 43
Thursday

"You two go into the cottage," said Harry to Mary and Luke. "I'm just going down the main street to the shops."

Harry walked from the police station around to Beardy Street and along to Richardson's store. After waiting on the footpath for a few minutes he saw the man he had passed while driving in the car. The man was standing inside the doorway of the store. Harry recognised him as Damien Strudwick, a former detective who had worked with him in the CIB before the war. Harry walked in and greeted him.

"Hello Damien. Long time no see. How have you been? Are you staying in town?"

"Hello Harry," replied Damien as he looked somewhat startled. "Yes, I'm staying at the Wicklow for a couple of days."

"It's great to see you again after all these years, Damien. Why don't we go across the road to the Empire Café and I'll shout you a cup of coffee?"

"No thanks, Harry. I'm pretty busy. Lots to do. Sorry."

Harry shifted around so that he stood straight-on to Damien and looked unblinkingly at him.

"Damien, I heard you are retired. You've booked into the Wicklow for a couple of days and you are wandering the main street of Armidale looking at clothing stores. So don't tell me you are too busy to have a coffee with a former colleague. Come on, mate. You and I worked well on those cases before the war, so let's go and have that coffee."

Harry took Damien's arm and led him out the door and across the road to the café.

"Now Damien," said Harry as they waited for the coffees, "we all know you were great mates with Sherman and Cross in the old CIB, but

I always saw you as being clean and honest; and you were a great detective. So why are you here in Armidale checking me out?"

"What do you mean?"

"You know exactly what I mean, Damien. You have been visiting Fred and Joe in the gaols and they have asked you to keep track of me so they can plan their next move against me. They thought that I would be too dumb to work out why you were in town. They had two hoons try to do me over recently, and that failed."

"I don't know what you are talking about, Harry."

"That's interesting, Damien, as I never saw you as being senile. You know exactly what I'm talking about. But never mind, mate, because I have most of Tony Jacobs's SIB team in town. I pointed you out to them. So if you see someone following you around town you'll know it is one of them."

"Why would you do that?"

"Because you are not as young as you used to be, and I wouldn't like to see you have a fall with nobody around to help you. How long, exactly, did you say you are you staying in town?"

"I'm leaving this afternoon," said Damien as he stood suddenly to leave. "I just remembered that I have to get back home."

"All the best, my friend," said Harry as he walked with Damien to the door. "Enjoy your retirement—and give my regards to your beautiful wife Mary. She is a wonderful woman. You two have earned a great retirement together without this nonsense. Give my regards to Fred and Joe."

***

"Where have you been, Harry?" asked Joe as Harry entered the station.

Harry told them about his meeting with Damien. "Fred and Joe will never give up. All the team will have to keep their eyes open because any of you could get involved if they see you as supporting me—but enough of that."

Graham McInnes came into the room. "Bonnie Munro phoned to say the officers in charge of the SUR parade will be available to see you now."

"Let's get back to work," said Harry. "Luke and Mary, I want you to come with me back to the university."

***

Arriving at the university, Harry, Mary and Luke walked to the agricultural science rooms. There they met Paul Rundell, the major in charge of the Sydney University Regiment unit. Paul was dressed in a dark-blue pinstripe suit and red silk tie. He was a tall, well-groomed and good-looking man with an upright posture. His fine and well-trimmed moustache completed the image of a man well suited to lead a regiment. He invited them to sit in the vacant laboratory.

"Thanks for seeing us at short notice, Paul," said Harry. "You already know what happened to young Stephen Parker. Could you talk to us about him?"

"Certainly," replied Paul as he stroked his forefingers across his moustache. "He was one of the brightest students I ever taught. He was a certainty to win the academic medal this year and I was hoping he was going to do his doctorate, and then, after a few years of practical experience, return here as a lecturer."

"How did the other soldiers in the unit find him?" asked Mary.

"At last night's parade they were all so pleased for Stephen," said Paul. "Last night we gave him his second insignias, promoting him to first lieutenant. He was a natural leader. He had a fine record of leadership throughout his life at school, in the community and here at the university. If we had to go to war I'd have wanted him next to me."

"But someone didn't want him," said Luke. "Why would someone want to kill him?"

Paul ran his fingers across the tops of his ears and smoothed the hair on each side. "Envy. As you know, people in authority and those with extraordinary talents are often attacked by those who can never live up to the same high standards."

"Think about all the people in your department, the army unit and in the general university community where Stephen was well known. Who would you suggest hated Stephen the most?" asked Mary.

Paul stammered. "Well certainly nobody in agriculture or the SUR unit. We all get on well and we all respected Stephen. We were all proud that someone close to us was so successful. Success breeds success.

There could be others in the university who would have been very envious of Stephen, but I couldn't name anyone who would go as far as wanting to kill him."

"How did the other senior officers and Non-Commissioned Officers get on with Stephen?" asked Harry.

"Hamish Mackenzie is the second in charge. He is an excellent officer. He is very strict with the troops and that is not a bad thing because—as you very well know, Harry, from your recent experiences—discipline is what saves lives at the front. He was always tough on Stephen because he saw him as a potential officer and he couldn't stand slackness. Lieutenant Richard Watkins is a bit more casual but he is excellent in the field. Sergeant Barry Case is strict on parade but mixes well with the troops away from the unit, and they respect him. Joe Cameron and Charlie Mitchell, the two corporals, are good men. I could depend on any of them in a crisis. I've never heard them complaining about anything Stephen made them do or how he treated them. "

"Could you suggest anyone who might have wanted Parker dead?" asked Harry.

Paul looked at the ceiling as he thought. "It's only my personal opinion, because there is no proof, but I'd say that it was more likely to be someone else from the university like a jealous student or a staff member but not someone from the SUR unit and certainly not the officers."

"How did you and the other officers get along?" asked Mary.

Paul chuckled. "Oh, Hamish would just love my position here as officer in command of the unit, but he'll have to wait his turn. I'm not intending to resign."

Upon Harry's request, Paul provided him with a list of the soldiers in the SUR and their academic departments. Also on the list were the names of four members of the unit from Armidale who were not students or lecturers at the university. Harry thanked Paul for his time and he, Luke and Mary walked to the psychology department building where they met with Hamish Mackenzie. Hamish invited them into his office.

"Thanks for meeting with us, Hamish," said Harry. "What can you tell us about Stephen Parker?"

Hamish sat upright in his chair as if coming to attention. "I didn't lecture to Stephen but he was in my unit in the SUR. He was an outstanding soldier. I heard that he was an exceptionally bright student and was very much involved in activities in the university."

"Relax Hamish," said Luke. "I know this must be a shock for you all, but what was he like as a person?"

Hamish sat back in his chair and looked out the window. "He came from a highly respected and well-to-do local family and he had a wonderful, caring upbringing."

Luke continued. "Yes, we know that, but what I'd like to know is how he got on with the other students?"

"He was captain of the rugby and swimming teams."

"Yes, we are aware of that, but that doesn't tell us how he got on with the other students and staff here at the university. Was he liked by the other students?"

Hamish paused before answering. "I hate to talk ill of the dead but many of the other students thought he was a bit of a snob; a bit up himself. He mostly mixed with those from the upper class of society, and particularly with others with better-than-average intelligence."

"As captain in the SUR, you must have had a lot to do with him in a variety of situations. How did he perform in the army?" asked Harry.

"He was well accustomed to army drills before coming here, having reached sub lieutenant in the cadets at Farrer Agricultural High School. And in a tough boarding situation like that, it was no mean feat."

"At last night's parade he was promoted to first lieutenant," said Harry. "Was he promoted on your recommendation?"

Hamish paused again and sat forward with elbows on the arms of the chair. He cradled his chin on his interlocked fingers. "No. Stephen had passed all the officer examinations and had participated in the required field work. He was highly recommended by Paul Rundell."

"Why didn't you recommend him?" interrupted Mary.

"I felt he was too young and that he needed to be more considerate of others and not so much up himself. Pride to him was more important than performance and, in many situations, he wanted to blame others rather than himself; especially those in the lowest ranks."

"Was he inclined to take credit rather than acknowledging the contributions of others?" asked Mary.

"Yes," replied Hamish emphatically. "That message was the focus of Reverend Charles Aitken's sermon last Sunday. He said that it is better to be of a humble spirit with the lowly, than to divide the spoil with the proud. It was a strong message and it was a pity that Stephen wasn't there to hear and take heed of it. And I'm not that surprised that someone slipped him a loaded Mickey Finn."

Harry sat upright. "Why would you say that he was slipped a Mickey Finn?"

Hamish shrugged his shoulders and turned to look out the window. "It's well known around town that the other victims were poisoned; it was reported in the newspaper, so I just assumed that Stephen was also poisoned. That's all."

Harry stood, thanked Hamish and led Mary and Luke to the history department rooms where they met Pat Murphy, Richard Watkins and Ken Salisbury. Pat and Ken were in the SUR and rugby team with Stephen. Their names were on the list given to Harry by Paul Rundell. Harry invited them to comment on Parker.

"He was a great bloke," said Pat. "We'll all miss him. It was such a shock that someone like Stephen was targeted by this killer. He was so talented and he could handle himself. A couple of weeks ago, two blokes took him on outside the dance hall because he had danced with one their girlfriends. Stephen belted both of them and left them bleeding on the footpath. We just stood back and watched. He didn't need our help."

"There was no way anyone would take us on when Stephen was with us," said Ken. "They knew what would happen to them."

"You three were bits of bullies, were you?" asked Mary.

"Definitely not," exclaimed Pat, "but we wouldn't take any nonsense from others."

"Stephen was a first-class officer," said Richard, "and thoroughly deserved his promotion last night."

For the next five minutes there was general discussion about Stephen, after which Harry thanked the three of them for their cooperation.

***

Harry drove Mary and Luke to the teachers college where they met Colin Barr and Howard Bulcock, whose names were on the list of non-university members of the SUR.

Colin started the description of Stephen. "He was a ponce. He was conceited and had a sense of superiority. He was always seeking recognition. It was more important to him to be seen in the presence of Major Rundell than any of us. His mates tell us that his room at home was covered with all the medals, ribbons, trophies and certificates he had won since he was a young kid, and the walls of the house are covered with photographs of him. He was thoroughly spoiled by his parents and he lived up to it. He tended to look down on us because we were only teachers college students and not studying at the university."

Howard Bulcock agreed with the comments of Colin. Following that conversation the team left to return to the station.

***

After Rita and Jack returned from the funeral parlour they, with Harry, Mary and Luke, joined Joe, Rita and Jack in a meeting with Ray Johnston for a final briefing of the day.

"At our meeting with Hamish," said Harry, "he said that he was not surprised that someone had given Stephen Parker a Mickey Finn. He claimed that it was no secret around town that the other victims were poisoned saying that it was reported in the newspapers. And he was right about that because James Bolton published his article in the *Sunday Truth* about the victims being poisoned. And there was that incident a couple of weeks ago at the Wicklow Hotel where Stewart Miles thought that out-of-towner had tried to poison him. We don't know where Bolton got his information about the poisoning. It is so easy for any of us to mention things like that when talking to friends and family and for them to carry that further to others. I must caution everyone again at our next superintendent's meeting. If I have to repeat it until I'm blue in the face I'll do so, because it is most important to withhold certain important information so that we can weed out the attention seekers from the real culprit when they contact us about these murders."

As Harry was about to leave the station he was handed a telegram by Pat Casey at the desk. It read:

> *In Armidale tomorrow morning. Will try to catch up.*
> *Will check at the station at 9am.   Father Ambrose.*

Chapter 44
Friday

Harry arrived at the station in time for Ray Johnston's early morning briefing. He sat with the SIB team who had just walked from the hotel. Ray asked Harry to bring everybody up to date with his investigations.

"Thanks everyone for your support for the team. I want to bring you up to date about our most recent murder."

Harry spent the next ten minutes detailing the circumstances of the Parker murder.

"Holy hell Harry, how many more will this bloke kill?" said Lars van Dyke.

"You all know how serious these cases are. It is complex because, other than the fact that some of the victims are students at the uni, there is little evidence to connect them and the other victims socially or through family connections. I would say that this man definitely lives in Armidale, or close by, and is well known to many residents in this city. I believe that he not only lives in this district but that he is actively involved in the community. He is not just a recent blow-in who has gone on a killing spree. The fact that, in every case, he has sat down with the victim and had a casual drink shows that he was known to the victims and probably had a reasonably close association with each and every one of them."

Keith Blackmore spoke up. "That wouldn't be unusual because this is not a big city and most people know lots of other people in town. We're getting a lot of calls here at the station but they are mostly from people who want to get back at others they don't like. When we interview them, it is obvious that they have little knowledge of the circumstances of the murders other than what they have read in the newspapers or heard over the radio."

"So, let's all look at any common links between the victims," said Harry. "Petherby, O'Sullivan, Slaughter and now Parker were all students of the university but they came from different departments such as psychology, zoology and agricultural science. And we have found no evidence to connect them through their studies or through other pursuits at the university or in town. They might have met casually but there is no evidence yet that they met regularly at the Bevery for meals or at a hotel for drinks. Winton was an SP bookie and was involved with loans to students but there is no obvious association with the murdered students. Gladstone was at the teachers college as a student and, because of his personal preferences, probably never played sport against the university students. Brouwer was a shopkeeper from South Africa but there is no evidence that the other victims shopped at that delicatessen. Can anybody show a connection between any of the victims?"

"Could there be a connection with some community groups like the Church, sport or other social groups?" asked Pat Casey.

Joe spoke up. "You can wipe out sport because Petherby was so fat and unfit that he could hardly stand, let alone run the length of a football field. And Slaughter was just lazy."

"What about churches?" asked Mervyn Leech.

"The only reason Winton would go to a church was to rob the day's takings, so you can eliminate that bloke," said Eric Talbot. "Gladstone and Jan van Brouwer were involved and Petherby was in the church choir but there is no evidence that the others went regularly to church,"

Mary Rutledge put up her hand to get attention. "Maybe we are coming at it from the wrong direction. Taking Harry's idea, we should stop thinking about all the victims knowing each other or being in the same social or other groups and start thinking about how the killer knew each of his victims."

Mary walked to the blackboard and wrote the word *Killer* in the centre and then the words *psychology, philosophy, English, biochemistry, zoology, agric sc, churches, teachers, hotel betting, choir, delicatessen, SUR, farms, love of food, students, sport, team mates* and *drama groups* around the edges of the board. The team members suggested others which Mary added to the board such as *Scouts, band, reptiles, Sunday school, horse racing, neighbours, clubs, money-lending, hotels, university* and *teachers college.*

290

"Now try to think of anybody at the centre who could have been connected with all of them," said Mary. "For example, the killer might know one victim through university, another through sport, another through church, another as a neighbour, another through a club like Apex, and another through some other social group. And you can add to the list, a family member. Our killer must have had a direct connection with each of his victims; otherwise, they wouldn't be sitting down with him to have a casual drink, would they?"

"Excellent suggestion, Mary," said Harry. "And while you people think about that, I want to bring to your attention the fact that a person yesterday mentioned to us that he was not surprised that the latest victim was given a Mickey Finn. We know the newspapers reported that the victims were poisoned but we must be careful in what we say about these cases."

Pat Casey put up his hand. "Remember when Stewart Miles punched that truck driver at the Wicklow pub because he thought the bloke had poisoned his drink? He said that it had been reported in the paper at that time that all the victims had been poisoned. I don't read the papers but, if that was true, people around town would be talking about it."

"That's a good point, Pat," said Harry. "But we must not mention that it was by phenobarbital."

"The difficulty I have," said Pat Casey, "is that this killer must be so cold and calculating to have committed seven murders in the last month and yet he has been able to charm each victim into accepting a friendly, let's-sit-down-and-have-a-chat invitation as if they are the best of mates."

"Good point, Pat. If I set up a portable table and chairs in the park on the banks of the creek, together with a couple of glasses and a bottle of beer, how many of you in this room would come and join me?"

Greg White burst out laughing. "No way, Harry, because you'd make me pay for the bottle before you'd pour me a glass."

"If you're paying, Harry, we'll all be there," said Pat.

The group joined in the joke and it helped to lessen the seriousness of the situation.

"And I'd charge you all double," said Harry. "And none of you would get a drink unless you brought some hot chips and crusty pies to go with the beer. Seriously though, Pat has a good point. The killer must have already had a close enough association with each victim to the extent that all of them trusted him enough to have a drink with him."

Ray Johnston tapped the table. "I think the killer was smart enough to choose the setting that suited each victim according to their particular interest or involvement in the community. Let's look at Splinter Winton as an example. He seems so different from all the others but the killer took him out the back of the Empire Hotel where Splinter did his regular SP betting. The killer might have enticed Splinter out the back on the pretext that he wanted to make a special big bet away from the customers, or, more likely, to arrange to fix a race at the next meeting."

"Or look at Jerome Slaughter," said Rita. "His only interest in life was the study of reptiles. So where else would the killer go to have a friendly chat and drink with him other than the snake farm? However, I can't see Jerome being relaxed with the killer even in his special place if he didn't also have a close relationship with that person. Jerome was very insular and was not normally comfortable in other peoples' company unless it was a close relative or a special friend or mentor. He would have been very suspicious of anyone he didn't know well who arrived at the snake farm. But he told his mother that he would be late home because he was meeting a very special friend."

"To do what this man has done means that he must be mad—absolutely crazy with a capital C," said Joe. "He is one very sick man. A man who is mentally deranged to that extent, and is planning to murder soon, should be showing odd signs, and they should have been obvious to the victims as they sat there and had a drink with him. Why hadn't they become aware of that before taking that drink from him?"

"From my experience," said Ray, "killers who are mentally deranged might still be very much in control and display normal behaviour with friends. There are many different mental disorders. Every person is different and every condition is different. It can be very difficult for the average person to pick some of these illnesses. Many doctors can't pick them. You would be surprised at the number of highly respected members of the community end up being murderers. With some of these people even close family members do not suspect them of being involved in these horrible crimes. Luke might help us here."

Luke raised his hand. "It is very difficult assessing a serious mental disorder without knowing the person. For example, people with
292

schizophrenia may suffer from hallucinations, paranoia and anxiety without showing external symptoms. They might hear voices and perceive the presence of threats. They could fear for their life and decide to react by attacking anyone who they hate or fear. These people could also be suicidal."

There was a tap at the door and Graham McInnes from the desk walked in and addressed Ray Johnston. "Excuse me, sir, but there is a visitor here for Harry."

"Thanks, Graham," said Harry. "That would be my good friend Father Captain Ambrose. He and I worked together in New Guinea during the war. He was the Catholic chaplain but he also acted as a medic right up on the front line on the Kokoda Track. He is one of the bravest men I know."

"Ask Father Ambrose to come in here, Graham. We would like to meet him," said Ray.

Harry greeted Ambrose at the door and introduced him to the team.

Lars van Dyke spoke first. "Thank goodness you're here, Father, because Harry needs a lot of spiritual guidance at the moment. But could you start by telling us about all the sins Harry committed in New Guinea? I bet he had you working overtime in the confessional."

The room erupted in laughter.

"Thank you for your question, Lars," replied Ambrose with a smile, "but as you would know, what is said in the confessional stays in the confessional. Harry's secrets remain with me and God."

"Are you going to take up a ministry here in Armidale?" asked Pat Casey.

"No Pat. I'm still a Catholic chaplain in the army. I'm based at Holsworthy in Sydney but I have a lot to do now with the new Citizen Military Force units being set up around the country. I was in the Sydney University Regiment before the war and will be meeting with the officers of that unit here at the university later today. Last night I worked with the Hunter River Lancers at Tamworth because they want to move their headquarters from Muswellbrook to Tamworth. The troops in those units also want to hear about my experiences in the worst conditions at Kokoda. They are very much aware of the recent developments in Korea and the impending war there, as well as the recent actions in Malaya. There is a fear that Communism will spread quickly from Russia to Korea and China and on to South-East Asia in a domino effect. People are worried that it will eventually take over Australia. About two weeks ago, Prime Minister Menzies introduced a bill in the parliament banning the Communist Party in this country. We are in very uncertain times."

Harry escorted Ambrose out of the room. "I'll drop you out to the university. Joe and I have to go now to conduct another interview. You are sleeping at my place tonight. My friend Colleen is coming into town tonight and I'd like you to meet her. I'll pick you up at the university later this afternoon."

***

Harry and Joe took Ambrose to the university then headed back through the city and out along Bundarra Road to the property of Jock and Gladys McAuliffe. They were met by Gladys and her son Anthony. Harry asked them to talk about their next-door neighbour Stephen Parker.

"Who were his closest friends? Who did he mix with? Did he have girlfriends?"

"I was in the same class as Steve at the Dem School and we were great mates then," said Anthony. "He went on to Farrer for high school but I was happy to stay here and go to Armidale High School. When he started to act as if he was above us locals, I had less to do with him. When he came home in the holidays he never came over here like he used to do. It was always me going over there to catch up and I quickly got to feeling that I was intruding when I did so. He was always bright and was a champion sportsman but he started to look down on us blokes who weren't as skilled as him. Even a lot of blokes at the university thought he was a stuck-up snob."

Jock took a drag on his cigarette. "He thought his shit didn't stink, but I told him to blow his nose first and then smell what he had just dropped in the dunny. Go and talk to the Lyonses on the other side of them. They've known him for years."

***

Harry and Joe drove to the farm on the other side of the Parker's property to meet Arthur and Maureen Lyons. They gave a similar description of Stephen as the McAuliffes.

***

They returned to town, worked with the team until it was time to pick up Ambrose at the university.

***

At five o'clock, Harry drove Ambrose to the Wicklow Hotel where he bought a bottle of Mateus Rosé and a bottle of fine Scotch whisky. When they reached home they found Colleen in the kitchen preparing a lamb roast.

Ambrose took an immediate liking to Colleen and they talked while Harry had a shower and changed into casual clothes.

"I hope Harry hasn't got you here in the kitchen every day so that he has a good meal ready for him when he gets home?" said Ambrose.

Colleen laughed. "No. Definitely not. This dinner is for you, not him. If I left it to him you'd be eating last night's slops from his old army dixie. If he wants to join us tonight, we'll let him. If not, he can take a stale cheese sandwich and a glass of water out into the yard and eat out there with the mice and the dog next door."

Ambrose burst out laughing. "Oh, my goodness, lass. I think you two will get on just fine. I'll have another Scotch on that."

Harry, Colleen and Ambrose spent the evening enjoying the meal, with more than a few glasses of Mateus and Scotch, before retiring to bed at midnight. Ambrose went to the small second bedroom and Harry and Colleen to the main room.

Chapter 45
Saturday

At six o'clock Harry rose and turned on the radiator. The air outside was dry and brisk. The magpies on the fence warbled and carolled to greet the new day. Colleen prepared the bacon and eggs for breakfast. Ambrose came through the front door after his early morning run.

"Ambrose," called Colleen, "go straight into the shower. Breakfast will be ready when you get out."

When they were seated, Harry asked Ambrose about his trip to the university. "Who did you meet? And what did you think of them?"

"I met with Paul Rundell who is the major in charge of the unit of the SUR here. I've known Paul for a long time. He had an outstanding record in the North African campaign against Rommel. I'm in Armidale because the New England University is pushing to sever its former links with Sydney University and Paul is seriously wanting to transfer the local SUR unit to the more local regional Hunter River Lancers when they transfer to Tamworth just down the road."

"Did you have to go on parade with all the soldiers?" asked Colleen.

"No. I only met with the officers to discuss the possible changes."

Harry put down his cup and wiped his lips on the back of his hand. "How did you find the other officers?"

"Hamish Mackenzie is second in charge. He was interested to know how you and I knew each other. He mentioned that you had spoken to him and Aled Prosser to get their opinions about these cases you're involved with."

"Although Hamish was old enough, I don't think he ever served in the war," said Harry.

"You're right," replied Ambrose. "He told me that when the government insisted in 1942 that all single men were to be conscripted, he had broken his foot and was exempted, and they never chased him up later on. He said that joining the CMF now is making up for that."

"How did you find him as an officer?"

"Put it this way," replied Ambrose, "if you and I were in the jungle on the Kokoda Track, facing the Japanese twenty feet away across the creek, I wouldn't like to have to depend on him for my safety. I see him as an officer who likes to give orders and dish out penalties to those who don't obey, but will not be there when the lead is flying. Those types demand that you salute them even in the thick of battle. Harry, you and I have seen plenty of those types in battles and we survived by using our own initiative to protect ourselves and our mates. I hate to admit it but, I even saw some of those people killed by friendly fire."

"What about Watkins?"

"He is fairly young to be a lecturer but he's raw but eager and will be a good soldier if called upon."

"Did they talk about the cases Harry is working on?" asked Colleen.

"They certainly did. In fact, they talked more about them than about the army. I gather that it is the main topic of conversation in this city. This is also big news throughout the country and no town likes to be the centre of attention for something as nasty as serial murders. Armidale doesn't want to be remembered as the serial-murder city in this country. You certainly have a problem on your hands, Harry."

"Did they have any suggestions or bright ideas?" asked Harry.

"Paul seemed to think that the perpetrator might be someone associated with the university but not necessarily from the academic staff. He thinks the killer could be a lab assistant or kitchen or admin staff member, and someone who has lived in Armidale for many years."

"What about the others?"

"Hamish said that he had done a lot of study on mental illnesses as part of his postgraduate studies and he thinks that could be a major factor in these murders. He mentioned a German psychiatrist called Emil Kraepelin and the Swiss psychoanalyst Carl Gustav Jung who did studies into such illnesses earlier this century. They specialised in mood disorders in some patients whose emotions swung between the extremes. They used names such as cyclothymia and manic-depressive psychosis. He said that people suffering from these conditions can suddenly change from one phase or mood to another. While the person was in normal or good moods nobody would know that anything was wrong, but then they would suddenly switch into severe depression and their whole personality changed, sometimes becoming suicidal. Their behaviour when depressed is rarely aggressive but can be so. They are more inclined to calm isolation, and that period could be short or long in duration."

"Ambrose, you have had years of dealing with people with mental disorders during war as well as in peacetime. What advice would you give to me and the team?"

"I'm not an expert, Harry, but I've seen men deal with critical situations in the intensity of the worst hand-to-hand jungle fighting for weeks and weeks on end. I also worked with patients in mental hospitals such as Callan Park in Sydney. As the chaplain I met with the psychiatrists every day. I was regularly invited to sit in on their group meetings when they were discussing patients. It is a very difficult area to work in, and there are not always clear answers. I know about some of the mood disorders Hamish was talking about. I've seen many patients like that. Some days they are the nicest people around and then their whole demeanour changes. They might not be angry or aggressive when they are talking to you, but there is an underlying obsession to do damage to those who don't fit into their strict standards of behaviour. Under normal conditions when they are in a calm psychological state, they could still display controlling behaviour over others due to having very high expectations of them. Your killer could be like that. On a day-to-day basis they could present as very normal to their family, friends and workmates but could suddenly change."

"Our problem," said Harry as he put down his knife and fork, "is that the killer seems to carefully plan each murder down to the last detail even though each event might only occur as circumstances suddenly arise for him to take advantage of the situation. He is so meticulous in cleaning the sites of all identifying traces. So far we have no evidence of fingerprints, fibres or anything else that could identify him."

"Yes," replied Ambrose. "That is a similar behaviour to some of the people I'm talking about, like the ones at Callan Park. While some went through those mood changes they were also fixated on order. They are often anal-retentive and pedantic perfectionists who are intolerant of the faults or weaknesses of others. They are the ones who demand high standards of behaviour in others. They can be prissy and critical. Workmates and family members often ignore or tolerate them without reacting. Those same people, however, are appreciated by the wider community because they often become very much involved in local activities and help others. Because of that they remain above suspicion. No one would suspect them of committing a crime or even a misdemeanour."

"Are you saying, Ambrose," asked Colleen, "that the person committing these crimes could be someone like the local bishop, the mayor, the president of the Show Society or even the local superintendent of police?"

Ambrose reached out and held Colleen's hand. "Colleen, Colleen. The records of crime in Australia are riddled with cases involving the clergy, the police and politicians. Don't think it couldn't happen here in Armidale. I'm not implying that any of the people here holding those positions are guilty of these murders but we must keep our minds open. Status, titles, intelligence, positions of authority or commendations are not barriers to crime. In fact, those with authority or power have better means to control the situations surrounding those crimes. The other problem with this is the police often overlook those people because of their status, authority and the high regard with which they are held in the eyes of the community. People assume they are above reproach."

"That's a great point, Ambrose," said Harry. "You said a minute ago that Paul Rundell suggested that the perpetrator could be a member of the university but not from the academic staff, and that it would have to be someone on the lower scale such as a lab assistant, kitchen staff or administration staff. Obviously, he has assumed that those in authority could not commit such crimes."

"You might like to check on Ray Johnston as well," said Ambrose with a hearty laugh. "It's those calm, controlled, respected men like him you'll have to watch."

Colleen and Harry joined in the joke.

"I'll put him through the third degree when I get to the station," replied Harry. "Now Ambrose, you can stay here and talk to Colleen all day but I must get back to the station because we have a killer on the loose, and sitting here gasbagging with you two is not finding him."

***

When Harry arrived at the Sheriff's Cottage, he met with the SIB team and asked all of them to stay in the meeting room. He walked across to the police station and asked Ken Wright, Keith Blackmore and Graham McInnes to join the others at the Cottage. Those three had served in Armidale longer than the other officers and were involved in many community organisations.

When they had all settled in the room, Harry spoke. "I've had a long talk with my friend Ambrose overnight and he helped me broaden my understanding of people who might have serious mental conditions that can lead to violence. Those people might appear perfectly normal most of the time, contributing time normally to family, work and the community. But they can change when carrying out the murders. We need to focus our efforts on catching the killer by focusing on people who live or work in Armidale and who knew the victims. See if we can find out who might have been friendly enough with the victims to convince them to sit down to have a friendly chat and a drink away from their home or in hotels."

"Where do you want us to start Harry?" asked Rita.

"I know it appears that we are going back and forth over the same things but I want you to look again at Mary's list but try to come at it more from the killer's point of view. We must begin with the university because four of the seven victims were studying there. After that we need to identify locations or groups or clubs where the killer could have met, worked with or played with each of the victims. So, let's start by naming all the groups in this city where that might have happened. Joe will write them on the board."

University, Rotary, Apex, Masons, Order of Odd Fellows, Lions, Rugby, Rugby League, Soccer, Cricket, Tennis, Basketball, Softball, Swimming, Vigoro, Billiards, Golf, Hotels, Scouts, Cubs, Girl Guides, City Council, Red Cross, CWA, Race Club, Show Society, Ballroom Dancing, Pipe Band, Brass Band, Historical Society, Teachers College, Schools, Car Club, Churches, Sunday Schools, Orchestra, Choirs, Dance Halls, Dramatic Arts, RSL, Shops, Air Force Cadets, SUR, Pottery, Lapidary, Craft Clubs

"Holy hell, Harry," shouted Ken Wright. "You don't want much, do you? There are so many different people in all those groups. How do you expect us to identify one killer in amongst that lot? Look at the hotels alone; there are about thirty of them in Armidale, let alone in nearby Uralla, Walcha and Guyra."

"Thanks Ken. I appreciate the problem but we must now try to narrow the options. For example, Splinter Winton worked only a few hotels and other victims tended to frequent one or two or none at all. So concentrate on only those places or groups that you know where a victim was involved and then we can eliminate the rest."

"I think you could remove all the women's groups," said Rita, "because we have agreed that the killer is a man. And there is no evidence that the CWA members have beaten the victims to death with their sponge cakes or Swiss rolls."

The group had a giggle as Joe walked across to wipe off Rita's suggested items from the board.

"I suggest that you underline all of the educational institutions such as the university, teachers college and schools," said Keith. "Five of the victims have come from those places and the students are very much involved in sports and other groups such as art, drama and the choirs in the city."

"What about lodge members, Harry?" asked Luke. "I've always had my suspicions about secret societies like them where they practise rituals like riding billygoats blindfolded and rubbish like that. The members are sworn to secrecy."

"Good point, Luke. Let's keep them up there."

Keith pointed to the board. "I doubt that the choir would have serial killers in their midst."

"No, Keith. Don't forget that Petherby and Gladstone were members of choirs."

Mary pointed to the board. "From all of the opinions we've heard, it has been suggested that the killer is most likely very disciplined, maybe anal-retentive, probably highly intelligent and interested in organisations where discipline is a high priority. If that is the case then I'd put a strong link between the university and the armed forces such as the SUR or the air force cadets. Let's underline those organisations."

"Most of the cadets are school kids," said Keith. "I can't see any of them being involved."

Mary turned towards Keith. "You're right, Keith, but I'm not talking about the kids. I'd only be interested in those adult officers who run the air force or army units. Add to that the men who run the Scouts or Cubs. We know that Gladstone was a Cub leader and was on a weekend camp when he was killed. Could any of them be our man?"

Harry relayed Ambrose's comments at breakfast about the SUR officers.

Ken put up his hand. "I know that a few lecturers at the university and teachers college are involved in groups such as the pipe and brass bands, the historical society, Scouts, choirs and dramatic groups. I think some of the more senior ones might be elders in the churches."

Jack pointed at the board. "Most of the people in those groups are down-to-earth citizens who wouldn't hurt a fly."

Rita pointed to the board. "We should keep the race club up there because Winton was very much mixed up in that and probably was involved in race fixing."

"Yes," replied Harry, "but even if we could identify someone involved in illegal gambling or race fixing doesn't mean that they're also a murderer."

The door opened and Charlie Hanwright entered.

"Harry," he said, "we just got a call from the ice works. You and Joe are wanted at the corner of Brown and O'Dell streets, across from West Armidale Park. This is urgent. Another body has been found."

"Okay," replied Harry as he turned back to the group. "I want Jack, Rita, Mary and Luke to come with Joe and me. Ken, Keith and Graham, you can return to the station. Let's go."

Chapter 46
Saturday

The team arrived at ten o'clock and parked the wagons on the verge in Brown Street, next to the corrugated-iron gate leading into the freezing works. They were met by manager Geoff Digby and floor supervisor Max Hislop.

"Follow me, Harry," said Geoff. "You need to look inside at what we found when we got here about half an hour ago."

The manager led the team through the warehouse to the loading bay. There were large crates, cardboard and timber boxes, pallets and stainless-steel containers. Further into the building were overhead conveyor lines with the bodies of rabbits hanging from hooks ready for skinning, cleaning and preparing for the freezer. Towards the rear of the building were very large doors leading into the freezer rooms.

"Those rabbits were brought in about four o'clock yesterday afternoon, just before we knocked off. It was to be our first job this morning. The workers were coming in at ten o'clock this morning to do that small batch on the conveyer belt," said Geoff.

Geoff Digby walked towards a large, rectangular stainless-steel tank on the floor. It was about ten feet long by three feet wide and three feet high. As they got closer the team could see the body of a man. He was floating face up in the partly filled tank. He was dressed in corduroy trousers, a thick polo-neck sweater, a scarf and a worsted gabardine overcoat.

Harry put his hand into the water to check if there was a pulse on the body. "That is freezing cold. There's ice in there and this man has been dead for some time."

"We haven't touched anything, Harry, since we closed last night," said Geoff. "Max and I came in this morning to check on everything before the skeleton staff came in to process those rabbits. As soon as we saw the body in the tank, we rang the station to let you know and then contacted the staff to let them know not to come in today."

"Thanks Geoff. You did the right thing. What is this tank normally used for?"

"Sometimes we use it to clean the larger carcasses. On other occasions we use it for chilling meat ready for freezing, or for packing the chilled meat for transport."

"We'll have to stop others coming in here, Geoff—office staff, packers, buyers, truckies, anybody."

"Okay. Only Max and me will be here. Anyhow, the other staff don't normally come in on the weekend."

"How did this man get into the building?" asked Harry.

Geoff pointed to the rear of the building. "The back door was ajar. The padlock had been jemmied. The front pedestrian door was closed but the lock had been unlatched from the inside. The chain securing the lock on the loading bay roller doors was cut. I would guess that the intruder jemmied the outside lock on the back door first, then opened the front pedestrian door from the inside before cutting the chain on the lock to the loading doors. Look, there are some drag marks on the floor."

Rita pointed at the marks. "But those drag marks are only about ten feet long. So, if this man was murdered elsewhere, then the killer probably drove in through the open roller doors before pulling the body from his vehicle and dragged it to the tank. That meant he only had to drag the body a short distance before lifting it into the tank. There are a number of tyre marks there but one set are narrow and are probably from a car and not from the delivery trucks."

"Joe, can you get the camera from the wagon and photograph those tyre and drag marks over there and then take pictures of the doors, locks, the body and anything else of interest," said Harry. "Then I want Jack and Mary to go with Max through the rest of the building to check on doors, windows, machinery and anything else. Get Max to take you into the freezer rooms as well. Rita, Luke and I will cover this warehouse area."

"What do you want us to do first?" asked Rita.

"We need to get that body out to examine it."

"I think I could help you there, Harry," said Geoff. "Give me a minute."

Geoff walked towards the side wall, reached up to take hold of the overhead controls and pressed the green button. There was a whirring of a motor and an overhead belt moved. A long chain with a hook at the end hung from the moving track. Geoff stopped it over the tank, walked over and bunched up the top section of the man's gabardine coat behind the neck and attached the hook firmly under it. To ensure a better hold of the man, he reached over and looped a length of rope around the body and under the armpits. He tied the ends into a firm knot and looped it over the same hook.

"That should do it," said Geoff. "Now stand back while I lift him out and place him on the floor where you are standing."

Geoff worked the controls to lower the body to the floor, still face up. The cold water from the man's clothes washed over the concrete floor in front of the team. Geoff walked across in his gumboots and untied the rope and hook before returning the track to its original position.

"Wait a minute," he said. "I'll get the squeegee and get rid of the water. I don't want you slipping and falling on that concrete floor and breaking your back."

For the next five minutes, Geoff worked the excess water into the drain away from the body.

Harry pointed to the man's body. "I would say that this man has only been dead up to about twelve hours. There is little evidence of wrinkling of the skin on the hands and no discolouration that comes from lengthy immersion because the icy water would have slowed the deterioration. You can see the remains of small blocks of ice in the tank water."

"If this is the work of our serial killer, this man's face looks much older than most of the other victims," said Rita. "He looks more in his forties, or even older."

Harry turned to Geoff. "Could you go to the office and phone David Hobbs and Gregory Ebsworth and ask them to come here when convenient?"

Rita swept her arm around the room. "I can't see any tables or fold-up chairs or stools like those that were found at the other murder sites. Does that mean that this man's death is unrelated to the killer in the other cases? Do we have a copycat killer?"

"A fair question, Rita, but all we can say at this point is that somebody broke into the warehouse and we have a dead body in the tank of iced water," replied Harry.

As Geoff walked towards the office he stopped and pointed towards a nearby crate. "Hey Harry, would those pieces of cardboard stuck on that crate over there have anything to do with this man, because they certainly have nothing to do with our work here? I've never seen them here before, and I go around this place numerous times every day."

Harry walked over to the crate. There were three pieces of white cardboard stuck to the side, one smaller than the other two. Written on the smaller piece in bold letters was:

**Gratitude
and
Kindness**

On one larger sheet was written:

*Rid yourself of all
deceit, envy and slander.*

On the other larger sheet in fine handwriting was:

*The Good Lord
hath spoken:
thy work is done.*

Jack, Mary and Max returned to the group, followed soon after by Joe who had been photographing the areas in and around the water tank.

Mary pointed to the last sign. "This is definitely the serial killer. But does that mean that he has finished now? Did he have an exact number of victims on his list and he has now killed them all? Or has he now had enough and won't kill anyone else? Is he now sick of all this killing?"

306

"But why would the killer go to the trouble of dragging this man in here and lifting the body up and into that tank of ice if that was the way he was thinking?" asked Rita. "He should have just left him where he killed him."

"You raise an important question, Rita," said Luke. "In every one of the eight cases the victim has been left in a very unique position and I think that reflects the killer's attitude to each of the victims individually. In the order in which they were murdered, the first victim was covered in lard and left in a room full of rats; the second was in a bath of water; the third had stones placed on his back in the creek; the fourth suffered the fire and brimstone of burning sulphur; the fifth was found in a snake pit; the sixth was dismembered in a barrel; the seventh was tied to a wagon wheel; and now we have the eighth victim thrown into a tank of ice."

"Okay," said Harry. "Let's keep all that in mind as we examine this case further. We need to examine this bloke here now. I want Rita and Jack to fingerprint everything around here and note anything else like scuff marks, stains, fibres, blood, dust or prints. You're the experts so I'll leave it to you. I want Joe and Luke to help me undress the body, and Mary to note anything we find."

"The amount of rabbit fur in this place might make it difficult," said Rita.

"I understand, but do the best you can," replied Harry.

Harry stepped forward and removed the man's scarf. Around the neck of the sweater was tied a thin leather bootlace holding an enamelled copper pendant with the number 4 clearly marked on it. He carefully handed the bootlace to Rita to check the pendant for prints.

"Wow," said Luke. "We now have eight victims and eight pendants with no missing numbers."

"How does that fit into our earlier discussions about the deadly sins and all that rubbish?" asked Joe.

"Well," replied Luke, "all of our discussions have centred on the Pope's seven deadly sins and Dante's nine circles leading down to hell, but we now have eight victims. We could still have another victim to come if the killer was following Dante. Is he saying he has done his job and couldn't care less if he is caught? Is he now saying 'come and get me'? Is he saying 'I have completed my mission of getting rid of these sinners'?"

"Okay, that's all very interesting," said Harry. "but now we need to carefully take off all of this man's clothes."

Joe helped Harry remove the victim's arms from the overcoat, sweater and shirt, baring the upper body. Luke laid out the clothes on the dry floor away from the body.

"Joe, roll him over so I can see behind his head and down the back," said Harry.

Harry found a couple of minor abrasions on the man's back but no cuts or major injuries. "These marks could have been caused by being dragged across the floor, or, more likely, across uneven ground somewhere else before he was brought here."

Joe removed the shoes and socks and undid the loose braces from the trousers. He slid the trousers off and laid them next to the other clothes, leaving the man in his boxer shorts.

Gregory Ebsworth came through the door, carrying his Gladstone bag of instruments and medicines. "What have we got this time, Harry?" he asked.

"At the moment we have a dead body with no external signs of brutal force, cuts or broken bones. We found the body in that tank of ice and water over there. From what the manager Geoff has told us, it must have happened last night or in the early hours this morning. He's definitely dead, and David will be here soon to take the body to the parlour."

Gregory walked over to the body and did an examination. "Thanks Harry. I'll wait until I get a call from David and then I'll do a full autopsy. I'd be very happy if Rita and Jack assisted me again when that happens. They were a great help with the last victim."

"Thanks Gregory. I'll send them back with David."

As Joe picked up the clothes to bag them as evidence, he stopped.

"Look at this, Harry. The back of this man's overcoat has grass stains from the waist to the tail. Could that mean that he was killed somewhere else, dragged across the grass to a vehicle, driven here and then dumped into the tank of icy water?"

"Good thinking, Joe. And there is a park across the road. Let's all go over there to examine the surroundings."

Chapter 47
Saturday

The team was about to walk across to the park when David Hobbs arrived with the hearse. Harry guided him in. He reversed through the main doors towards the tank. David got out and walked across to the body.

"Oh my God," he said. "Someone has done him in at last."

"What are you talking about, David? Do you know this man?"

"Yes. His name is Victor James. He's a lecturer in psychology at the university."

"How do you know him?" asked Harry.

"He was in the West Armidale Rotary Club with me and was an absolute pain in the bloody neck. He was so miserable that he would complain about everything. His tea had to be the first poured and it had to be boiling hot. He couldn't stand any flavours in the meat dishes except a sprinkle of thyme with the lamb. He detested Asian food because that came from filthy peasants and was probably made from dog or bat meat. He desperately wanted to be elected president of the club but nobody would ever nominate him, and that made him critical of everything the current president and committee did."

"We didn't meet him at the university," said Joe, "but he must be in the same department as Hamish Mackenzie and Aled Prosser who we have already met."

"Yes," added David, "he often spoke about them. He was highly critical of the university when they appointed somebody else over him as head of the department. He considered he was more intelligent and had more worldly experience than the other applicants. He wasn't even invited to apply for the position. He tolerated Prosser because Aled joked with him, but he hated Hamish Mackenzie."

"Why was that?" asked Mary.

"He couldn't stand Hamish being involved in everything at the university and around town and getting praise for that. Hamish was intolerant of Victor because he was always complaining but doing nothing to contribute to the department. Hamish was highly disciplined and active while Victor sat on his bum and complained all the time. They both live alone in town but are as different as chalk and cheese. You wouldn't find a bigger contrast than between those two. Hamish runs bushwalks and camps for the students. He is in the Armidale Highland Pipe Band and is an officer in the army SUR regiment. He's an elder in the Presbyterian Church, is in the choir and helps at Sunday school. He was a leader of the Scouts and organised a lot of their activities. Hamish got all the praise while Victor wallowed in his own self-pity. Victor was more interested in reading and discussing academic psychological theories with like-minded individuals."

"While you are on the topic of Hamish," said Harry, "he obviously does good deeds, but I'm quickly coming to the opinion that he could be seen as an irritating little prick. Aled Prosser gets on well with him because he doesn't let him get away with anything, but to everyone else he seems to come over as an intolerant bossy-boots who wants to rule the roost in everything he's involved in. And when he comes across people like Victor here, it is going to end up with conflict of the highest order. If he and Victor are living alone as you say, David, they have nobody there to share emotions with away from work or to let off pent-up steam. It couldn't have been a good mix with both those two in the one department."

"Could we just put it down to the fact that those two were in the psych department at the university?" asked Mary. "You'd have to be a bit mad to work in psychology in the first place."

"How long has Victor James been in Armidale, David?" asked Luke.

"He came here after the war. As a fellow Rotarian, I invited him home on a number of occasions to help him settle into the life here, but my good wife Janice put a stop to that because she couldn't stand his whingeing."

"What's Victor's background?" asked Jack.

"From what he told me, he was raised in a town called Lewes in East Sussex. He was an only child and, from what I could gather from his conversations, he was abused by his lawyer father but thoroughly

310

spoiled by his mother. Spending a lot of time in his room, he developed an interest in the arts and classical music, and studied hard. After graduation he was appointed as a psychologist at Birmingham but left because he considered those people were of a much lower class and not deserving of his status and ability. In the thirties he worked briefly in Kenya and India but could not stand the food or the people, so went back to England."

"Where did he live?" asked Harry.

"He owned a small house in Mann Street between the Duffys and Coxes."

"Thanks David. We'll help you load the body before we go to the park. Rita and Jack can go with you and the others can come with me. We'll take the clothes and other gear with us. I'll phone the neighbours when I get back to the station. I'll want to talk to them tomorrow."

The remaining group walked across the street to West Armidale Park. Harry asked them to stop in front of a small pavilion facing the park. There they found a small folding table, two chairs, a half-empty bottle of red wine and two glasses, one with some remnants in the bottom. To the right of the table was a concrete-block incinerator for burning the rubbish from the park. Harry walked towards it and bent to feel the ashes.

"There are still some warm coals under the ashes. I'd say that the killer lit that fire last night to keep himself and the victim warm. It was quite cool last night. That looks like some bits of book covers in here. It looks like someone tried to burn some books here last night."

"What's that pile of timber over there towards the railway station?" asked Mary.

Harry looked up. "That's just a build up for the Empire Day fireworks. I remember at school we had to pledge our allegiance to the King and wave the Union Jack and then we got the afternoon off to build up our fires ready for cracker night. It was the very best night of the year with our bungers, jumping-jacks and rockets. The kids here have already been building up heaps of timber for weeks, ready for the big bonfires."

Joe dusted the bottle and glasses for prints and poured the remains of the red wine into jars. He dusted the chairs and table for prints.

Harry called for the team's attention. "I want you to start at the kerbside, walk again to the pavilion and incinerator and then across the park to the other side and back. Look for tyre marks in the gutter. Bag any rubbish. We don't know if he picked up the victim and drove him here first. Go to it."

Luke pointed down the road towards Butler Street. "What about that Morris Minor parked along there?"

"Let's check it out, Luke."

When Harry and Luke reached the car, it was locked.

"Go back to the wagon, Luke, and check the victim's clothes for keys."

The key Luke brought back opened the door. Harry checked inside the glove box and behind the sunshade.

"Here's the licence. It's in the name of Victor George James, and his address is in Mann Street. His date of birth is the 10th of January, 1905. That makes him forty-five years old."

Joe shouted out from near the pavilion. "Hey Harry, come and look at this."

When Harry and Luke reached Joe, they saw him holding a bottle clearly marked with the name PHENOBARBITAL. It was the same as the ones found near Richard Gladstone and Jerome Slaughter.

"Where did you find that?" asked Harry.

"Over in the grass on the other side. The killer could have thrown it there from the pavilion. It still has some fluid in it."

"Be careful," said Harry. "If the killer was so careless to throw that away, it might still have prints on it. Dust it carefully."

"The point that interests me," said Luke, "is that, when we have found most of the victims, there has been a small table and two chairs or stools. We already know that with Winton behind the pub there was no table or chairs but only a box to sit on. With Slaughter there was a blanket but no table or chairs, and there was no table in Brouwer's shop. The killer did not remove the table and chairs from each site but had new ones at the next location."

"Yes, Luke," said Harry as he tapped him on the shoulder, "so the killer either knew exactly what furniture was required at each murder site or he brought it all every time and only used what was needed, depending on the circumstances when he arrived."

Mary called out from behind the incinerator. "Come over here. Look at this."

She held up a canvas bag with a shoulder strap. It had prints of red roses on the outside and it was the type of bag women took shopping. She spread the handles to reveal four hardcover books.

"That's interesting," said Harry. "I wonder if they are connected to those remnants I found in the ashes in the incinerator. Could all of them have belonged to the killer? Or the victim? Were they burning books together? Lay them out on the grass."

The first book was titled *The Psychology of Religion* by J.B. Pratt. It was printed in 1908. The second book had the same title but was written by C.C. Josey in 1927. The last two were more recent publications by Knight Dunlap titled *Religion: Its Functions In Human Life* and *Mysticism, Freudianism and Scientific Psychology.*

Harry walked back to the incinerator and extracted the burned remnants of the other books. The covers and first few pages were too badly charred to identify the authors or titles but he turned some of the charred pages and skimmed over the chapter headings and paragraphs in the bodies of the books.

"It's interesting that all of these books talk about the relationship between religion and psychology," said Harry. "If they were planning to also burn those books in the bag, like they did with these ones in the incinerator, does that mean that they disagreed with the views or ideas expressed in them? Or did they agree that all these books were nonsense and needed burning? Could it be similar to the German students' book-burning rallies in 1933 that began the movement of state censorship in that country? I remember at that time Goebbels described the books as intellectual filth. Or maybe they were burned just to keep them warm last night. But the question remains: why would anyone be here to burn these books?"

Luke picked up one of the intact books. "Since the beginning of man's existence on earth, people have always questioned their own existence and how that relates to the surrounding environment. There have always been philosophers, theologians and writers who have studied the human condition. Over the centuries their insights and understandings blended into the study of psychology and its relationship to religion, anthropology, science and sociology. There was often disagreement and it was not uncommon for some to destroy the works of others."

"That's very interesting Luke," said Harry. "If these books belonged to either the killer or victim, or both, then they probably deeply opposed what was written in them."

"Of the eight victims we now have, five were involved at the university and one was at teachers college; all the types of people who might read books like these," said Mary. "Splinter Winton and Jan van Brouwer were the odd ones out, but Brouwer was involved in the Church. So, because of these books, should we now be concentrating our efforts back at the university and in the churches?"

"Good point, Mary," said Harry. "I'm going to contact Arthur McBryde, the general manager of the university, and demand he set up a meeting of all teaching staff from the relevant departments tomorrow morning."

"But many of those people will be at church on Sunday or at their parents' place for Mother's Day," said Luke.

"Well, they can go to the evening service tomorrow," replied Harry. "This will be an order, not a request."

For the next hour the team went over the park thoroughly, looking for any evidence, but found nothing more of importance.

***

They returned to the Sheriff's Cottage.

Harry phoned Arthur McBryde to arrange the meeting at the university for ten o'clock tomorrow. McBryde argued against it but Harry informed him that he would not like his name in the Sunday papers as being the person who would not cooperate with the police in the ongoing investigation of these serial killings.

The remainder of the day was spent sorting all the evidence from the ice works and park as well as contacting Gregory Ebsworth for the details from the autopsy.

***

The team had a quiet dinner at the hotel before retiring early.

Chapter 48
Sunday

Straight eight.
Eight citizens dead.
One killer alive

James Bolton: Special Crime Reporter

Eight people have been murdered in Armidale in the last four weeks but there is still one killer running loose in the city. He might be the person standing next to you at the post office or sitting next to you in church.

In Australia's history there have been some very nasty serial killers. In late 1825, long before Australia's Federation, a British convict named Thomas Jefferies murdered six people on the island of Tasmania. John and Mary Makin killed ten people, as did John Lynch, while Robert Burns killed eight. Just imagine the stress on the good people of Armidale, not knowing if this killer will strike again.

Sources close to the police have assured me that the killer is most likely a person living in the city or in the New England district and is most likely to be known to many in the area. He could be your next-door neighbour.

What drives a person to commit such horrible crimes is still a mystery. Top medical experts in Sydney believe that the killer has probably been affected by a

Harry read the paper before tearing it into squares for use in the toilet. He ate some cereal and a piece of toast and Vegemite before driving to the station to meet the others on the team.

***

"What is the plan today, Harry?" asked Rita.

"I want you to come with me to visit the neighbours of Victor James. I want you others to go over every piece of evidence again from yesterday and be ready to go to the university for our ten o'clock meeting with the staff."

***

Harry drove Rita to Mann Street. Harry knocked on the door of the house to the left of Victor James's house. They were greeted by Robert Duffy who invited them in and introduced his wife Peggy. Harry informed them of the death of Victor.

"We would like you to tell us about your relationship with your neighbour," said Harry.

Robert guffawed. "Relationship? What relationship? He was the most pig-arrogant bastard I've ever met. He took the prize for the worst whingeing Pom on this earth. I don't know why he ever came to Australia. He hated everything and everyone here."

316

Peggy sat forward. "When he arrived in Armidale we did everything to help him but he blocked our every attempt. He was an odd mix. On one hand he seemed so puffed up with his own ego, but on the other he seemed so hopeless and helpless."

"He was a constant miseryguts," said Robert, "and he was a bit of a coward. He was frightened of spiders, flies, ants and anything else that moved. He even hated being near our dog Spot, the friendliest beast that ever walked on this earth."

Harry sat forward. "Did he ever have visitors? Had you seen anyone strange around his house recently? Has anything unusual happened in the street lately?"

"Never seen anyone there," replied Robert. "But I'm not surprised."

The conversation continued for some time in the same tone. The Duffys were very down-to-earth people but couldn't find a positive thing to say about their neighbour. Harry thanked them and he and Rita walked to the Coxes house on the other side of Victor's. Harry explained the reason for their visit.

Mrs Vera Cox recalled her impressions of Victor. "I felt sorry for him at first, being new to the country and living alone. I took him cakes and biscuits and we had him in for dinner a few times, but Bluey made me stop."

Bluey Cox sat back. "That bastard was in another world. Half the time he couldn't even stop to say g'day. He seemed to me to be depressed and always sad and constantly complaining. Last week he complained that a couple of beautiful camellia flowers from our side were hanging over his side of the fence and he wanted them cut back."

Harry and Rita asked the same questions as they had asked the Duffys and got the same answers. They thanked Bluey and Vera and said their farewells.

***

Harry and Rita drove to the university where they met with the rest of the team in the meeting room of the Booloominbah building. On entering the room the team sat along the front. Arthur McBryde introduced them to the professors and lecturers present. He apologised that some staff members couldn't be there at such short notice. Some were not in Armidale this weekend.

Harry addressed the gathering. "I've called you here today because we have reason to believe that the recent serial murders are directly connected to this university. We also want to inform you of the death of Victor James from this university; although I'd already given Mr McBryde permission to pass the news onto you all when he arranged this meeting. You would have all known Victor well. Before we leave this room I want each of you to tell Detective Simms where you were on Friday afternoon and night and early Saturday morning."

"Excuse me, Detective," said Joseph Tannock, a senior physics lecturer, "but where we were on the weekend is private and none of your business. We were not at work so that is our free personal time."

"Thank you Joseph, but we are investigating a number of murders and, if necessary, we will take you to the cells until you cooperate with our investigations. The information you give to Detective Simms will be confined to our team. Is that clear?"

Joseph slumped back in his chair. "Yes, okay. If you put it that way."

Harry continued. "We'd like all of you to assist in our investigations. We want you to give us information about the university victims in particular, with emphasis on their friends and possible enemies. For example, have you noticed any unusual activity, fights or arguments between Victor and anyone else recently? Have you noticed any strangers in and around the university lately, and especially in your area of work? Did you notice any strange activity or behaviour of the other victims in the weeks leading up to their murders? To start, I'd like your comments about Victor James."

Professor Clarence Stringer spoke first. "Victor was a sad, melancholic man. From my conversations with him I concluded that he had a very difficult childhood and had never formed a close personal relationship with his parents since. I doubt that he ever contacted his parents, who still live in East Sussex. And he hadn't been back to England since he came to Australia. He also found it difficult to accept the reality of working in a rural university; so different to those he had experienced in English cities. He couldn't accept that this university was in a remote country region and not in or near a major city like Sydney. To see undergraduates not in academic gowns every day was

318

unacceptable to him; not like Eton or Harrow. He never accepted that he was not good enough for more senior positions here."

"I note," said Harry, "that Hamish Mackenzie and Aled Prosser are not here today."

"No," replied Kathleen Underwood, a psychology lecturer. "Hamish said he had to go yesterday afternoon to Tamworth to attend to his sick father who is the veterinary surgeon there. He arrived back here early this morning before he and Aled took a group of third-year psychology students on the bus to Lennox Head for their field studies."

"What time did they leave?"

"About nine o'clock," replied Kathleen.

"We saw Hamish at the rat shed after young Jonathon Petherby was found dead there. We also sought the advice of him and Aled to gain a better understanding of the psychology of the serial killer. How did those two get on with Victor James?"

Joseph Pearson, a lecturer in philosophy and education, raised a hand. "Aled always tried to jolly Victor up with his jokes, but Hamish was intolerant of his complaints and constantly lectured him about his state of mind. I found it interesting, psychologically, that Hamish, although much younger than Victor, took the stance of an older brother giving advice and direction to his younger sibling about his behaviour. On some days Hamish and Victor would sit together and have serious conversations over a cup of tea or a glass of wine, while on others they couldn't tolerate each other. They also clashed on their different beliefs regarding various psychological theories. When they were together it was a battle of wits, with each one trying to outsmart the other and gain supremacy."

"You mentioned Hamish's father," said Harry. "With all of Hamish's other interests, does he have a close relationship with his parents?"

"Oh yes," replied Joseph. "Hamish never married so his mother, sister and father are his close family. He spends some weekends and holidays at Tamworth helping his father in the veterinary clinic. They are very close."

Paul Rundell, senior lecturer in agriculture, coughed to get attention. "I know that the killer took our star student, young Stephen Parker, who was also promoted to first lieutenant in the SUR, but I can't see how we can be of any use to your other investigations. I've already talked to you about Stephen and I can't think of anyone on this campus who would go about killing people. I think you are barking up the wrong tree, Harry."

"I don't think you fully appreciate the purpose of this meeting, Paul. This is not just about your prize student, Stephen. It's about all of the victims, many of whom were from this university. Paul, we want your full cooperation. Now tell us what you know about those university victims you know and remind us again about the relationship between Stephen Parker and Hamish Mackenzie, your second in command in the SUR unit."

"Why would you ask that? Hamish and Stephen were both outstanding officers."

"Were they close friends?"

"They worked well as officers. Both were very efficient and they both carried out their responsibilities according to regulations."

"Were they close friends away from the unit?" asked Rita.

"No, but then each had their own interests and were both very much involved in the community."

Harry stood, turned and whispered to the team. "I'm going to take Rita now to Tamworth to talk to Hamish's parents. I want you all to remain here and continue to give everyone in the room, including McBryde, a chance to comment on the victims and their place in the university."

***

In the car Rita asked "Why are we going to talk to Hamish Mackenzie's family?"

"Just a hunch. All the victims have been poisoned. And in each case it has been phenobarbital. You and I know that the only people to legitimately have supplies of that drug are doctors, pharmacists, hospitals and veterinarians. And this morning we learn that Hamish's father is a vet and that Hamish occasionally helps his father. It also disturbs me that Hamish mentioned that Parker was given a Mickey Finn. It might be a wild-goose chase, but I want to investigate."

***

320

An hour later Harry and Rita were met by Marjorie Mackenzie, Hamish's mother, who invited them into the bedroom where her husband Andrew was lying in bed.

"Sorry to disturb you, Andrew, when you are not well, but we are conducting a routine investigation into some matters that relate to the recent spate of killings in Armidale. They told us at the university this morning that your son visited you yesterday because you are not well."

"It's nothing, really. Just a virus which I probably picked up from one of the animals. How can I help?"

"During the course of our investigations we have found bottles of phenobarbital and we have been visiting all the doctors, pharmacists and vets to find if there have been any unaccounted losses in their supplies."

"Isn't that interesting?" replied Andrew. "It was about five or six weeks ago that someone broke into the surgery over the weekend while Marjorie and I visited our daughter in Newcastle. Hamish was here looking after the animals for us. When we returned he showed us where the intruder had jemmied the lock on the back door of the surgery and forced open the door to the medicine supply cabinet. Hamish said he had been for a walk down the street and when he returned he found the door of the surgery open."

"Was anything stolen?"

"Yes. Six bottles of phenobarbital."

"Was anything else taken?"

"No."

Andrew turned to his wife. "Marjorie, take Harry and Rita to the surgery and show them the doors and where the medicine cabinet is in the storeroom."

Marjorie showed them the locks, the register of drugs and the book entry that noted the theft of the phenobarbital. In the cabinet Harry saw two bottles of phenobarbital.

"We told the Tamworth police and gave them a written statement, but they didn't seem interested. They said they had higher priorities."

Harry returned to Andrew's bedroom. "By the way, Andrew, how much phenobarbital would it take to kill an animal like a small pig with the weight of a human?"

Andrew looked to the window as he thought. "Phenobarbital is a barbituric acid derivative and occurs as white, odorless, small crystals or crystalline powder that is very soluble in water or alcohol. The amount varies so much on the animal and its condition, but a dose of ten grams would more than do the job. Here at the clinic we prepare the liquid form by dissolving phenobarbital in ethanol."

Harry thanked Marjorie and wished Andrew a quick recovery.

***

They left to drive back to the station.

In the car Harry raised the matter of the bottles of poison. "Six bottles were stolen from Hamish's father. Three bottles were found with Gladstone, Slaughter and James. If the bottles stolen from the veterinary clinic were those used in the murders, then there are three more left. But from what Hamish's father said, one bottle would be enough to kill many victims. Does that mean that the killer used a much higher quantity for each victim than what was required for a lethal dose?"

That's a big unanswered question," replied Rita.

As they were passing through Uralla, Harry stopped the car at a phone box outside the post office and phoned Ray Johnston at home. He asked if he could have an urgent meeting with Ray and Ken Wright as soon as he arrived back in Armidale.

***

"I know it's Sunday and Mother's Day," said Harry when the two senior officers entered the room of the police station, "but I want you to call an urgent special meeting with the magistrate, Gregory McMaster. I want a warrant to search the property of Hamish Mackenzie, a lecturer at the university. I have good reason to believe that we will find evidence on his premises relating to these murders which will lead to an arrest."

"Why the urgency? Gregory won't be happy. He always plays golf on Sunday afternoons."

"Which is more important—eight dead bodies or a little white ball? I can't just break into the house by myself. I need a warrant from the magistrate to search the premises and I can't get it without your recommendation."

"On what grounds?" asked Ken.

Harry took five minutes to outline the matters relating to Hamish, his connection to the victims and their visit to Tamworth.

Ray stood and stared at Harry. "I'm uneasy with this, Harry, and I'm not sure that Gregory will be sympathetic, but let's go. You stay here, Ken. I'll take Harry to the golf course."

***

It was a very angry magistrate who dragged his golf buggy back to the clubhouse from the 15th green at the far end of the course. He demanded a beer before he would talk. Ray handed him a written request for a search warrant of Hamish Mackenzie's property.

Harry spoke. "We believe that Mackenzie stole bottles of phenobarbital from his father's veterinary surgery and has used them to kill people he does not like. We believe he had the motive and the means to carry out all the murders. He knew all of the victims and had close contact with most of them. We have strong evidence that Mr Mackenzie is the killer or is an accomplice. I believe that the evidence in that house will confirm this. Mackenzie is in Lennox Head at the moment and will not return for a few days."

The magistrate sipped on his beer. "I'm very reluctant to issue search warrants when the owners are not present."

"Sir," said Harry as he tapped his closed fist on the table, "what is more important—the sensitivities of the owner having his house searched while he isn't there or another murder? If you insist that he returns from Lennox Head to be present at the search he will be forewarned and is likely to take off and disappear."

After a pause the magistrate spoke again. "I'll consider this request overnight. I'll give you the decision at nine o'clock tomorrow morning in my office. Now, let me get back to playing my interrupted round of golf."

Harry could hardly contain his anger at the delay but there was nothing he could do but wait. Ray didn't say anything to help.

***

Harry went back to the Sheriff's Cottage to meet up with the rest of the team to tell them of the latest developments.

Chapter 49
Monday

Harry was on the doorstep of the magistrate's office at nine o'clock and followed Gregory McMaster into his office on his arrival.

"I'm not happy with this request, Harry. I really don't like approving warrants when the owner of the premises is not present. It sets a precedent for every cowboy police officer to do a search on a whim, or because they don't like the owner and they might be inclined to add items to support their case while the suspect is not there."

"Yes," replied Harry as he anxiously rolled his open right hand over his closed left hand, "but surely my request surpasses the everyday cases involving theft or embezzlement or divorce settlements. We have eight murders by a serial killer. There are strong enough grounds to investigate whether Hamish Mackenzie is the perpetrator or is closely associated with the killer. I believe the conclusive evidence will be in his house. We need that evidence to wrap up these cases and prevent any further murders."

"Okay Harry. I'll grant it just this time. You have a very flimsy case but I'm willing this time to allow it. But don't think you can come in here at any time in the future and get another warrant."

"Thank you, sir."

***

Harry sprinted back to the Sheriff's Cottage to get the others. Harry drove his MG while the team took two wagons and drove to a neat small cottage on Butler Street. It was constructed of reddish bluestone bricks with a red tiled roof. There was a very large painted weatherboard garage set back behind the house. The garden was manicured. Harry called Joe to the front door.

"Do your best, Joe. Pick the lock. I don't want to break down the door."

Joe pulled a lock-pick set from his pocket and had the door open in two minutes.

"Now," said Harry, "I want you all to spread out. Check every room. Go through everything—every cupboard, under the beds, in the garbage bins. Bag anything suspicious. Rita and Jack will take prints around the house. Give a yell if you find anything."

A few minutes later Mary shouted from the main bedroom. "Come and look at this. This jerk starches and irons his own underwear. And look at how he does his wardrobes and drawers; everything is packed so neatly that there is not a tenth of an inch out of place. Just look to those shoes and army boots; they are all polished to a mirror finish. No wonder this jerk doesn't have a wife. They couldn't keep up with that."

Luke pointed down the corridor. "It's the same in the kitchen. I reckon he gets out the tape measure to check the alignment of the baked bean tins in the cupboard."

"In the laundry," said Joe, "there's three different packets of washing soap as well as some Reckitt's Blue rinse."

"Come on, come on," shouted Harry. "I'm not interested in his nappy rashes. Get on with it."

Mary was in a room with a single bed and a desk and chair. She called to the others. "Come in here. This could be important. Here are some sheets of white cardboard which look similar to those found at every site with the messages written on them. And on the shelf is a set of old-style calligraphy pens of various sizes next to a bottle of Indian ink. I'll lay money on one of the larger nibs being used to write those messages. Also, look at the penholder. That gold Parker fountain pen is top class and I suggest that was the pen used to write that last message in cursive script on the sheet found at the freezing works. We'll need to run them through some tests."

Harry asked Rita and Jack to check the pens, brush, inks and cardboard for prints. The others returned to the other rooms to continue their searches.

Fifteen minutes later Harry called them all back into the kitchen.

"Other than the cardboard and writing equipment, is there any other evidence that could tie Hamish to these murders?"

"No," replied Jack. "But isn't that enough to go on to get him into court and locked up while we finalise our investigations?"

"Definitely not," replied Harry. "McMaster would throw us out of court, and deservedly so. We need more evidence. Let's all go to the garage out the back."

The two large doors at the front of the garage were secured by a large brass padlock. Joe picked the lock.

Harry spread his arms. "Stop here and take in everything in this space before we enter."

There was no vehicle in the garage, and no indication that one had ever been parked there. The concrete floor was spotlessly clean. The interior walls had been plastered and painted stark white. Against the left-hand side of the back wall was a steel workbench with a vice. Above that bench were many tools neatly arranged according to their individual black silhouettes painted on the wall. Between the bench and the right-side of the back wall was a door that was closed and locked.

"Look over to the right side back corner," said Mary. "There are three folding tables and some chairs with some bottles of beer, wine and whiskey on the tables. They look similar to those used at the murder sites and some of the glasses on that table also are similar."

Joe pointed to the left wall. "Who the hell is that bloke in that large frame?" said Joe.

They all looked in that direction. A bright light mounted on the roof beam shone directly onto a large-framed black and white etching of an ancient human figure. Either side of the etching were sheets of white cardboard with writing on them.

Luke pointed to the etching. "I think I've seen that image before. When I did philosophy in my undergraduate years, we spent a lot of time studying the development of religious principles. We studied the ancient philosophers and prophets. I am fairly certain that etching is of an ancient Christian prophet by the name of Evagrius of Pontus. I think it came from an ancient Armenian manuscript. Evagrius had a lot of influence on the Eastern or Orthodox Church at that time, but his writings were looked upon with reverence by scholars and all churches for many years after, including the Western or Roman Catholic Church."

"Why the hell would Hamish have this image under lights in his garage?" asked Joe.

"I can only think that Hamish must have a deep respect for the ideals promoted by the teachings of Evagrius," replied Luke. "Hamish would likely have come across him in his studies and may have specialised on him in his honours, masters or doctoral studies."

"That's out of my league," snorted Joe. "Couldn't he think of someone more famous to study?"

Luke tapped Joe on the shoulder. "Evagrius lived in the fourth century after Christ and he wrote about the eight evil thoughts that the monks of the day, and man in general, must avoid if they were to get to heaven. Later, in about the sixth century, those ideas were picked up by Pope Gregory the Great who rearranged them into what we still know today as the seven deadly sins, also known as capital sins or cardinal vices. I kick myself for not seeing earlier that there might have been a connection between the systematic behaviour of the killer and the philosophy of someone like Evagrius."

"What were the sins the old bloke listed?" asked Joe. "I might have been guilty of one or two myself."

Harry clapped his hands for attention. "Let's all walk over here to the left-hand wall. There are eight large panels of cardboard; four on either side of that etching. Each sheet appears to deal with one of those ancient sins. Study each one."

The team moved to the first panel. At the top of the panel was written in large letters:

Gluttony

"Look at those photos pinned to the top," said Joe. "That one is Jonathon Petherby at the Bevery with three plates of food in front of him, feeding a large spoonful into his mouth. The other photo is Jonathon lying on the floor of the shed with rats running in all directions."

Written at the bottom were the words:

Salvation: Temperance
Punishment: Force-feed rats or toads. Philippians 3:19

"Let's move to the second panel," said Harry.
At the top was written:

Avarice: Love of Money

There were two photos of Splinter Winton; one of him counting pound notes at the end of the bar in the Empire Hotel, and one of him with a fistful of notes at the picnic races at Tamworth, standing next to his bookmaker and father.

Written at the bottom was:

Salvation: Charity
Punishment: Bath of water. Luke 12:15

"This bloke is a nut-case," said Jack. "But he is a dangerous one because he has taken it upon himself to get rid of all the people who don't live up to his ideals and the principles laid down by some unknown monk back in the fourth century. Why would he listen to this ancient bloke as his guide for what we should and shouldn't do today when we are well into the twentieth century?"

"But," said Mary, "he has taken it to the extreme because even the main churches today preach about the seven deadly sins as only guidelines for our behaviour. For God's sake, we are a long way past the Spanish Inquisition."

"Right," said Harry. "Move to the next one."

It was headed:

Vainglory

There were two photos of Julian O'Sullivan; one dressed in his dinner suit and the other driving his expensive Jaguar XK120 car.

Written at the bottom:

Salvation: Humility
Punishment: Weigh down with stones in the water.
Psalms 119:37

The team moved to the next panel. It was headed:

Lust and Fornication

There were two photos of Richard Gladstone; one in his Rover Scout uniform and one lying in a tent with a young Cub.

Written at the bottom was:

Salvation: Chastity
Punishment: Fire and Brimstone.
Revelation 21:8

They moved to the first panel on the right of the etching. It was headed:

Sloth

There were three photos of Jerome Slaughter; one of him sitting alone in the Bevery, another of him in his Riley car and another of him at the snake farm.

Written at the bottom was:

Salvation: Diligence
Punishment: Throw into snake pit.
Proverbs 21:25

On the sixth panel was written:

Anger and Wrath

There were two photos of Jan van Brouwer; one waving his finger at his wife and another one showing him pushing a customer out the door.

Written at the bottom was:

Salvation: Patience and respect
Punishment: Dismember.
Matthew 26:52

"Come on, Joe," said Harry. "Keep up. Let's look at them together as a team."

The next panel was headed:

Pride

One photo showed Stephen Parker being awarded medals and ribbons. The other one showed him pointing to the new pips on his shoulder when he was promoted to first lieutenant in the Sydney University Regiment.

Written at the bottom was:

Salvation: Humility.
Punishment: Tie to the wheel.
Romans 12:16

Everyone moved to the far right in front of the last panel. It was headed:

Sadness and Envy

There were two photos of Victor James; one in a tweed suit and bow tie and the other waving his hand in dispute at a meeting.

Written at the bottom was:

Salvation: Gratitude and Kindness
Punishment: Tank of ice.
1 Peter 2:1

Luke waved his hands across the panels. "You must realise that the words written here are almost the same as those written by Evagrius. I'm convinced now that Hamish was obsessed by the philosopher and used him as his own guide and justification for his recent murder spree in Armidale. It must be his way of trying to cleanse the world of sinners."

Rita pointed to the etching. "Did Evagrius ever demand the death penalty for anyone who committed those sins?"

"No," said Luke. "Evagrius did not propose severe punishments for the sins. His list was only intended to be a guide to the monks at that time on how to overcome the thoughts of temptation that inevitably arise in the human mind. It was centuries later that other church leaders referred to them as the deadly sins. It probably reached its pinnacle during the Spanish Inquisition from the 1400s when they held public ceremonies devised to reinforce the Church's power and the monarchy's control. The accused were paraded, confessions made and the guilty were turned over to civil authorities for execution although their crimes were not necessarily associated with the seven deadly sins. Maybe Hamish was inspired by Evagrius's ideas but took it further."

"It is interesting," said Mary, "that the order of the panels on the wall is the same as the order of the murders."

"So, if we believe that all eight murders are related to the philosopher-monk of Evagrius and his eight evil thoughts, then can we assume that the killing spree is over now? Maybe we should keep our minds open until we're sure."

Harry pointed towards the workbench on the back wall. "Let's move on. Gather around the workbench. Look carefully at everything on it. Tell me what you see."

Chapter 50
Monday

"What are all those bottles with bright coloured powder in them?" asked Jack.

There were seven bottles, each containing a different colour: red, orange, yellow, green, blue, white and black.

Mary stepped closer to the bench. "My uncle who lives in Epping has always been interested in copper enamelling as a hobby and I've seen similar materials in his workshop. I think those bottles contain finely ground coloured glass."

"You mentioned copper," said Joe as he pointed to the end of the bench. "There is a thin sheet of copper leaning up against the end of the bench."

"Yes. And look," said Mary. "There are some small copper shapes lying on the shelf under the bench."

Harry picked up one of the pieces in his handkerchief. It was circular in shape, about three inches in diameter and with a small hole cut in near the edge.

He pointed to the left of the bench beside the copper pieces. "There are some leather bootlaces, similar to the ones attached to the enamelled pendants we found on each of the bodies."

"But hold hard," said Joe. "All those other pendants we found on the victims were roughly oblong in shape and about three and a half inches by one and a half inches. These pieces are round. Does that mean that these have nothing to do with the murders?"

"Not necessarily," replied Harry as he turned the piece over in his hand. "He could have cut those circular discs as a trial run before deciding to go with the oblong shape."

"Or he could be just making pendants to sell at the craft fair," said Rita.

"Or he might be preparing new pendants for his next group of possible victims," suggested Luke.

Jack pointed at the bottles. "How do you get those coloured powders to look like the polished enamel effect on the pendants found on the victims?"

Mary stepped forward. "I used to watch Uncle Angus do his enamelling. He started by cleaning the copper plate. He then drew a pattern on the surface. Next, he would work the powder into the patterns he wanted before he put it in the kiln for firing. Sometimes he would overlay that pattern with more colours before firing it again."

"Unless there is a kiln behind that door over there," said Rita as she pointed to the right, "Hamish would have to do that somewhere else. I can't see any around this space, and there wasn't one in the house. However, he could be a member of a pottery or lapidary group where they have a kiln."

Harry pointed to the end of the bench. "Look at the end of those tubes attached to that large gas tank. There is a welding torch, and on that hook on the wall is a welder's shield and some heavy-duty gloves. It appears that Hamish had skills well beyond his academic pursuits. The heat from that torch would be more than enough to melt that glass powder to produce an enamelled surface. If that was so, he didn't have to risk using a club with others looking on. Now let's move on."

Harry pointed to the closed door on the back wall. "Joe, undo that lock, please."

Joe picked the lock and opened the door. "The window in here is painted black and that light bulb above the bench is red. Is he afraid that the neighbours will look at him?"

Harry stepped into the room. "Look at the items on the bench. There is a half-filled tank, scissors, thermometer, metal dish, a wire with clips stretched across the room and a bottle of film developer. There is a strip of negative film clipped to the wire up here. This room has been used as a darkroom for developing photographs. Hamish must do his own developing."

Harry unclipped the strip of negatives and walked back into the main garage where the light was better to look at the images. "It's hard to see what's on these negatives, but the person in this first one looks like Paul Rundell, the senior lecturer in agricultural science and major in the SUR unit at the university. He's not looking at the camera."

Luke took hold of one end of the negatives. "If my eyes are not deceiving me that last image looks like you, Harry."

"That's all very interesting," said Harry. "I wonder why he would have a photo of me?"

Harry returned to the darkroom. Rita pointed to the ledge below the window. "The label on that bottle there says it is phenobarbital."

Rita undid the lid. "It is full of crystals. The bottle is the same shape, colour and size as the ones we found at the murder sites."

"What's the quantity on the label?" asked Jack.

"One hundred grams," replied Rita.

"Wow," exclaimed Luke, "you could easily knock off a few victims just from that bottle."

"Bag everything in this room, Joe," said Harry.

Harry led the rest of the team from the small room back into the main garage and towards the opposite side wall. On that wall, from left to right, were three large sheets of cardboard similar to the ones on the other side of the garage.

"Look at the photos pinned to the top of the first one," said Harry. "That's Paul Rundell. One shows him in full uniform in front of the unit at the parade ground. The second one shows him leading the unit marching down the main street of Armidale. You can see the courthouse in the background. The third is a casual shot of him having a beer at the hotel."

Luke pointed to the other sheets of cardboard. "The photos on the next one are all of Aled Prosser and the third sheet has photos of Charles Aitken, the Presbyterian minister."

Harry spread his hands wide to show the width of the three large sheets of cardboard. "These don't seem to have any connection to the eight pieces on the other wall. It seems that Hamish was firstly obsessed with killing eight victims to match the evil thoughts laid out by Evagrius. It appears that he has now lost his mind completely and wants to continue his killing spree to target others with whom he has had difficulties."

Mary waved her hand around the room. "I think he lost his mind well before he put up these last three."

Luke tapped his nose with his forefinger. "I'd agree that he has a serious mental condition but there are a number of mental conditions we don't fully understand yet. Schizophrenia is one such condition but there are others where the person goes in and out of highs and lows. They might appear on the one hand to have delusions of self-importance with high levels of creativity, energy and activity. They can be highly irritable, impatient and aggressive but then change to become depressed and withdrawn and in some cases become suicidal. Hamish could fall into one of these categories."

"Thanks Luke," said Harry, "but put that aside for the moment and let's concentrate on the first of these cardboard sheets on this wall. Look at what is written."

The first sheet was headed in large writing:

Power

Underneath that heading was written:

Salvation: Grace
Punishment: And whosoever will be
chief among you,
let him be your servant.
Matthew 20:27

For there is no power but God.
Romans 13:1

On the next sheet the photos of Aled Prosser showed him lounging back, dressed untidily, with bottles and glasses of wine.
It was headed:

Blindness

Underneath was written:

Salvation: Truth
Punishment: The sword comes and
takes any one of them.
Ezekiel 33:6

The photos of Charles Aitken showed him in the pulpit or at the altar with head up and arms raised, engaged in a lofty and powerful sermon.

The sheet was headed:

Hypocrite

Underneath was written:

Salvation: Righteousness
Punishment: And they will go away
into eternal punishment
Matthew: 25.46

For if a man thinks himself
to be something,
when he is nothing, he deceiveth himself.
Galatians 6:3

Mary pointed at the wall. "Those sheets of cardboard have been written in the same style as the ones on the other wall. Those eight people on the other wall have all been murdered and we have concluded that they were related to the eight sins as written by that ancient philosopher-monk Evagrius. Now we have three new panels. How do we explain that?"

"Could it be that we were wrong about Evagrius?" asked Joe who had finished in the darkroom and returned to the group. "Are we barking up the wrong tree?"

"Right now, Joe," said Harry as he pointed to the three news sheets, "I couldn't care less about Evagrius. We have three new potential murder victims and we have to protect them at all costs. Joe, you are coming with me right now. We have to set up protection for those three people. Get in my car."

"What about us?" asked Mary.

"I want the rest of you to go over this whole property with a fine-tooth comb. Collect all the evidence and then return to the cottage to prepare your reports. After Joe and I see the superintendent we'll go to Lennox Head to pick up Hamish, if he's still there."

***

On entering the superintendent's office Harry quickly summarised the details of the search at Hamish's house.

"What is your next move, Harry?" asked Ray Johnston.

"Firstly, I want you to arrange continuous protection for Paul Rundell, Aled Prosser and Reverand Charles Aitken. I want an officer with each of them at all times. Joe and I will take off to Lennox Head to arrest Hamish Mackenzie. Don't tell anyone that we are going there. I don't want him alerted to our intentions."

"Drive safely, you two."

Harry and Joe jumped into the MG and drove off.

Chapter 51
Monday

Harry pushed the MG to the limits on the drive down from the tablelands, through Ebor to Dorrigo and down to Bellingen. For most of the trip, Joe hung on tight as Harry took the corners at speed. Harry was confident that the low-set car with its direct rack-and-pinion steering could handle the winding road with ease. They continued through to the coast where they turned north, went through Coffs Harbour and on to Lennox Head.

At Woolgoolga, Joe turned to Harry. "How long will it take for us to get to Lennox Head, Harry?"

"It's now twelve o'clock. We should be there well before three this afternoon. Hopefully, the students and lecturers will be back in camp soon after we get there."

"How will we play it when we get there, Harry?"

"From memory, the first army hut is the administration office. Let's go there first and check where everyone is and what huts they have allocated to them. We don't know if the lecturers are in a separate hut or are rooming with the students in the main huts."   Just   past Woolgoolga it started to rain so Harry stopped and he and Joe put up the hood. They walked into the bush for a quick toilet stop before heading off again.

They drove through Ballina and on to Lennox Head, arriving just before three o'clock. They drove through the town, past Lake Ainsworth and on to the sport and recreation centre.

As they entered the camp grounds Joe looked at the wooden ex-army huts. "Is this it?"

"Yes," replied Harry. "The government set up this centre so that country kids could come here and enjoy the surf, sand and sun even in the winter. It's perfect because they also get health and fitness checks while they are here. I also know that the Armidale Teachers College students come here every year to do practice teaching at the local schools. Remember that Hamish told us that they brought the third-year psychology students here to survey the locals on a range of social issues."

"But there is nothing else around," said Joe.

"That's the beauty of this place. But enough talk. Let's get out and find our man. Be prepared for anything. This man is highly intelligent and, as we saw this morning at his house, is very well organised. I hope that he hasn't anticipated that we would have gotten onto him by now. If so he could be waiting for us or has already moved on."

Harry and Joe got out of the MG and walked to the first hut. They found an office where they were greeted by a woman dressed in a casual cotton shirt and shorts.

"How might I help you gentlemen?" she asked.

"I'm Detective Senior Sergeant Harry Taylor and this is Detective Joe Simms. We would like to meet with Mr Hamish Mackenzie. He is a lecturer from the university in Armidale and is here with a group of students. Could you please let us know where he is?"

"I'm Shirley. Pleased to have you here. Yes, Hamish is in the hut next door with Aled Prosser, the other lecturer. I'll take you there now. Please come with me."

As they walked out of the door, Shirley stopped and pointed towards the surf. "Look, there is Hamish now, doing his daily march along the beach dressed in his kilt, sporran, feather bonnet, dirk, badge and brooch. Doesn't he just look so grand? I took his photo yesterday to show to my Scottish mum. Every year that the students come here, Hamish plays his bagpipes on the beach every afternoon, much to the thrill of the students and staff and some of the locals. Someone said he was in the Armidale Highland Pipe Band. He's a wonderful player. And the sound of his pipes ring out right along the beach. It is quite a moment."

Hamish turned towards the surf as he played the last notes of the *Skye Boat Song*. As he stopped playing he pulled the blowpipe aside and turned towards the office hut. He stiffened as he recognised Harry and Joe standing next to Shirley on the verandah. Hamish turned quickly back towards the ocean. He reinserted the mouthpiece, paused and commenced playing the lone piper's rendition of *Lord Lovat's Lament*.

340

He marched straight into the surf, fully clothed in his complete band outfit.

Harry ran down to the beach. He stripped off his coat and boots along the way. On reaching the water he dived in and swam towards Hamish whose music had by then gone silent. The surf was very rough and Harry was dumped back into the shallows three times before he could break through the lines of steep waves to reach Hamish who, by that time, was being carried quickly away from the shore in a rip.

Harry took hold of Hamish's collar and tried to sidestroke back towards the shore, pulling Hamish behind him, but the rip carried them further out. He changed direction and swam across the current for about thirty yards to get out of the rip. He left behind the inflated bagpipes being tossed in the angry surf.

Harry struggled to keep afloat because Hamish's kilt kept dragging them under. It was made from eight yards of heavy Scottish wool.

Joe took off his boots and ran into the surf to help Harry drag Hamish to the sand. Harry immediately sat astride Hamish's prone body and started resuscitation using the Schafer method of pushing down on the small of his back to pump in air and drain water from the lungs.

"Joe, check there is nothing in his mouth. Straighten his tongue so that it is not blocking his airway."

Joe turned Hamish's head to the side and cleared some sand from the mouth. "All clear."

"Now go up to the office and call the ambulance and the local doctor. Get them here now. Also contact the local police station and tell them to get somebody here immediately with a wagon. Then come back here to help me."

Harry worked on Hamish for the next twenty minutes.

When Joe returned he took over the resuscitation on Hamish for another twenty minutes. Water drained from Hamish's mouth in short dribbles.

When Harry took over again, Hamish gave a weak cough. A mixture of foam and water drained from his mouth. Harry rolled him onto his back. There was a bluish tone to his skin and tongue. Hamish's eyes started to move slowly from side to side.

Harry looked up and saw Shirley with her hands over her face, shocked at what she had just seen. Surrounding her were the students; most of them in shock. None came forward to assist.

"Shirley, go to the office and get some blankets," shouted Harry. "You others stand right back."

The students stepped back.

Aled Prosser ran down the beach. "What happened?"

Harry wiped the water and sand from his face and hair. "Get the students back to the huts."

Aled turned and gave directions to the students who reluctantly turned to leave. As they walked across the sand they kept turning to see what was happening with Hamish. Most of the girls were crying. Others hugged each other for support. A siren was heard approaching the camp.

Clarrie Wakeling, the ambulance officer, ran down the beach with a mask attached to a small oxygen tank. He placed the mask over Hamish's face and turned on the oxygen. He had to stop a couple of times as Hamish coughed and vomited. Hamish eventually looked up, somewhat confused, and became agitated.

Harry placed a firm hand on his shoulders. "Just stay still, Hamish, and do what the ambulance man tells you."

Joe walked back up to the huts as a police wagon pulled up. He met the local constable, Dick Owen, and they carried a stretcher from the back of the ambulance down to the beach. When Clarrie removed the mask and put the oxygen tank aside, Joe and Dick helped place Hamish on the stretcher.

Harry took Clarrie aside. "Where is the nearest hospital?"

"Ballina. It's only three miles from here."

"I want Joe to go back with you in the ambulance. You must go straight to the hospital because this man is suspected of committing serious crimes and he must remain under constant police guard."

He turned to Dick. "I am sending Joe in the ambulance to stand guard over this man in hospital. This man is the serial killer we have been searching for and he must have round-the-clock supervision by a police officer. You follow the ambulance to the hospital and get him into a private room. Don't let anyone into his room other than doctors and nursing staff. You and Joe stay with him until I can get relief for you. I'll
342

arrange for a roster of police to supervise him in the hospital until he is fit enough to go to gaol."

Harry walked up the beach to the administration hut and asked Shirley to get Brian Sayle, the police inspector at Lismore, on the phone. A minute later Shirley handed the phone to Harry. He explained the situation to Brian.

"I will have Dick Owen guarding him at Ballina hospital but there must be a police officer with this man at all times until he is released from hospital. When he is fit to travel I'll arrange his transfer to Grafton Gaol down the highway where he will stay until his trial."

"Great work, Harry," said Brian. "It must be a relief to have finally caught this killer. Leave it to me. I'll organise a roster of officers to cover him until he's in Grafton."

Harry walked back to the beach to collect his gear. He met Aled Prosser who had waited patiently to talk to him.

"We came here to question Hamish regarding the serial killings," said Harry. "I won't discuss the details here but, when Hamish saw us, he just walked into the surf playing his bagpipes. It looked to me as though he made a deliberate attempt at suicide."

Aled stepped nervously from one foot to the other. He looked down at the sand and shook his head from side to side. He rubbed his left hand across the back of his neck.

"I feel terrible. Are you saying that Hamish was guilty of those murders in Armidale?"

Harry placed a hand on Aled's shoulder. "We have sufficient evidence to prove that he was involved in the deaths of those eight victims. I am going now to the hospital to charge him with those crimes."

Aled shook his head in disbelief. A tear ran from his left eye. He removed a handkerchief from his pocket and wiped it slowly from his cheek.

"I knew Hamish had a troubled mind but, as much as I tried, I couldn't help him. I always tried to humour him to get him to relax, but he was so pedantic and such a perfectionist that he couldn't see that other humans couldn't or wouldn't live up to the standards that he so often preached. He was more stubborn than any man alive. Hamish never did anything by halves. I have been concerned about him for some time now, but very little I said had any effect on him. I tried to get him to see a specialist but he refused. He saw himself as above all that. I knew he was on medication given to him by a doctor in Tamworth but I'm convinced that he had stopped taking it. He told me that the drugs had impaired his normal functioning. He said they deadened his enthusiasm to do everything on his demanding agenda. Occasionally he would flip into deep, dark moods for periods lasting from a few hours to a few days before reverting to his regular active and engaging self."

"Thank you, Aled," replied Harry. "I knew that you and Hamish were close, and I appreciate your honesty. I want you now to get all the students back to the huts and explain what has happened. You will need your best counselling skills. After you have explained it, send them on a run or walk to the end of the beach and back. That will help them to sleep better tonight. Now I must be going to the hospital."

Aled touched Harry's arm. "I'll take care of the students. I'll encourage them to have an open discussion tonight after dinner. It will be a good lesson about the realities of life and death. They'll learn more in those few hours than all the rest of this week talking to people about their piddling anxieties."

Harry returned to the hut and towelled down as best he could.

Chapter 52
Monday

Harry drove to the Ballina hospital where he met the local physician in charge of the wards. He explained the need to have a police guard at all times outside Hamish's room. Harry and Joe were escorted along a corridor to a room at the end where Hamish was recovering. Harry moved to the side of the bed. Dick Owen had cuffed Hamish's left wrist to the bed frame close to the wall.

Hamish lay on his left side, facing that wall. His complexion was pale. He continued to glance back towards Dick Owen who was standing at the foot of the bed. Harry walked to the bedside and tapped Hamish on the shoulder to get his attention.

Hamish turned slowly towards Harry who waited until he had Hamish's full attention.

"Hamish Mackenzie, I am charging you with the murders of Jonathon Petherby, Samuel Winton, Julian O'Sullivan, Richard Gladstone, Jerome Slaughter, Jan van Brouwer, Stephen Parker and Victor James. Further, I am charging you with a threat to kill a further three people. Those people are Paul Rundell, Aled Prosser and Reverand Charles Aitken. Following your recuperation here, you will be transported to Grafton Gaol where you will remain until your court hearing at a date to be decided. Do you understand the charges? Do you have any questions?"

Hamish rolled away from Harry without a word. Harry walked to the end of the bed where Dick Owen was standing. He thanked him and assured him that the inspector at Lismore would arrange a roster of relief. "Would you mind waiting outside for a moment? Joe and I need to talk to this man."

Harry pulled up a chair and sat facing Hamish. "I wish to inform you that we obtained a warrant to search your premises which included your garage. Both myself and Doctor Luke Dearing from our scientific investigations unit were fascinated with your interest in the ancient philosopher Evagrius of Pontus and his teachings. Did you specialize on him in your post-graduate studies?"

Hamish tried to turn onto his right side toward Harry but the cuffs on his left wrist prevented him from doing so comfortably. He lay on his back, stared at the ceiling and remained silent.

Harry tapped him gently on the shoulder. "I'm not an expert on Evagrius like you Hamish but I believe that his preachings about the eight sins at that time were no more than advice to the monks to avoid committing those sins if they wanted to get to heaven. I can't find any evidence of him suggesting death to those who committed those sins. In fact, it wasn't until about ten centuries later in the Spanish Inquisition that the Church executed people for committing various sins at that time. Please tell us why you used Evagrius to justify the murders of those eight people in Armidale?"

Hamish opened his eyes. His body stiffened before he suddenly swung his free right arm and grabbed Harry's arm. Harry stayed still and waited.

"That's the very point you people don't understand," said Hamish as he gritted his teeth. "Evagrius was brilliant enough to identify the eight evil thoughts and to alert everybody about them, but the powers in the churches took a long time to see the seriousness of his revelations. Eventually they translated those evil thoughts into sins. But after the Spanish Inquisition the powers went soft again and they stopped executing the guilty ones. Now we go soft on everyone and the criminals are locked up for a few days and then released back into society. I have now shown you what should happen to them."

Harry put his hand on Hamish's and loosened his grip. "But surely, Hamish, you would have to agree that the death penalty was too severe a punishment for such things as gluttony, pride or even anger? Why did you kill those people?"

Hamish released his grip from Harry's arm, swung it back across his body and slammed it down hard beside him on the bed. "That's the trouble with you police, and you wonder why we have so many criminals wandering the streets. If you had done your job I wouldn't have needed to do your job for you."

346

"In your garage you have clearly identified each of the eight sinners and the reason they were killed. Each was guilty of one of the eight sins or evil thoughts set out by Evagrius. But on the opposite wall you have three more people identified. Why are they there? What have they done to be on the wall of your garage?"

Hamish gritted his teeth again. "Because they, like the others, have committed serious sins, and you police have done nothing to bring them to justice."

Harry placed his hands behind his neck and sat back, exasperated. He waited for Hamish to continue but nothing more was forthcoming. He stood. "We are leaving now, Hamish. I'll see you in court."

As Harry reached the door, Hamish let out a raucous laugh. "Just to let you know, Harry, yours was the next photo to go on my garage wall."

Harry paused at the door and considered a response. "The difference between you and me, Hamish, is that most of our work is spent trying to prevent crime, not to carry out punishments. You can spend your days in Grafton thinking about that."

Before Harry and Joe left the hospital, Harry went to the main desk where he phoned Ray Johnston to inform him of the outcome of their visit to Lennox Head. He then phoned Rita at the Sheriff's Cottage to let the team know about the events on the beach and the situation at the hospital.

"We are leaving Ballina now. We'll be back in Armidale about ten or eleven tonight. Save some food and drink for us at the hotel. We've had nothing to eat since breakfast. We'll need it by the time we get back."

***

When Harry and Joe arrived in Armidale there was lots of clapping, cheering and back-slapping at the hotel. Ray Johnston and Ken Wright had been invited to join in the celebrations. The team had also invited Colleen to join the group. She gave Harry a big hug and kiss, cheered on by the team.

Harry and Joe sat there for another two hours as they nibbled the food and drank the many glasses shoved in front of them while they described every detail of the trip and the capture of Hamish.

It was almost one in the morning when Harry and Colleen got into the MG to drive to Harry's house. Before taking off, Colleen put her hand on Harry's arm and pointed up the hill.

"Darling," said Colleen, "you need to have a few minutes to relax and slow down after everything that has happened today and being back with the excited team tonight. It's a clear autumn night. Could you please drive to the top of the hill to look at the stars?"

Harry wiped his weary eyes and looked at Colleen with a smile. "Sure. Why not? I think it'll do us both good to relax for a minute or two. I couldn't think of anything nicer; especially with you beside me. Let's go."

Harry drove up Dangar Street past the teachers college and turned right over the bridge and parked. They looked down over the city lights and up to the sparkling stars. It was an idyllic scene.

"I'm so proud of you, darling, for what you have achieved today," said Colleen. "I only hope that the powers that be appreciate the pressure you have been under."

Harry stretched his arm behind Colleen, turned and gave her a long loving kiss and hug. The kiss lasted for what seemed an eternity.

"I've been waiting for that all day," said Harry.

"I've also been longing for that all day and night," replied Colleen as she eased away but still focused on Harry's face.

"Don't give a second thought to what the top brass think. They probably won't even remember my name," replied Harry. "They'll be just so happy that the press will take the pressure off them for a while. Besides, I don't want to have anything or anyone else interrupting us here. This moment is just for us. Let's enjoy just being together here by ourselves on this crystal-clear night."

He leaned over again for another prolonged gentle kiss.

Colleen eased back and, with both hands, gently pushed the hair away from Harry's eyes. "Well then, darling, if they are not going to give you good news, I will."

"What do you mean?" replied Harry as he looked expectantly into Colleen's eyes.

"I'm pregnant."

****

On Monday the 14th of August, 1950, Hamish Mackenzie appeared in the Supreme Court of New South Wales to face eight charges of murder and three charges of threat to kill other people.

Hamish pleaded guilty to the eight murders but not guilty of a threat to kill another three persons. Following discussion between the prosecutor and Harry, the threat to kill charges were dropped.

The defence lawyer pleaded for a custodial sentence as an alternative to the death penalty on the grounds of Hamish's mental condition.

The judge rejected that plea and handed down a guilty verdict with a death sentence. As Hamish was escorted from the courtroom, the judge unscrewed his pen and dropped the parts into the waste paper bin under the bench. Having just written the death penalty with that pen, he didn't want to use it again.